EXTREME VETTING

EXTREME VETTING

A THRILLER

ROXANA ARAMA

OOLIGAN PRESS - PORTLAND, OREGON

Extreme Vetting
© 2023 Roxana Arama

ISBN13: 978-1-947845-38-1

Ooligan Press
Portland State University
Post Office Box 751, Portland, Oregon 97207
503.725.9748
ooligan@ooliganpress.pdx.edu
www.ooliganpress.pdx.edu

Library of Congress Cataloging-in-Publication Data
Names: Arama, Roxana, author.
Title: Extreme vetting / Roxana Arama.
Description: Portland, OR : Ooligan Press, [2023]
Identifiers: LCCN 2022026956 (print) | LCCN 2022026957 (ebook) | ISBN 9781947845381 (trade paperback) | ISBN 9781947845398 (ebook)
Subjects: LCGFT: Thrillers (Fiction). | Legal fiction (Literature) | Novels.
Classification: LCC PS3601.R3449 E98 2022 (print) | LCC PS3601.R3449 (ebook) | DDC 813/.6--dc23/eng/20220608
LC record available at https://lccn.loc.gov/2022026956
LC ebook record available at https://lccn.loc.gov/2022026957

Cover design by Frances K. Fragela Rivera
Interior design by Frances K. Fragela Rivera

References to website URLs were accurate at the time of writing. Neither the author nor Ooligan Press is responsible for URLs that have changed or expired since the manuscript was prepared.

Printed in the United States of America

This is a work of fiction. Names, characters, business, events, and incidents are the products of the author's imagination or are used fictitiously. Any resemblance to actual persons, living or dead, or actual events is purely coincidental.

Content Warning: language, violence, guns, death, trauma, illness, depression, self-harm, attempted suicide, racist attitudes expressed by some characters.

To my father

ǀ

ON THAT WEDNESDAY morning in February 2019, Laura Holban arrived at the Seattle Immigration Court determined to fight like hell for Felix Dominguez's children. Seventeen-year-old Cruz and thirteen-year-old Clara sat beside her at the counsel's table, looking terrified of being sent to Honduras, a country they didn't even remember. At the government's table, Immigration and Customs Enforcement trial attorney Josh Peterson appeared relaxed, as if he'd already secured the kids' deportation.

"Any submissions for today's individual hearing?" Judge Carolyn Felsen said.

Laura handed over a manila folder with pictures from Felix's murder scene. He'd been Laura's client prior to his deportation. He was a good man who'd lived in Washington State for many years, worked hard, and paid his taxes, but last October, Judge Felsen had denied his asylum application and ordered him deported to Honduras. By mid-November he was dead—murdered in his hometown of Choluteca as a warning for those who thought they could escape the local gangs by fleeing north.

Judge Felsen leafed through the photos. The courtroom was so quiet that Laura could hear the ceiling lights buzzing. A bench squeaked as someone from the children's foster family shifted in an otherwise empty gallery. In the corner of Laura's eye, Peterson was adjusting his tie, as if getting ready for his performance. He had a reputation for using technicalities and precise legal terms to counter the flesh and blood of the cases presented by immigration lawyers.

Laura took a deep breath to quiet her nerves. When her emotions ran high, her brain sputtered, unable to find the right words in English and reverting to her native Romanian. In immigration court, the government didn't have to prove that Laura's clients should be deported—she had to prove they shouldn't. Keeping her cool in stressful situations was vital because her well-chosen words could make a huge difference in the lives of her clients. And at the moment, she was anything but cool.

She'd cried last night while printing the murder scene photos. Felix had been found in the driver's seat of a gray Toyota pickup, head tilted back, eyes closed. There was a gunshot wound in his throat, and his white shirt was covered in blood. Close-ups showed a red-spattered hand clutching the steering wheel. Two bullet casings on the sidewalk. A blood-stained picture of Cruz and Clara taped to the truck's dashboard. For contrast, Laura had added to the file a cheerful selfie of Felix in a green-and-blue Seattle Sounders T-shirt, a busy soccer stadium in the background.

Cruz bit his lower lip. Clara stared down at her chewed fingernails. Laura imagined her own fifteen-year-old daughter Alice sitting terrified at a table like this while a judge decided her fate. As an immigrant herself, Laura knew how awful it was to be at the mercy of a bureaucrat while her life hung in the balance.

Judge Felsen rubbed her forehead. "Let me get this straight, Counsel. Are you implying I'm responsible for the murder of your former client?" Her voice was calm, but her hand shook a little on the manila folder.

"No, I'm not implying that at all," Laura said, now worried. Had she gone too far by sharing the photos with the judge? "Those pictures are…they show what might happen to Cruz and Clara if they're deported." She hated saying that in front of the children.

"Your former client," Judge Felsen said, "he was just…unlucky. The asylum rules changed shortly before his hearing." She tapped her finger on the bench. "As you may recall, the US attorney general wrote a formal legal opinion stating that victims of domestic and gang violence no longer qualified for asylum at that time."

"Felix Dominguez was unlucky, yes," Laura said. "Especially since a federal judge later struck down the asylum rules invoked to deport him. But by that time, my client—"

"This is preposterous, Your Honor," the government attorney said.

"Don't call me Your Honor, Mr. Peterson," Judge Felsen snapped at him. "This isn't a court of law. It's an administrative tribunal."

"I'm sorry, Judge," Mr. Peterson said, sounding contrite.

Laura braced herself. Most judges didn't mind being called "Your Honor," so for Judge Felsen to point out that immigration courts operated under administrative law rather than the formal judicial system, applying rules and procedures created by government agencies—that meant she was angry. "I hate to bring up Mr. Dominguez's tragic story with his children present, Judge. But if their application is denied, they…" Laura swallowed her words. Cruz and Clara looked terrified enough already. "The evidence I provided at their father's hearing last year is just as relevant today. Perhaps even more so."

"Circumstantial evidence, at best," the government attorney said with a smirk.

"Circumstantial, Mr. Peterson?" Laura said, slowing down so she wouldn't make mistakes. "At the hearing last October, I entered graphic pictures of my client's stab wounds into evidence. I even asked him to lift his shirt and show his scars. Those wounds had been inflicted in Everett, Washington, long before his deportation."

"Because he was involved with PSB," Peterson said, meaning the Puget Sound Barrios gang, which was active in the Pacific Northwest and had connections with Mexican and Central American cartels.

"No. He was terrorized by PSB. He fled Honduras because he didn't want to work for a drug cartel there. They found him here and—"

"And you believe that?" Peterson said.

Judge Felsen rapped her gavel. "Order! This is the last time you interrupt, Mr. Peterson." She turned to Laura but didn't look her in the eye. "And you, Counsel, make your arguments without throwing accusations at the court. Or it will not bode well for this asylum application or any other you may bring before us in the future. Because…" Her voice cracked. "I want you to know that I do my best to follow the law. Even when it breaks my heart."

"I know, Judge," Laura said, trying to sound warm. Judge Felsen could be fired if she didn't meet the standards of efficiency set by the current administration. It was a conflict of interest challenged by lawsuits that would remain unresolved for years.

"No, you don't know," Judge Felsen said. "Day after day, I handle death penalty cases in…in a traffic court setting."

Laura couldn't agree more but remained silent.

Judge Felsen cleared her throat. "Please continue."

"If my clients are deported to Honduras," Laura said, "their lives are at risk. And one can hardly argue that they're involved with PSB." She pointed at the folder before the judge. "I think we've established a higher than ten percent likelihood of harm in this case. Under current law, Cruz and Clara Dominguez should be granted asylum."

Cruz stared at the judge, begging with his eyes. Clara's lips moved a little, as if in prayer. Laura remembered the phone call she'd received last November, the second worst call of her entire life. Cruz was choking on tears as he told her that his father had been killed in Choluteca. Everyone knew the narcos would kill him, so why had the government sent him back?

"What does the government have?" the judge said.

Peterson still looked confident, though he'd lost the smirk. "Judge, to your previous point about Mr. Dominguez's deportation, neither you nor the Justice Department are in any way responsible for his tragic death in Honduras. Mr. Dominguez never reported the PSB death threats to the police in Everett. Therefore, I must ask: is this how someone in fear for his life behaves?"

Laura thought to argue that undocumented immigrants avoided the police because local authorities cooperated with the Immigration and Customs Enforcement and because the current administration allowed ICE to arrest undocumented immigrants who had never been accused of any crimes.

"Trying to get on my good side, Mr. Peterson?" the judge said. "Do you think I was born yesterday?"

"Judge," Peterson said, "there's no proof that Mr. Dominguez's children will be targeted by drug cartels in Honduras. As far as we know, they've never been threatened by PSB in Everett. And Honduras is their home country after all."

"For God's sake, they're just kids, Mr. Peterson," Judge Felsen said. "Mr. and Miss Dominguez, this is your home country." She banged her gavel.

Laura could breathe again, but the children looked confused. They rose to their feet, and she gave them a hug. "You're safe now," she told them, and they broke into timid smiles. She sent them over to where their foster family was waiting. When she turned back, Judge Felsen had already left, and Peterson was closing his briefcase.

"You're going to appeal?" she asked him.

"I'll let the boss decide," he said, heading for the doors at the back of the courtroom.

The man who nodded at him in passing was Mason Waltman, Seattle chief ICE prosecutor. He wore a black suit with a blue tie but didn't look much different from the people he deported for a living—dark eyes and tanned skin, dark curly hair, short-cropped and graying.

Laura finished packing her leather tote bag, when Waltman stopped at her table.

"You might've won your case, Counsel," he said. "But you've made an enemy today."

"I thought we were already enemies," Laura said. She'd never stood so close to Waltman before. She noticed an old scar on his left cheek.

Waltman laughed without mirth. "I'm not your enemy, Ms. Holban. I actually admire your idealism, though I don't appreciate your lack of respect for the law."

"Outdated law, Mr. Waltman, passed to protect people against oppressive governments. Now refugees need protection from gangs and cartels their governments can't control. The law hasn't kept pace with the times."

"I meant you've made an enemy of Judge Felsen. She'll go home tonight and tell her family that an immigration lawyer with an accent accused her—to her face—of murdering an applicant."

Laura's stomach turned cold. "That never crossed my head." She heard herself and hurried to fix the Romanian leaching into her English. "Crossed my mind. Judge Felsen—"

"Judge Felsen is a human being." Waltman smiled with the excitement of a kid plucking wings off a fly. "Word will reach the other judges, here and in Tacoma. They'll blackball you, Ms. Holban."

"Are you implying that our judges cannot remain impartial, Mr. Waltman? If word of your doubts gets around, they may blackball you."

"Very funny, Ms. Holban."

But his threat felt real. The five judges assigned to Seattle and Tacoma were a tight-knit group.

"Will you appeal today's decision?" Laura said.

"Appeal? Haven't you heard the good judge? They're just kids, Ms. Holban. What kind of man do you think I am?"

The kind who destroyed families for a living, Laura wanted to reply. No, that wasn't quite true. Waltman also deported dangerous criminals and disrupted international trafficking of drugs, arms, and people. There was nothing simple about what either of them did for a living.

"I'll see you soon, Ms. Holban. Because ICE never rests in its mission to clean up the country."

He said "clean up" as if immigrants like Laura and the Dominguez children were filth. But after her nerve-racking exchange with Judge Felsen, Laura was too spent to come up with a clever retort. Next time, maybe.

But if Waltman was right, there might not be a next time. Or a next win, anyway.

2

EMILIO RAMIREZ WINCED when he heard the Thursday morning weatherman predict a record snowfall for February. He'd lived in Everett, Washington for more than two decades, long enough to know that snow meant trouble. He worked as a general contractor with Fernando's Home Improvement, and snow meant icy roads, which meant halting construction because equipment and supplies couldn't reach the job site. These were worries he'd never had back in his native Guatemala, the land of eternal spring.

For the moment, the ground looked dry. Emilio's sixteen-year-old son David grabbed the keys to their Ford truck and announced he'd be driving. His younger brother Jacob didn't seem to care who took him to school. After a bit of haggling, Emilio agreed to let David drive and followed his sons to the garage. He checked the mailbox on the way there and was glad to see it empty.

He climbed in the passenger seat of the four-door pickup. "Careful, careful," he said in Spanish, one arm thrown over the front seat, head turned to look behind. "Watch out for the garbage bins."

Fourteen-year-old Jacob settled in the back seat with his phone and earbuds, nodding to his music. Emilio corrected David's grip on the steering wheel, and the rear of the truck eased out into the driveway. He then put the truck in drive for his son, who snorted with annoyance.

Emilio's wife Blanca watched from the house, one hand over her mouth. She crossed herself as she always did when David took the wheel, then waved goodbye.

David stepped too hard on the gas, snatching away Emilio's wave to Blanca. Moments later they were on Olympic Boulevard. They hadn't seen the sun in weeks, but there was no ice on the road. David drummed on the steering wheel.

"No, no, no," Emilio said. "Keep your hands steady. Eyes on the road. Check both ways. Your eyes should scan those mirrors all the time. Left, up, right—then again."

"Like a Cylon, you mean?" David said. They'd all watched *Battlestar Galactica* when the boys were younger.

"Exactly," Emilio said, checking the mirrors. He was always alert outside the house, monitoring the people and cars around him.

His cell phone vibrated in his pocket, and he answered.

"A black SUV," Blanca said in breathless Spanish. "It passed our house right after you left."

Emilio turned in his seat and saw a black Chevy Suburban some fifty feet behind them. Blanca didn't have to say the words. It could be ICE.

"Don't worry, my love," he whispered into the phone. "No one's following us." If she worried too much, she'd get a migraine. She'd had the worst attack in years when David took his driver's license test. She'd lost four days of work then.

Behind them, the SUV turned right on a side street and disappeared. Emilio listened to Blanca's high-pitched advice: stay alert, make sure David didn't cause an accident or get a traffic ticket, drop the boys off at the high school, watch for that black SUV on his way to work. He hung up after one last "No te preocupes, mi amor."

"What shouldn't she worry about?" David said.

"You know your mother," Emilio said. "Hey, eyes on the road!"

He turned to check behind again. Everything looked clear, and he felt silly for worrying a moment before. He had a valid Washington State driver's license. He'd bought his Social Security number on the black market more than twenty years ago and had been working and paying taxes with it ever since. His job was on the books. He owned his house and paid property taxes. He shouldn't have to worry so much.

"So, Dad," David said, "can I take that job?" He meant bagging food at Grocery Outlet after school, three days a week.

"You don't need it, son. Worry about your homework and your boxing."

David passed Our Redeemer's Church and turned the corner onto West Mukilteo Boulevard. The turn was smoother than Emilio expected. David was getting better at driving.

"Sorry, Dad, but I need a paying job."

"Why? I give you an allowance. I let you drive my truck. I just bought you that new guitar." He realized he shouldn't have said that. David walked dogs and mowed lawns because he wanted to feel independent. Emilio understood that. But David's teenage needs shouldn't interfere with more important things like school, family, and community.

The church they'd just passed had welcomed Emilio years ago and helped him make a home in Everett. Father Nicolas taught him how to buy the rundown bungalow on the secluded plot at the top of the hill. After Emilio tore it down, Father Nicolas blessed the foundation of the new house and lent a hand during construction. He then married Emilio and Blanca and baptized their children. If David had time to spare, why not use it to volunteer at Father Nicolas's church?

"He wants to buy a better phone, Dad," Jacob said in English from the back. "To shoot better videos of his band."

Emilio sighed. When he was sixteen, he was harvesting ramón seeds in the rainforest of Petén and dodging recruitment by Guatemalan drug gangs. David's biggest concern was a phone with a better camera. That wasn't right. Instead of a job at Grocery Outlet, he'd better stay in school, get an education, and start a good career.

Emilio felt the pickup drifting toward the middle of the road. "Watch out!" he said and corrected the wheel just before they crossed the centerline. The truck swerved back with a screech.

Emilio glanced in the rearview mirror. A blue Nissan and a delivery truck followed them through Forest Park. Was there a black SUV behind the truck? Emilio's pulse quickened. David was driving a bit over the speed limit, but Emilio didn't tell him to slow down.

The delivery truck fell behind, and no other vehicle passed it to follow them.

"Why do you keep looking back?" Jacob said.

"Don't worry, son," Emilio said.

Whatever Blanca had seen, it wasn't ICE. But it could have been Evelyn Brunelle, a real estate agent who also drove a black SUV. She'd been leaving letters in Emilio's mailbox for months now. Heartwarming stories: Two newlyweds hoped to start a family in Emilio's perfect house on the hill overlooking Possession Sound. A retired couple dreamed of spending their golden years watching the ferries from Emilio's living room window. An enthusiastic gardener would work miracles on Blanca's hillside orchard. Sometimes the letters told him how the greater Seattle real estate market was booming and what an awesome time it was for him to cash out on his house. Emilio had thrown away the letters before Blanca could see them. But now he wished he hadn't, because one day he'd found a single page in the mailbox with the words:

DOES ICE KNOW YOU'RE AN ILLEGAL? CAFÉ ABDUL,
TOMORROW, 9:00 A.M.

No, ICE didn't know. They had limited resources, and there were millions of undocumented immigrants in the US. But this pushy real estate agent seemed ready to put Emilio on their radar. Once alerted, they'd investigate.

Emilio had no choice. He'd met with Evelyn, a blonde American with perfect white teeth. He sat in a wooden chair for a painful hour, listening to her talk about the tremendous opportunities of the amazing real estate market. When Emilio had bought his land almost twenty years ago, he'd never imagined that the neighborhood—next to the bay, though far from downtown Everett—would become expensive. But then the tech boom happened, and the greater Seattle area prospered. Because he had no mortgage to pay, he could afford his property taxes, though they kept going up.

"You wouldn't know 2008 ever happened around here," Evelyn said. She used the word "opportunities" a lot, but what she didn't say was that someone like Emilio shouldn't be allowed to own a large piece of property in a good neighborhood. Or any neighborhood.

Evelyn talked about the money they could both make off a sale, but Emilio made enough money already and had good benefits. Thanks to an article in *The New Yorker* about the Big One—an earthquake expected to hit the Pacific Northwest at some point in the future—there were enough seismic retrofits to keep Fernando's Home Improvement going strong for the next decade.

When Emilio finally spoke, he told Evelyn that the house on the hill was his only home. That his house in Guatemala had been torched, and that, when he first came to the US, he'd lived in shelters. He couldn't sell his home, with Blanca's mature garden and the new sunroom he'd built for the boys.

Evelyn had seemed moved, and Emilio thought he'd convinced her to look for "opportunities" somewhere else. But he still worried.

The truck swerved again, but David brought it back fast.

Emilio stopped himself from cursing. "You almost hit that parked car back there."

David kept driving as if nothing had happened.

"The signal?" Emilio said when they turned left.

"I forgot."

"Forgot? Tell that to the police."

"Relax, Dad, we're almost there."

"You drive like crap," Jacob said from the back seat.

"Jealous much?" David said over his shoulder.

Jacob scoffed. "Why drive when you can Uber?"

They turned right, tires bumping into the curb, then left, and Everett High School came into view two blocks ahead. It was a 1909 building with white facades and wrought-iron doors, a well-crafted thing of beauty.

When they passed the last intersection, a black SUV turned in and followed a short distance behind. It looked like a Ford. Emilio couldn't remember which make Evelyn drove, but if she'd followed him to his sons' school, he needed to set her straight once and for all.

They turned onto a side street to park, while the SUV drove on. David climbed the curb while attempting to parallel park. Once in the space, he got out and headed for the school. Jacob slammed the back door and dashed after his brother.

Emilio killed the engine, locked the truck, and followed.

"What are you doing?" David said when Emilio caught up.

"I have a meeting with your admin. The school wants to upgrade the gym and needs an estimate."

They cut across the open campus. At the main entrance, Emilio glanced back and spotted the Ford SUV parking across the street. He followed his sons inside the school. David vanished into the crowded hall. Emilio said goodbye to Jacob, then hurried back along a hallway thick with students. The admin would have to wait while he found Evelyn and had a quiet word with her. They'd agreed the house was not for sale. Why wouldn't she just leave him alone? But whatever he said to her, he'd have to do it in a nice way or risk getting in trouble for attacking an American.

"Dad," Jacob called behind him.

Emilio turned.

"I need some pocket change."

Emilio was reaching for his wallet when someone called out his full name. Students cleared the path for two ICE officers dressed in black fatigues and body armor marked with the word "POLICE."

One of them grabbed Emilio by the arm. "We've got an arrest warrant for you."

The officers turned Emilio around and cuffed his hands behind his back. The cold metal dropped heavy around his wrists. All around him, kids watched, whispering, phones up, recording. Emilio needed to think, but all he could do was feel: a sudden chill expanding from his chest to his limbs.

"Leave my dad alone!" Jacob cried.

Emilio jerked his head back and met his son's eyes, wide with fear. His whole body sought to go to his child's rescue, but in the next moment, he was pushed and pulled along as if sucked away by a riptide.

"What are you doing to him?" a girl called. "Leave him alone!"

Others joined in, jeering at the officers, but it all sounded garbled to Emilio. He wished he could tell Jacob not to worry, that ICE would release him soon, but he had no words.

3

ONCE HOME FROM another day in court, Laura went for a run, though it was a bitter-cold afternoon. She was upset about a client's rejected asylum application but couldn't do anything about it until her paralegal Jennifer Snyder prepared the paperwork for the appeal. A run on the streets of her Capitol Hill neighborhood would make her feel better.

She wore a double-sided sweatshirt, wool cap, and sunglasses. The sound in her earbuds was a random mix of '90s music chosen by the streaming service on her phone. A few minutes into the run, she wished she'd worn gloves. She'd been so upset about her lost case that she'd forgotten them at home. In her eleven years of practice, she'd won plenty of applications, and lost a few as well, but losing Gabriela Izquierdo's case today was hard to swallow. And Laura had lost on all fronts: asylum application, cancellation of removal, even withholding of removal.

Judge Derek Brown Gibson of the Tacoma Immigration Court had never been unfair before this morning, when he'd ignored all of Laura's arguments. And they were solid arguments. Gabriela Izquierdo had escaped a sex trafficking ring in Sinaloa, Mexico when she was twenty-two. She was married to an American citizen, had a five-year-old American son, and owned a Mexican restaurant in Issaquah, where she served her award-winning barbacoa. She hadn't broken the law since crossing the border years ago. Laura argued that if Gabriela were deported to Mexico, she'd be persecuted or worse, and her child would suffer extreme hardship. But the judge denied everything, and he shouldn't have.

Laura stopped to catch her breath at the top of the stairs on Broadway East, rubbing her cold hands. She noticed the snowdrops and purple crocuses poking through last fall's shriveled leaves, and she hoped for spring and warm weather. No more snow. She hated snow.

And she hated feeling powerless, the way she had during her first years in the United States. In 2001, her boyfriend Adrian was offered a job at Microsoft, and after a hasty wedding they left Romania for Redmond, Washington. But in the wake of 9/11, their corporate-sponsored green card applications—and Laura's work permit—were delayed for six long years. While Adrian grew in his job, Laura was legally forbidden to work. She'd given up a good law career in Bucharest to be with Adrian, and until Alice was born, she had little to live for in Redmond.

By the time her work permit arrived in 2007, she'd earned a paralegal certificate, was fluent in Spanish—another Romance language, like Romanian—and was finishing up her JD at the University of Washington School of Law. Her first job interview was for a paralegal position at an insurance law firm. It ended as soon as it began.

"Language," the middle-aged male interviewer told her, "is our professional tool, ma'am. I'm sorry, but we can't possibly offer you a position here. If our clients hear your accent, they won't take us seriously."

Laura found plenty of accents and more meaningful work in immigration law. Still, after years of accent-reduction classes, once in a while she'd see a judge squint and lean forward as if making an extra effort to understand her English. Had Judge Gibson this morning been too annoyed with Laura's pronunciation to consider her arguments on their merit? Or...

Laura felt the sting of Mason Waltman's warning again. Had she really turned the immigration judges against her yesterday? Was this the end of her career?

Laura started running again, the music in her ears more annoying than comforting. The system was already rigged against immigration lawyers. Every Friday afternoon, the Justice Department released updated rules meant to keep lawyers guessing—and making mistakes— when they filed their cases the following week. ICE prosecutors could derail cases without consequence. Well, almost without consequence.

A few years back, one of Waltman's trial attorneys had gone to prison after he was caught falsifying an undocumented immigrant's signature on an official form.

The immigrant in question had allegedly been arrested while driving under the influence and had initialed the Request for Disposition box on an I-826 form. That box said:

> I admit that I am in the United States illegally, and I believe I do not face harm if I return to my country. I give up my right to a hearing before the Immigration Court. I wish to return to my country as soon as arrangements can be made to effect my departure. I understand that I may be held in detention until my departure.

Waltman's trial attorney had been caught not because of any internal audit, but because a smart immigration lawyer figured out that the form I-826 that his client had supposedly signed didn't exist at the time of the alleged DUI.

No one on the government's side verified Waltman's work or his team's, and that made Laura's job tougher than it should have been. Now she wondered if she'd pushed Judge Felsen too hard for Cruz and Clara's asylum. She didn't regret it, but what about Gabriela? What about Laura's other clients? And how would she pay the bills and take care of Alice if her career was over?

She spotted a hawk circling high over Lake Union, the Space Needle in the distance. She remembered her first Fourth of July fireworks at the lake, how she couldn't stop gasping because she'd never seen anything so magnificent in her life.

She balled her hands into cold fists and sped up, her thoughts returning to Gabriela's appeal. Judge Felsen's vengeance—if that was the explanation—might not reach all the way to the Board of Immigration Appeals in Falls Church, Virginia.

Laura felt better by the time she got home. The house was warm and smelled of books. She dropped her things on the entry table, slipped off her running shoes, and grabbed her laptop. There were no urgent emails from work, but someone named David Ramirez had written her a message with the subject: "Please help my dad!!!" It sounded urgent enough. She opened it.

Dear Ms. Holban,

My friend Cruz Dominguez gave me your email address. My dad was arrested by ICE this morning when he dropped me and my brother off at Everett High School.

Another child with a parent snatched by Immigration and Customs Enforcement. But arrested at school? Local authorities had asked ICE to avoid arresting people at sensitive locations such as schools, churches, and hospitals. ICE was getting more brazen every day.

His name is Emilio Luis Ramirez Garcia

Ramirez Garcia was such a generic Latin American name that Laura wondered if it might be borrowed, which wasn't unusual. Many of her refugee clients had created new identities in the US, choosing names that were easy to write on government forms—definitely no diacritics or accents—names that allowed them to blend in rather than stand out.

and he crossed the US-Mexico border illegally in January 1998. He's loved and respected in our community in Everett. I don't know who could've alerted ICE about my dad. He's at the Tacoma Northwest Detention Center now. His deportation officer is Ken Masters. We've already raised the $15,000 bond with family savings and a loan from Father Nicolas Zapata at Our Redeemer's Church here in Everett.

Father Nicolas had been born and raised in Guatemala, arrived with a scholarship in the United States, and was now a citizen. Over the years, Laura had helped a few people from his church with asylum, green card, or citizenship applications. She didn't know him well, but he always had a friendly word when they met at immigration events.

My dad's employer Fernando Harris is a natural-born citizen so he'll take the cashier's check to the ICE offices at NWDC tomorrow. I started an online fundraising campaign to pay back our congregation: $1,160 so far.

I checked out your website and I know you've helped families from our church over the years. My dad is from Guatemala and my mom from El Salvador (also undocumented), but I was born here. And so was my younger brother Jacob, who witnessed the arrest this morning. It's our right to live in our country with our family, isn't it? Please help us stop our father's deportation. We worry our mom might be next.

I can assist you in any way you need. I'm good with computers and the internet and I have an unrestricted driver's license.

Please help us,

David Ramirez

If David's father was getting out on bond, his case couldn't be too complicated. Any lawyer could handle it. Still, Laura felt she should at least take a look at this case. But then she'd just lost Gabriela's without a clue why the judge had ignored strong evidence favoring their application. Like missing a step and then feeling wobbly, she'd now have to double-check everything she was doing for her other clients, all fifty-two cases. Fifty-two was a lot of cases anyway, and Laura only had Jennifer to help with that load. *Sorry, David, can't help you*, Laura thought. She'd refer him to a few immigration lawyers she trusted.

She threw the sofa blanket over her shoulders and began typing her email. It was a sweet, encouraging message containing the words "unfortunately" and "best of luck." She hit send, closed her laptop, and headed upstairs to take a shower. Alice would be back from school soon and starving, as always. Tonight, Laura would make her daughter's favorite dinner: chicken strips and fries.

×

Mason Waltman's team of ICE prosecutors had done excellent work today, but he was glad to be home, helping his wife Helen prepare dinner. He set the tomato on the cutting board and first sliced it in half, then quarters, then each quarter into four rounded wedges. He tipped the cutting board into the salad bowl and picked up another tomato, when he heard a cough coming from the living room. He put the knife down and went to check on the kids.

His eight-year-old twins Chloe and Oliver sat on the couch with their new Pokédex, a Pokémon encyclopedia he'd bought on the way home from work. Orsetto, the family's golden retriever, lay at the kids' feet, watching everything they did. He still looked like a little bear—the name Mason had given him when he saw him at the breeder. It was the nickname Mason's Sicilian-born mother used to call him when he was little.

"No, that's not right," Chloe told her brother. "Igglybuff evolves into Jigglypuff—"

"Yes," Oliver said, "that's what I said: Jigglypuff, not Wigglytuff." He coughed again.

Mason dreaded colds—the kids struggled to breathe and eat, and no one got much sleep. He checked his son's forehead.

"Look at this," Oliver told Chloe, pointing at an open page. "Eevee can take not one, not two, not three, but eight rad forms."

Chloe scrunched her nose. "But it can't evolve into a Poison type like Arbok."

Orsetto let out a short bark, as if taking Chloe's side.

Oliver's forehead didn't feel warmer than normal. Maybe they'd all be spared another miserable cold. They'd had quite a few already this winter.

Mason lingered in the room for another moment, watching his beautiful children chat about Pokémon. They both had blue eyes and light brown hair, like Helen. They'd never be bullied by other kids for their looks, the way young Mason had been because of his dark Sicilian skin. They were happy and innocent, and Mason worked hard every day to keep them safe.

The kids babbled on, excited. If they fell asleep early tonight, maybe Mason and Helen could retreat to the master bedroom and close the door. He went back to the kitchen, smiling.

Helen put her mitts on to take the baking dish out of the oven. "Your phone's ringing," she told Mason. "Hasn't DHS heard of email?"

Except it wasn't the Department of Homeland Security. The ringing came from Mason's brown leather briefcase and the disposable cell phone he kept to communicate with Javier Saravia. That phone wouldn't ring at this hour without a good reason. Maybe Saravia had questions about the data Mason had sent earlier: a new ICE arrest and three detainees scheduled for deportation.

Helen placed the glass dish on the stove. The kitchen filled with the aroma of oregano, roasted garlic, and sizzling chicken fat. Mason's stomach rumbled, but he made a sad face at Helen, who shrugged like "What can you do?" He fished the burner from his briefcase, grabbed his fleece vest, and stepped into the dark backyard. He waited a moment for Orsetto to follow, but man's best friend chose the warm house instead.

In the distance, Bellevue's lights glimmered on the black waters of Lake Washington—the bridges between Seattle and the Eastside two lines of colored light across the dark expanse.

Mason answered the call, cold biting at his fingers.

Javier Saravia spoke in his distinct smoker's voice. "I hope I not interrupt your dinner." He called from Chiapas, Mexico. He was a man in his fifties, and Mason had met him a few times in Seattle, always at the Jade Jaguar Gallery. "Emilio Luis Ramirez Garcia," Saravia said.

The man arrested today after a concerned citizen called the ICE hotline. As soon as Ramirez had been processed at NWDC and assigned a nine-digit Alien Number, Mason had accessed his information through the Automated Biometric Identification System, or IDENT, and generated a report. He printed the first page—the one containing Ramirez's picture, date of birth, country of origin, and biometric markers—and took it home. Before helping Helen with dinner, he'd logged into a secure site through an encrypted connection and uploaded the document for Saravia. It had become standard procedure.

"I want him," Saravia said. "As soon as possible." His voice was never hurried because people had no choice but to listen to him. He spoke only English during conversations with Mason, his accent soft and dull.

Usually, Saravia provided valuable information on arrested illegals, gleaned from sources throughout Latin America. Such evidence helped Mason's team expose fake names or criminal histories, ensuring deportation. Sharing information with foreign intelligence providers was in line with the new "extreme vetting process" the administration was pushing for immigrants—though Saravia was a shady provider whose arrangement with Mason was far from official.

"You have anything on him?" Mason turned against the icy wind and began pacing.

"Nothing," Saravia said. "I want him in Nuevo Laredo." That was his favorite drop-off in Mexico, just across the border from Laredo, Texas. "When he's to arrive there?"

"A few months, I guess."

"I want sooner. The end of the month."

Mason hated that commanding tone. He'd entered this relationship as an equal because it gave him something he couldn't get just by sending illegals to countries from which they could return whenever they pleased.

Saravia was a data broker for criminal organizations in Latin America. He provided intel that allowed transnational drug cartels, sex trafficking rings, and other criminal organizations to avoid the law and thrive. And such organizations paid good money for the people who'd once escaped their grip. Wanted fugitives were picked up the moment they arrived home—and made into examples. Crushing people's hopes for a better life somewhere else was critical to keeping them afraid and obedient. The examples sent a clear message: There is no escape. Not even in America.

Mason understood that awful reality, but it wasn't his problem. His job was protecting the United States of America. And it wasn't like everyone ICE deported was wanted by some cartel somewhere. Most of them just returned to their homes and plotted another trip to El Norte, "The North." Mason didn't keep track of those ICE deported and didn't want to know what happened to them. But once in a while he'd hear something. Yesterday in court, for instance, he'd found out from Laura Holban that Felix Dominguez had been murdered by local gangs in Honduras. Mason remembered who Dominguez was because, at the time, Saravia had been very interested in his biometrics report.

Mason told himself it was all worth it. He received great intel about his arrestees, which helped win case after case. Until recently, anyway, when ICE had begun arresting too many working people. People who'd been in the country for decades, had no criminal record, and were of no interest to Saravia or his friends. "Chaff," Saravia complained. "Too much chaff." He'd even hinted that he might stop paying Mason by the number of detainee profiles he provided. Once in a while though, a name or a picture popped up that made Saravia happy. A few months ago, it was someone named Gabriela Izquierdo. Today, Emilio Ramirez.

Mason needed Saravia but hated being treated like a subordinate. He was the Chief Counsel for ICE's Office of the Principal Legal Advisor in Seattle, with a team of trial attorneys at his command and enforcement responsibilities over four states. His territory—Alaska, Idaho, Oregon, and Washington—was thirty times larger than Chiapas, Mexico, where Saravia was based. And his territory was American, not Mexican, damn it.

"Sir," Mason said, because he never used Saravia's name on the phone, "Ramirez will be on his way as soon as his hearing lands on the court's calendar, plus three weeks for deportation formalities."

"How much time to the hearing?"

"Up to three months."

"Not okay."

"I can't change processing times. That's in the judges' hands."

"Hands can be greased."

"Not that easy in the US, sir. But this should be an easy case. Ramirez doesn't even have a lawyer." The right to an attorney applied only to criminal cases, and immigration was civil. If Ramirez wanted a lawyer, he'd have to pay for one or get in line at a nonprofit.

"The end of the month," Saravia said. That was less than three weeks away. "Make Ramirez ask for deportation."

"Why is he so important to you?" Mason's voice had an edge to it now.

"Not important. And no bail for him. Or he run away."

So Saravia knew enough to assume that Ramirez would flee if released on bond. An important client wanted Ramirez, and Saravia needed to deliver. Mason would make sure the deportation happened, just like he was doing now with Gabriela Izquierdo. But would Saravia's reputation be on the line if Ramirez didn't arrive in Nuevo Laredo by the end of the month? This was the first time he'd asked for a sped-up process.

Mason thought about ways to get Ramirez into deportation proceedings fast and with no recourse. He preferred to supervise removals that went through the Seattle Immigration Court, but those were for non-detainees only. Ramirez was locked up at NWDC, a private for-profit ICE processing facility, where Mason had less reach. Since the immigration court in Tacoma and all the necessary ICE offices were located inside NWDC itself—which saved the hassle of transporting detainees—Ramirez would stay put until deportation. That was a plus. Also, processing times were shorter for arrested immigrants because detention space was limited.

"The end of the month," Saravia said and hung up.

Mason pocketed the burner and rubbed his cold cheeks. He pulled his work cell phone from his slacks and dialed Noah Sheldon, a junior trial attorney in the NWDC ICE office, too green to ask inconvenient questions. "Eager to please his boss" was what Mason had wanted to write on Sheldon's annual performance review. Instead, he'd written "dedicated to serving the law" or something like that.

Mason shivered in earnest now, ready to go back into his warm house to that mouthwatering dinner. "Emilio Ramirez," he told Sheldon, skipping the evening pleasantries. "I need you to make sure he stays at NWDC until he's deported. If he deserves to be deported, of course."

"They all do, sir," Sheldon said. Eager to please.

4

EMILIO'S FIRST NIGHT in the low-security pod at the Tacoma Northwest Detention Center was short on sleep. His top bunk was in the middle of a wide-open space with dozens of men stirring in their beds. The detainee pod smelled of disinfectant and sweat, which Emilio's brain translated as imminent danger. He forced himself to keep his eyes closed, but then the odor shifted to wood smoke and cracked clay—the smell of a house burning thousands of miles away in Guatemala, where homes weren't built with drywall. He decided to keep watch, his back pressed against the lumpy pillow.

Then the bright lights came on, and he stared at the metal tables bolted to the cement floor below his bed, trying to remember how he got there. He'd somehow fallen asleep. The smell was different now: the coffee on the breakfast cart rolling through the detainee pod. Once he was allowed to move around, he bought some mints from the commissary for three times their grocery-store price. The combination of strong coffee aroma and fresh spearmint scent managed to banish those tormenting smells, at least for a while.

Back in his bunk, he thought about Blanca and the kids. Had she developed a migraine last night? Made it to work today? Her income at a residential cleaning company wasn't much, and he hoped to return home soon. That look on Jacob's face yesterday had broken his heart. What were Fernando and the guys at work doing now? They were supposed to start renovations on a 1905 mansion in Queen Anne.

Emilio closed his eyes, trying to kill time with some sleep, but the noise around him was too much. A rowdy crowd watched a wall-mounted TV tuned to Telemundo. Another group argued over a game of cards. A man sitting at the computer yelled in a foreign language at his out-of-state family. The guards' heavy boots slammed against the concrete floors. Their keys jangled. Metal doors opened and closed in the distance. Every noise echoed off bare walls. The din started at five thirty in the morning with a loud all-call asking people if they needed to visit the medical clinic and didn't stop until lockup and lights-out at eleven thirty at night. Only six hours of quiet time.

In the afternoon, Emilio sat up, hung his legs over the side of his bunk, and rubbed his eyes. His head was foggy from lying in bed when he should have been up and working. He wasn't sick, but he felt terrible. His lower back was stiff, and it wasn't just the bad mattress.

But he wouldn't be here for long. Last night on the phone, David told him they'd raised the bond money. The first thing Emilio wanted to do when he got home was talk to Jacob about the arrest. Jacob was delicate like Blanca, who never recovered after witnessing her brother's murder in El Salvador. Things David shrugged off with ease would send Jacob into a depression. In middle school, when a classmate told him to go build the wall, he wouldn't talk to anyone for weeks. Blanca took him to a therapist when she discovered he was cutting himself. Jacob was doing better now that he was in high school, keeping busy with homework. But what if a bully made fun of him because his father had been arrested in front of the whole school, not to mention the video that was posted on the internet for everyone to see?

Emilio's pod mates Arturo and Marco played cards on the next bed. Like Emilio and everyone else in low security, they wore dark-blue uniforms.

"You want to play?" Arturo asked him in Spanish.

Both he and Marco were from El Salvador, like Blanca, and both were in their twenties. They had arrived at the southern border a few months apart, asking for asylum. Arturo had traveled alone. Marco was separated from his wife and daughter, then sent to NWDC. He had no idea where his family was now.

Emilio slid down from his bunk to the one below. "What are you guys playing?" It didn't look like poker, and the cards were from two different decks.

"Uno," Marco said. "My daughter's favorite." He smiled.

"I hope it's not raining." Emilio slipped into his black sneakers. "Maybe we can grab the soccer goal out there."

"Nah," Arturo said. "Can't get past the Mexicans."

The door at the far end of the pod opened, and a guard with a clipboard walked in. Arturo put the cards down.

Marco stood up. "He's announcing the jobs," he told Emilio, who had already decided he'd never work for just one dollar a day.

Though the law said detainees couldn't be paid more than that for their work at NWDC or other immigration centers, such a low wage was no better than slave labor, in Emilio's opinion. Arturo and Marco had told him that his resolve would soon disappear. There were twenty-three hours of inside time in that one-dollar day, and he couldn't sleep them all off. Arturo had spent one day in the laundry center, the shortest day he'd ever had at NWDC. Marco had served once in the barbershop, which he loved, and twice in the bathrooms, which he didn't. The jobs were limited to detention center maintenance, so they felt more like communal work than forced labor.

"They should pay outside contractors," Emilio had told them after their well-intended explanations.

"That's at least minimum wage, man," Marco said. "And NWDC is for-profit. Listen, when they order you to do the work, you do the work, or they'll take away your phone and recreation time."

"Say no," Arturo added, "and you'll get pepper sprayed. Then there's solitary confinement. Don't forget you're in jail now."

So far, no guard had bothered Emilio, and he hoped to get out before they even learned his name.

"Come on," Arturo said under his breath, staring at the guard with the clipboard. "Give me something to do until you deport me."

"Why think they'll deport you?" Emilio was sure he could convince the judge to let him stay. If it turned out that Evelyn Brunelle had called the ICE hotline, he'd just explain how much heart and sweat he'd poured into building his house, which was now home to his American children. He'd show pictures of David and Jacob under the flag at school. The American dream was about hard work and equality, not greed and injustice. Any honest judge would agree.

"Everyone gets deported," Marco said. "Getting asylum is like winning the lottery. Sure, it can happen to someone. Just not you. Never you."

Marco's words sounded like a curse, but Emilio had survived Guatemala in the '90s, crossed the Sonoran Desert, and made a home in America. He'd raised a family and paid his taxes. He'd earned the right to be here.

A familiar sense of danger—something he'd lived with for years during and after Guatemala's civil war—stirred in his chest.

"Ramirez!" the guard called out. "Visitors!"

It had to be David with Fernando as his adult chaperone. They must have posted bond. Emilio couldn't help but smile.

The guard checked the name and picture on Emilio's wristband, then sent him to another guard, who unlocked the door with a key chained to his belt. Emilio glanced at the guard's nametag: Svenson. But that didn't matter now. He was going home.

He followed Svenson through a hallway that smelled of more disinfectant. The booming of the guard's boots covered the whisper of Emilio's rubber soles. They passed an impressive mural depicting a bald eagle and an American flag. The bright reflections on the bird's yellow pupil, the fine lines on its white feathers, and its shadow against the fluttering red stripes had probably been painted by a skilled inmate, working for a dollar a day.

The visitation area was behind two metal doors. The guard unlocked the first, and Emilio waited for him to close and lock it before approaching the second, which would not open until the first was secured.

Fernando sat on the far side of the plexiglass barrier, phone in hand. David stood behind him. But the look on their faces…

Emilio sat down and lifted the heavy handset from its socket on the wall. "What happened?" he said in Spanish. "Is it Blanca?" Had she missed work because she'd been worried sick about him? When Fernando shook his head, Emilio blurted out, "Is it Jacob?"

"Don't worry, they're both fine." Fernando sighed. "It's just…We don't know what happened. We showed them this." He pressed a document against the window: Notice of Custody Determination. "It says here that ICE has agreed to your bond, but today…"

David's big brown eyes were swimming in tears.

Fernando rubbed at the back of his neck. "Officer Masters just said no. He told us they changed their minds. Told us to take it up with the judge."

Emilio slumped in his chair and stared at his faint reflection in the plexiglass.

"But don't worry," Fernando said. "We'll find you a good lawyer and get you out of here."

A lawyer. A bond hearing in front of a judge. How long would that take? What would it cost? Where would the money come from?

"Tell Blanca I'm fine and not to worry," he said, motioning to David to come closer.

Fernando passed the handset.

"David, make sure your mother and brother are okay," Emilio said. To his own ears, he sounded like a man who knew he'd never go home. "Do your homework. Don't skip your boxing practice. Make sure Jacob does his too."

David ran his hand through his short black hair. "Don't worry, Dad. We'll get you out." He tried to smile, but his voice caught. "Like you always say, this is America."

✕

David rode back to Everett in Fernando's truck, replaying the NWDC conversation in his mind. He'd never seen his dad so defeated before. Emilio Ramirez could do anything. Always. How could a setback crush him like that? Because he definitely looked crushed.

David wasn't giving up though. Laura Holban's email said she was too busy to take Emilio's case and that other lawyers would be just as good, maybe even better. But Cruz had told David how Ms. Holban had fought for him and Clara, and that was the kind of lawyer David wanted for his dad.

Fernando's truck pulled up under the leafless oak tree in front of the house, and David got out. His mom wasn't home. In the kitchen, he made himself a cheese, salami, and mustard sandwich, then studied a map of Seattle on his phone while he ate. Laura Holban's office was south of downtown, in Pioneer Square.

He called her number, but her paralegal Jennifer said she wasn't in. Would he like to leave a message? David said he'd try back later.

He finished the sandwich and went to his room to look for his laptop. He found it on the bed, under the new guitar he'd strummed before the NWDC trip. He'd heard of online directories, websites that aggregated all sorts of public records—property, traffic, phone, voting, financial, criminal records, and so on—to create huge databases of contact and background information. After a bit of research, he created a free trial account with one of them and looked up Laura Holban. She was forty-five and related to someone named Adrian Holban. She used to live in Redmond and had no criminal record. Not even a traffic ticket. Now she lived in Seattle on Tenth Avenue East.

David went to listen outside Jacob's door. Just a few days ago, his brother would have been playing Xbox at this hour, but the videogame racket was absent today. The lights were on though, so Jacob was either in bed staring at the ceiling or doing homework. David hoped for homework. Just not trigonometry. He wouldn't wish that on anyone.

A trip to Seattle might make Jacob feel better, but David didn't know how long he'd be gone. Besides, he didn't want to fail with an audience. He had to do this alone. He'd check on Jacob again later.

He found a bag of pretzels, filled his water bottle, and grabbed the keys to his dad's pickup truck. The driving app on his phone kept him in heavy traffic on I-5 South. His hands sweated on the steering wheel, and his jaw hurt from clenching his teeth, but he made it all the way to Seattle and the Lakeview Boulevard Exit, where he relaxed a little. He even took a moment to check out the Space Needle and the skyscrapers in the distance.

He drove past homes with expensive views of Lake Union, then up a hill so steep he feared he'd lose control of the truck, slide backward, and crash through the concrete barrier onto I-5. The pickup's engine groaned in protest, but he made it all the way up, where he parked in a two-hour spot on Tenth. His heart jumped when a bus zoomed by, inches from his side mirror. At last, he checked the street, picked up his backpack, and set out on foot.

The lawyer's small house was set back from the busy street, beyond a paved front yard with a parking spot surrounded by rhododendrons.

David had seen a picture of Laura Holban on her law firm's website and another in an article in *Crosscut*, a regional nonprofit news site. She was a middle-aged White woman with high cheek bones, dark hair, and brown eyes. She looked friendly, like maybe she'd help him after all.

He climbed the wooden stairs and rang the bell. A moment later, the door cracked open, and a White girl with glasses, a bit younger than he, peered out at him.

"I'm here to see Ms. Holban," he said, pretending he had an appointment.

"My mom's not home." The girl shut the door.

David thought about returning to his truck, but then he might miss the lawyer's car pulling into the driveway, so he sat on the front steps, his backpack next to him. It started raining, but the porch roof kept him dry.

He watched buses come and go and checked his phone to see what his friends were up to on Snapchat. He answered a text from Cruz about their next boxing practice, played a few rounds of Candy Crush, and was soon bored. He stood up when he felt too cold, paced the front porch for a while, then returned to the front steps. He thought he saw the girl spying on him from the living room window, but he ignored her.

He liked that Ms. Holban's front yard was covered with interlocking stone pavers. It was the best kind of yard, with no lawn to mow. Just when he sat down again, he heard the door unlock. He jumped to his feet, dusting the butt of his black jeans, and slung his backpack over his shoulder.

The girl opened the door. "You said you know my mom?"

"Um, yeah." David pulled out his phone and opened the email Ms. Holban had sent yesterday.

The girl propped up her glasses and glanced at the screen. She puckered her mouth, as if thinking hard, then opened the door and let him in.

"Shoes off," she said, pointing to a small closet by the entrance. David counted four pairs of Converse sneakers in different colors. The red ones looked brand new.

The girl wore skinny blue jeans and a graphic sweatshirt with monsters. David smiled, but she didn't smile back. She was tall for her age, and her brown hair had purple highlights. Or lowlights, whatever. And she'd taken pity on poor him, waiting in the cold like a loser.

"I'm David." He held out his hand.

She shrugged. "Alice. Want some water?" She hit the lights along the way, as the afternoon was dark and getting darker.

David followed her. His dad would really like this house, even though it was small. It had nice pine floors, high ceilings, and tall windows with glass sconces that mirrored the shape of the trees outside. The furniture was sparse. Or maybe the people living here were too busy to bother filling out the floorplan. A digital piano stood in the window nook between the living room and the dining room. It was a dark-brown, compact instrument with five hundred prerecorded voices. David's school had one just like it, and he'd tried it out a few times.

The kitchen was its own room, with sliding doors and counters finished in white granite. The cabinets were stained wood and wrought iron.

"Beautiful house," David said.

Alice filled a glass from the fridge dispenser and handed it to him. "What do you want with my mom?"

"She can help my dad." He took a sip of water, feeling strange under her questioning gaze. "I hope—"

Alice turned around, leaving him there. For a moment, David didn't know what to do. He took another gulp of water and set the glass on the counter. He followed her into the living room. He realized he still carried his backpack, so he dropped it by the coffee table. Alice said nothing, so he sat down on a brown leather sofa facing a fireplace flanked by built-in bookcases.

He craned his neck to look at the windows. The house was quiet, as if the busy street outside didn't exist. "Your walls," he told Alice. "They're at least six inches thicker than normal."

She shrugged again. "Our house was a project of the School of Architecture at U-Dub," she said, meaning the University of Washington. "It's small and sturdy, and it's supposed to be the last building standing in case the Big One hits."

"Cool." He didn't know what else to say.

"But that's not why my mom…and my dad bought it. When they first moved to Seattle, they were afraid Mount Rainier might erupt and trigger a mega-earthquake. They'd watched a Discovery Channel documentary that said the volcano erupts every five hundred years, and the last time was around the year 1500. You do the math." She rolled her eyes, like that was the silliest idea ever.

"Any day now," David said, though it did sound silly.

"And she doesn't let me go up the Space Needle. Because earthquakes."

David felt himself blush. "Um, I've never been up there either. I guess that's for tourists?" He glanced at the mantelpiece, where a younger version of Alice smiled from a framed photo. No glasses then. "Fourth grade?"

"Fifth. The last time they pinned me down for a school portrait."

She dropped into a leather wingback chair and flung her legs over the armrest. David sighed. Seattle kids were the coolest. They had style. They had better taste in clothes and music. Sure, plenty of bands stopped by the Everett Theater, but they were always heading for Seattle, which had ten times more venues, all of them bigger and better. Alice's sweatshirt had probably been bought in some rad Seattle boutique. And she probably had better friends than David did in Everett. Between the naval station, government contractors' apartments, and housing for Boeing employees, people were always coming and going. Except for his friend, classmate, and boxing buddy Cruz.

"So," David said after a long silence, "what kind of name is Holban?"

"Romanian."

"That's where you're from?"

She looked at him as if he'd spit on her polished pine floor, then she peeled herself off the armchair and headed for the kitchen.

"Wait," David said. "I didn't mean it like that. Of course you're from here. I'm from here, but my dad's from Guatemala, mom from El Salvador." His voice was pleading. "I was just curious, that's all."

He should have known better. It wasn't as if he and his brother hadn't put up with this kind of shit all their lives. As though he hadn't landed some punches and Jacob hadn't shed gallons of tears over being called "wetback" or "filthy Mexican." That was why they'd both taken up boxing, not just because their dad wanted them to.

David looked around, desperate to find a change of subject. "Do you play?" He pointed to the piano in the window nook.

Alice turned around as if favoring him with a second chance. David felt so grateful.

"I told my mom I quit." She lifted the keyboard cover and did a quick succession of chords that David recognized as the inversions of G. "She made me take lessons, ever since I was four. All because they had, like, one piano in all of Bucharest. That's the capital of Romania."

David didn't know that but nodded as in, "Obviously!"

Alice went on, "When my mom was little, her parents couldn't take her to piano lessons at the Pioneers' House. That's some communist clubhouse for kids." She played a short glissando. "She bought this for me when I was one—one!—but she had to wait until my fingers grew big enough for the keys."

"My dad wants me to be a boxer because he didn't get to do it back in Guate."

She looked at him with renewed interest. "You box?"

"Yeah…Won a few tournaments."

She turned back to the piano and plucked a thin book of Bach from a woven basket on the floor. She opened it to the Minuet in G Minor and began to play.

She was really good. David leaned against the bookshelf by the piano to listen. For a moment he was all ears and no thoughts. He could see how tricky the music was. She was better with the piano than he with the guitar. She played two pages, then finished the piece with a flourish.

David had forgotten to blink. "I…" He cleared his throat. "I'm in a band, with some friends from school." Though they didn't practice much. What would it be like to have this kid on keyboard?

"Cool," she said.

He looked around. "Do you have a guitar around here? Or drums?"

Alice laughed. "If you knew my mom, you wouldn't ask about drums. Even though our neighbors wouldn't hear zilch through these thick walls."

"There are drums you can only hear with headphones or speakers."

"The expensive kind?"

David nodded, glad she wasn't a spoiled rich brat. "I can text you a rad video of our band—if you want. We played at school. For Christmas."

"Sure. I'm also on Instagram." Of course. No cool Seattle kid would be caught on Facebook.

They'd just finished exchanging phone numbers when the front door opened.

David stood still, holding his breath.

Ms. Holban unzipped her boots. She looked a bit like her daughter but was thin and pale, and she seemed stressed and hurried.

"Mom," Alice said, "this is David."

5

A JOLT RAN through Laura's body. The boy wasn't one of Alice's classmates. Who was he then? Dark hair, light-brown skin, a weak smile—he looked anxious standing by the sofa, playing with his hoodie's zipper.

"What's going on, Alice?" Laura didn't want to overreact.

The boy stepped forward with his hand extended. "My name is David Ramirez. I need your help to stop my dad's deportation."

The boy who'd sent the email about the dad who'd crossed in 1998. "David," Laura said, throwing a hard glance at Alice, "this is not how I do business. I already wrote to you and said I can't help you. Have you tried the lawyers I recommended?"

"My dad's in more trouble than we thought. We raised the bond money, but ICE changed their mind. They wouldn't take it." His brown eyes filled with tears. "We need a lawyer, Ms. Holban. A great lawyer, like you…Cruz Dominguez—we're both juniors at Everett High School, same boxing team. He said you'd know what to do."

The kid seemed shaken. Having ICE revoke the initial bond was a sure sign they had something serious on his dad, but Laura was already juggling fifty-two cases.

"Please," David said.

On the other hand, the number of detainees granted bond had fallen from over ninety percent a few years back to almost zero. Detained immigrants were less likely to find lawyers. Immigrants without lawyers were less likely to win their cases and more likely to agree to deportation. It was an intentionally vicious circle.

"Please, Mom," Alice said.

"Du-te la tine în cameră!" Laura told Alice in Romanian.

"You can't send me to my room," Alice said. "I'm not a baby."

"Așteaptă până te chem eu." Laura didn't raise her voice, but her command to wait until called on had the force of a sledgehammer.

"Nu-mi spui mie ce să fac," Alice said, but turned around and started up the stairs.

David shot Alice a worried look, and then Laura realized that the "do" in Alice's "Don't tell me what to do," must have sounded like the f-word to him.

"You were saying?" Laura asked him.

"My dad, he loves this country. He always says this is America, the land of opportunity."

Laura cringed at his words. That was what her father's doctor had said back in 2005: in America they could fix anything. If only Laura had taken her father to see American doctors while there was still time. Because she hadn't, he died in Romania, and it was all her fault.

Laura walked past David, heading for the kitchen. She needed a glass of water to help her swallow the knot in her throat. She saw Alice on the upper landing, listening.

"To your room," Laura called up. "Now." She went to the kitchen, filled a glass from the faucet, and drank it all up.

"Ms. Holban?" David said.

"Something's not right with your father's case." Laura leaned against the counter. "To be granted bond means you're no flight risk, you're no danger to the community, and, as the law puts it, there isn't 'anything else relevant.' A revoked bond means one of those three boxes got ticked." She'd pronounced "three" like "tree," and the slipup bothered her for a moment.

"My dad, he's not going to run away on us, and he's no danger to the community."

"Then it's the third thing. There's something else going on, and I'm not the best lawyer to dig into that right now." She had to go over the most current DOJ updates and make sure none of her current cases was jeopardized by the latest weekly rule changes.

"But you are the best lawyer, Ms. Holban! Cruz says so."

Now here was this boy, barely older than Alice, doing everything he could to save his father. If she turned him down and he didn't find another lawyer, or worse, if he went to one of those notarios who'd take his money and do nothing for him, he'd end up blaming himself for his father's deportation. Guilt over letting a parent down was hard to live with. Laura knew that better than most.

She wanted to help him, but then there was Judge Felsen. And Waltman's warning. And whatever the hell had happened with Gabriela's case yesterday. With Laura as his lawyer, David's dad could end up spending months in jail.

"I'm sorry, David."

"We have the bond money. We'll raise more. I'm good with computers—"

"That's not it." It was hard to watch him beg like that.

"Cruz's dad," David said, his voice breaking, "he was killed in Honduras."

"Yes, I know!" Felix wouldn't wait for an appeal. Some people couldn't deal with months and months in jail.

"Ms. Holban, please. I don't want that to happen to my dad."

Would anyone want to kill this kid's dad? "Do you know why he fled Guatemala?" Laura heard herself asking.

"Not exactly." Hope appeared in David's eyes. "I guess I've never really asked him. Wasn't there a civil war or something? He must've run away from that war!"

"The war ended in '96, and you said in your email that your father crossed in '98."

"You remember my email! Yes, '98, January." He spoke fast, as if he didn't want to give her time to say no again. "Maybe he fled because life was too hard after the war and he wanted a better future? He was only nineteen when he crossed, I know that."

The Guatemalan Civil War ended in 1996, but the country didn't reach real peace in the aftermath of the Peace Accords. Crimes against the Indigenous population, and women in particular, continued for years. Even now, Guatemala was plagued by gang violence, weak governance, corruption, and poverty—all solid reasons for migration north. US government statistics pegged Guatemala as one of Latin America's most violent nations, which Laura always quoted in her clients' asylum applications.

"Any relatives still living there?" she said.

"They all died when my dad was young. Probably in the war. My dad was away, I don't know where, and couldn't go to their funerals. He still tears up because he missed their funerals."

Laura understood that burden all too well, though she hadn't cried when her father died. Couldn't, for many months. Not one tear.

David was watching her with anticipation. She couldn't turn him down now, but she didn't even know the details of his father's case.

"Do you have any documents with you?" she said.

David dashed to his backpack. A moment later he was shaking its contents out over the dining room table. Laura slid a yellow folder from under a bag of dog biscuits. Inside, she found the cashier's check for the bond in the name of Fernando Harris—the American employer—made out to the Department of Homeland Security.

She looked through Emilio Ramirez's W-2 tax forms from different employers, going back twenty years. His Social Security number seemed real, but he'd probably bought it from people who recycled SSNs and sold them on the black market. His 1040s had a real federal tax ID. There were a couple of expired driver's licenses and a few IRS receipts and refund notices. Also, a six-year-old check stub from the Washington State Department of Labor and Industries, covering medical costs after a work accident at Fernando's Home Improvement. Emilio's brand-new Alien Number was written on a yellow Post-it note.

"Would the money we have now"—David pointed to the $15,000 cashier's check—"be enough to hire you? I mean, your services. As our lawyer?"

"My fee is six thousand, and it covers all hearing statements and court appearances. Filing fees are separate."

David smiled. "So you're going to help us?"

Laura couldn't believe it either. She nodded.

"Yes!" David pumped his fist. "I'll bring a check from Fernando tomorrow."

Laura put the folder down. "Here's what I need you to do, David. Ask everyone who knows your father—at church, work, school—to write letters of support for his asylum application. Have them explain how important he is to your community."

"I can do that. I'll get you lots of letters. We'll win this, right? And when I'm twenty-one, I'll sponsor both my parents for citizenship."

Laura avoided answering that one. Even in the best of circumstances, a sponsored application wasn't guaranteed to be approved. Because David's father had crossed the US border illegally, he'd have to go through consular processing in Guatemala. And when he left the US, he'd trigger a ten-year entry ban because he'd been in the country illegally for more than a year. In addition, the citizenship process itself took ten years to complete. David's family would never be the same, but the boy didn't need to know that now.

David re-stuffed his backpack and put his shoes on. He thanked Laura, looking both relieved and proud of himself.

"Please don't be angry with Alice, Ms. Holban. She couldn't stand to see me freeze out there. She's really kind." He opened the door. "And super talented with the piano."

Alice had played the piano for David? The last time she'd touched it was before an ugly fight where she accused Laura of forcing her to learn out of misplaced ambition. Adrian never forced her to do anything because, of course, only he understood her. But if Alice played the piano for David, then maybe she hadn't quit for good?

Laura closed the door after him and kept her smile to herself as Alice came down the stairs.

"What's for dinner, Mom?" As if nothing had happened. As if she hadn't been told to wait until Laura called her downstairs.

But the news about the piano was too good to let anything else spoil it. "Salmon and salad," Laura said, opening the fridge. She took out a cucumber and a plastic box of cherry tomatoes.

"Mom, I told you, it's pronounced SA-mon, not SAL-mohn."

"SA-mon," Laura said, crossing the kitchen. She knew that, damn it, but her English had slipped because she was tired. As with any other skill, from tennis to skiing, she was sometimes better at English and sometimes worse. English didn't inhabit the same part of her brain as her native Romanian. Had she learned it earlier in life, she'd manage being drunk in English and sleep-deprived in English and, most of all, angry in English. As things now stood, she could have a good fight with her mother in Romanian, but only a crappy one with her daughter in English.

"Can you slice the cucumber?" she said.

"Slice" was the right word. Laura remembered a Microsoft party where she and Adrian had arrived early, and Laura offered to help the host in the kitchen. He showed her the cutting board and a block of hard cheese, and Laura got to work. Newcomers passed through the kitchen on their way to the back porch, greeting Laura and asking about her task. She told them all she was "cutting the cheese." Everyone smiled, a few even laughed, but no one told her that "cutting the cheese" was slang for farting. For the next year or so, Laura never cut anything again. Everything was sliced. She sliced deals, sliced her losses, and sliced through red tape.

Alice took the vegetables to the sink to wash them. "So," she said, failing to sound casual, "did you take David's case?"

"Never ever unlock the door for a stranger again. You hear me, Alice? It's not safe."

"Yes, Mom." Alice turned the water on. "But did you? Take the case, I mean."

Laura nodded. Alice smiled, and Laura knew, as only a mother could, that her daughter was proud of her in that moment. She wanted to dart across the kitchen and give her child a mama-bear hug, but she knew Alice wouldn't like it.

6

AT THE END of her Saturday morning run, Laura had a plan for the Ramirez case. Her house was as quiet as when she left it an hour earlier, with the dawn. Alice was probably still asleep upstairs. Laura took off her shoes, wool cap, and gloves and sat at her laptop in the dining room. There were no urgent emails this early, but before going upstairs to take a hot shower, she just had to type up some notes for her upcoming interview with her new client.

She was almost done when Skype launched its annoying jingle. The video chat screen showed Claudia Florea's picture. It was close to six in the evening in Bucharest, Romania. Laura didn't feel like talking to her mother. She needed a coffee and a shower first, but she also could never let a call go unanswered on the chance that Claudia might be trying to reach her from a Bucharest hospital.

The worst call of Laura's life had come from such a hospital in December of 2005, at two in the morning, noon local time. Her father had been admitted with stomach pains the day before. They'd run some tests but wouldn't tell him anything about the results. He handed his cell phone to a male doctor, who took it out of the room.

"His condition is very serious, ma'am," the doctor said, sounding panicked. "Your father is bleeding internally, inside his abdomen, and we can't stop it. To make matters worse, Mr. Florea has a rare blood type, AB negative, and we don't have enough blood to keep replacing what he's losing. We can't get more because it's snowing here, and the roads are closed. We gave him hemostatic medicine to force rapid blood coagulation, but for the moment that's all we can do."

"Is there any hospital that can deal with his condition?" Laura's voice was calm, but her insides were twisted with dread.

"Maybe where you live in the States, ma'am, something could be done. But here, no. We can't move him. We can't operate on him. He has a pancreatic tumor, very advanced and tangled with blood vessels. All we can do is pray for a miracle."

To Laura, the doctor's words sounded like an accusation, not a prayer. As in, had Laura taken better care of her father—had she brought him to Seattle months ago and taken him to doctors here—he wouldn't be in mortal danger now.

"How long do we have?" she said.

"A few hours, ma'am. A few weeks if he's lucky and we stop the bleeding. We need a miracle now. And we need this damn snow to stop."

Laura found airplane tickets for a British Airways flight with a layover in London. She packed a small bag for her and fifteen-month-old Alice, making sure everything, including the car seat, fit in the stroller. They crossed the Atlantic and would have made it to the hospital in time had it not been for the snowstorm that closed the Bucharest airport.

The laptop kept ringing. Claudia's call was probably nothing, just her wanting to chat, but Laura had to make sure. She clicked the green button to answer.

Claudia came online with a blast of static. Her face, lined from years of squinting and frowning at blueprints on her architect's drafting table, filled the screen in poor resolution.

"What happened to your hair, Laura?" she asked in Romanian, pronouncing the name as they did back home: La-ooh-rah, with a rolling *r*.

Laura smoothed her matted hair. "I went for a run."

"Did you take a shower?"

Laura put on a thin smile. "Why? Can you smell me all the way from Bucharest?"

"Now don't be testy," Claudia said. "I called to ask if you watched that video I sent you."

Laura had received the video last night, a public service announcement recorded by Romanian media personalities, urging citizens to vote in the upcoming European Union elections. "We must all come together for our children to preserve this beautiful and blessed country," said an elderly actress sitting in a theater chair. "Indifference enables thieves to rule us," a middle-aged male singer added. "Do you think anyone has ever left Romania because things are just too good here?" asked a beloved children's author. An opera singer with a magnificent hairdo appeared next. "Do you think the people who live abroad and work from morning 'til night to send money home wouldn't love to return to a fair and democratic country?" Scenic images of Romania filled the screen as people spoke together, "I'm not ready to give up on Romania. Are you ready to abandon Romania, to give up on the graves of your loved ones, on your language, and your parents?" Laura knew why she'd been sent that video.

"Sorry, didn't have time," she lied.

"Well, don't forget to vote this spring. You still have a valid Romanian passport, no?"

Of course Laura had her passport. Yes, she'd go to the expats' voting station in Kenmore, Washington and make her father proud. Romanian democratic elections had started after the 1989 anticommunist uprising, and he'd voted in every one of them.

Laura blurted out, "But you didn't go last time," and regretted it the next moment.

"Because I'm too old, and I have to walk to the voting station alone. What if I have a heart attack waiting in line?"

At sixty-seven, Claudia wasn't considered too old by US standards, though Laura's father had died at fifty-eight.

"Go with your neighbors then," Laura said. "And take a cab." Her sweatshirt felt cool against her skin. Soon she'd start shivering.

"You want me to waste money on cabs?" Claudia said.

Laura took a deep breath, as she'd learned from her last therapist. "There's enough money on the card, Mama." She'd opened a debit card in her mother's name soon after her father's funeral.

Claudia made an incredulous face. "People don't just take cabs in Romania. You forget what life is like for the rest of us here."

Laura rubbed her temples. She'd stepped into another of her mother's guilt traps. "So, what are you watching these days?" she said.

To her surprise, Claudia accepted the change of subject and began talking about a Romanian-subtitled South Korean TV show she'd been watching on a pirated videos website. The characters were high schoolers. The boy was involved with street gangs, the girl was an honors student in a starched uniform, and they of course fell in love. The girl was going to help him get out of trouble, but not before getting in trouble herself.

"Alice would like it," she said, "now that she's in high school."

Laura doubted it. Claudia barely knew Alice's tastes.

And whose fault is that? Claudia would say. *Whose fault is it that I don't spend enough time with my granddaughter?*

Laura started to shiver in her damp clothes. "That sounds fascinating," she said when her mother reached a natural break in her South Korean story of teenage love. "I'm sorry I have to go, Mama. I have a prehearing statement to finish today."

"Always your work...And for people who aren't even your people."

Laura's pulse quickened.

"Don't forget to take care of Alice," Claudia said and waved goodbye.

Laura didn't need reminding. She'd been taking care of Alice by herself for years. Ever since the divorce. Even more after Adrian had moved back to Romania to marry someone ten years younger and start a tech company there. No, she didn't need reminding she was a single mom. Alice still blamed her for the divorce and punished her with a cold and defying attitude.

And why is it you have no help with Alice? Claudia would say. *Your whole family is here. Home. Why are you still there?*

Because Laura and Alice were American citizens, and their lives and their home and work and school were here in Seattle. They lived alone because it was the right thing for Alice. Laura's last affair had been a couple of years ago, with Gordon—a retired Amazon software developer working on a tech-thriller. Some of the tech industry characters in his novel were immigrants, so he had hired Laura to consult on immigration issues, and one thing led to another.

Before Gordon, there'd been Tadelesh, an Indian PhD student at the University of Washington, who moved to Colorado after Laura helped secure his green card. Before him, there'd been Mike, a photographer who grew up in Hong Kong and had moved to Seattle as a teenager. Mike, Tadelesh, and Gordon often complained that Laura never invited them to her home or made time for them on weekends. But that was her way of protecting Alice, who would have found her mother's relationships with men confusing, especially after the inevitable breakup. And so, Gordon, Tadelesh, and Mike all left in the end, just as Laura had expected them to.

But she couldn't explain that to Claudia, who disapproved of both divorce and dating—and everything else Laura did with her life in America.

"Bye, Mama," she said instead.

"Don't forget to eat or you'll get stomachaches." Claudia made a long kissing sound.

Laura echoed the kiss, waved, smiled, and clicked the red button. Claudia vanished from the screen, but her PSA echoed in Laura's mind: *Are you ready to give up on the graves of your loved ones?* She remembered the white marble cross at the cemetery and the oval picture of her father in a black cowboy hat. She'd bought that hat from a tourist souvenir shop in downtown Seattle and taken the photo in Bucharest. Her father was smiling at the camera, trying on his new hat, never imagining that this picture would one day mark his grave. Laura felt a painful lump in her throat—then and now. She would have made it to Bucharest and her father, if not for the snow.

That PSA was not just a plea to go out and vote, it was also a warning to people like Laura, who'd never be forgiven for abandoning their parents and their country.

...to give up on the graves of your loved ones...mormintele celor dragi...

Laura wiped her eyes. Enough with all that. Better to think of the here and now. Shower first to clean up and warm up. For breakfast, she'd make bacon and eggs for Alice. Maybe a batch of blueberry muffins too. Then she'd start outlining the Ramirez prehearing statement. Emilio Ramirez, one of the people who weren't even her people, as her mother would say.

7

DAVID COLLECTED LETTERS of support from churchgoers before the Sunday sermon at Our Redeemer's in Everett. Father Nicolas Zapata had written three stapled pages. Once David had the letters in hand, he stayed close to his mother and Jacob. Every time someone stopped by to tell them how sad they felt about Emilio, his mom nearly burst into tears. David worried that the stress might trigger one of her migraines, so he kept an eye out for the usual symptoms: pale lips, squinting, shallow breathing. For the moment she seemed okay.

Father Nicolas had delivered a sermon about standing together to help those in need. "Brother Emilio is one of us," he said in closing, his voice loud from the pulpit. "He met Blanca in this church, married her here, baptized his two boys here."

The congregation nodded and murmured their support.

"Let us all pray now," Father Nicolas said, "for the swift return of Brother Emilio. His family needs him." He motioned to the pew where David sat with Jacob and their mom. "His workmates need him." He nodded toward Fernando and his men at the back of the church. "His neighbors—and all of us—need him."

"Amen," people said.

"And if you feel so inclined, please write a letter of support, telling ICE how important Brother Emilio is to our congregation and this community. You'll find pads and pencils at the back."

David locked arms with his mother, and they headed for the writing table. Jacob sidled alongside, frowning.

Fernando caught up with them. "From all of us at work," he said in Spanish, giving David's mom a plastic bag with what looked like an inch-thick stack of dollar bills. She thanked him and put the gift in her purse.

They waited around a while to collect more letters, thanking the people who wrote them.

Outside, the sky was cloudy, with snowflakes swirling in the air and melting on the pavement.

"Want to play Xbox when we get home?" David asked Jacob as they walked to the truck.

"Sure," Jacob said.

David was glad his brother felt better, but before he could say something, he heard the purposeful clacking of high heels behind them.

"Mrs. Ramirez!" a woman's voice called out. The clacking sped up.

The family turned to look. "Do you know her?" David asked his mom, who shook her head. "She doesn't know your name."

But they stopped and waited for the woman. She was tall and slim, with long blond hair. She wore a fancy coat over a red business suit and looked out of place.

"Mrs. Ramirez," she said. "My name is Evelyn Brunelle. Has your husband ever mentioned me?"

"No…"

"You can call me Evelyn. Is there a place we can talk? You'll be interested in what I have to say."

David didn't like this Evelyn. Her perfume was too sweet, and whatever she wanted to talk about sounded like bad news.

She searched through her red leather purse and took out a business card, handing it to David's mom, who shook her head.

"Real estate agent? We are not interested."

"Where can we talk?" Evelyn said.

David's mom just said, "We are going home."

"Awesome. I'll meet you there." Evelyn unlocked a black Mercedes SUV. The vehicle stood out among more humble cars and trucks.

"How does she know where we live?" David said, climbing into the driver's seat of the family pickup.

"She'll just follow us, duh," Jacob said from the back of the crew cab, earbuds already in place.

"Should I lose her, Mom?" David said.

"You drive safely, you hear me?" she said.

David drove slower than usual, keeping Evelyn's SUV in his rear-view mirror until he pulled up in front of the garage. Evelyn parked behind them, and they all went inside the house. They left their shoes in the mudroom except for Evelyn, who kept her red pumps on. Jacob went to his room and slammed the door behind him.

"What do you want?" David's mom asked Evelyn, who was looking around the kitchen.

"Great cabinets…Beautiful quartz countertops…The fridge and the oven might need upgrading."

She edged into the sunroom, a recent addition hugging the side of the house like an L-shaped Lego piece. David's dad had finished it the previous summer with tall windows and skylights. His mom had bought a large sofa and a wooden table at a garage sale, plus a few mismatched wing chairs from a church auction, and made the place feel cozy. The walls were hung with planters holding flowers, cacti, and other green stuff. David could see how Evelyn might appreciate the space.

The new sunroom was the family's favorite spot in the house. That was where Jacob sat with his tablet on weekends, where they all played board games, where the parents admired the blue waters of Possession Sound and the islands in the distance.

"I want to buy your beautiful, amazing house," Evelyn said, sitting on the sofa. "I already have a few developers interested in the orchard plot. Someone is thinking a restaurant by the beach."

"Sorry, ma'am," David said. "Our house is not for sale." He glanced at his mom to see if she looked okay. She sat down in a chair and touched her temple. Was she feeling ill? Was that why she let this horrible lady walk all over their house like that?

"I've heard about your husband," Evelyn said. "In church, today. And I thought, what a great opportunity to help my neighbors, as Father Nicolas said."

David's mom squinted. "You live in this neighborhood?"

Evelyn laughed. "The greater Seattle is my neighborhood. When was your house built?"

David's mom didn't answer. He wanted to take that obnoxious lady by the arm and show her the door, but he wouldn't make a scene and upset his mom. Not yet anyway.

Evelyn smiled. "Do you have enough money for the bond and a lawyer?"

David balled his hands into fists to keep his anger in check.

"The people at our church," his mom said, "they helped us more than we hoped."

"Your husband's legal expenses will soon be beyond what your congregation can help with."

David noticed she'd forgotten to say "our congregation."

"In fact, Mrs. Ramirez, you're one trip to the ER away from having no money left at all. You lost your health insurance when your husband was arrested, didn't you? The medicine you need for your migraines costs money too."

David's mom winced. She was getting ill. "How do you know all this about us?" she whispered.

"People talk, Mrs. Ramirez, and I listen. But I can help. I can buy your house for close to market value and not charge agent fees, which means more money for you. Half a million dollars in cash, part of it upfront as a non-refundable deposit. I can have the money in days. And I'll take care of all the paperwork."

David's mom rubbed her forehead. "That is…less than half of the market value."

David could no longer watch this evil woman torment his mom. "Get out," he told Evelyn.

"David…" his mom said.

"No, get out," David told Evelyn. "And don't you dare bother my mom, ever again."

Evelyn dropped a business card on the coffee table. "Think about it, Mrs. Ramirez," she said, leaving the sunroom.

David hurried to open the front door for her. "I'm not shook, Ms. Whatever. You think you can mess with my mom, but you can't mess with me. I know my rights, and I'll defend my home with the full backing of the law."

Evelyn burst out laughing. "People thought that in 2008 too." She called over David's shoulder, "You need a friend out there, Mrs. Ramirez." And then she was out the door, her too-sweet fragrance lingering behind.

"Her name is Morales," David yelled after her.

He then went back to his mom. "Are you okay?" But he knew the answer.

"We'll lose the house," she whispered in Spanish.

"Mom, that's not going to happen. We'll raise more money."

"The people who support us now, they'll get tired of our begging."

"Can we get a mortgage from the bank?"

"I'll try tomorrow," she said, squeezing her eyes shut. "I have to lie down."

Her day was ruined. She'd take a migraine pill, close the blinds in the upstairs bedroom, and grow too weak to get up. David would make dinner, no problem. There was some chicken soup in the fridge, and he'd go to the grocery store for the rest, before snow covered the roads.

He went to Jacob's room and cracked the door a little. "You want to go to the store?"

Jacob was in bed, earbuds on, eyes closed. Tears on his cheeks. David wished he could do something for his little brother. At school, a couple of teachers had already told David that Jacob stared out the window and refused to answer questions. David told them something had happened to a relative. He wasn't sure why he'd lied—it wasn't like people didn't know about his father's arrest.

"You okay?" David said.

Jacob turned on his side. "I wish I was dead."

David wanted to smack him over the head. "Dude, this isn't about you. It's about Dad. And Mom. And our house. Just this once, can you not grab the center of attention?"

"Like I said…I'm useless to y'all."

"I don't have time for this," David said, surprised at his instant anger. "I have to get some bread and milk before the snow starts for real. You want anything?"

Jacob didn't answer.

Back in the living room, David pulled out his smartphone. He'd normally hit up Cruz to vent, but he wouldn't mind chatting with Alice Holban right now. They'd texted a few times, and she seemed friendly. He'd also sent her that video of his band, and she'd replied with a smoking-hot emoji. Her joining them someday still sounded great to him.

He typed, *An awful woman wants to buy our house*

Did you kick her ass? Alice texted back.

You bet

Though he hadn't, not really.

8

ON MONDAY, LAURA went through the security station at the Tacoma Northwest Detention Center, showed her attorney ID, and gave Emilio Ramirez's full name and Alien Number. She then received an invisible-ink stamp on the back of her left hand. The guard at the check-in desk was a new face—faces changed often at NWDC—a woman in her thirties with blue eyes and sandy hair.

"Where're you from?" she asked Laura, smiling.

Ah, the question that always drew a line between Laura and the other person. Sure, it stemmed from well-intentioned curiosity, but it also stated that Laura was from somewhere else. Not from here, not one of us. Though after two decades in the United States—most of Laura's adult life— she no longer thought of Romania as home. She wanted to explain to this affable woman that immigrants often left their native countries when they didn't feel at home there, usually because of mortal danger or lack of economic opportunities. It took years—at least seven, psychologists said—for a new country to feel like home to an immigrant. And then *the question* reminded them that they still didn't belong.

But she said none of that. Instead, she pressed her lips into a polite smile and said, "Romania."

"My mom's from Germany," the guard said, "moved here in the '80s. Funny thing, I didn't realize until I was maybe fifteen that she had an accent."

"That's…interesting." After all these years, Laura still didn't know how to continue such conversations.

Just in time, another visitor needed checking for guns and drugs, and Laura moved aside.

That guard's mom had left Germany—East or West?—to move to the United States around the time Laura's father had tried to flee Romania for West Germany. Back then, life was getting worse in Romania, with no end in sight. Everything was rationed or missing altogether, and the police state was vicious. Laura was thirteen when her father left home one summer morning, heading for the Danube and Yugoslavia beyond. He promised to call as soon as he found a phone in Serbia: three rings, then he'd hang up. He wouldn't risk a conversation that could be intercepted. Once he arrived in West Germany, via Austria, he'd find a way to bring Claudia and Laura there too.

Claudia spent the next few days waiting by the phone, but instead of three rings, eventually there was a knock on the door, and two militia officers informed her that Tudor Florea was in jail. Laura and Claudia took a train to the border town where Tudor was held. When they reached the jail, they were shown to the infirmary.

Laura screamed when she first saw her father. He was so scary-looking, all purple and broken-faced. He could speak, but he sounded like his mouth was full of cotton balls.

Claudia took his hand. "Did it hurt, love?"

"Only when they hit me the first time…then that spot grew numb…"

He came home after eighteen months of hard labor, mixing cement at construction sites around Bucharest. The three of them sat together in their tiny living room, and Laura asked her father how he'd been arrested. Claudia said that was a conversation for when she was older, but Laura said she was old enough at fifteen. She needed an explanation for her father's purple face, which had haunted her nightmares since the arrest.

"I'm one of the lucky ones," Tudor told her. He'd arrived at the Danube in the evening and spent the next two days camping in nearby woods, learning how the border patrol guarded that area. He chose to cross on a moonless night at a spot hidden by trees. He put his clothes and wallet in a plastic bag, which he tied to his back, and dipped into the Danube. The water was calm and lukewarm, and the whole world was silent. He could see lights across the river, on the Serbian shore. He was a strong swimmer and thought he could make it.

But the lights on the Serbian shore were reflected as straight lines on the water's smooth surface. The border patrol watched those lines—if one was crooked, that meant there was someone in the water. And they pounced.

Tudor was making good progress when a spotlight snapped on about a hundred meters ahead. It was mounted on a speedboat, though pointing away from him. He noticed people in the water up ahead. He heard their terrified, pleading voices.

Frightened, he stopped swimming and treaded water, watching. A soldier stood at the bow, holding something in his hand—a harpoon or a spear. He threw it at the people in the water. The anguished cry that followed made Tudor lose his composure and sink for a moment. When he came back up, he saw the soldier pulling the line in and retrieving his spear, then throwing it again. Another shriek sounded from the group in the water. The swimmers thrashed wildly, trying to get away, but the boat followed.

Tudor swam back to the shore as quietly as he could and hid among the trees. He put his clothes back on and started for the nearest village. He didn't get far. Soldiers with flashlights and dogs surrounded him. They threatened to shoot, so he didn't resist arrest. At the jail, they handcuffed him to a radiator and started punching and kicking him. They enjoyed it but had to take turns. Hammering a grown man was hard work, even for seasoned border patrols.

Claudia sobbed through most of Tudor's story while Laura listened, unable to blink. Not having her father home had been hard. Claudia was always tired and snapping at Laura over the smallest mistakes. They'd lost Tudor's adult food rations. They went to bed hungry and cold as life got worse all around them. Kids at school made fun of the girl whose father was in jail. But now she felt bad for thinking she'd had it hard.

She wrapped her arms around her father's neck. "I'm so sorry that happened to you, Tata."

"Don't ever try that again," Claudia said. "Never put your life in danger like that. Promise me."

He promised. But in December 1989, no such promise could keep him from joining the people in the streets to bring down President

Ceaușescu and the communist regime. He took a bullet to his thigh and never walked the same after that.

When Laura told him she planned to move to America with Adrian, Tudor smiled and said, "Good for you, kid, go see the world."

What would her father say now if he saw the world Laura dealt with in her day-to-day job? She took a seat in the NWDC waiting room and worked on her laptop for the next hour. She read through documents on two other cases, which Jennifer had emailed the night before. One would be heard by the Seattle Immigration Court, the other would be reviewed by the Board of Immigration Appeals in Falls Church, Virginia.

At last, her name was called. She stashed her laptop in her leather tote and presented herself at a secure door that buzzed a moment later. The white hallway beyond smelled of cleaning products, plastic, and pain. Laura's low heels echoed under harsh ceiling lights. At the end of that tunnel-like hall, she stopped in front of the guard stationed at the security room. Despite years of coming here, Laura still dreaded being trapped inside that tiny space.

She showed the guard her ID. He nodded and called her name into the radio mic on his shoulder. When the door buzzed open, she entered a room no bigger than an elevator. In two steps, she was at the black light lamp by the opposite door and made her left hand into a fist. The round stamp with the NWDC logo showed in pale white. The guard on the other side of the door nodded through the window and said something into his mic.

Laura imagined that, somewhere up in the sky, a man sat in front of a wall of TV monitors and pressed a giant red button—always the same red button—that granted admittance to those deemed worthy. She'd had this red button fantasy since childhood, when she and everyone else had been forced to wait in long lines for just about everything.

Today, the man with the red button was taking his time. Laura shifted from foot to foot. She felt her chest tighten. At least she was alone and could take a few steps. When she was crowded in with others, she had to stay put, focusing all her energy on not screaming.

She reminded herself that she wasn't on an airplane flying from Seattle to London in the middle of winter. Not trapped in a box in the sky where she didn't know whether her father was alive or dead. Not replaying the doctor's words in her mind: *Maybe where you live in the States, ma'am, something could be done.* Not fighting off the conjured-up image of her father's body on a morgue table, his cheeks a sickly shade of gray, his lips purple, his eyes—

Open up, open up…

Laura's fingers felt cold and tingly. She pushed out a breath, mouth round, eyes fixed on the guard beyond the window. He gazed in the distance, as if she were no longer his problem.

One step back, one forward. She forced herself to remember her father alive. She grasped for a good memory of him. Watching him fish under a willow tree on the banks of the Dâmbovița, the river crossing Bucharest. Summer days filled with the smell of fish and mud and sea-weed. Sometimes she'd throw rocks in the water to scare her father's fish, but he never got angry. He smiled and told her to return to what-ever book she was reading. And then he'd go back to catching perch or carp, bream or pike. He kept them alive in a mesh bag in the water until it was time to go home.

In the afternoon, Laura would sit at the kitchen table while he cleaned the fish. He'd light a cigarette, and the smoke would rise against the yellowed ceiling. He scraped the scales off and opened the bellies with a sharp knife. Laura would always get the air bladders—transpar-ent organs filled with air—and share them with the other kids in the apartment building. They all loved stomping on them, the way Alice had loved bursting bubble wrap when she was little.

Her father seasoned the fish with salt and pepper, coated it with egg and flour, and fried it in a cast-iron skillet. Sometimes he boiled it with noodles and broth. Other times, he put it in a dish with parsley, dill weed, and lovage, then baked it with potatoes and carrots.

Laura closed her eyes. She could smell the open oven in their tiny kitchen in Bucharest. Her panic loosened its grip. A deep breath. She could see the small table, crammed in a corner, so it only had three seats. But that was all the space their little family needed to enjoy their baked fish with veggies on a summer evening.

Another deep breath.

The lock buzzed, and Laura shoved the door open. She stood in the hallway for a minute, composing herself.

The doors to the visitation rooms were up ahead. Today she was going to number four. There were five such rooms in the detention center, but two were always occupied by a nonprofit that helped those without legal representation.

Inside, Emilio Ramirez was already at the table, holding his I-862 form in one hand. He was in his forties, with short brown hair and a face hardened by sun and wind. He had the distinct air of a longtime immigrant arrested for the first time in his life. He knew he'd broken the law by crossing the border illegally, and there was guilt in his eyes, but Laura could also read his disbelief at what was happening. His wide, strong shoulders—the build of a construction worker—were hunched like he'd been beaten, though the beating was only emotional at this point. He was calm and subdued, more so than Laura would have been in his place. He was probably thinking about his family and wondering what his arrest would mean for them. Laura knew from experience that there would come a time when he'd start thinking about his own survival in this cage, but that was still in the future for Emilio Luis Ramirez Garcia.

She took a seat and introduced herself. She then checked her new client's full name, Alien Number, and the picture on his wristband. Dark-blue band, like his jail uniform. The color marked him as the lowest security risk at NWDC and allowed him the greatest number of rights as a detainee, such as they were. The other colors—dark green, orange, and red—turned the screws on a detainee's rights until his treatment was no better than solitary confinement.

"Thank you for taking my case, Ms. Holban," Emilio said with a mild Spanish accent. "It means a lot to my wife Blanca. And to my sons, who are such good boys." He sounded fluent.

For Laura, language was the biggest barrier when working with her clients—many of them needing interpreters if they didn't speak Spanish, which she knew well, or English. Language was a bigger hurdle than their level of education or the fact that many of them had lost their papers while traveling to the US. When Laura was still in law school, a visiting lecturer had told her class that those who didn't go through school didn't have the same level of respect for papers. Laura had then remarked on the lack of good schools in war zones and the difficulties of keeping one's papers in order while fleeing death and destruction. That conversation hadn't ended well.

"Is your real name Emilio Ramirez?" Laura said.

He nodded. "Everybody calls me Emilio."

"Then you can call me Laura. I'm here to do your intake, Emilio," which meant figuring out his legal situation, "and to see what forms of relief you might qualify for. Do you think you have a claim based on belonging to an Indigenous group?"

He squinted at her question.

"Are you Mayan by ethnicity?" Laura explained.

"No. Ladino." He meant of mixed European and Indigenous heritage, someone who couldn't claim Mayan customs and tribal ties, and whose primary language was Spanish.

Laura made a note. "Thank you, Emilio."

They agreed he'd call her from NWDC because lawyers weren't allowed to place phone calls to the detention center. Because Emilio's wife Blanca was also undocumented, Laura advised against her visiting him here, where ICE had offices and officers.

"It would be like marching straight into the wolf's mouth, as they say in Romania."

Emilio nodded, looking resigned. "She hasn't come here yet. Only my older son and Fernando, my boss. Can they arrest Blanca too?"

"If they do, we have a strong case for her release because your American sons would be left without a caregiver." She went back to her checklist. "For most of the filings, I'll have to work with Blanca since detainees can't keep documents in here—with some exceptions." She pointed to his I-862 form. "Like your NTA. May I see it?"

Emilio passed her the paper titled Notice to Appear. "Blanca, she gets migraines. She won't be able to help you always. But David can."

"As little as possible, I hope. He's only a child." Laura scanned Emilio's charging document for prior convictions—none—and legal charges based on the Immigration and Nationality Act of 1965 and the Illegal Immigration Reform and Immigration Responsibility Act of 1996. Emilio's entry date into the United States was January 14, 1998. "'It came to the attention of Officer Masters,'" she read in the NTA, "'that the respondent might be in the US illegally, and the allegation was confirmed upon further investigation.' But how had it come to their attention?"

Emilio rubbed his shaved cheek and sighed. "I was going to meet with the high school admin for an estimate. Maybe the meeting was a setup? Or, it could have been this real estate agent…Evelyn Brunelle. She wanted to buy my house, and I said no."

Laura made a note to track down the school admin and Evelyn Brunelle and talk to them. "About your bond, because ICE refused you one, we can now petition an immigration judge. ICE and the judge, they both work for the government, but if the judge finds you're not a flight risk or a danger to the community, they'll approve it. With one exception: Can this Evelyn provide the judge with 'anything else relevant' that might make them reject us? Could she be the reason ICE refused to grant your bond?"

"I don't know. I only met her once, and I was very polite to her."

"Why did you meet with her?"

"She threatened to alert ICE if I didn't."

Laura noted the time and place Emilio had met with Evelyn Brunelle. She'd check with the staff at Café Abdul in Everett to see if they remembered any arguments that day.

"Why did you leave Guatemala, Emilio?"

"I…"

Despite the warden's assurances, Laura still wondered if there were microphones in the visitation rooms. But if she couldn't talk openly with her clients here, where could she? Not on the phone—those conversations were recorded, and she kept them short, only making arrangements for the next meeting.

"Don't worry, no one is recording us," she said. "I'm trying to understand what kind of deportation relief you qualify for. There are three types: asylum, cancellation of removal, and withholding of removal. I'll explain them in more detail later. So, why did you leave Guatemala?"

Emilio sighed. "My father, he was a border patrol officer. He was killed after he arrested…some traffickers. Then they came after us, his family." He looked away, as if not wanting to remember. "I was home when they came. My mother and my brother…They were killed. I got away. They burned down our house."

There weren't many details to that awful story, but Laura could fill them in later.

"I went north with a pollero," Emilio said, meaning someone who brought undocumented workers to the US. "First by bus, then on foot through the Sonoran Desert. All the way to a place near Nogales." He meant the two cities with the same name in Mexico and Arizona.

"Any way to document your story?"

Emilio took a moment to answer no.

"And you never applied for asylum? I mean affirmative asylum, which must be filed within the first year of arrival in the US."

He shook his head, a dejected look in his eyes.

"We'll now apply defensively," Laura said, "because now the government is suing us in immigration court, and we need legal protections while we're in deportation proceedings."

Before she could explain more, the door opened.

"Time for the counting," the guard called, meaning Emilio and the other detainees had to return to their pods for lockdown and attendance.

Laura never knew when NWDC would schedule its counting. It seemed to change every week. "Can we have an extra minute?"

"Not today," the guard said.

After leaving the visitation room, Laura went straight to the immigration court clerk to apply for Emilio's bond. A more inexperienced lawyer would have waited to find the school admin and Ms. Brunelle first, to make sure her client was beyond reproach and eligible for bond. But that would add precious days to an already lengthy stay in detention. "Apply anyway" was Laura's strategy, which had served her well so far.

×

Mason sat in his ICE office in downtown Seattle. He'd just secured a three-million-dollar settlement with an Idaho apple farmer who'd used hundreds of illegal aliens in his orchards. It'd been a good day, but Mason was exhausted. He hadn't slept much the night before, not with his son Oliver's constant coughing. Helen had kept the twins home from school today, and she was sure to be tired, which meant no rest for Mason when he arrived home.

He was browsing emails, looking for the next big case, when the burner phone rang in his briefcase. *Shit.* Too busy with the orchard settlement, he'd forgotten to check for updates on the Ramirez case. He answered the phone.

"Why Ramirez meet with a lawyer this morning?" Saravia said. He sounded calm, but his words jolted Mason. "You say he not have a lawyer."

Mason didn't know anything about a lawyer. He moved the burner from one ear to the other, rose from his ergonomic chair, and closed the office door. "How do you know that?" He sat down again and swiveled toward the rain-streaked windows overlooking Elliott Bay.

"I have eyes and ears everywhere."

Mason didn't like the sound of that. "Nothing can happen to him in detention, are we clear?"

"Then send him to me. The end of the month." Saravia hung up.

Mason felt like cursing out loud, a habit he'd broken after the kids were born. He dropped the burner in his briefcase and used the desk phone to call Noah Sheldon at NWDC.

Sheldon answered on the first ring. Yes, he was up to speed with the case and knew that Ramirez had hired Laura Holban. He was going to put that in his daily report.

Mason cursed under his breath. Holban had a history of suing the Department of Homeland Security when things didn't go her way. When local immigration judges ruled against her, she took the case to the Board of Immigration Appeals in Virginia. If she wasn't happy with that panel's decision, she upped the ante with the Ninth Circuit Court of Appeals in the judicial branch. DHS held no sway there, and she wound up winning most of those cases—or having them sent back to the Board of Immigration Appeals. She was bright and adept and a freaking pain in the butt. He'd have to keep an eye on her this time, or he'd be dealing with a very unhappy Señor Saravia.

He decided to go on the offensive. "Who called our hotline on Ramirez?"

"I know this…" Sheldon sounded like he was leafing through a notebook. "One Evelyn Brunelle, real estate agent in the greater Seattle area."

"And who's Ramirez's deportation officer?"

"Ken Masters."

Masters was in his late fifties and very much hoping for a promotion before he retired. But he was also an honest man, and if Holban asked him why ICE had changed its tune on the Ramirez bond, he'd tell her the order came from above.

"Tell Masters to refuse any contact with Ramirez's lawyer," Mason said.

He hung up and stared at the somber clouds, the gray waterfront, and the ferries in the distance. Now that Ramirez had his lawyer, he'd be processed in the backlogged immigration system instead of being fast-tracked toward deportation. Saravia would hate that. If Mason were to speed up the case though, his prints could be nowhere near it.

He turned back to his desktop and clicked on the folder named AILA for American Immigration Lawyers Association. He opened the speech he was scheduled to give at their monthly conference and found the paragraph where he quoted the new efficiency standards imposed by the Justice Department. "To get a 'satisfactory' rating on their performance evaluations, judges will be required to clear at least 700 cases a year and to have fewer than 15 percent of their decisions overturned on appeal." The new rules forced judges to choose a time-saving denial of application over a time-consuming hearing and to cover each other's backs. Mason added a sentence to his speech, urging his trial attorneys—and the immigration lawyers in attendance—to help the judges in Seattle and Tacoma reach their DOJ-mandated quotas.

He massaged his temples. This veiled order to prosecute faster wouldn't move the needle much for the Ramirez case. He needed to speed up the court's calendar, which was impossible. At best, he might be able to influence a decision if he was consulted on a case. But Saravia wouldn't care about the inner workings of the Justice Department.

"Motherfucker," Mason whispered to himself. Yes, he was trading immigrants' personal information for money deposited into an offshore bank account. Yes, he was selling it—indirectly—to organized crime and breaking the law he'd sworn to uphold. But he refused to get his hands even dirtier. If he could find someone else...

He picked up the phone and dialed Lieutenant Mike Greene at the Seattle Police Department. He needed a background check on Evelyn Brunelle.

9

LAURA'S TUESDAY MORNING case involved arguing for a Chinese student's visa before Judge Felsen, who approved the request but still refused to make eye contact. At least she'd been professional and not taken her dislike of Laura out on an innocent client.

By the time Laura got back to downtown Seattle, it was too late for a proper lunch. Jennifer had called Evelyn Brunelle a few times the day before at the number listed for her real estate agency and only reached her voicemail. This morning Laura had called the same number and left a message about needing an agent to help her buy her dream home. She may also have said that money was not an issue, which, under the circumstances, happened to be true. Two minutes later, Evelyn called back. She had a warm, professional voice, said "awesome" a lot, and promised to visit Laura's office at 1:00 p.m. If Evelyn had nothing to do with Emilio's arrest, Laura would contact the high school admin next.

Pressed for time, she walked up Second Avenue to the Chicken & Stuff food truck parked in front of the Norton Building. On the way, she glanced at the window of the souvenir shop where she'd bought her father's black cowboy hat many years ago. A three-foot-tall Space Needle dominated the display, and Laura smiled at the thought of sending something like that to Claudia.

The line for the food truck was short. Laura ordered a chicken burrito, left a good tip, and headed back to Pioneer Square. The front door of her century-old building was hard to open with food in one hand, and she squeezed inside before it swung shut on her. She could take the stairs, but she was working on controlling her claustrophobia, so she waited for the old elevator in its blue wrought-iron cage. The more time she spent in small spaces with nothing bad happening, the better. That was the theory.

Riding upward, she focused on her breath. The floors rolled by with echoless *dings*. She was not on an airplane to London. She was not trapped in a box in the sky without knowing whether her father was alive or dead...Deep breaths...

Her office was on the fifth floor at the end of the hallway. Inside was a small lobby with a couch, a few chairs, and a water cooler. Beyond that were two offices—one for her and one for Jennifer—and a smaller room that housed file cabinets and a printer. There were already people waiting in the lobby, huddled together on the couch and leaning against the wall, all there without appointments, since Laura's roster was already full. She'd let Jennifer sort them out, knowing she'd probably end up with a desperate new client by the end of the day.

The view from Laura's office window probably looked oppressive to her visitors: a red brick building with a wrought-iron fire escape that zigzagged down to an alley. She sat at her computer and clicked on the current folder in her work queue: a family of Somali refugees looking for asylum.

She took a bite of her burrito—spices and cheese and roasted chicken—then remembered Ken Masters, Emilio's ICE deportation officer. She'd been trying to get hold of him to find out why Emilio's bond had been rescinded. She dialed the NWDC number again and was again put on hold at the switchboard. Per new ICE regulations, she had no access to a direct phone number or an email address for Ken Masters or any other ICE officer.

She was still waiting to get through to Masters when the real estate agent arrived. Evelyn Brunelle was tall and athletic with long, wavy blond hair. Her plum-colored business suit was complemented by a black-and-gold purse and pumps. Her handshake was firm. She carried a wool coat over one arm.

"I detect a slight accent," she said after introductions. "Where're you from?"

Laura would have answered Seattle but didn't want to sound snarky. She needed Evelyn's cooperation. "Romania," she said.

"Awesome." Evelyn sat down in one of the upholstered chairs. "So, what kind of house are you looking for?"

"Emilio Ramirez."

Evelyn's face lost its plastered smile. She made to get up, which Laura had expected.

"I need your affidavit about your encounter with my client," Laura said. "I can get it now or ask an immigration judge to call you as a witness during Mr. Ramirez's individual hearing."

Evelyn sat back down.

"A hearing can last for hours and be scheduled at all sorts of inconvenient times," Laura said. "But since you're here, we can get it out of the way." She picked up her desk phone and asked Jennifer to join them.

When the door opened, the lobby looked just as packed.

"Among other great things," Laura said, "my paralegal Jennifer is also a notary public."

Jennifer took a seat and opened her laptop.

"I felt it was my patriotic duty to report an illegal," Evelyn said, her tone defensive.

Jennifer started typing. She asked a few basic questions, and Evelyn supplied the details.

"Let's start with how you figured out Mr. Ramirez was undocumented," Laura said.

"I didn't know. Until he showed up at Café Abdul." Evelyn smiled, looking pleased with herself.

"Tell us about the meeting at Café Abdul, please," Laura said.

Evelyn explained her bewilderment at Emilio's stubborn rejection of an "awesome opportunity" to make money in a hot real estate market. "He's sitting on a lot of land."

"Anything else Emilio Ramirez did or said to you that day?" Laura said. "I've already checked with the staff at the café, and they don't remember any disturbances or customers having arguments."

"Because there weren't any." Evelyn ran her hand through her hair. "I was supporting our administration's efforts to rid our country of bad hombres."

Jennifer rolled her eyes while making a note of Evelyn's contradictory comment.

In law school, Laura had studied a clip from a presidential debate between Ronald Reagan and George H.W. Bush. Both men agreed the country should treat undocumented immigrants as humanely as possible. They used words like "sensitive" and "understanding" when discussing immigration policy. But that was a different time, when seasonal farmhands returned to their families in Mexico at the end of each harvest season, knowing they'd be welcomed back in the spring. That was before immigration became politicized, like everything else in America. Migrant workers grew afraid to go south in the winter because they might not be able to return to work the following spring. Instead, they stayed put and tried to bring their families to the US. Things escalated from there and, in the process, immigrants had become bad hombres.

"Did Mr. Ramirez at any time threaten you in any way?" Laura said.

"Do I look like someone who gets threatened?"

"Yes or no, please."

"No."

"Then you just need to sign the affidavit," Laura said.

Jennifer printed two copies. As soon as everyone signed, Evelyn was out of the office—plum, gold, and all—and Jennifer returned to the potential clients in the lobby.

Laura hadn't uncovered anything damaging about Emilio, which was good. But even this exoneration might not be enough. A few years ago, an undocumented immigrant had to commit a felony to be deported, but now all bets were off, and a family man like Emilio with no criminal record whatsoever could be kicked out of the country after being reported by a self-proclaimed "patriot" like Evelyn Brunelle.

×

The blonde woman standing in Mason's office doorway looked impeccable but harassed. He glanced at the clock on his wall: still two hours before the end of his workday. He was ready to go home and check on Oliver. He worried Chloe might get sick next, and then no one would get any decent sleep for another week.

The woman walked in. "Evelyn Brunelle. Your message said it was urgent. I don't understand why. I already gave a statement to the other lawyer." She plopped herself in a chair before Mason's desk.

"The other lawyer?" Then he knew. "You mean Laura Holban?"

She nodded.

"We're the government's prosecutors, ma'am. Ms. Holban is the defense."

"Awesome." She looked past him as if bored. On that dark afternoon, lights were already turning on along the piers. "Well, here's a copy." She opened her purse and produced a few printed pages held together with a paperclip.

Mason glanced at it. "You signed an affidavit?"

"Is that bad?"

Mason read the section about the meeting between Ramirez and Brunelle a few weeks before. He saw nothing he could use—no proof Ramirez was a dangerous man who'd yelled at Brunelle or attacked her. But he knew there was always room to insert doubt about the "good moral character" of an illegal, some plausible reason for a judge to deny a petition.

In immigration court, where an applicant had to prove he was worthy of not being deported, details like notarized affidavits didn't count for much. If the government contradicted Holban's story, she'd try to disprove a lie. But all that mattered was muddying the waters. Immigration judges didn't have time to wait for the waters to clear. They had quotas to reach.

Mason leaned back in his chair. "Are you saying, Ms. Brunelle, that you never felt threatened by Ramirez?"

"Never." She ran a hand through her hair, a stubborn expression on her face.

"Think about it, Ms. Brunelle. It wasn't just greed that drove you to pick up the phone and report Ramirez."

She looked offended now.

"It was apprehension," Mason added with an understanding smile.

She didn't take his cue. "It was patriotism, Mr. Waltman."

"Yes, of course, but also apprehension. Ramirez is a dangerous man, Ms. Brunelle. You're lucky you got away unscathed."

She seemed concerned. "You think so?"

"I'm sure he made threats against you. Maybe not in so many words."

"I didn't do this because I'm a coward." Her voice rose. "There were no threats."

Mason had hoped he wouldn't have to work this hard to convince her, but she seemed to have issues with her self-esteem. The patriotism thing particularly annoyed him. If there was a patriot in the room, it sure as hell wasn't her.

He gestured for her to wait a minute and searched his inbox until he found Officer Mike Greene's email. He printed the background check submitted by the Kirkland Police Department and forwarded by SPD. It contained a complaint logged three years before, in which a home buyer alleged that Ms. Brunelle had failed to disclose a defective boiler on a property she'd sold, despite knowing about it before the sale. When the new homeowners took their first tour of the house, champagne flutes in hand, they found the basement flooded with rusty water. KPD subsequently uncovered a shady arrangement between Ms. Brunelle and the property inspector, but the charge had been dropped when Ms. Brunelle agreed to pay for the installation of a tankless water heater.

Her background check also contained a note from Ms. Brunelle's bank, stating that she'd periodically withdrawn large sums of cash, all just under $10,000. That in itself was not illegal, but it could suggest that Ms. Brunelle was building a rainy-day stash. Mason wouldn't mention it just yet for fear of causing her to cover her tracks, but it was something he might examine more closely if need be.

"Here, Ms. Brunelle." He handed her a page from the background check. "I'm sure there are more broken boilers out there, should anyone care to start looking."

She read the page, biting her lip. "Those charges were dropped." She looked up, defiant.

"Ms. Brunelle," Mason said with a smile. "I have friends in high places who can go after your predatory tactics with everything they've got."

She lowered her eyes, scanning the background check again, but Mason could see her resolve had been broken. She was hiding something, and she didn't want the police nosing around.

Time to go for something big. "Say he tried to rape you."

"No way, Mr. Waltman." She stared up at him. "I'm not going to describe those kinds of things in a statement. Give me something else to work with."

In truth, if the victim wasn't convincing, a rape accusation could backfire big-time. He just needed to cast some doubt on Emilio's character, and the immigration judge would order his deportation. His biggest problems were smart-ass immigration lawyers, like the one who'd exposed his former trial attorney for falsifying documents.

"Say he shoved you against a wall and tried to choke you."

"Where? Not at the coffee shop. His lawyer said she checked with the staff, and there were no disturbances that day."

"No, not there. If we can find a place where we can say he attacked you…"

She nodded, biting her lip. "There was another time. I went to his house. Thinking to convince him with honey instead of vinegar."

Mason perked up. "Was he home?"

"Yes, working in the garage."

"Anyone else at home?"

"I don't think so."

"Any cameras on the property?"

"No, not in the usual spots."

"Did you talk to Ramirez?"

"No. I…decided to call the ICE hotline instead."

"Good. That's good." Mason rubbed his hands. He could accuse Ramirez of assaulting Brunelle, and it'd be a "he said, she said" situation. No cameras, no other witnesses. An assault in the second degree. An alleged class B felony sure to destroy Holban's argument for "good moral character" of her client. It would also explain why Brunelle called ICE when she did—because she was frightened.

Mason turned to his computer, typed up a page, and printed it for her. "How's that?"

She read the text but looked uneasy. "What would the other lawyer say?"

"Don't worry about her." That was why he'd have Brunelle sign a witness statement instead of an affidavit. A witness statement was not a sworn document, making it easier to argue that the signer had misremembered things.

"I don't know," Evelyn said, shifting in her chair. "I still want to buy that house. If I'm the plaintiff against the homeowner, and I also offer to buy his house, that has to significantly affect the criminal case, doesn't it? And won't it make it impossible for me to get the house? It'll look like I'm just saying this bad stuff for my own benefit."

"That's a good point, yes," Mason said. "Except, there will never be a criminal case. It's all being decided behind closed doors, and Ramirez will soon be deported. You'll be free to pursue the house, if that's what you want."

Evelyn nodded at last and signed, then let herself out.

Mason emailed the scanned witness statement to Sheldon, who'd sign it as the trial attorney assigned to the Ramirez case. In the email, Mason wrote, "Let NWDC know he's been credibly accused of assault."

Even an aggressive lawyer like Laura Holban wouldn't appeal for an assault perpetrator. That should guarantee Ramirez's deportation as fast as the choked-up immigration bureaucracy allowed. Hopefully that would take care of the bug up Saravia's ass. Ramirez might not be out of the country by the end of the month, but it shouldn't take much longer.

There was of course a risk in what Mason was doing with Brunelle, but he found it exhilarating. He touched the scar on his cheek. Sometimes, like now, it felt tender under his fingers. He'd picked it up in the '80s in Yakima County, land of White farmers and seasonal Mexican farmhands. The White kids there used to tease Mason and his sister Margot about their dark skin. To make her feel better, Mason told little Margot that, because their mother had been born in Italy, they were descended from Roman emperors.

When Pa Kirk got drunk, he cursed them and their mother, even though he must have once been in love with her dark Sicilian looks. "A weak gasbag," he called Mason. That was what 1930s Americans used to call Italian immigrants, who ate lots of garlic and beans.

There had been a girl once, fair-skinned and blue-eyed like Helen, who'd liked Mason's dark looks. She went out with him once, but her redneck father brought his shotgun to Kirk's house and threatened to kill "them Mexicans."

"We're no fucking Mexicans," Kirk bellowed at the girl's father, shooting his rifle in the air. But he still used his belt on Mason that day and gave him the scar on the cheek. "That's for letting people think you're not a real American."

Mason touched his scar again—the only scar anyone other than Helen could see. The thrill of doing something he wasn't allowed to and getting away with it...Mason was even better at that than Pa Kirk, who'd died on his way home one evening, drunk out of his mind. The old bastard fell on the side of a dark road and froze to death. He died doing what he loved best, but before he was forced to pay for the scars he'd left on Mason's body.

For years, Mason had been a model student and citizen, never breaking the law, never even getting a speeding ticket, always separating his recyclables from the garbage. But what really brought him joy these days was mastering what Pa Kirk had once done as an amateur: breaking all the rules from a position of power where no one could hurt him. For that, ICE was the perfect employer.

10

AFTER HER CHAT with Evelyn Brunelle, Laura drove south to Tacoma. At NWDC, she entered another visitation room, pulled out a chair, and sat down across the table from Gabriela Izquierdo. Gabriela was in her late thirties, and her long dark hair was just starting to gray. She wore a yellow uniform and had a sad, resigned smile. Worse than that, it was a forgiving smile.

Laura spoke English per Gabriela's initial request to work together on her language skills for court appearances. "Let me do this for you, Gabriela. Let me file an appeal."

"No te preocupes por mí, Laura." She pronounced "Laura" the Spanish and Romanian way. "I am…all right. I'm going home." She seemed ready to go back to Mexico, to be with her mother and grand-mother and all the cousins and aunts she'd missed over the years. And with the graves of those lost in other people's drug wars.

…*the graves of your loved ones…mormintele celor dragi…*

"Home?" Laura said. "Your home is here, with your son and your husband."

Gabriela had already said she wouldn't take her family to Mexico, where their lives would be in danger. "When I come back, I show picture of mi niño at the border, maybe they let me back in."

"This is not the old times, Gabriela. You can't haggle your way back in with pictures of your American family." It pained her to say the next words. "They don't want you here—at all. But we can fight them, together." She knew she was asking her client to remain in jail and slog through the American immigration system for years to come.

"I come back. I find a way."

Laura believed her, but she also feared for Gabriela's life. "I understand why you want to walk out of here, I do."

Gabriela had a hard time being in lock-up even though she wore a yellow uniform—the women's wing equivalent of Emilio's dark blue. She wasn't used to not working, so she took every dollar-a-day job that came her way. She couldn't stand the food and had lost so much weight she looked gaunt. In January, she'd had bronchitis and had recovered in her bunk with no medical attention.

"You think you'll get out of here," Laura tried again, "and go see your family in Mexico, then come right back, but you'll attract attention back home. One of my clients was killed last year in Honduras." She hated to mention Felix Dominguez, Cruz and Clara's father, who'd also refused to wait for an appeal and had been shot dead just weeks after his deportation. And Gabriela was going to a worse place than Felix's Choluteca. She was going to Culiacán, Sinaloa, a crossroads of drug and sex trafficking routes. The people who'd forced her into prostitution when she was around Alice's age were probably still there. "Please, let me file an appeal. You just hang tight."

Gabriela shook her head. "How long, Laura? How long?"

Because of the backlog in Virginia, made worse by the recent government shutdown, the date for an appeal brief could be months or even years in the future. And because a case filed with the Board of Immigration Appeals resulted in a review of paper briefs rather than an actual hearing, rejection was all but certain. Laura would try to overturn that decision in the Ninth Circuit Court of Appeals, but it could take seven years to get there. And all that time, Gabriela would remain locked up at NWDC.

Laura's long silence was an answer in itself.

"No. I want deportation. I want out from this cage." Gabriela's sad smile was infuriating.

"You're not walking out of here tomorrow," Laura said. "It takes weeks for your paperwork to be processed and for ICE to prepare a flight out of Boeing Field."

Gabriela shrugged. "Weeks, sí. Then I go. Then I come back to mi niño."

Laura was losing Gabriela like she'd lost Felix. She felt the grief like a hook through her gut. "Maybe wait a little longer to decide? We have thirty days to file the appeal."

Gabriela touched Laura's hand. "Estaré bien."

No, Gabriela wouldn't be fine.

The only thing left for Laura to do was beg. The last time she begged, her father had laughed at her. It was in October 2005, during a video chat. Tudor looked thin in his T-shirt, the skin on his arms hanging from the bone. Laura sat on her kitchen floor with her laptop next to her thirteen-month-old's baby bouncer.

"Please, Tata," she said, playing with Alice's tiny fingers, "you don't look so good. Please go see a doctor."

She knew what he'd say. He hated doctors since doing time for his attempted border crossing in the '80s. The doctors at his hard-labor prison camp had been among the worst abusers there, refusing help when someone broke a bone or got an infection or needed medicine for some other illness. Their role was to give inmates methadone to control their libido and to write death certificates.

"Doctors?" Tudor scoffed with an infuriating grin. "They're crooks. I don't need doctors."

"It's just that you've lost a lot of weight," Laura said with an appeasing tone.

Alice grabbed Laura's shirt and pulled, fussing. No way the conversation could continue if the baby didn't get nursed. And it was important to convince Tudor to get a medical checkup. Laura picked Alice up from the bouncer. She made sure the webcam only saw her from the neck up, then she lifted her shirt and felt the baby latch on.

"You worry all the time," her father said, his voice warm. "About everything."

"Please, Tata. I can't come help you right now. I can't leave my baby, and I can't travel with her either." Alice was in the thick of her night terrors—long wailing episodes with tight-shut eyes that lasted for hours. Adrian needed to function at work, so it was always Laura spending the night with a screaming Alice and the day taking care of the baby, cleaning and cooking, and studying for her law degree. She was so sleep-deprived that she'd had two minor car accidents in six months. One of them was on Alice's first birthday, at the Guitar Center. Laura had folded the back seats of her Toyota Prius, pushed the box with the digital piano from the cart into the trunk, then backed out of the loading bay, across the sidewalk, and into a streetlamp she swore she hadn't seen.

Tudor laughed. "Who says I need help? Take care of your baby and don't worry about me, I'm fine." He stood up and grabbed his black cowboy hat. He wore it everywhere, and his neighbors had taken to calling him "the American." He put it on and tipped it toward her, like J. R. Ewing on the *Dallas* TV show. "I have some errands to run now."

"Tata, please, go see a doctor."

He waved his thin arm. "I'm fine." He smiled. "And I'll be fine until the day I turn two hundred."

Two months later he was dead.

Laura saw the same resolute smile on Gabriela's face now. All the begging in the world wasn't going to change her mind.

×

David skipped his Tuesday afternoon boxing practice to make the long drive to Ms. Holban's house. It was dark when he got there. A text message from his mom told him to hurry home. He wrote back *On my way!* then took a moment to work up the courage to knock on Ms. Holban's door. With a little luck, he'd see Alice again. They'd been texting for the last few days, and he thought he'd managed to sound Seattle-cool in his funny, short remarks to her.

When she opened the door, the words rushed out of his mouth. "Hi, I'm here to pick up the power of attorney for my dad. I won't be long—I have a lot of homework for tomorrow. I can get through Spanish fast enough, but trigonometry is a whole different ballgame."

He sounded as cool as melted ice cream.

Alice smiled and waved him into the warm house. "We just finished dinner."

The place smelled of sautéed onions and stir-fried meat and veggies.

"David!" Ms. Holban stepped out of the kitchen, wiping her hands on a towel. "I have the letter for your father," she said and went downstairs.

Alice returned to rinsing plates and putting things in the dishwasher. David followed her into the kitchen, wondering how to start a real-life conversation.

After a long moment, he thought of a reasonable question. "This delicious smell, is it Romanian food?"

Alice peered over her glasses. "Do people always ask if you eat Guatemalan?"

"I mean…" David couldn't believe he'd done it again.

"I know what you mean." She softened her tone. "At school, they ask me about my ancestry, like, all the time, you know? Celebrating diversity and all that. Since you asked," she said, emptying cups, "Romanian cuisine is not that exciting. Cheesy polenta and stuffed cabbage rolls and eggplant salad, yum. Lots of overcooked meats. And pickled stuff. I'm lucky my mom doesn't cook any of that. Not ever. I only have to endure it when I go to Romania, and that's usually just for a few days."

"Got it." He was glad they were still talking.

"Tonight, we had Thai food my mom picked up on her way home. You hungry?"

David was hungry, but he wasn't going to chew and swallow while Alice watched. Even if he managed to do it well, he was sure to end up with something stuck in his teeth.

"No, thank you." He looked at a wooden spice rack on the counter and picked up a small glass jar with a foreign label. It was half full with flakes of a dark green herb. "What's this?" He turned the jar around and saw the expiration date. "2006?"

"Put it back," Alice said, glancing at the door. "It's my mom's."

"What is it?"

"Lovage. Leuștean. They use it in soups in Romania."

"What does it taste like?"

"Parsley, celery, I don't know. Kind of strong. But this one's dead. My mom won't throw it away because her father gave it to her a long time ago. He was a great cook, I heard. Anyway, that's dry as dust, but she still keeps it with the rest. Just put it back."

David returned the jar to the spice rack as if handling a relic. "So, have you been playing the piano?"

She shrugged. "Not since the other day." But she seemed intrigued by his question.

He decided to ask. "Have you thought about joining a band?"

"Here," Ms. Holban said, coming up the stairs. "This is a specific power of attorney. The warden at NWDC will let your dad take it to the law library there, where a notary will certify it. Then your mom should be able to negotiate a mortgage with the bank on your dad's behalf."

David took the envelope but didn't start toward the door. He hadn't come here just for the letter. He cleared his throat. "Ms. Holban, please give me something to do. I can't just sit idle while my family's hurting."

Alice glanced at him and smiled, but Ms. Holban frowned.

He felt emboldened. "I can investigate whatever you need me to. And I can drive."

"Well," Ms. Holban said, "be careful on those roads tonight, with the coming snow."

David ignored that. "I can send emails, use listservs, create pages to spread the word about our case. I'm good with all kinds of social media. I can raise awareness about my dad's good deeds and this…injustice."

Ms. Holban smiled at last. "I don't doubt that, David. But your dad's story is just one of thousands. There have been protests outside NWDC for years. People just don't pay attention. And it won't help to antagonize the judges. Just let me do my job, okay?"

"Please let me help," David said.

"You can't," she said, adjusting that old jar of lovage on the spice rack. "I'll handle Mason Waltman on my own."

"Who's Mason Waltman?" David and Alice said at the same time.

"Nobody. Never mind." She patted David on the shoulder. "Focus on school instead."

Alice mouthed the words, "She always says that," then rinsed a bowl and put it in the dishwasher.

"How's your brother doing?" Ms. Holban said.

She wouldn't know about Jacob's struggles, would she? "He's fine, but I need to help."

Alice turned off the faucet. "Come on, Mom, let David help."

"He can't, Alice."

"Just because you say that doesn't make it so." She groaned big time. "Nothing gets done in this world because of people who call themselves adults." She made air quotes around the last word. "You say you're in charge, but you always want us to fix your messes. Like climate change."

David could tell they'd had this fight before.

"Go to your room," Ms. Holban said in a calm voice.

Alice made like she was going to say something, then she strode from the kitchen. "Bye, David," she said as she stomped up the stairs.

David headed for the door.

"Careful on those roads," Ms. Holban said. "And don't worry, I always stay in touch with your mother."

"My mom can't always handle things. She literally gets sick with worry."

"Then take care of her and your brother. As for your father's case, I got it." She walked him to the door and said goodnight.

A thin layer of powder covered the pavers in the front yard, and David was careful not to slip. His truck was parked in front of the house, and he hurried to get inside and start the engine. A flurry of snowflakes dotted the bright shafts of his headlights. The ground was still warm and the flakes melted on contact, but if it was snowing in Seattle, it was probably worse up north in Everett. David had to get home before snow covered the roads.

His phone pinged just as he was ready to shift into drive. A text from Alice.

You don't need my mom's permission to help your dad

David sent her a thumbs-up emoji. He wished he had a clever remark but was afraid of saying something about Ms. Holban that could sound disrespectful.

He put on his turn signal and joined the slow-moving traffic.

He drove for a while, watching for cars and lights until he found the ramp to I-5 North. No snow survived on the highway, so he could relax a bit and let his mind wander. Alice was right. He didn't need anyone's permission to help his dad. But what could he do? Maybe check out Mason Waltman, whoever that was.

II

IN THE MEN'S wing of NWDC, Emilio was doing his best to kill time. He'd read all the newspapers left on tables and spent twenty-five minutes on the stationary bike. He'd borrowed a Rubik's Cube from a Honduran who had gone to his shift in the kitchen. He'd then done a complicated sudoku puzzle from the book Father Nicolas had brought him. He'd talked to a few people and listened to their stories, which had trauma and cruelty in common. And all that time Emilio worried about Jacob and Blanca, and about David, handling everything by himself though he was just a boy. He'd already found a lawyer who seemed to know what she was doing. He should now focus on school and his and his brother's boxing practice.

When the doors banged open and Marco and Arturo returned from their laundry shift, there was still an hour to kill before dinner.

"You want to play cards?" Arturo said in Spanish.

Playing cards would be just what the guards wanted them to do. Play cards and stay out of the way. Emilio was surprised by his sudden anger. "No, thank you," he muttered and climbed to the top bunk.

Marco shrugged and sat down on the lower bunk of Arturo's bed. "Having another bad day? Just go with it, man."

Emilio lay on his back, arms folded under his head on the thin pillow. As if he hadn't had enough time to sulk all day. Why take his anger out on his buddies? He should climb down and join them, but something held him back.

He was now angry with himself. He'd been a fool not to apply for asylum in 1998, his crucial first year here. Sometimes he told himself he'd been too busy staying alive and scraping out a living. Sometimes he blamed the people he'd met in the beginning, other Guatemalans who hadn't steered him right. He didn't know the language or the law and had no money for a lawyer. Years later, when he had a family, he was too scared to attempt legalizing his status for fear he'd be deported.

Back then, he didn't think it was dangerous to remain undocumented. It was a way of life. Not perfect, but possible. His kids were citizens. The government wasn't after him. He'd always stayed on the right side of the law and taught his sons to do the same. He'd been a fool all these years. Reckless.

"Lockdown," a guard announced from the other side of the pod. "Counting," said another. Emilio recognized them: Kaminsky and Lonsdale. Kaminsky was a thin man with a receding hairline who compensated for his insecurities by constantly tensing the muscles in his face. But he wasn't a bad guy. Lonsdale was there to pass the hours and get to his next paycheck, which bought him enough beer to keep his potbelly round. Emilio hoped it'd be an easy counting.

He slipped down and put on his sneakers. Arturo and Marco left their Uno game and stood at attention between the beds, arms at their sides. The guards moved methodically, checking wristbands and calling out the detainees' names.

What would David feel, seeing his father like this? On the phone today, Emilio thought he'd heard disappointment in his son's voice when he said the bank refused to consider Blanca for a mortgage. She had a valid-looking SSN, just like Emilio. But the bank didn't refuse her because of her immigration status. They did because her name wasn't on the title to the house—another stupid mistake on Emilio's part.

Kaminsky checked Emilio's wristband and moved on.

Emilio had bought the big plot and the rundown bungalow before he had a family, with cash he'd saved working two and sometimes three jobs at a time. Then he met Blanca. But he'd never thought to add her name to the title. There were so many things he hadn't thought of. He should have known he might be arrested one day.

Such a fool.

"At ease," Lonsdale said at last.

"Not you, Ramirez," Kaminsky said. "You're coming with us. Pick up your stuff. Don't forget your toilet paper." He pointed to the roll tucked behind Emilio's pillow at the corner of his mattress.

Emilio glanced at his buddies, who shrugged. "Where am I going?" he said.

"You've been upgraded," Lonsdale said, fingers tapping on the belt under his potbelly. "You've got an orange uniform now, and you'll be sharing a pod with hardened criminals like yourself."

In a daze, Emilio grabbed his toiletries and said goodbye to Arturo and Marco. The walk to the orange pod took him and his escorts through locked doors and long hallways.

Just as Kaminsky pulled his long keychain out of his pocket, the door before them burst open, and two guards pushed through, carrying a naked, unconscious man between them. His skin was pale as a fish's belly. His lips and his fingers were blue, and there were purple marks around his neck. His head lolled as the guards rushed him toward the medical ward.

"No phone calls for anyone today!" one of the guards yelled at Kaminsky on the way past.

Emilio couldn't swallow, his tongue dry in his mouth. "What happened to him?"

Lonsdale grabbed the door and held it open. "Nothing. Just move."

×

When the breakfast trolley pulled into the medium-security pod on Wednesday morning, Emilio got in line, still thinking about the man he'd seen yesterday. Maybe people here knew who he was and what had happened to him.

When his turn came, he loaded his blue plastic tray with a bread roll, a tablespoon of strawberry jam, a skinny sausage, and black tea, then scanned the tables in the pod for an open seat. They all disappeared at his approach.

Emilio had heard of PSB—the Puget Sound Barrios gang—but hadn't met any members in the low-security pod. Now they were everywhere, and they didn't seem to like him. He looked around again, accepting he might need to eat standing up. He was tired. He'd had a nightmare last night about being stung by scorpions in the desert, and after that he couldn't go back to sleep. He'd never been afraid of snakes on his journey to America, but the thought of scorpions had kept him up at night. Then and now.

Someone pushed him from behind. Emilio held onto his tray, but a young man with a tattooed neck flipped it out of his hands. Food and tray crashed to the floor.

A guard stood ten feet away, pretending not to notice. No point in complaining to him. Maybe he was part of whatever this was.

When a detainee dropped his food, that was it. There'd be no replacement. And what if his next meal also wound up on the floor? He could go hungry for days. As awful as the food was here, it kept Emilio alive. He knew from his days in the Sonoran Desert that a starving man could think of nothing but food. His stomach growled.

The tattooed guy smirked and walked off. Emilio pulled a few paper towels from the dispenser on the nearby wall and began cleaning the floor. The strawberry jam stuck to the concrete, so he dipped a towel in the tea puddle and wiped the red off the gray. When he was done, he put his tray on the dirty dishes rack and turned to leave.

The tattooed guy blocked his passage. And again, the guard looked away.

Emilio couldn't let the PSB goons see how scared he was, so he stared hard into the young man's small, mean eyes.

The man leaned close and whispered in Spanish, "Go back to Guate, you bastard!"

A swift punch in the ribs stole Emilio's breath. When he looked up, the guard was still there, still seeing nothing. But he tilted his head, urging Emilio to move along.

Emilio limped past him, heading back to his bed to wait for the guards to take him to his bond hearing.

12

THIS WAS MASON'S chance to get rid of Ramirez—fast. He stopped in the doorway of Judge Edward Hwang's NWDC office. The walls were covered with plaques and framed awards. There was one from US Citizenship and Immigration Services, dated a few years back, when the organization's mission statement still included the words "USCIS secures America's promise as a nation of immigrants." Last year, Mason worried that people would protest the statement's change to "administers the nation's lawful immigration system," but soon learned that Native Americans and African Americans didn't mind the revision, as they'd never felt included in the term "nation of immigrants." A nice surprise that took the sheen off the word "immigrant."

"Mr. Waltman," the judge said.

It was hard to believe that the soft-spoken, middle-aged Hwang had once worked for Mason. As a trial attorney, Hwang had been ruthless in his prosecution of illegals, but as a judge, he showed too much independence. Mason had hoped for Judge Derek Brown Gibson on Ramirez's case, a cautious man easily swayed. Hwang was going to be much tougher to influence.

Mason cleared his throat. "I'm here this morning to check on my team."

"I remember how that felt." Hwang never smiled. "Come in, Mr. Waltman." After all those years working together, they were still on a last-name basis. "We almost canceled today on account of the snow."

It was rare for the Justice Department to take a snow day, which meant rescheduling the day's hearings months into the future. Mason was glad they hadn't, even though he'd almost crashed his Audi on a patch of black ice on the way here.

Hwang hated to be told what to do, especially by his old boss, so Mason picked his words carefully. "Since I'm here," he said, sitting down in a stiff chair and unbuttoning his jacket, "there's an application I wanted to flag for you. It's on your master calendar hearing for today. One Emilio Ramirez, represented by Laura Holban."

Hwang leaned back in his seat. The lawyer's name had made an impression.

"She'll ask for release on bond," Mason said. "You'll hear from Sheldon that Ramirez poses a grave danger to society. We have a statement from a real estate agent he assaulted. Bond should be out of the question."

Hwang frowned. "You don't trust Sheldon to make his case to me? Most people arrested by ICE are criminals. They crossed the border illegally, didn't they?"

Mason smiled. "Here's the thing, since Ramirez is a danger to the community and doesn't qualify for bond, his asylum application is dead in the water. You think you could tell Ms. Holban to stop wasting our time?"

"I'm a judge now, Mr. Waltman. My priority is to let the law run its course."

If only Saravia understood that. With the end of the month less than two weeks away, Mason needed to report some progress.

"Okay then," he said in a conciliatory tone. "Could you perhaps give Ms. Holban a call-up date to brief the issue instead of a full individual hearing?"

An individual hearing would be scheduled months away, and Holban would be able to argue on the merits. She could present favorable evidence and call in friendly witnesses. She could cast doubt on Evelyn Brunelle's accusations. And she was resourceful enough to maybe pull it off. Mason knew it wasn't a good idea to ask a judge to deny an individual hearing, but he wanted to give Hwang the satisfaction of turning him down a few times.

Hwang pursed his thin lips. "If we don't give her an individual hearing, she'll sue us and win. And deservedly so." He waved a hand. "No. Let her have her hearing."

"All right." Now for the favor Mason really needed. "But can it take less than three months to get it on your calendar?" In the old days, that wouldn't have been exceptional. "Can you schedule it for next week, say?"

Hwang looked annoyed. "You know our backlog is at an all-time high and growing?"

Mason knew that immigration judges didn't have much say in their own caseloads. They didn't even oversee their staff and resources and were forced to prioritize the current Justice Department immigration policy, but he hoped Hwang could still move things around. Unless he really couldn't, in which case he'd go on the attack to hide it.

"If you don't want to wait," Hwang said, "I can always skip the hearing and offer them withholding of removal." Which meant Ramirez could remain in the US with a work permit for years. Not what Mason wanted to tell Saravia.

"If you offer withholding," he said, "Ms. Holban will sue you because a judge shouldn't be part of the pleading process."

Hwang nodded. "But after she wins, she must still argue the asylum case in my courtroom. I'm not worried. So, do you want withholding of removal?"

Mason scoffed at the proposal. "You have your quota, and I'm trying to help you process this case quickly."

"Don't worry about me, Mr. Waltman." Hwang pointed to his mounted awards.

"Come on, Judge. I've never asked you for a favor before."

"You didn't need to. You could just order me around."

Mason sighed. "Just process Ramirez fast. Please. This comes from the top."

"You're bluffing, Mr. Waltman. I've had years to observe you, and I know." He leaned in, elbows on his desk. "Ramirez will get his individual hearing. In three months' time."

Mason left the judge's office and plodded down the hallway, quietly cursing himself. Why had he bowed to Saravia's threats and tried to alter Ramirez's deportation schedule—only to be humiliated by a former subordinate? He'd set Judge Hwang on edge, which could hurt Sheldon at today's hearing.

Now he had to find a creative way to convince Saravia to wait.

×

Laura's drive to Tacoma took longer than normal, owing to cautious drivers on slushy streets, but she managed to arrive on time for Emilio's first court appearance, which combined his bond hearing with a master calendar hearing. He and other detainees would stand in turn in front of Judge Edward Hwang for the equivalent of an arraignment. As usual, Laura might have three minutes to make her case and hopefully get Emilio out on bond.

The Tacoma Immigration Court was housed inside NWDC but, unlike normal courtrooms, its hearings were closed to the public. To see the judge, Laura had to pass through three locked doors: one into a waiting room, a second into a long hallway, the third into the courtroom itself.

The guard at the last door demanded Laura's credentials and took his time to check the name Emilio Luiz Ramirez Garcia on his list, as if Laura were there to stealth-represent someone else. Once his inspection was complete, he waved Laura on with a look that reminded her of communist Romanian bureaucrats. In those days, when Laura had been faced with clerks who held all the power, she used to feel some messed-up sense of gratitude when they finally deigned to grant her what was already hers. Today was no different.

Inside the windowless Tacoma courtroom, the hostile atmosphere persisted. In municipal or superior court, people would be talking, looking up court records, taking notes, or just hanging out. But not here, where people sat in silence and where pen and paper were allowed only to lawyers and accredited members of the press.

Noah Sheldon hadn't arrived yet. Two other trial attorneys sat at the government's table. The right side of the courtroom was packed with detainees in color-coded uniforms. Laura searched for Emilio's dark-blue shirt but couldn't find him. She was beginning to panic when someone in orange waved at her from the back row.

It was Emilio. In a uniform marking him as a serious criminal.

She hurried to him. "What happened?" she called over the heads of the other detainees. Whatever the reason, wearing orange pretty much killed Emilio's bond chances today.

"They didn't let me call you," he said.

"What? Why?"

A guard steered her back to the left side of the courtroom, reserved for lawyers and nonprofit personnel. Laura took a seat in a front row, still stunned that Emilio was wearing orange. She wished she had Jennifer with her to discuss this awful new development, but paralegals weren't usually allowed in immigration court.

The day went both fast and slow. Fast because Judge Hwang didn't spend much time on any given applicant, only explaining the government's charges, informing the detainees of their rights, and refusing bond to most of them. At some point, Sheldon joined the other two attorneys at the government's table, muttering something about the snowpocalypse.

When Emilio's turn came, he and Laura advanced to the attorney's table. Emilio was limping a little. He might have got into a fight in jail, but Laura didn't have time to ask.

The judge opened the bond hearing. "Any submissions for today?"

Laura submitted the defense's stack of documents, while Sheldon gave the judge and Laura a statement she had no time to glance at, with only a few minutes to make her case.

"Mr. Ramirez doesn't have any criminal history," she hurried to say. "No convictions, no encounters with the police. He's clearly not a danger to his community. He's in fact a pillar of his community. He works and pays his taxes. He provides for his teenage sons. He volunteers at his church." She pointed to her thick bond submission, which the judge was leafing through. "We have twenty-eight letters of support from Mr. Ramirez's neighbors, one from the pastor at Our Redeemer's Church in Everett, two from teachers at his sons' high school, and five more from his coworkers at Fernando's Home Improvement. With two children and a wife with disabilities, he's also not a flight risk."

The judge looked Emilio up and down as if to point out the color of his uniform.

"This must be a mistake, Judge," Laura said. "Mr. Ramirez was in low security just two days ago. His orange uniform is news to me—and intentionally so—because he was not allowed to call me." She wished she could be granted a continuance to adequately prepare, but that wasn't how things worked in immigration court.

"Government?" Judge Hwang said, reading Sheldon's document.

Laura glanced at her copy: something about Emilio attacking Evelyn at his house? That wasn't possible.

"Here," Sheldon said, "we have a witness statement from a well-respected real estate agent named Evelyn Brunelle, who alleges that Mr. Ramirez attacked her not long before he was arrested. Hence the orange uniform."

Emilio shook his head in panic. "But I didn't!"

Laura scrambled to find her words. "I have an affidavit—an affidavit, Judge, not a witness statement—from this same person, Evelyn Brunelle, and she's saying in here..." She corrected herself. "She states in this affidavit that my client never threatened her." Her hand was shaking. "She also says, and I quote, 'I informed the authorities about Mr. Ramirez's immigration status based solely on my duty as a concerned citizen.' The witness statement and the affidavit cannot both be correct, Judge. This is clear evidence that Ms. Brunelle lied. My client never assaulted her."

Sheldon stepped up. "We think Ms. Brunelle was too scared the first time around and needed assurance from our office that she wouldn't become a target of Ramirez's violence if she came forward with the truth."

"Or maybe," Laura said, voice rising, "she was intimidated into giving a false statement the second time around."

Judge Hwang looked bored, cleaning his teeth with his tongue inside his closed mouth. "Did the people who wrote your letters of support know of these accusations, Counsel?"

"I've only heard these allegations just now," Laura said. "Mr. Sheldon didn't share them with me, and my client wasn't allowed to call me—on whose orders, I don't know. But they're obviously messing up..." Another slip. "Manipulating things to influence the outcome."

"We had nothing to do with Ms. Brunelle coming forward," Sheldon said.

"Mr. Sheldon," Judge Hwang said, "we'll hear from Ms. Brunelle at Mr. Ramirez's individual hearing, and we'll learn then whether she told the truth. Ms. Holban, someone has accused your client of being a danger to the community. As you can see"—he indicated the dozens of detainees awaiting their turn before him—"there's no time to investigate what kind of danger he poses. Bond denied. Let's move on to the master calendar hearing. How does Mr. Ramirez plead to the government's charges as listed in the Notice to Appear?"

Laura cleared her throat and pulled herself together. "We admit the charges and concede removability, Judge," which was customary. There was no point in arguing that Emilio didn't break the law in 1998 and wasn't therefore removable. But Emilio's application for asylum was a good defense against imminent deportation. "We're applying for asylum and cancellation of removal because Mr. Ramirez is afraid to return to Guatemala where he could be killed by his family's killers."

Judge Hwang set Emilio's individual hearing for late March and gave Laura ten days to file the application. But without the bond, Emilio was locked up for the foreseeable future. Laura tried to catch his eye as a guard took him back to his seat, but he sat down with his head in his hands. Another guard showed Laura out, then the troll at the door waved her down the hallway toward the waiting room.

What the hell had just happened? Maybe Emilio had lied to her. Maybe Evelyn Brunelle had indeed been too scared to tell Laura the truth. In any case, she had work to do. Jennifer would make inquiries at the Everett Police Department to see if there'd been any complaints ever filed against Emilio and then dropped. But if Emilio was guilty, why hadn't ICE asked Evelyn to sign an affidavit?

Laura hurried to her green Prius in the parking lot, dialing Evelyn's number. It went straight to voicemail.

"Hello, Ms. Brunelle," Laura said, her voice bitter. "This is Laura Holban, and I'm calling to ask why you changed your statement about Emilio Ramirez. It couldn't be a lapse of memory, could it? In case you don't know, what you did is very much against the law. And I won't let it stand. Give me a call when you get this." She hung up but didn't expect to hear back any time soon.

She got in the car, wishing she could talk to Emilio, but he was stuck in the day-long hearing until all the applicants were processed. She'd have to come back first thing in the morning. And still no word from Emilio's deportation officer, the elusive Ken Masters.

A knock on her door startled her. "David?" she said, lowering the window.

"Did they approve my dad's bond?" David said.

Laura shook her head. "A woman accused your father of assault, so the judge turned us down."

"Assault? How? What's her name?"

"Evelyn Brunelle. She's a real—"

"She came to talk to us at church last Sunday. Said she wanted to buy our house."

Maybe that was why she'd changed her statement, to corner Emilio and force him to sell. Still, something didn't add up. "Is it possible, David, that your father really did attack her?"

David shook his head. "She's lying. My dad doesn't attack people. He never hit me or my brother—ever. He always goes on about not breaking the law."

Laura believed him. "I'll see what I can do," she said.

×

In his office in the Seattle ICE building, Mason was anxious for news about the Ramirez hearing but didn't want to appear too interested. He'd wait for Sheldon's report.

Midday, an email arrived from the *Seattle Times* with a request for an interview. The reporter wanted to talk about the collaboration between ICE's Homeland Security Investigations and the local police department—a taskforce that had just concluded a monthlong enforcement operation. It had netted a dozen arrests while executing state search warrants related to ongoing drug and money laundering investigations. The haul had been impressive, mostly fentanyl. Intel provided by Saravia had been crucial to the operation. On days like this, Mason knew he was in the right line of work.

Helen called a few times to tell him that Chloe had a temperature but Oliver was doing better. Both Mason and Helen had taken turns looking after Chloe last night, propping her up on pillows so she could breathe through her stuffy nose. At lunch, Mason had another coffee to stay alert through the rest of the day.

When Sheldon finally called in the afternoon with an update on Hwang's master calendar hearing, Mason learned they had six weeks instead of three months until the individual hearing, which was worse because now Ramirez might wait for his day in court instead of choosing deportation. Would he agree to leave in return for a promise of asylum for his also-illegal wife? But the thought of watching her swear allegiance to the American flag at Seattle Center on the Fourth of July, with the mayor and the governor shaking her hand and the Space Needle in the background—it just made Mason's skin crawl. He could arrest the wife, but a jailed couple with two American teenagers raising hell on social media could backfire, drawing unwanted attention. With two parentless minors to yap about, Holban would have the wife out on bond in no time. But there was another way to pressure Ramirez to agree to deportation.

Mason dialed Evelyn Brunelle's number on his cell. "I need you to file a complaint with the Everett police against Emilio Ramirez."

"Are you serious? You said no criminal case."

"And there won't be one. Listen, do you want to get your hands on that house or not? This would speed things up."

She didn't answer.

Mason pressed on. "With Ramirez deported and his income gone for good, the family will have to sell the house. And you'll be right there with an offer."

"I'm the last person they'll sell to now."

"Not if you can close the transaction faster than anyone else." The cash withdrawals flagged by her bank could come in handy here. "Can you?"

Evelyn was quiet for another long moment. "I see."

"Then you'll do it?" Mason hoped he didn't need to threaten her with a probe into her banking habits.

"I guess."

"Make sure you tell the police he tried to strangle you." That would give them at least a second-degree assault to work with.

After hanging up with the "patriot," Mason called Sheldon, who picked up from his car on the highway.

"Trying to get home, sir. It's snowing hard in Redmond."

"Brunelle is going to file a criminal complaint against Ramirez in Everett," Mason said. "Make sure you ask Snohomish County to file charges against him based on that complaint."

"Will they listen to us?"

"Filing charges costs them nothing. Tell them it's the smart thing to do in this case."

"Shouldn't there be an investigation first?" Sheldon said, his voice unsure.

"They can do the investigation in parallel. Be persuasive, Sheldon. Who are they going to believe: a good-looking American woman or a law-breaking illegal?"

"Okay, so with charges filed, any judge will then reject his relief from deportation as a matter of discretion. Even if his lawyer paints him as a saint at the hearing."

"Yes, yes, Sheldon, but that's not what you should focus on next."

"Sir?"

Mason sighed. "Once the charges are filed, go have a chat with Ramirez. Explain to him that deportation is preferable to ten years in prison for aggravated assault. Make sure he knows that he only gets deported after he serves his sentence. Throw in a line about what a criminal conviction would do to his sons' future."

"Oh."

Mason felt exhausted. "Bye, Sheldon. Careful on those roads."

13

BECAUSE OF LAST night's heavy snow, Laura couldn't drive to Tacoma to see Emilio when he needed encouragement the most. He seemed resilient in general, but the way he'd bowed his head after yesterday's court decision broke her heart.

Laura had grown up with harsh Romanian winters, but Seattle under snow was a different kind of beast. Two inches of powder and the city people called it a snowpocalypse. Like every new immigrant in the area, Laura had first scoffed at that silliness only to soon learn that in the Pacific Northwest the ground never properly froze. So when snow first fell, it melted and turned to ice, which was then covered in more snow, up and down the hilly face of the city. Cars without chains lost traction and slipped into each other. City buses slid downhill. Drivers abandoned their vehicles on the road. Because it seldom snowed, the city never had enough plows and sanders. Schools closed, stores ran out of goods, hospitals operated with skeleton staffs. The first serious snowfall after Laura moved to Seattle reminded her of the Romanian food and power shortages in the '80s.

She finished her coffee and was contemplating cleaning the snow off her sidewalk when the video app on her laptop rang. She hoped it was her college friend in LA calling to make fun of Seattle's snow. But, alas, it was her mother Claudia, who had also typed a message on the app in Romanian: *Are you okay? I saw on the news that you had a lot of snow. Call me or I won't be able to sleep tonight.*

Laura groaned and answered the call.

"Is Alice safe?" Claudia said. "Did you let her go to school today?"

"She's upstairs. Snow day." Laura took the laptop to the French doors to show her mom the white rooftops stretching all the way to Lake Union.

"That's beautiful…" Claudia said.

"Beautiful if you don't have a job to go to," Laura said. "We're stuck in the house." She turned the camera to the other windows, showing heavy snow on pine trees and bamboo hedges. For a moment, Laura remembered why she liked this house so much. Despite being in the heart of the city, it was quiet and secluded. She didn't even need curtains.

Then she realized that Claudia was quiet too. She was leaning to one side of her swivel chair, tinkering with something off camera.

"What's wrong with your chair?" Laura said.

"There's a loose screw here. I push it back in, but it keeps coming out. My fingernail isn't strong enough to twist it into place."

"Your fingernail? Don't you have a screwdriver?"

Claudia straightened up. "Your father had a screwdriver in his toolbox, but I can't stand to go through his things."

"Well, if you can't fix it, get a chair from the kitchen."

"It needs to swivel."

"Then go buy a new one."

"You know I can't do that on my own!"

Laura had no time for another fight with her mother. "If there's nothing else, I have to clean up the snow on my sidewalk."

"I did hear something you might want to know."

"Yes?"

A strange look came over Claudia, something Laura could only describe as smug concern. "Adrian's wife is pregnant."

Laura felt like she'd been knifed in the stomach. She could tell her mother was enjoying delivering the news. "Good for them," she managed to say.

"He's rebuilding his life here. I don't see why you can't do the same. Just move back to Bucharest and find yourself a nice, strong Romanian man."

There she went again. Laura steeled herself for what was sure to follow.

"You've been single for too long," Claudia said. "No American is interested in you. You've got big bones. Not their type."

Laura let out a loud sigh. What was the point in arguing?

Claudia went on, "Adrian is doing so well here. People look up to him because he's an experienced American businessman. Alice would have her father and her new brother or sister close by. And her grandmother."

Laura reminded herself she had to call Jennifer to find out if Everett PD had any complaints against Emilio.

"I'm not saying you couldn't live in a different country," Claudia continued, her tone a bit warmer. "But you could have chosen London or Paris or Rome or Cyprus, like most children. Not Seattle, where the world map ends." She rubbed her eye. "I don't ask for much. I can take care of myself but—"

"I have to go," Laura said, unable to listen any longer.

"And leave me upset? You want to give me a heart attack?"

Laura scoffed. "You can't give people heart attacks."

"Then why have it in all those movies?"

"Bye, Mama."

She closed her laptop, though she'd meant to only close the video app. She'd been ambushed, again, and had to bring herself back from a state where her mind was wholly occupied by a fruitless argument with an imaginary Claudia. The real one was exasperating enough.

After a call to Jennifer—no complaints against Emilio on file, no records of dropped ones either—it was time to shovel snow off the sidewalk. Laura put on her waterproof hiking boots, her raincoat, and a wool cap. It took a bit longer to find the thick gloves she'd worn when skiing with Adrian at Snoqualmie Pass before Alice was born. Before she hated snow.

"I'm going outside," she called at Alice upstairs.

Just as she opened the door, her cell phone rang in her pocket. She stashed her gloves under her arm and picked up.

It was Blanca. "I need to make sure they don't take me too. For my boys. Can you help me file documents, so I'm not in trouble?"

"Sure, we can talk. You might qualify for a special type of visa based on your history, but I won't know which until I do a thorough intake and I walk you through your options."

Blanca agreed to call Jennifer and schedule a consultation.

Gloves on, Laura found the shovel and the broom under the front porch. She looked forward to the workout since she hadn't run in a while. She thrust the shovel into a bank of snow and emptied it on the side. Her mind went straight to Adrian.

She hadn't thought of him in a while, but now she remembered how torn she'd been when he proposed. It was soon after he'd interviewed with Microsoft in Bucharest, at a time when Laura was just getting to know him. Sure, she enjoyed their weekend trips through the Carpathian Mountains in his Dacia sedan, shopping with him at the new supermarket near his apartment building, and biking together through Bucharest's old streets and public parks. But getting married? Was he the right man for her? He sometimes snored, and did she really want to listen to that for the rest of her life? Then there was the relocation to a foreign country that had no use for a Romanian lawyer's skillset, and Laura loved her budding law career in Bucharest.

But when they leafed through the glossy Seattle photo album he'd brought with him, she forgot her doubts. The images were breathtaking: glass-and-steel buildings in bright daylight, old neighborhoods of red brick, mountains, and beaches. The image of a couple—a woman with flowing hair and a man with perfect teeth—rolling their classy luggage through Sea-Tac Airport, a cloudless sky through the huge windows behind them, that image stole Laura's heart. Then there was the Space Needle, Pike Place Market, boats on lakes, bikes on trails, and fields full of tulips.

That was the world her father had almost died trying to see. She wanted to go there, live the life advertised in those pictures, try all those new experiences. The thought of Adrian traveling alone to America—a faraway land filled with Hollywood stars, shiny cars, and color-display cell phones—was bad enough. But what if he met one of those impossibly beautiful American women, better-looking than Laura, with her slightly crooked front teeth and the chickenpox scar on her jaw? She looked at Adrian as he sat next to her—a victorious warrior returned from battle—and her whole body filled with a warmth and a joy she'd never felt before. And the way he looked at her when he took her hand and said in English, "We're going to America, baby!"

Now Laura was alone in America with Alice while Adrian was having another child, with another woman, on the other side of the planet. She threw another shovel of wet snow under the rhododendron bush. She remembered Claudia's tears when she heard of Adrian's proposal. No words of wisdom about marriage or wishes of good luck, just the same heartbroken look as when Tudor had been arrested.

"We'll send money home," Laura whispered.

"I don't need your money," Claudia said. "Our pensions will be enough. What we need is someone to bring us a glass of water when we're old and bedridden."

"Don't worry, Mama, we're only a couple of flights away. We'll be home in no time."

Another assumption proven wrong a few years later, when a Romanian doctor informed Laura that her father was bleeding to death in a Bucharest hospital. Adrian couldn't take a leave from work—his team was shipping a new version of Windows soon—so Laura flew to London alone, with a fifteen-month-old Alice suffering from night terrors.

During a ten-hour flight, Laura couldn't sleep, always on the brink of panic, imagining her father's dead body on a morgue table. Alice had one of her screaming episodes, eyes and fists shut tight. Laura latched her on to shut her up and pacify the annoyed passengers around them. When she tried to move the baby back into the car seat, the screaming restarted, so she spent the next few hours with Alice sucking on her breasts until they hurt. The engines hummed around them, the sound frightening, not soothing. Laura was trapped in a box in the sky, checking the time, terrified that her father had already died, while her thoughts circled back to that imagined morgue table.

But that was a long time ago. Laura picked up the broom and began sweeping the snow left behind by the shovel. When her then-boyfriend Gordon had asked her years later why she took Alice on that horrendous flight to London, Laura was speechless for a moment.

"You mean," she said, "I should've left my baby behind and boarded a one-way flight? Abandon my child for weeks or months? You know babies are not like puppies, right? They need their moms to survive." But those words failed to capture the chasm between Laura and Gordon—and many others who'd had opinions on the matter since.

It had been daytime when Laura and Alice landed in London. Laura called Claudia, who told her the doctors had stopped her father's internal bleeding. They now said he had five months to live. Laura could breathe again. Five months seemed like an eternity.

She pushed the stroller packed with Alice's car seat and a small bag through Heathrow Airport, thinking she'd get to Bucharest and talk to the doctors and figure out the best treatment for her father. It wasn't until she reached her boarding gate that she learned about the snowstorm. Her flight was delayed because nothing could land in Bucharest that day.

Time crawled. It was getting dark again. Laura had been up for more than twenty-four hours. Without one good night's sleep since giving birth, the jetlag hit her that much harder. She felt dizzy and nauseous. While Alice napped in the stroller, Laura bought a sandwich and took a few bites, hoping it might help.

A few minutes later, she wheeled the stroller into the restroom and puked in the nearest stall. The whole room was spinning. She splashed cold water on her face and returned to the gate. She took small sips of water every few minutes and closed her eyes to stop the spinning. She needed sleep but couldn't let herself drift. She had to watch Alice.

An hour later, the baby woke up for a diaper change. Then she wanted to nurse, so Laura latched her on under a poncho, wincing. Then she wanted to move, so Laura let her toddle for a while. Alice giggled at her own reflection in the dark windows, while Laura trudged after her daughter, stopping to breathe her nausea away.

At some point, she went to the counter and asked about her flight again.

"We don't know yet," the attendant said. "But it looks like the flight might head to Budapest, Hungary instead. There's a train from there to Romania." That kind of trip—crossing Hungary, Transylvania, and the Carpathian Mountains—would take at least two days.

After she fed Alice apple sauce and crackers, Laura called Adrian. It was midday in Seattle. "There's a snowstorm," she said. "It'll take another two days to get there. Maybe more. My hands are shaking. I threw up, and I can't eat. I must stay awake, but I need to sleep." She kept her eyes closed, holding Alice by the hand. "I'll figure out a way to go see my dad. They say he has five months. There's time."

Laura put Alice in the car seat, but the baby began to cry. A few people glared at her, but Laura ignored them. She pushed the stroller to an internet kiosk with a printer. Two electronic tickets were already waiting in her email inbox. They must have cost Adrian a fortune on such short notice. She printed the tickets. Her flight back to Seattle was in three hours.

Just then, a voice came over the PA system announcing they were boarding the flight to Bucharest. All around Laura, people grabbed their luggage and headed for the gate.

She closed her eyes and took a few deep breaths, then went back to the attendant. "Is the snowstorm in Bucharest over?"

"If conditions at destination worsen, the plane will be rerouted to another airport."

Laura dropped in a chair, baby Alice crying beside her. She took more deep breaths. What did a snowstorm even look like? She imagined the whole plane shaking in the sky, people screaming, oxygen masks dropping, Alice strapped in her car seat, all of them crashing into a mountainside. She knew she wasn't thinking straight, but she couldn't think at all. Should she press on, get on a plane headed into a snowstorm, and put Alice's life in danger? Or should she take Alice to safety and miss some of the remaining time with her father?

She looked at her daughter. Alice was howling, tears and boogers dripping down her little puffy face. The terminal spun around them.

Five months left to live. That was what the doctor had said. There was time to reach Bucharest. Adrian would come with them next time.

Laura chose Alice.

Her father died a week later, and Laura wasn't there.

For months after, she was grief-stricken, and she needed someone to blame. "You weren't there to help me," she accused Adrian. "At Heathrow, I had to buy a scarf to tie around Alice's waist, to make sure she wouldn't fall from my lap if I fell asleep for even a second. Had you been there, we could've taken turns."

"I had to work," Adrian always responded. "I bought you expensive airplane tickets. Don't put this on me! The airport in Bucharest was still closed when you arrived home."

Their fights became routine. No matter his arguments, she couldn't shake the belief that, had Adrian been with them, they would have made it there in time to say goodbye to her father. To bring him a glass of water if he needed one. She wouldn't have let her mother down.

"You're a coward," Adrian told her once. "You were too scared to watch your father die, so you used Alice as an excuse to turn tail. And now you're trying to pin your guilt on me."

"That's ridiculous. I needed you there with me, I was sleep-deprived."

"Sleep-deprived? You didn't work back then. You stayed home all day."

"With a baby who didn't let me sleep at night! And it wasn't like I wanted to stay home."

"Not my fault you didn't have a working visa. Blame the government."

"I gave up my law career to be with you, Adrian. But you always put your work before your family."

"My work keeps this family fed and clothed."

And on and on and on, with contradictory accusations on both sides, until one day Adrian slammed the door and the house fell quiet, except for Alice's little whimper. Their common Romanian friends in the Seattle area chose his side, and Laura became estranged from that community. Soon, Alice learned to love the weekends when Adrian took her skiing or swimming and bought her sweets her mother wouldn't allow. The way she cried when he brought her home was heartbreaking and infuriating—and Laura could do nothing about it. She wanted Alice to have a good relationship with her father, so she never said a bad word about him.

Laura wiped the sweat off her forehead. She was thirsty, and her back ached. She assessed her work: the sidewalk was as clean as it could be. She stashed the broom and shovel under the porch and climbed the front steps. She was about to open the door when she heard a faint sound coming from inside.

The piano.

She put her ear to the door. Yes. She recognized the tune from one of Alice's practice books. A variation of Chopin's Concerto no. 1.

Maybe everything else was wrong with the world. But that, right there, made her day. She sat down on the porch, leaned her head against the door, and let Alice play.

14

DAVID WASN'T GOING to waste a school-free Thursday. Like Alice said, he didn't need anyone's permission to help his dad. His mom was at work, so she couldn't stop him, and he had an all-wheel drive pickup truck. He also had a name: Mason Waltman. A little online research told him that Waltman was the boss of all ICE trial attorneys in the Pacific Northwest, including Noah Sheldon. The same online directory David had used to learn Ms. Holban's address told him where the big boss lived. Next, he checked out Waltman's family on Facebook: wife Helen, eight-year-old twins Chloe and Oliver, and a golden retriever named Orsetto.

David eased the truck out of the garage and headed to Seattle. Early commuters had already cleared the snow off West Mukilteo Boulevard. He took I-5 South—also clear—and then Seattle surface streets, which grew worse the farther he drove from the freeway exit. He felt his wheels spinning and sliding at turns and stops. Cruising was sluggish, as if he had low-pressure tires. And when he hit the gas, the truck seemed to have a mind of its own, so he kept his speed under twenty until he turned onto Mason Waltman's street: Hillside Drive in the Madison Park neighborhood.

The houses looked really nice and the cars expensive. The blacktop was covered in packed snow. David rolled past the Waltman house, then parked across the street, two doors down. Not far ahead, a green yard-waste bin had been stuffed with broken tree branches next to another big pile on the ground. The heavy snow had done quite a number on the trees on that property.

David pulled his baseball cap low, zipped up his windbreaker, and got out of the truck. His sneakers slipped every few steps.

Waltman's house was white with green shutters and giant Roman columns. A shiny array of solar panels covered part of the roof. Tall, pruned hedges fronted the house, and the yard was protected by a black fence with a sliding gate. Through the open space between Waltman's building and the one beside it, David glimpsed a foggy sliver of Lake Washington over treetops going down the hill. A security company sign told him the property was monitored, but he couldn't see any cameras around.

The snow outside the gate hadn't been disturbed, which meant Waltman was still home. Maybe if David waited around, he'd catch a glimpse of the ICE man. Maybe he could tail a car that pulled out of the double garage. But what he couldn't do was keep standing around looking suspicious. He glanced up and down the street for nosy neighbors.

The world was white and quiet. Even so, he didn't dare climb the fence.

After a moment, his mood deflated. He'd come all the way here for nothing. And he couldn't wait around much longer because his sneakers and windbreaker were no match for the chill. But who'd think to buy winter clothes in the Pacific Northwest? It wasn't supposed to be this cold. His fingers and toes were already numb.

There must be something he could do though. He couldn't just give up when his dad needed him. He strolled past the gate, all the way to where Hillside met Lake Washington Boulevard. He stopped behind the metal guardrail at a sightseeing spot and looked at the fog hiding Bellevue's skyscrapers across the lake. On clear days, Mount Rainier would tower over the region from the south, but today the mountain was missing from the low gray sky. David eyed the slope leading to McGilvra Boulevard, maybe a hundred feet down the hill. What if he walked down Lake Washington to McGilvra and then climbed up the hill through the trees to Waltman's backyard?

Just then, a mail truck passed him and pulled up to the curb farther down the street. Rain or shine. A woman in a blue uniform stepped out with a mailbag and began her rounds. He followed her from a distance.

Waltman's mailbox was by the front door—inside the gate. Now that was interesting.

David waited until the woman delivered the mail for Waltman's neighbor. He then crossed the street and found a spot from which to film the carrier punching in the gate code. He set his zoom to maximum, wishing he'd had that sick new phone with extra cameras that took awesome pictures, even at night.

He focused his phone's lens over the woman's shoulder. He couldn't quite catch the numbers while she pressed them, but he hoped to pick them one by one when he watched the video in slow motion.

When she was done, he climbed behind the wheel and settled in the cold cabin. He played the video, zooming in. He followed the carrier's gloved finger on the panel in the grainy image. 6–5–1–0–#. That looked like a birth date. Aww—Waltman's twins. Touching, but not very secure. David typed a note on his phone.

But should he make his move now or wait? He'd accomplished something already, something big. Maybe he shouldn't push his luck. Better to come prepared and maybe with help.

He couldn't wait to tell Cruz of his cool stunt. He started the engine, put the truck in drive, and pressed on the gas. He must have parked on ice though, because as soon as he started moving, the truck swerved to the right. The fender hit the green yard-waste bin and the heavy pile of broken branches. David slammed on the brakes, but the truck wouldn't stop. It slid on for another few feet, grinding against the overturned bin and the sharp branches until David turned the wheels into the curb.

He jumped out and checked the damage: a large scrape down the whole right side of his truck and a dent by the headlight. He looked around, panicked. No witnesses. The mail carrier's truck was driving away, thank God, but David was in trouble. What would his dad say? Was David supposed to call the police and report the accident? Right across the street from Mason Waltman's house? No way—Ms. Holban would be furious. Nothing was damaged though, other than his truck and his confidence. The green bin looked fine, though branches were scattered everywhere. Maybe he should call the insurance company, but would they increase his premium? Would the accident go on his driving record? Maybe he could find some scratch-off solution at a hardware store and fix the paint, though scratch-off wouldn't take care of the dent.

David climbed back in, pressed his head against the steering wheel, and began to cry. It came so easily, and the sobs built so fast. He remembered how his mother could always make his heartbreak go away when he was little. Not this time. She'd be so scared that it could have been worse, that he could have been injured.

He sat up and wiped his eyes. At least he had the code to Waltman's gate. He put the truck in gear and very carefully pulled out. For the first time, driving felt like pain.

×

Emilio's new pod was always full. Detainees in orange uniforms didn't get day jobs, so there was nowhere to go.

After a breakfast he ate standing up against the wall with his tray, he returned to his bunk and read a copy of the *Seattle Times* he'd found on a table. No mention of the Russian who'd killed himself at NWDC a couple of days ago—the naked man Emilio had seen carried down the hall. But in here, everyone talked about him. They said he'd been tortured by the Russian police for disagreeing with their government. Somehow he'd managed to get on a ship to Mexico, then turned himself in at the San Ysidro checkpoint and asked for asylum. Sent to NWDC, he'd been here for the better part of a year. When his application was denied, he spent weeks on a hunger strike, being force-fed in solitary. And on suicide watch. He warned that if they sent him back to Russia, he'd be killed. He hung himself with a blanket.

The newspaper was instead filled with politics, sports, movie and book reviews, and restaurant openings. That all seemed so impossibly distant now. There was an untouched crossword puzzle; no one at NWDC—detainee or guard—had the language skills for that.

Emilio turned another page. The word "Guatemala" caught his eye. Two Dutch archeologists and a local diver had been murdered in Flores, El Petén, soon after recovering some Mayan artifacts from the bottom of the sacred Lake Petén Itzá. They'd been killed for a few obsidian blades and ceremonial bowls used for animal sacrifices. The article then explained that long ago, King Pakal the Great used to kill his war prisoners to repay the Mayan gods for their own sacred blood, which they'd mixed with maize flour to create humankind at the beginning of time. Had the stolen artifacts been used for human sacrifices, they'd be worth a fortune on the black market.

"Outside," a guard called.

Emilio put the paper down. Being outside with the PSB crew for an hour was dangerous, but he had no choice. He picked up his flannel jacket and headed for the door.

There was snow on the ground. His feet were cold in those flimsy canvas sneakers. He zipped up his jacket and jogged around the perimeter to stay warm. On his second lap, a basketball found the back of his head. The blow scrambled his vision and made his ears ring. He stumbled but managed to remain upright.

He rubbed his head and looked at the men by the basketball hoop. The tattooed guy was staring back at him, hands on his hips. Something in his stance said he was just getting started.

Emilio wished he could go back inside, but yard time wasn't up yet.

Someone pushed him from behind and hissed, "Self-deport, motherfucker."

Emilio ran on, dizzy and stumbling.

Yesterday in the visitation room, Father Nicolas had spoken about God, who saw everything and would protect Emilio. But he wasn't feeling very protected right now. He'd accepted a long time ago that God didn't meddle in human affairs. Otherwise he wouldn't have let Emilio's family die the way they did.

He spent the rest of the hour standing in a corner, his back to the wall, shivering and waiting for the next attack. He blew on his hands and rubbed them together. His toes were numb.

Soon he'd go inside and then what? Would the PSB guys attack him that night? Drag him out of his bunk and beat him in the dark? He wished he knew how to box, like David and Jacob, but he'd never had time or money for hobbies.

At the end of the hour, he was stiff cold. And he'd made up his mind to do something about his situation.

Once inside, he went to the first guard he saw, Svenson. "They're… after…me," Emilio said, his words hard to utter with a frozen face.

"Who is?" Svenson looked like he'd seen a lot but retained his humanity.

"PSB," Emilio said, shivering. And he told him what had happened.

"Go back to your bed," Svenson said. "It's counting time."

Emilio stood for the count, shivering, the PSB goons scowling at him. They'd seen him talking to the guard.

Svenson returned with Warden John Goins, a tough-looking guy with blue eyes and wide shoulders, who looked ready to knock teeth out on short notice.

"You sure they attacked you?" Goins said. "As opposed to, I don't know, just innocent accidents?"

Emilio nodded.

"Can you show me who?" He turned to face the room, gazing left and right.

Emilio shook his head. "Can't remember."

"Can't remember," Goins said with a chuckle. "Well, then."

Emilio saw himself thrown to the wolves. He looked the warden in the eye. "No one listened to the Russian either," he whispered.

Goins scowled. "What did you just say?"

Emilio knew he'd been heard.

Goins turned to Svenson. "Stash him away." And he left, cursing and shaking his head.

"Gather your things," Svenson said.

"Where am I going?" Emilio said.

"Solitary. Call it protective custody."

Emilio sighed with relief. After what had happened to the Russian, the guards didn't want any more drama and attention.

"Can I call my lawyer?" Emilio said.

"Shut the fuck up."

He took that as a no.

×

David pulled the truck up the driveway and parked beside the hedges so no one would see the damage. His mom would park her car in the garage, and that would buy him some time to figure out how to tell her about the accident. Good thing she was still at work and wouldn't—

David's stomach sank. The front door stood wide open. Tire tracks and footprints in the snow. ICE couldn't just break in, could they? Had they taken Jacob? He bolted inside and rushed to Jacob's room, panic choking him. There were muddy shoeprints all over the house. Like everything else, Jacob's room was a mess. Drawers pulled out, stuff all over the floor. Even the posters had been torn off the walls. But Jacob wasn't there. They'd taken him!

A knot in his throat, David dialed his brother's cell.

"I'll be home in a sec," Jacob answered and hung up.

Jacob was fine. David's fingers missed once while dialing his mom.

"Are you okay?" she said.

"Sorry, butt-dial." David hung up before his shaky voice could betray him.

He went through the house. Scattered things all over. Lamps knocked to the floor, slashed sofa pillows, broken plates in the kitchen, but he couldn't tell what was missing. He stood in the living room, hands on his head, wondering what the hell it all meant.

It was more than he could handle. He needed an adult to take care of things, just this once, so he phoned Ms. Holban.

"How bad is it?" Her soothing voice made him tear up.

He cleared his throat so he could speak. "Um, they didn't destroy much. Almost anything, really. Was it ICE?"

"I'll check. Did you call the police?"

"No. I'm scared they'll arrest my mom."

"The police won't check your mom's immigration status. But ICE might take a look at recent police cases."

"Then I won't risk it."

"Okay. Take pictures of everything."

David had an idea. He looked around to make sure Jacob hadn't arrived. "These people, they also dented and scratched my dad's pickup truck in the driveway."

Ms. Holban was quiet for a moment. "Take pictures of the damage and call the insurance company."

"Okay." So much for his clever idea. He wasn't going to lie to the insurance company; that was probably a crime.

Calming down at last, he took pictures around the house with his phone. It seemed like everything had been opened or turned over, from cabinets to furniture. The watercolor paintings in his parents' bedroom had been taken off their hooks and the paper backings had been slashed open. But his mom's jewelry was still there. Weird.

"Hot mess…What happened?"

David turned to see Jacob standing behind him. "Where have you been?" he said.

Jacob took off his windbreaker, and David noticed a bruise on his brother's neck. It was mostly covered by the hoodie. David moved in for a closer look. The bruise went down Jacob's chest, and it was purple.

"Today?" David said.

"Yesterday." Jacob pulled the hoodie tight and zipped up the neck. "I got into a fight with Kingston at school. Don't tell Mom, but I've been suspended for three days. Not sure if the snow days count." He glanced over his shoulder to make sure their mom wasn't around. "He made fun of Dad for being arrested at school, so I punched him in the face."

David had also been treated to mean comments about their dad. He tried to ignore them. Fighting just made their family look bad. Those kids were a bunch of assholes who didn't know any better.

"What happened here?" Jacob said.

"Someone broke in. Ms. Holban is looking into it."

"You didn't call the police, did you? They'll take Mom too!"

"Don't worry, I didn't."

Jacob sighed, then his eyes opened wide. "She can't see the house like this. You know how she gets."

They started cleaning up right away and agreed it wasn't a normal burglary. Otherwise the TV and the jewelry would be gone. Two hours later, they'd straightened everything up. Except for the slashed sofa pillows, a broken lamp, and a few broken plates in the kitchen. Then they vacuumed and mopped. There was no way to know if they put their parents' clothes back in the drawers right, but other than that, David thought they'd done a pretty good job.

"What was the point of all this?" he asked Jacob. "Trying to intimidate us? Or were they looking for something and couldn't find it?"

Jacob was sweaty from his housecleaning efforts. He pushed up his sleeves and fanned his face.

David gasped. "What's that on your arm?"

Jacob pulled his sleeve back down and didn't answer.

David grabbed his brother's arm and pulled the sleeve up again. There were thin red slashes on the skin. "You're cutting yourself again? What the fuck, Jacob?" His stomach tightened as it always did when he saw his little brother hurt.

"Leave me alone." Jacob pulled away, ran to his room, and slammed the door.

David went after him, but the door was locked. "That's bullshit, man."

Jacob cracked open the door. "What do you know? This"—he slapped his forearm—"this feels real. Everything else is just like, I don't know. Like we're all living a big fat lie."

David couldn't argue with that. They'd just covered up a break-in, and he'd just lied about the truck to Ms. Holban. "You want to come with me to buy a new lamp?" he asked Jacob. He had four hundred dollars and change on his debit card, money saved from odd jobs in the neighborhood.

Jacob pushed past him and headed outside without a word. David followed. Jacob squeezed past the hedges to get into the truck, then stopped by the door, looking at the dents and scratches.

"Get in and I'll explain," David said.

They found everything they needed at Everett Mall. Tape for the slashed paper behind the watercolors, replacements for the sofa pillows, and white plates just like the ones they already had. They couldn't find the same lamp, so they bought the closest thing. Jacob would say he broke the old one by accident.

Back home, they got to work again and made sure everything was where it should be.

"I know things are shitty," David said. "How can I help?"

Jacob shrugged. "I don't know."

"Talk to me, man. Please."

Jacob shrugged again. "I dream of them at night. Always in their black uniforms, like when they took Dad. I see them arresting Mom too."

"I still have some money," David said. "We could make an appointment with Dr. Berger." He was the therapist who'd helped Jacob in middle school.

They heard the front door open and close. "Children!" their mom called in Spanish.

"We have something to show you," David called back.

She brought her grocery bags into the kitchen and started putting things away. "The house looks so clean. What's going on?"

"Snow day," David said. "We wanted to surprise you." He picked up the new sofa pillows and brought them to the kitchen. "And how do you like these?" He held them up for her inspection: light-brown fabric with curly green vines.

"They're beautiful," she said, "but—"

"We found them at a garage sale for five dollars each and thought you might like them. The other pillows were faded and stained, so we got rid of them."

She looked at him for a long while, hand over mouth. "I know what you're doing."

David thought it best to remain silent.

"Jacob, the principal called me today," she said.

Damn snow day, it gave the principal time to call parents.

"He said you've been suspended for fighting with Kingston. I know you're upset about your father, but you shouldn't fight." She seemed so matter-of-fact about it.

Jacob just stood there, looking at the floor.

"Come, love, let's talk." She put the empty grocery bags away and took Jacob into the sunroom.

David watched her, with her small shoulders slumped from hours of scrubbing and vacuuming. He hoped Jacob wouldn't say anything to upset her—or show her the cuts.

David had so little control over the world around him that he wanted to scream. But there was something he could still do. He went to his room, turned on his laptop, and started shopping for a motion-activated camera to install in the living room. He found one small enough to fit inside the air vent, high up on the wall. If he got a wide-angle camera and positioned it right, it would show most of the living room, the dining room, and the kitchen. And if the camera had Wi-Fi, he could watch its output on his cell phone from anywhere. The camera he was looking at had all those features, plus an SD card that held a ton of footage—for under fifty bucks. He placed an order with overnight delivery and closed his laptop.

He wanted to text Alice and ask her to join his band, maybe in the summer. Though the matter seemed unimportant, thinking about the future felt pretty good right now. He started typing when he heard Jacob yell, "Just leave me alone!" Then a door slammed shut.

15

LAURA ARRIVED AT the Washington State Convention Center in downtown Seattle at eight in the morning for the monthly gathering sponsored by the American Immigration Lawyers Association. She pulled down the hood of her black raincoat and shook melting snow off her shoulders. The place smelled of wet carpet and muddy shoes.

Hundreds of lawyers, prosecutors, and government officials were there. Laura scanned the busy lobby and spotted Noah Sheldon. She went straight to him, interrupted his conversation, and pulled him aside. He looked too surprised to object.

"Did you send your officers to ransack my client's house yesterday?" she asked him.

Sheldon pulled back, frowning. "You mean Ramirez? We don't have a search warrant for his property, so no. What's this about?" He sounded sincere.

"If you get a warrant, you're required to inform me."

"Sure," Sheldon said and walked away, shaking his head.

Laura waded back into the crowd. She said hi to a few people but didn't stop to chat.

"Ms. Holban?" a man called her. He looked somewhat familiar. Tall, Black, early forties. Handsome too. "I really enjoyed your talk at the WDA conference last year."

That was a presentation Laura had given to the Washington Defenders Association about the importance of the words used in court by criminal defense attorneys. She'd explained that if attorneys weren't careful with their language, they could jeopardize immigrants' chances for citizenship later on.

The man offered his card, and she noticed he didn't wear a wedding band. She took the card and read aloud: "Kyle Jamison, criminal defense attorney." She'd heard of him, but they'd never crossed paths, as he moved in different circles than immigration lawyers. His work address was close to Pioneer Square, in the Norton Building on Second Avenue, where Laura sometimes visited the food truck.

"Your presentation," he said, "was eye-opening. I just wanted to say thank you." He smiled. "See you around, Ms. Holban." He turned away, a youthful spring in his walk.

When was the last time she felt youthful? Laura put his card in her wallet and headed upstairs to the glass-covered walkway over Pike Street. The crowd there was sparse. Most people went directly to the conference hall, so it was hard to miss Mason Waltman as he headed her way.

He was invited to all AILA events to speak on behalf of ICE and its affairs in his jurisdiction. Today's program said he'd appeal to all immigration lawyers to help Seattle and Tacoma judges reach their assigned quotas of processed cases. As if people like Laura would ever short a client to help a judge. "Efficiency" was the word he'd picked for the title of his lecture, but it should have been "expediency."

He didn't seem happy to see Laura. The feeling was mutual. Still, she smiled and said she was looking forward to his presentation.

"I've been watching your case with interest," he said. "As I watch all of my TAs' cases," he said, referring to his trial attorneys. "I admire your dedication, but really, what's the point of fighting for someone like Emilio Ramirez? An illegal who assaulted an American citizen."

Laura was unfazed. "My client is innocent of these new allegations. The same Ms. Brunelle who gave your office a witness statement also gave me an affidavit saying that nothing bad happened between her and my client."

"These new allegations are not covered by your affidavit, as far as I understand."

Laura shrugged. "I don't want to bore you with the details. Suffice it to say that Mr. Sheldon and I will relitigate Ms. Brunelle's allegations at my client's individual hearing."

Waltman twitched with a hint of annoyance that soon turned into condescension. "Ms. Holban—may I call you Laura?" Using a vulnerable person's first name would make her feel comfortable and more prone to mistakes.

"Sure, Mason." Her tone was sharp.

He leaned in. "Laura, you don't have a case, and you know it."

She scoffed. "I can build a whole case on the unfair treatment my client has received while in ICE custody. You know he's been roughed up by PSB gang members, I assume."

"Fighting happens all the time in vermin nests like NWDC."

"Did you just say vermin? That's Nazi talk."

Waltman stiffened up. "The easiest insult in the book: go for the Nazi comparison. I'll let it slide." He smiled. "Inmates then."

"Detainees."

"Detainees. They fight all the time, don't they?"

"Then why would PSB tell my client to self-deport to Guatemala? That's not usually what detainees fight about, is it?"

Waltman shrugged it off. "Laura, my presentation here today is about helping our judges go faster through their caseload. I'm afraid people like you are the cause of their missed quota."

"And why should I care about their quotas?" She felt her blood rushing to her cheeks. "What I care of—about—is that my client has been harassed at NWDC and is now locked in solitary."

"Protective custody—"

"Good morning, Mr. Waltman," a man said in passing.

Laura realized she and Waltman now stood close to each other by the glass wall, whispering in each other's faces. She pulled back and spoke in a normal voice. "I'm filing a lawsuit against the NWDC warden. If he can't protect his own detainees, he shouldn't be in the business of housing them."

Waltman rolled his eyes. "That's a long shot."

"Not after the state AG's lawsuit about the conditions at NWDC and their egregious dollar-a-day pay policy. Or after that Russian's suicide and this morning's article in *Crosscut*."

If she followed through on her threat—which she hadn't thought of until a few seconds ago—she'd be invoking habeas corpus and suing in federal court, which meant the Western District of Washington State, a bench not particularly friendly to NWDC. And why shouldn't she follow through? Even if there was nothing she could do right now to free Emilio, the publicity from such a case might secure better treatment for him.

"And I can add damages too," she said. "My client's house was ransacked because he's in jail. Some lowlifes in his neighborhood thought they could mess with his house because he's away. Thanks to you."

Waltman inched in again and touched her elbow. "Your client is a criminal, Laura. You know you can't get his asylum application approved. The waters have been muddied by Ms. Brunelle."

She pulled back. "I'll un-muddy them because my client is innocent."

The scar on Waltman's cheek grew darker. "Well, even if he is, you aren't."

"What are you talking about?" Laura wasn't sure what he meant, but he sure meant business.

Waltman closed the space between them and whispered in her ear, "You lied on your green card application."

That was the last thing she expected to hear. She knew the current administration wanted citizenship applications going back ten years to be reevaluated if there was "good cause," the definition of which was left to the trial attorneys' discretion. More extreme vetting nonsense. Lying on an official form meant the green card was not lawfully obtained, which meant the citizenship wasn't either. But some of those "lies" were really splitting hairs.

"What are you speaking—talking—about?" Laura said, flustered.

"Were you never associated with a communist organization?"

Laura had answered "No" on her own application. Had she answered "Yes," she would have had to explain more and submit a waiver of some sort.

"Every child in communist Romania was a...um, Pioneer." Words were now failing her, though she knew what she wanted to say. No one from Eastern Europe had ever filed a waiver. Organizations like the Pioneers were both mandatory and meaningless. Belonging to one didn't mean a person actually had communist sympathies, just that they lived under a communist regime. And no one had ever explained it on their green card application because, until 2017, no US administration had expected them to.

Waltman smirked. "But how old were you when you were last a… um, Pioneer?" He parroted her and stressed the *r* at the end of the word.

Laura was sixteen at the time of Romania's uprising, no longer a Pioneer but a member of the Communist Youth Union, the mandatory organization for high school students. "My father," she said, her throat tight and dry, "was a member of the Communist Party. But that doesn't mean he…My father went out in the streets with the rest of the people." The words felt like rocks on her tongue. "He was shot fighting to rid Romania of—"

"Your father," Waltman said with a sudden smile, "he went out *into* the streets."

He was right, of course. Those goddamn prepositions. Laura was mortified. Her misstep was tiny, but it pointed out that she hadn't mastered Waltman's language. She was an outsider with no place or business here.

"Besides," he said, "sixteen is considered adult for the purposes of that question."

Laura composed herself. "I dare you to do that. I'll go after you for unlawful retaliation. All the way to the Supreme Court."

"Yes, yes, yes. But how many years will that take? For my part, I'll only be doing my job. But you, you'll be fighting for your life. And your daughter's future."

"Leave my daughter out of this."

"Or you can accept your defeat and advise Ramirez to ask for voluntary deportation."

"Not going to happen."

"I can even put in a good word with Judge Felsen." He took out his wallet and produced a business card. "Here, call my cell phone when you make up your mind. But don't make me wait too long." His eyes narrowed. "I hate waiting."

He brushed past and joined a group of men who welcomed him with pats on the back.

16

EMILIO'S NEW CELL was only four steps across, and it had a bunk bed, a table mounted on the wall, and a toilet. He wasn't allowed outside anymore. After just one day here, his thoughts swirled in a painful jumble. What use was he to his family locked up in this box? At least they had the house. Laura said ICE didn't do house raids. Blanca knew how to keep a low profile and her job. Her cleaning company hired mostly undocumented workers and knew how to stay under the radar. As for Emilio, he'd do what PSB wanted and self-deport.

He thought of the people locked up in solitary for months on end, some on hunger strike because of poor living conditions, bad food, and the lack of medical attention. Now they protested on behalf of the Russian who'd killed himself the other day. But that wasn't Emilio's fight. He was going to Guatemala, a place he hadn't seen since 1997. His next fight could be there.

Back then, he was called Miguel and had been a janitor at the Maya Biosphere Reserve in Petén for almost a year. He'd hoped to work his way up to an assistant.

One humid, mosquito-infested summer, he was home in Bethel to celebrate his nineteenth birthday with his parents and his brother Antonio. He'd brought with him a disposable camera with a twenty-four-shot film roll, a present from his coworkers. He'd used half the shots at the reserve and at the party thrown by his former schoolmates at home and saved the rest for his actual birthday.

In the morning, Mamá made him his favorite treat for breakfast, rellenitos de plátano. Black bean paste with cinnamon and chocolate, wrapped in plantain dough, rolled into balls, and fried. He and Antonio gobbled them up, while she gave him the warmest smile for a photo.

Then Papá took him on a ride in an armored Jeep to check on his squad at the Guatemala-Mexico border. Miguel looked through his camera's eyepiece but only pressed the shutter once for an impressive portrait of Papá driving to work with a rifle on his knees.

Papá parked the Jeep at the end of the dirt road by the stairs leading down to the Usumacinta River. People and cars crowded the place. Miguel took a photo of the trees on the shore with boats on the water and Mexico in the distance. Then he heard yelling and followed Papá down the slope.

Two handcuffed men were shouting at the soldiers who guarded them. One had wild brown hair and a mustache, the other a full, black beard. Miguel assumed they'd been arrested by Papá's squad for drug trafficking and that the drugs were inside an open backpack he saw on the ground. He snapped a photo of the scene to show his buddies at the reserve.

"Cocaine?" Papá asked his border guards.

"Come see," one said.

The guards' names were Rafa, Tito, and Chema, young men like Miguel, sent there from a military unit in Petén. They shook hands with him, but there was no time for small talk because the two traffickers kept yelling, offering bribes, and threatening retaliation.

Miguel crouched next to the backpack to take a better look. A dozen obsidian arrow points were scattered on the ground next to a clay figurine of a kneeling warrior. A sacrificial dagger, its jade handle carved like a Mayan god's head. Two lifelike eyes stared at him from an object loosely wrapped in brown paper. He pulled back, his jaw tight with dread. A Mayan death mask.

He'd seen stone replicas at traveling fairs but never the real thing. This one looked old and imperfect, made of small jade squares. It had the rusty smell of cinnabar, a sign of Mayan royalty. For the scent to be that strong, the mask must have been removed from a tomb and not too long ago. The eyes had brown irises surrounded by white stone, and the mouth was slightly open, which made the mask look alive and menacing.

Back at the Maya Biosphere Reserve, Miguel worked with archeologists exploring unearthed ruins. They'd want to see this. A real Mayan royal death mask! Miguel peeled off some of the paper and took a photo, trying not to touch the artifact.

"Janaab is coming for his cargo," the mustached man told the guards.

Miguel didn't know who Janaab was, but Papá's face changed, if only for an instant.

"Rafa, Tito," he told his men, "take them and the cargo to the Jeep. Chema, keep an eye on the people at the checkpoint."

"Fuck you!" the bearded man said, spitting.

Miguel took a picture of Papá staring down the traffickers, his rifle slung over his shoulder. This could become deadly at any moment. Miguel's hands became sweaty, and he gripped his camera.

"He's going to kill you all," the bearded man said.

Papá shoved him against a tree, turned him around, cuffed him, and marched him up the stairs to his Jeep while Miguel followed, not knowing what else to do. People blocked his sight ahead, some yelling. He saw Tito pushing the other man into the Jeep while Rafa started the engine. Papá instructed the people to move away, and the Jeep had enough space to make a U-turn and drive off to the nearest police station.

Miguel followed Papá back down to the water to check on the river traffic. Just when he thought that the exciting but scary incident was over, a blue lancha—a narrow motorboat with a domed sunroof—came up to the shoreline. Miguel took a picture.

"Stay back," Papá said.

A man in his thirties got out and strutted over. He had thick eyebrows and slicked-back hair.

"Janaab," Papá said, rifle at the ready.

"Where's my stuff? Where're my people?"

Papá's rifle was trained on Janaab.

Miguel glanced around, worried. Rafa and Tito had already left. A few steps away, Chema held the only other weapon, a pistol pointed at Janaab. Miguel stood there, fidgeting with his camera.

Janaab's face was twisted with anger, but he kept his voice low while arguing with Papá.

Miguel pressed the shutter—only three shots left.

For an instant—when Janaab poked him in the chest—Papá seemed frightened. His mouth was downturned, as if he'd been poisoned by a scorpion. But all the while, the muzzle of his rifle was inches from Janaab's chest.

A few brave people gathered around to watch the argument. Miguel snapped another picture. And then it was over. Janaab went back to the lancha and was gone.

"You can lower your rifle now," Miguel told Papá after heaving a sigh of relief.

Papá's hands shook a little, and his forehead was covered in sweat.

"Who is this Janaab, Papá?" Miguel said.

"Nobody."

Two days later, Janaab was all but forgotten. For Miguel, the morning was busy with saying goodbye to the neighbors. Papá was away on a night raid along the border. Mamá cooked while Antonio bought supplies for Miguel to take with him to the reserve.

"Another photo," Miguel said, huddling with his mother and brother, their heads pressed together. He grinned at the camera, and just as he pressed the shutter, he thought he heard Papá coming home. He had one shot left, then he'd be able to develop the film. One last shot of Papá.

He rushed to the door, but the crunch on the gravel outside sounded deeper than the Jeep's tires. He slipped the camera inside his jacket and opened the door. There was a black van outside. Three men got out: the two traffickers Papá had arrested the other day and Janaab. All three pointed their guns at the house.

"Down! Get down!" Miguel called to Mamá and Antonio, slamming the door. He dropped to the floor just as the first bullets whizzed through the open window shutters.

Mamá's surprised face turned to him, his name the last word out of her mouth before her cheek was ripped off in a spatter of blood and flesh.

Miguel screamed in terror, but the sound was lost in the explosion of bullets, wood chips, and clay shards. His head was pounding. He was short on air. He crawled away from the window and into the kitchen, but Mamá was already dead. Antonio fell to the floor with chest and stomach wounds, dying in front of him.

Miguel cried out for help, but no help came. Only bullets. Once in a while, a dip in the noise meant someone was reloading. The air smelled of dust and blood.

How long had it been? A minute? An hour? Miguel covered his head while bullets ricocheted off the walls above him. A Molotov cocktail crashed through the window and burst on the table, fire slithering over the floor.

Miguel scuttled away and fell out the back door into the narrow alley. He stumbled along until he found a familiar space between two houses and squeezed through. He was in Tía Celia's backyard now. Beyond it, rows of corn stretched as far as the eye could see. A good hiding spot. Dizzy and stumbling, he parted the corn plants, pushing deeper into the field. Thick smoke rose in the blue sky. His house was burning.

Deep between yellow stalks under a darkening sky, Miguel dropped to the warm dirt and wailed into his fists, but all the crying in the world couldn't put things right, couldn't make Mamá and Antonio alive and whole again.

After sunset, he found his way to the migration office. Papá's friend Lucio was outside, standing under the blue arches with DELEGACION DE MIGRACION written across in white.

"You're alive!" the officer said, his voice trembling. He pulled Miguel close and looked him over, as if checking for wounds.

"They killed them," Miguel said. "Mamá and Antonio. They killed them…"

Lucio nodded, rubbing his eyes. "Your house is gone too."

"Janaab's men, why aren't they in jail?"

Lucio looked away, chewing on his white mustache. "We were going to send them to Flores, but we let them go last night when we got word that Janaab had your father."

"They have Papá? Let's go get him!"

Lucio shook his head and put a hand on Miguel's shoulder. "Come."

Miguel grew weak in the knees as Lucio led him inside. Papá's body lay on the cement floor. He was covered in a dirty sheet drawn up to his chest. And his face was…not his face. His eyes were swollen shut like those of a newborn. A bruised, dead newborn. His face had a faint reddish tint, as if he'd been covered with paint and then washed.

Miguel picked up a corner of the sheet, working up the courage to look at what they'd done to Papá's body, but Lucio said, "Don't. They cut his heart out."

Miguel's stomach lurched. He dashed to the nearest corner, where the yellow bile in his stomach hit the wall.

"They dropped him outside," Lucio said, his voice quivering. "I cleaned him up. I couldn't stand to see him like that."

Miguel heaved some more.

"This Janaab," Lucio said, "he's sick in the head. Trying to copy Mayan sacrificial ceremonies. He could've been obsessed with other parts of their great culture. Math, architecture, astronomy. But no, it had to be human sacrifice. Slashing the belly to get to the heart through the diaphragm." He crossed himself. "And this sick bastard, he doesn't even know what he's doing. He rubs his victims' faces with cinnabar, but cinnabar was for Mayan royalty, not war prisoners. He should've used blue pigment or nothing."

Miguel couldn't follow. "Who is Janaab?" he whispered, wiping his mouth and inhaling hard.

"He's big in Mexico," Lucio said, rubbing his eyes, "but no one knows his real name, only that he's from Yucatán. This last year, he's made a name for himself along the border because he never leaves the family of an enemy alive. Not even the newborns."

Miguel was in a bad dream that would soon be over. It had to be.

"This note was pinned with a knife on his chest." Lucio held out a blood-stained piece of paper.

TELL THE REPORTER TO BRING HIS CAMERA TO FRONTERA.

Frontera Corozal was the closest town across the border, in Chiapas, Mexico.

"They thought I was a reporter…" Miguel felt sick again. His camera was the reason for all this carnage? Janaab had thought Miguel was a reporter taking photos for a newspaper?

"That makes some twisted sense," Lucio said. "These cartel guys, they hate to have their picture taken. Ever since Pablo Escobar's mugshot ended his political ambitions in Colombia. Janaab must've thought a photo of him at the border crossing in Bethel could damage his front business, whatever that is."

Papá had died without telling them the truth about Miguel. Somehow, he'd led them to believe his son was a reporter. He'd died trying to keep him safe.

Miguel reached under the sheet and took Papá's hand, the way he used to when he was little and scared. But now the hand was cold and rigid.

"If Janaab finds out you're alive," Lucio said, "he'll come after you. You must go somewhere safe. Not back to your job, no."

"Not leaving them here like this. Their funerals…"

Lucio picked up a canvas rucksack from somewhere. "Your father was dear to everyone in town, Miguel. We'll take good care of him and your mother and your brother. Don't worry. But you must go on living. For them. And you won't if you stay." He opened drawers and rummaged through them, picking up things to throw inside the rucksack. "We'll spread the word that the reporter went back to Flores. But if you stay here, you put the whole town in danger." He grabbed Miguel's arm and pulled him away. "Your father, he'd never forgive me if I didn't make sure you're safe."

"Wait." Miguel's hand was shaking, but he managed to pull out his camera and take one last photo of Papá. He heard the film roll hit its end.

"Hurry," Lucio said. "If anyone saw you coming here, and if Janaab gets word…"

In a daze, Miguel followed Lucio outside and climbed into a car parked on the street. Lucio told him to lie across the back seat, out of sight. Miguel sank into a muffled place inside his mind, where Mamá's wondering face exploded, Antonio's chest spewed blood, and Papá had been robbed of his heart.

Miguel's camera held the last images of his family—and their killers.

When Lucio finally stopped the car, it was close to midnight. "Here, take this." He gave the rucksack to Miguel. "Some money and a pistol. Get as far away from here as you can."

A world away in solitary confinement, Emilio wiped his eyes. Once they deported him, he'd finally go to the graves of his mother, father, and brother. Then he'd find a way to return to Blanca and the boys. If Laura refused to file the Stipulated Order of Removal—the self-deportation document he'd read about in the NWDC law library—he'd work directly with Ken Masters, his deportation officer. But he'd rather she filed it on his behalf and continued to watch over his family while he was away. He'd probably be deported in a few weeks. Whenever ICE scheduled the next plane to Guatemala City.

He'd ask Laura not to tell Blanca about his voluntary deportation though. Not until he was out of the country. Otherwise she'd risk everything to come and say goodbye. And she'd be arrested too.

17

DAVID PARKED THE truck on Hillside Drive and showed Jacob the white house with the Roman columns and the black gate. There was snow under the trees, but the street was clear. Three other pickup trucks were parked nearby. A few houses away, a construction crew was up on scaffolds despite the cold. For a moment, David feared they might be Fernando's guys, but no. Then his heart sank again. Not long ago, his dad had been one of those construction workers.

"What now?" Jacob said, leaning back in his seat.

"Now we wait. Cool thing contractors are everywhere. Makes us blend in."

David had taken his brother out of school that Friday to cheer him up. They told the teachers they felt the flu coming, and no one objected. Now he and Jacob were partners in crime. It was midday, a good time to investigate someone's place when they weren't home.

Jacob whistled. "Waltman's house must be worth a couple million. At least."

The whole neighborhood was full of big houses with lake views and professional landscaping.

"How much money does ICE pay?" Jacob said.

"Not enough for this."

"Let's take a look."

Ms. Holban would be angry to know they were here. But David didn't need her to tell him that snooping around someone's house was probably illegal. "Let's make sure no one's home first."

Waltman was at a conference today—David had called his office in the morning and found out—but his family could be home if the kids had another day off. Some schools feared slabs of melting snow sliding off roofs and trees, hurting people and breaking power lines.

Jacob put in his earbuds. David watched the house for half an hour while scrolling through Snapchat stories on his phone.

"Wow, check this out!" He showed Jacob a video of Cruz's dog doing a 360-flip.

"Hashtag killing it," Jacob said, smiling.

It was good to see him smile.

A swirl of snowflakes came and went across their windshield.

Alice texted that her school was closed and she was bored, but no snow would keep her from a classmate's Dungeons & Dragons party on Saturday morning. David was pretty sure she wanted him to meet her there. She hadn't said the words, but she had provided the address of a house in Seattle's Magnolia neighborhood. Maybe he could talk to her about the band tomorrow.

He checked outside. Still no movement at Waltman's house.

Jacob shivered and rubbed his arms.

"I can't idle the engine, sorry," David said.

Jacob paused his music. "We could walk around a bit, scope out the neighborhood."

"Fifteen more minutes. Got to make sure no one's home."

Jacob turned his music back on and slumped in his seat. Not long after, the door to Waltman's house opened, and a woman came out with an empty cardboard box. Helen, the wife. David recognized her from Waltman's Facebook page. She took the box around the left side of the house into a narrow alley by the property fence, then came back without it.

"They're home," Jacob said with a pout. "Today's busted. Can we go now?"

"This takes time and patience." David scratched his cheek to hide his annoyance. "See why I don't usually take you with me?"

"Usually, you need a plan," Jacob shot back.

David was cold too, though he wouldn't admit it. "A bite to eat?"

They took out the ham and cheese sandwiches they'd bought at Café Abdul that morning and began eating in silence.

"The gate," Jacob said, his mouth half-full.

David looked up as the metal gate slid aside and a blue Volvo SUV pulled out of the double garage. Helen was driving. Through the tinted window, David saw a girl in the back seat. He watched the SUV until it disappeared around a corner.

"The gate's closing," Jacob said.

David wrapped up the rest of his lunch and threw it in the back seat. "No worries."

He couldn't help strutting half a step ahead of Jacob as they walked to the house. He stopped at the gate and punched in the code he'd learned from the mail carrier: 6510#.

Nothing happened.

A chill ran down David's spine. He tried the code again. Still nothing.

"I thought you knew the code," Jacob said. "We've got to move. We look suspicious."

"I know that, Jacob." David tried to stay calm.

The video on his phone, he still had it. He scrolled through pictures and videos and found the one with the mail carrier.

"Hurry," Jacob said.

David watched with tensed breath as the mail carrier pressed each number with thick gloved fingers.

6–5–1–0. Maybe the second digit was a 4?

Hand trembling, David punched in 6410#. Nothing.

"Hurry, David," Jacob cried.

It had to be one of those digits around 5. Which was all of them. David tried 6610#.

Nothing.

"Come on, man," Jacob said.

6810#. The pedestrian gate buzzed and unlocked.

"Yes!" Jacob slapped David on the back with excitement.

They crossed the yard and moved to the porch, where they were mostly hidden by evergreen hedges. David didn't see any cameras, but that didn't mean there weren't any. He looked inside through a window. A hallway led to a bright room with a view of the lake. No one else seemed to be home. He turned to Jacob and pointed to the thickest tree in the front yard, a Douglas fir twice as tall as the house.

"Keep lookout over there."

Jacob nodded and hurried to his post. They were lucky the Waltman kids and the dog had tramped through the yard minutes earlier, leaving footprints everywhere. No one would notice two more sets in the snow.

David followed Helen's earlier route into the narrow alley on the left side of the house. Definitely no cameras there, but he found the garbage bins, always a good source of intel. He raised the lid of the blue recycling bin and propped it against the fence, then moved the flattened cardboard box aside to see what he could find: children's drawings, empty bottles and jars, a chewed-up dog-food bag, plastic containers. He opened the green bin next: yard waste and compostable bags of food leftovers. The small black garbage bin was empty. Now what?

David found a tree branch in the green bin and went back to the recyclables to dig around. No sheets of paper anywhere. That was unusual. Could it be...He moved to the green bin again. One foot down, between a greasy pizza box and a bag of chicken bones and paper towels, he found another green bag, this time filled with shredded paper. Yes! He pumped his fist, excited. Waltman might be a tough guy at ICE, but at home he put his shredded paper in the compost bin. David pulled the bag out and dropped the lid.

"The gate," Jacob called from his lookout spot under the tree.

David peered around the corner and saw the gate rolling open. He waved Jacob over. His brother crouched down and ran along the fence to join him. At the other end of the alley, they tried the backyard gate but found it locked.

David set the compost bag down. "Give me a hand."

Jacob made a step with his interlaced fingers. David planted one foot there and swung the other over the narrow gate, then slid down. He undid the latch, which was too low on the gate for someone to reach from the alley. Jacob grabbed the bag and hurried through.

They were on Waltman's terrace now, a low wooden fence separating the property from the hillside slope. They'd barely closed the gate behind them when a dog raced up the side alley, barking up a storm. It had to be Orsetto, Waltman's golden retriever. The dog threw himself at the gate, making even more noise. Whoever had just come home was sure to investigate.

"Do you have any dog treats in your pockets?" Jacob said.

It was too late for treats even if David had any left from walking the neighbors' dogs that week. Someone was coming.

"You really are a shitty planner," Jacob whispered.

"Come here, Orsetto," a man's voice called from the alley. Mason Waltman, for sure.

David held his breath as the voice drew closer. They had to get out of there. He motioned to Jacob. "Go, go, go." They sprinted across the terrace—Jacob first, David after him—and jumped over the fence and the hedges at the top of the hill slope.

The dog was still barking, and now Waltman sounded angry.

David and Jacob slid down the steep hill behind the house, toward McGilvra Boulevard about a hundred feet below. There were enough trees and vines in the way to make it a slow descent, though snow and ice turned the ground slippery at times.

A branch poked the green bag, and a few small bits of shredded paper flew out.

"Leave them," David cried. "We've got to move."

After what seemed like forever, they reached the sidewalk on McGilvra.

Jacob grinned. "That was fun," he said, panting.

David looked for Waltman or Orsetto, but no one seemed to be following. Now all he and Jacob needed to do was walk back up to Hillside Drive, find their pickup, and drive back to Everett. Simple enough.

"You bring the truck here," Jacob said, "and I'll go get the paper bits we dropped."

David agreed and started climbing the hill on Lake Washington Boulevard. At the top, he ran along Hillside to his truck. He turned on the engine and rubbed his freezing hands, then pulled toward the street. A blaring car horn made him slam on the brakes as a white sedan drove past. He'd forgotten to check the mirrors. Heart racing, he looked both ways and stepped on the gas again.

In the rearview mirror, he saw a silver Audi pulling out of Waltman's driveway. Was Waltman coming after him? David couldn't speed up though. The construction crew's vehicles parked on one side of that residential street turned it into a one-way for long stretches.

David turned left the first chance he got and headed west, hoping to hit Madison Street, where he could hide in city traffic. He was almost too afraid to look in the rearview mirror.

The Audi was catching up with him.

David's hands turned slick on the steering wheel. He knew he was in trouble. What happened if Waltman—a government attorney— caught him? Jacob was still waiting at the bottom of the hill.

He turned right and saw East Madison a couple of blocks away, but his truck was no match for the Audi. It was right behind him, with Waltman at the wheel. No way David was engaging in a car chase. He didn't drive that well anyway. There could be icy patches ahead, between here and the main street. And if he crashed the truck, his mom would be sick for days.

He pulled over by a green hydrant. He kept his shaking hands on the wheel, feeling like he was going to throw up. The Audi parked right behind him. David took one deep breath and let it out in a loud exhale. He didn't want to look scared.

Waltman knocked on the window. He was a White man with short hair, a nice suit, and a scar on his left cheek. Taking him on was out of the question. David's coach had warned him that someone with scars might strike faster and harder than a boxer who'd never fought outside a tournament ring.

Waltman motioned for David to roll down the window. David lowered it halfway.

"Who are you?" Waltman said. His teeth were pretty crooked. His folks must have been too poor for braces when he was little.

"David."

"David who?"

Could Waltman force David to show his driver's license? He wasn't the police.

Waltman cocked his head. "Where're you from?"

"Around here."

"Do I know you?"

"No, sir."

"Then what were you doing at my house?"

In his hurry to get away, David hadn't thought of a lie. "Nothing."

"You were in my backyard. That's trespassing. Were you trying to get into my house?"

"No, sir."

"How old are you?"

"Sixteen."

"A good age. At which boys can be prosecuted as adults. Can you even drive alone?"

David felt the blood drain from his face. "Yes, sir."

"A great way to start your life, kid." Waltman paused. "What's your father's name?"

David was going to get his dad in trouble too. Before he knew it, he had tears in his eyes.

"What's your father's name, David?"

"My father's dead."

Waltman took a small step back and scratched his chin, looking away for a moment.

David wiped his eyes and waited. He didn't know what else to do. If Waltman searched the truck, he'd figure out who his dad was.

Waltman leaned into the window. "If I see you at my house again, I'll have you arrested, you hear me?"

David nodded and sniffled.

"Now get the hell out of here."

David shifted the truck into drive and took off. When he couldn't see Waltman anymore, he pulled over and phoned his brother. "I'm coming," he said and hung up.

He saw a text from his mom asking what he and Jacob wanted for dinner. His fingers hovered over the screen without typing, then he threw the phone on the passenger seat and started crying.

Mason got back in his car, grateful Helen had taken the twins to the pediatrician and missed this strange scene. Chloe needed a prescription of steroids for croup cough. She should be better in a day or two, and maybe they could all sleep for a few uninterrupted hours tomorrow night. After the AILA conference, Mason had picked up Orsetto and taken him to the vet because the dog had started wheezing—as if there wasn't enough sickness in their family already. The vet had prescribed an anti-inflammatory and recommended they wait a few days to see if the condition improved.

Mason drove home, staying under the speed limit advised by the "20 is plenty!" neighborhood signs. He parked in the garage by the door to the kitchen but remained in the car for another moment. Still thinking about the terror in that boy's face. Mason knew he was frightening to many people, but they were mostly adults who'd sneaked into his country and deserved to be terrified and punished.

But this boy? Sure, he'd sneaked into Mason's backyard, but he was only a kid. He did look Latino, but people had once thought Mason was Latino because of his Sicilian blood. And this kid had no accent. When Mason caught up with the Ford truck on the street, he was ready to bring the law down on that troublemaker. But then the look on that boy's face weakened his resolve.

Mason remembered Pa Kirk's twisted mouth and heavy fist. He remembered his mother whimpering on her knees, her face swelling from hard slaps.

Kirk towering over her in their small kitchen. "Pathetic. Useless. You and your ugly gasbag spawn."

With all the courage his twelve-year-old heart could muster, Mason had yelled back at him. "She's a good mother. And we're not ugly. Mom, can't you just grab a chair and throw it at him when he tries to hit you?"

Kirk glared at Mason with pure hatred, the kind he showed when talking about the Vietnamese soldiers who'd kept him prisoner until the night he escaped by snapping the neck of the boy who brought him food. Mason was about the same age as that dead boy. He knew Kirk could snap his neck—and he sure looked like he wanted to.

Mason's courage melted away. He turned on his heels and ran to his room, thinking Kirk would go back to hurting Mom—and that maybe for once she'd grab a chair and throw it at him. But Kirk came after Mason instead, feet stomping on the hallway floor.

The bedroom door flew off its hinges and slammed against the bookshelf. Kirk grabbed Mason, threw him on the bed, and pinned him on his stomach. Then punched him in the ribs, neck, head. It hurt like nothing else ever had.

Mason heard his little sister screaming, "He's killing him. Help! He's killing him." By then he felt numb and dizzy. Margot swatted at Kirk. "I'm calling the police! I'm telling the neighbors! Just stop hurting him!"

Mason couldn't remember where his mother was during that nightmare, before everything went black.

Judging by the fear Mason had seen in David's eyes, the boy's late father must have never raised a fist against him. Kids who'd been hit before had a defiant attitude and not a trace of shock that something as terrible as being attacked could happen to them. They knew how the world worked, and they snarled at it.

But not young David in his dented pickup truck. He had the same innocence Mason had nurtured in his own children. And today, for some reason, he couldn't take that away from a child. Though most days he had to, as he deported children and adults alike to their own damn countries.

"Shit," Mason whispered. He was growing soft.

×

Laura was now forced to explore more of NWDC than she'd cared for. Because Emilio was in protective custody, he was kept away from other detainees, which was why she had to go to his cell instead of meeting him in a visitation room. They sat on the hard bed while the guard watched them from the open door. Emilio seemed better than last time she saw him.

With Mason Waltman threatening to go after Laura's citizenship, she felt even closer to Emilio now, though she would never burden him with her problems. She was ready to go through her task list—get an affidavit from Emilio saying he'd never attacked Evelyn Brunelle; tell him she'd found no incriminating evidence against him at the Everett Police Department; explain his bond appeal, and more—when she saw tears in his eyes.

"What happens if I ask for deportation?" Emilio's voice broke a little. Laura drew back, waiting.

"I can't help my family from inside here," he said. "I'm not really in jail if I can ask to leave, no? All I need to do is say the word. I'll even pay for my plane ticket."

"And your family?"

"I'll come back, like I did before."

Laura remembered her conversation with Gabriela. "A few weeks in detention and people start dreaming of walking out of here and coming right back. It doesn't work that way, Emilio. You can't come back at the border and ask for asylum, not anymore."

"I'll cross the border through the desert again. I'm still strong. They can't keep me away from my family."

The guard at the door shifted in place.

"We're not having this conversation," Laura whispered, then added in her normal voice, "Now, before we run out of time, I have some bad news. Your house was broken into yesterday."

Emilio's face changed to dread. "Blanca and the kids?"

"They're fine. Everyone's fine. Nothing was stolen as far as David could tell. And we haven't told Blanca yet. The boys fixed everything up."

"It must be Evelyn Brunelle then. You said nothing was stolen? The house isn't burned, just messed with. Because she wants me—my family—to move out and sell to her."

"I didn't say anything about burning." That was an odd detail. "And no, it's not Evelyn Brunelle. At the time of the break-in, she was showing houses to one of her clients in Lake City. She posted pictures on Facebook about her big snow day."

"Maybe she paid someone?"

"That'd be too risky."

"Then who?"

"I don't know. But David said they were looking for something in your house. They slashed pillows and ripped the backs off wall hangings. But they didn't take Blanca's jewelry. Why? What were they looking for?"

Emilio didn't answer.

"Emilio? Do you have any important objects in your house? Things you brought from your country, maybe? Something valuable?"

He looked away. "No, I brought nothing with me."

Laura could tell he was hiding something. But then, most of her clients did, and she had no magic truth potion to extract it from them. She was just an immigration lawyer, and the break-in didn't concern Emilio's asylum case—other than eliciting sympathy from a judge.

18

DAVID DIDN'T WANT to be late meeting Alice at her Saturday Dungeons & Dragons party. The moment he finished walking his neighbors' dogs, he got in his pickup and drove to Seattle. He parked in front of an eggshell-blue house, turned off the engine, and texted Alice. A light snow had started while he was on the highway and was still going. The pavement was slushy. A dusting of white covered everything: roofs, patio furniture, cars parked along the street.

If Ms. Holban knew about them seeing each other like this, she might drop David's dad as a client. To hear Alice tell it, Ms. Holban was a kind of mama-bear, always watching over and protecting her daughter even when she didn't need protecting. Like now.

While waiting for Alice to respond, David thought of the slow progress he'd made last night, scanning bits of shredded paper from Waltman's compost bag. It would be days before he could feed the scanned images through a reconstruction program.

Soon Alice stepped from the house in her puffy coat, skinny jeans, and tall boots. David waved, and she smiled when she saw him. He leaned over to unlock the passenger door and pushed it open.

Alice grabbed onto the seat and hopped in with a pocket of cold air. "Tall truck," she said.

"Helps with the glutes."

She laughed, settling in. "The scratches on your truck? Was it those guys who broke into your house?"

"Ah-ha," David said, not wanting to lie more than he had to. "Won't they miss you in there?"

"They're fine for now. My barbarian just passed out in a tavern. Too much honey ale. I have a few minutes."

Then neither of them knew what to say. David focused his attention on the shape of his steering wheel. He wanted to talk to her about his band but hoped the subject would come up naturally in conversation. So he kept his mouth shut. Still, it was great to be sitting with a cool Seattle keyboard player in his crew cab, watching the snow fall.

Alice took off her foggy glasses and cleaned them with the hem of her sweatshirt. She smelled nice, like fruit and mint, which made David's heart jump. Based on his experience of high school parties, he had to ask, "Your friends, what are they drinking in there?"

She put her glasses back on and gave him a smile. "Just bubble tea, no alcohol. The parents are upstairs. You vape?"

David didn't know the correct answer. "Should I?"

"My grandpa died of cancer. From smoking his whole life. My mom is against anything resembling a cigarette." She gestured toward the blue house. "They wanted me to try vaping, but I didn't. I just…My mom—she gets really upset about smoking."

"You said vaping."

"My mom thinks there're bad chemicals in those too."

"I tried it once," David told her. "Tangerine flavor. It was okay." He wanted to say vaping was an expensive habit, but he didn't want to sound poor. Before his dad's arrest, he'd been saving money to buy a better smartphone. Now everything was about bills and legal fees.

"What phone do you have?" he said.

Alice reached into her jacket and took out her phone. She unlocked it with her thumbprint and gave it to him.

David weighed it in his hand: the latest iPhone, heavier and with a bigger screen than his. He opened the settings and looked through the options to find all sorts of rad features for creating music videos. And much more. "This would be perfect to control the camera I just installed."

"What camera?" Alice said.

"Security camera. In our living room. To catch them if they break in again." David passed the phone back, before he looked like he was snooping.

Alice put it back in her jacket. "What are you doing after this?"

He shrugged. "I was thinking of going to the gym. It'd make my dad happy if I keep up my boxing practice." It made him sad to say those words.

Alice glanced at the house. "My friend's dad!" She ducked. "I don't want him to see us." A man in a denim jacket climbed down the front steps.

David was glad he had the chance to show Alice he could cover for her. Like he did when Jacob was in trouble.

His heart jumped when the dad headed their way. He held his phone in front of him as the guy walked past and continued down the street.

"All clear," David said.

Alice sat up. "I should go."

"You want a ride home?"

"My mom's picking me up."

The windows were fogging up, but David didn't want to turn on the engine. It would make Alice think he was in a hurry to leave. He thought about getting the guitar from the back seat. He'd been planning to show Alice a few tunes his band rocked, but the idea seemed ridiculous now.

Alice clasped the door latch but didn't open it. "How's your brother?"

The question jolted David. "Good. Why?" Alice didn't know Jacob, did she?

"My mom talks to your mom, and I overheard that he's really upset about your dad. If that happened to my dad…"

"Where's your dad?" David said, happy to change the subject and keep talking.

"My mom ran him out of town. Out of the country, really. He's back in Romania." She seemed to be getting sad. "He has a new wife, Vera."

"That sucks," David said. "Does he come to visit?"

Alice nodded. "He usually comes in winter to take me skiing at Snoqualmie Pass, but I don't know what happened this year. I bet my mom said something to upset him."

"I love skiing," David hurried to say.

"Me too. But my mom hates snow, so she never takes me." She sighed. "Daddy always buys me a hot cocoa after a hard run."

"I love their hot cocoa, yeah," David said, almost tasting the vanilla milk and the dark chocolate.

She pushed the door open and cold air hit him, coupled with regret. She'd be gone in a moment, and he hadn't talked to her about the band.

"Next week, my barbarian could travel to a faraway town to see a legendary blacksmith," she said, almost like a question. "Our Dungeon Master won't mind if I step out for fifteen minutes...if you feel like driving here again."

"Sure, yeah." David was so glad she liked hanging out too.

×

While Alice was out with her D&D friends, Laura called Blanca to check on Emilio's family. Before she knew it, their conversation turned into a consultation about Blanca's undocumented status. Laura sat down at the dining room table to take notes for a thorough intake of a potential client. She hoped to find good cause for a U-visa, given to victims of crime who cooperated with US law enforcement agencies, or for a T-visa, awarded to victims of trafficking—or even to unearth a pending green card application filed long ago in Blanca's name by some family member. What she found instead was troubling.

Eighteen years ago, Blanca had been arrested in Bellevue for drunk driving. She'd arrived with a tourist visa from El Salvador the year before and had remained in the US after her visa expired. She found a job as a busser at a restaurant and started saving money. She made friends in the Pacific Northwest's Salvadorian community and through them found Our Redeemer's Church in Everett. She bought a clunker of a car and even sent some money to her parents back home.

But young Blanca had trouble sleeping at night. She kept dreaming about her brother dying in her arms after being gunned down in front of their home in El Salvador. To control her anxiety, she started drinking. On sleepless nights, she drove her car up and down the freeway to calm her nerves. That was when the migraines started.

One evening, she was pulled over and given a breathalyzer test. Back then, the police didn't ask federal authorities about people's immigration status, so Blanca spent twenty-four hours in jail, paid a thousand-dollar fine, and received a five-year probation. She never broke the law again.

"What are my options?" Blanca said, sounding worried.

"I'm sorry, Blanca. I'm afraid there's no path to legalization for you. The only way you could get documented is if the government puts you in removal proceedings. That's when they send you notice to prepare for deportation. Then you're allowed to appear in front of an immigration judge and defend yourself."

"Defend myself?" Blanca's voice caught. "And they arrest me first?"

"Not necessarily, but that's one way."

"I can't do that. My boys need me."

"I know." Laura had had this tough conversation with many undocumented immigrants before. She waited for Blanca to say something, but there was only silence. "The letter the government sends you is called Notice to Appear. If you receive an NTA from USCIS, you'll let me know right away, okay?"

There was a faint "yes" at the other end, then the line went dead.

✕

Mason bundled the twins and took them to the Woodland Park Zoo, to give Helen a chance to rest at the end of a rough week. After being cooped up in the house for days, Chloe and Oliver were over the worst of their colds. They bolted as soon as they passed through the zoo's gates.

Chloe ran ahead, yelling "Confusion attack, now!" and Oliver followed with "Gust attack, now!" It was another Pokébattle, interrupted only by shouts of admiration for the snowmen built by the zoo staff.

Mason remembered being close with his sister Margot when they were kids. Things had soured between them after he joined ICE and she accused him of adopting Kirk's xenophobic worldview. Years later, she blamed Mason for government policies that allowed asylum-seeking parents and children to be separated at the border—the children sent to government custody or foster care, the parents to jail. Margot thought he should resign in protest. He tried to explain that he had nothing to do with kids in cages. But she wouldn't listen, and they hadn't spoken since.

Mason followed the Pokébattle calls for vine-whip and razor-leaf attacks and caught up with his kids at the carousel. The historic 1918 building had a pointy, round roof covered with solar panels. The kids kept the glass door open for Mason. He exchanged bills for golden coins at the token dispenser while the twins waited at the gate, watching painted horses circle around to the sound of carnival music. Mason gave them tokens for two rides—enough time for a call to Saravia.

He watched the twins pick their mounts. Oliver climbed on a red horse with a silver mane and blue-jeweled harness, Chloe on a black horse with a garish saddle. Mason waved to them as their horses began moving, then he headed for the door.

Outside, he paced while waiting for Saravia to pick up. He stepped off the sidewalk and kicked a patch of dirty snow to relieve his tension. Sheldon had told him of the break-in at Ramirez's house. At last, Saravia answered.

"You're supposed to respect my turf," Mason said instead of hello. "Not send your thugs here." He didn't sound as impressive as he hoped. More like a kid whining at his dad before slamming the door.

"What are you talking about?" Saravia said with a most insincere tone.

Mason stared at the clouds as he spoke. "You sent your people to ransack his house, didn't you?" He hoped he was right.

Saravia said nothing.

"Why did you do that? Intimidation? Because nothing was stolen."

"You are a test of my patience."

"And having PSB harass him in detention? What if he fought back? They would've killed him. But you need him alive, don't you?"

Saravia's sigh sounded like a sudden gust of wind. "I begin to believe you cannot handle this case."

Mason spotted Chloe smiling and waving and then Oliver, solemn in the saddle.

"I've always been upfront with you," Mason said. "Our friend will be charged with aggravated assault on Monday. No judge will grant him asylum then. He'll be deported."

"When? I want him at the end of the month."

That wasn't going to happen unless Ramirez asked for deportation. And not even then. "Trust me, sir," Mason said, "I want him out of my country as much as you do."

"Not as much as I do."

"You'll have to wait though. I can't make the judges move any faster."

"Maybe I work with a judge then."

"No need for threats between us." Mason started back to the carousel.

"This is our last nice conversation about Ramirez."

"What's that supposed to mean?"

Mason listened until he heard the three beeps that meant Saravia had hung up. He should have known they'd clash one day. A couple of years ago, the two of them were at a party after an opening at the Jade Jaguar Gallery in Pioneer Square. It was one of Saravia's Mayan artifacts shows, featuring pieces from his large collection. After a few drinks, he started talking about his ancestors' history.

"When I was very young," he said, while Mason pegged his age at early fifties, "I like to see people from everywhere come and admire our Mayan cities and pyramids. All scientists know that Maya is a superior civilization."

Mason wasn't going to debate whose ancestors were better. The Romans, obviously.

"Think about it, Mr. Waltman," Saravia said, "when Europe was in her dark ages, the Mayans build a golden civilization. You ever hear of K'inich Janaab' Pakal of Palenque?"

Mason had heard of the king, yes, from a book about a time-traveling brother and sister he'd read to the twins. The king's name meant "shield" in Mayan.

"When Pakal has twelve years," Saravia told Mason, blowing blue smoke from a cigar, "it is time to repay the gods who grant him his royal power. The price is paid in Pakal's own blood. Priests with demon masks take him to a chamber under the ground, torment, and bleed him with stingray spines. You know how?" Saravia pointed to his face and crotch. "From his tongue and…"

Mason laughed but squeezed his legs together.

"They keep him in the dark until the gods take his gift of blood and show their faces to him. Only then the priests bring the child out in the light. They put him on the throne and lift him for the crowd to say he is the king." Saravia took a deep drag from his cigar. "Some of my collection pieces, they are from that sacred ceremony, Mr. Waltman."

Mason had seen the obsidian blades and the ceramic bowls but was fascinated by a jade death mask made with small tesserae in different shades of green. The mask's irises were brown semiprecious stones, and the whites of its eyes were bright white tile. The realistic eyes made the open-mouthed face look so alive it was spooky.

"Did the jade mask belong to King Pakal then?" Mason said.

"I wish," Saravia said. "But to other royals, I am sure."

At the end of that memorable evening, one of Saravia's men, an American with a funny name, like a city or a state, got very drunk. "The boss," he said, spilling whiskey on Mason's shoes, "he thinks he's the second coming of King Pakal. Never get on his bad side, or he'll tear your heart out. And kill your entire family. And burn your house down. Oh, he loves to burn down homes. He's a fucking homeless machine."

Mason shook off that memory. He watched the twins get off their horses, thrilled and unaware of how terrible the world could really be. Would Saravia send his thugs to break into Mason's house next? That possibility seemed all too real. He should have known better than to associate himself with a man obsessed with his ancestors' pure blood. He'd learned that hard lesson from Pa Kirk, but then somehow, he'd ignored it.

He'd let his guard down, and now his family could be in danger. The thought of Oliver and Chloe getting hurt put a painful knot in his throat. Their house alarm system hadn't been upgraded in years. He also needed cameras on his property—made obvious yesterday by that kid David. He should call the company first thing on Monday. He didn't know anything about guns either. He remembered reading in the news about some Dutch archeologists killed in Guatemala for their discovery of Mayan artifacts. That was something Saravia would do. Mason hadn't been scared in a long time.

If only Sheldon could convince Ramirez to ask for deportation.

19

LAURA WENT INTO the office on Sunday afternoon to pick up some documents she wanted to work on in case of more snow days ahead. A short email from Noah Sheldon was waiting in her inbox, informing her that Emilio would be indicted in Snohomish County for assault in the second degree against Evelyn Brunelle. The speed with which the government was moving from accusation to indictment was frightening. There hadn't even been time for a proper investigation.

She read the email again. There was no date provided for the filing of said indictment. Maybe Sheldon was just trying to intimidate her, show her the hurdles awaiting her if she kept representing Emilio. It cost prosecutors nothing to file charges even when they didn't have a case. Maybe the prosecutor in Snohomish County thought Emilio would plead guilty for a reduced sentence—as ninety percent of people did these days, without ever going to trial.

Laura started typing her angry reply—why did Sheldon need to go after her client like that, and why did his boss need to go after her?—when her cell phone rang. She glanced at the screen but didn't recognize the number. The phone assigned it to Issaquah, WA. Another spam call. She let it go to voicemail and finished typing, then listened to the message.

"Ms. Holban, please call me back," said an agitated voice with a Spanish accent. There was traffic noise in the background. "My name is Pedro Izquierdo. I'm Gabriela's cousin. Is important."

Probably another referral for an immigration lawyer. But something in Pedro's voice—the kind of panic Laura always feared from Claudia's voicemails—made her hit the call button.

"I thought you should know," Pedro said, his voice breaking, "Gabriela was killed last night. Shot dead outside a friend's house in Durango."

Laura felt sick to her stomach. When had Gabriela been sent to Mexico?

"Who killed her?"

"Her old bosses. They made an example of her, for the other women."

Laura was speechless. "I…I want to help the family, with the funeral." She wrote down the address of a crowdsourcing page set up in Gabriela's memory. "Thank you, Pedro."

She opened her browser, went to the website, and stared at a photo of Gabriela in a flower-print dress at someone's quinceañera. Gabriela loved parties, carnivals, and dancing. And she liked cooking for big crowds.

Tears blurred Laura's vision. She'd lost two people in less than a year. Sure, it could be a coincidence, but what were the odds that two of her clients would be hunted down and murdered—and so soon after being deported? There was no apparent connection between them. One was from Honduras, the other from Mexico. One had been killed by narcos linked to PSB, the other by a local sex-trafficking gang.

Had Laura done everything in her power to save them? She'd given up on convincing Gabriela to wait for an appeal because begging hadn't convinced her own father to see a doctor years ago. She should have begged, goddamn it. And if Emilio was deported, were there people in Guatemala waiting to kill him too?

She discarded her reply to Sheldon and printed his message instead. She might be just an immigration attorney, but she could still fight the government's intimidation tactics. What she needed now was a criminal defense attorney.

She took Kyle Jamison's card from her wallet. She'd googled him yesterday. He was from New York and had been serving at-risk Black communities in Seattle for the past ten years. He knew his way around police departments and government agencies all over Washington State. His website boasted of his investigative skills and extensive knowledge of obscure legal precedents.

Laura called his number to leave a voicemail, but he picked up right away.

"Um, Mr. Jamison?" She had no words, again. "My name is Laura Holban. I need help with a client. A consultation on criminal charges, if I can schedule one."

"Ms. Holban, what a surprise!" His voice was joyful. "Let's hear it, let's hear it."

"I'd rather talk in person. Can I make an appointment?"

"I'm in my office. Want to come in now?"

Laura didn't expect that. "I'm in my office too, about two blocks away. I'll be there in ten minutes." She put Sheldon's email printout in her bag and headed for the door. Riding the elevator down, she used each ding to take a breath and stay calm while thoughts of Gabriela threatened to overwhelm her.

Outside, she braved a freezing wind as she walked to First Avenue past mounds of packed snow, then up Columbia to the Norton Building. She found the lobby deserted and rode the elevator to the eighth floor, focusing on her breath. The waiting room in Jamison's suite was empty, so she took a seat and texted him.

Up on the wall, a TV was tuned to a talk show with the sound on mute. Two men sat at a table, chatting. One seemed to be the host, the other a vaguely familiar actor saying something about his wife. But the subtitles were all wrong.

"My wife green solar ten years sing." The words came letter by letter as the actor uttered them. "I don't think night books then we went clothes building yes…Seventeen soldiers."

This reminded Laura of her first days in Redmond. She and Adrian lived in a one-bedroom apartment provided by Microsoft, not far from the Redwest Campus. One morning, she dropped Adrian off at work, then drove their rental car to the grocery store to buy a broom. She hadn't yet discovered the vacuum cleaner in the closet. She was still figuring out the basics: Why there was standing water in the toilet when, in Romania, the bowls were almost empty. And how they shouldn't take showers back-to-back because the hot water tank ran out. In Romania, the hot water came from the neighborhood water-heating station.

She had parked the giant Oldsmobile between two empty spaces to be sure she wouldn't hit anything and entered the huge supermarket.

She spent a few minutes reading signs and navigating aisles but soon felt overwhelmed.

"Need anything?" said a middle-aged woman with a nametag.

Laura couldn't quite remember how to say "broom" in English. "Um…I need a groom?"

The clerk frowned.

Laura made it look like she was holding a broom. "To swipe the floor?"

The clerk looked like she'd just smelled something rotten. "It's called a broom." Her voice was low and stiff. "To sweep the floor. Aisle seven." She walked away, shaking her head.

It was the first but not last time Laura felt out of place in America. For years she needed a chart to translate Fahrenheit to Celsius and miles to kilometers, and she always carried a dictionary in her purse. And then there were the Microsoft launch parties, where she laughed at South Park jokes she didn't understand. And Adrian's Texan work-mate who, whenever he saw Laura, asked her to say the words, "I want to suck your blood!" with a Russian accent. She'd only heard of vampires a few years before, when Bram Stoker's *Dracula* had finally been translated into Romanian. She told him that Romania wasn't Russia, and that she hadn't had a chance to visit Transylvania, but eventually gave up trying to explain. One day she'd even uttered his cherished phrase, pronouncing "vahnt" instead of "want."

Jamison appeared in the hallway, wearing the same carefree smile that had intrigued Laura before.

His handshake was warm and firm. "Follow me, please." He wore slacks and a cashmere sweater, both in shades of gray.

He led her down a hall lined with closed doors. When they reached his office, he took her coat and offered her a chair. She paused for a moment to take in the impressive view of Elliott Bay meeting downtown Seattle.

Jamison sat behind a mahogany desk. "How can I help?"

Straight to business, Laura liked that. She wanted to begin with the terrible news about Gabriela but thought she might get too emotional. Her English would slip, and she'd make a bad impression. Better to keep things simple. She pulled Emilio's folder from her tote.

"Thank you for seeing me on a Sunday afternoon." She showed him Sheldon's email and explained Emilio's case in as few words as possible.

"This assault case they have?" Jamison said after a moment. "Seems unconvincing."

Exactly what Laura wanted to hear. "Would you be available to help us fight this? My client needs a spotless criminal record to secure relief from deportation."

"We should go to trial, not take a guilty plea."

Laura liked that he'd said "we." They'd still have to figure out his retainer, and she didn't know if Blanca could afford Jamison, but she wanted to hear everything he had to say.

"May I call you Laura?"

She didn't sense a need to dominate coming from him, as she had when Waltman had asked the same question. She nodded and glanced around the office. No pictures of a partner or kids. But no, she wasn't looking for a relationship now. Especially when she was still rattled by her ex-husband's baby news.

"Laura. Is that the correct pronunciation?"

No one had cared in a long time how her name was pronounced. "Um, it's actually La-ooh-rah, but don't worry about it. Whatever works."

"Of course I care. It's your name, and our names should be treated with respect. Laura."

It sounded beautiful. "Thank you, Kyle." She hoped she wasn't blushing. "So...they don't have anything on Emilio?"

"Other than Brunelle's witness statement," Kyle said, "they don't have anything on Mr. Ramirez. But you have an affidavit, which makes her an unreliable witness. Does she have an ulterior motive?"

"Emilio's son said Brunelle offered to buy their house."

"Ah. Good. Maybe Brunelle will recant her witness statement. It shouldn't be hard for my private investigator to figure out whether Sheldon convinced her to lie, and if so, how."

"Thank you, Kyle." Laura didn't want to go. "Please bill my office for the consultation."

"It's going to be hella expensive though," he said with a mirthful laugh. "I'm kidding. This consultation is free. To thank you for your formidable WDA presentation."

Laura sighed with relief. "Thank you, Kyle!"

"We should meet Mr. Ramirez's wife and see if she wants me onboard."

20

EMILIO SAT ON the bed in his solitary confinement cell, while Noah Sheldon delivered news of a criminal indictment in Snohomish County. The guard watched them from the open door, hands clasped on his truncheon.

"I want my lawyer present," Emilio said.

"And I want rainbow-farting unicorns," Sheldon said. "Most people here don't even have a lawyer. You're not entitled to one when you talk to an ICE official in an ICE facility."

Emilio clamped his mouth shut. With that attitude, Sheldon wouldn't get another word from him. He folded his arms across his chest and waited for Sheldon to be gone, but the attorney lingered.

"It would be easier if you just ask for deportation," Sheldon said in a low voice, as if he didn't want the guard to hear. But he needn't worry. The guard, a young, Black man named Perkins, assumed the worst about all detainees and wasn't about to create problems for an ICE attorney.

Three days ago, Emilio would have begged Sheldon to let him leave the country, but once he heard about the house break-in, how the intruders had looked for something specific, everything changed. Could Janaab have found him after all these years? Even when he was using a different name and had gone as far north as he could short of Canada? Unless he knew for sure the break-in wasn't Janaab's doing, he couldn't return to Guatemala. Janaab always went after the families of his targets. Emilio had to stay here to protect Blanca and the kids in any way he could. He'd already called Fernando and asked him to change the locks and make sure they were sturdier than before. And David had installed a camera on the main floor.

"The sentence for aggravated assault is ten years in prison," Sheldon said. "You're sure you don't want to go home instead?"

Emilio let out a deep sigh but still said nothing. He'd ask Laura what to do about this indictment, but a criminal case would take months to develop. If Janaab had found him, he wouldn't have months to worry about indictments. He'd have days, at most, to prepare for an attack. He'd thought about telling Laura about Janaab, but what could she do to stop him? And if this wasn't Janaab, complaining to the police about an old-time trafficker might create even more problems for Emilio's asylum application.

He needed proof. Maybe Janaab would send a message. Maybe PSB was connected to Janaab and they'd reach Emilio.

"Think about your wife, Ramirez," Sheldon said. "We can arrest her too, and then your children will be placed in foster care."

Sure, but Laura would be there to help them. This prosecutor was wasting his time. Right now, Emilio wasn't scared of anyone except Janaab.

×

Laura sat behind the desk in her office, facing Kyle and Blanca. It was an awkward seating arrangement, as if she were directing things, when in fact she was waiting for Kyle to speak. His smile gave her stomach butterflies. She hadn't felt that way for years, not since she and Adrian had paged together through that Seattle photo album. The realization that it had been that long annoyed her.

Blanca clutched her humble purse in her lap. Her eyes were red-rimmed, as if she'd been crying.

"You good?" Kyle asked her, and she nodded. "I think your husband is innocent, Mrs. Ramirez."

"My name is Blanca Morales Camacho," she said in a soft voice, as if apologizing. Married women in the Spanish-speaking world didn't always change their surnames the same way American women did.

"Ah. Ms. Morales," Kyle said with a gracious smile, correctly addressing her by her father's surname and not her mother's. "I don't believe your husband ever attacked Evelyn Brunelle."

Blanca nodded. "It all started with that woman, no?"

Laura worried Kyle might not understand Blanca's strong accent.

"I lost everything because of her," Blanca said. "My husband. And my job."

Blanca still had a job last time she and Laura talked on the phone.

"My boss told me yesterday," Blanca answered Laura's unasked question. "He said I was a risk now, with Emilio in jail. He's right."

That was exactly what Emilio had worried about. It also explained how Blanca had been able to come to Laura's office on such short notice on a Monday. But if she was unemployed, how would she be able to pay for food and utilities, let alone attorney's fees?

Kyle explained that if they didn't go to criminal court to answer the charges the prosecutors in Snohomish County had filed against Emilio that morning then the charges would remain pending and his asylum application would be denied. He'd be deported, but only after serving the sentence—a maximum of ten years in jail if convicted.

Of course, the prosecutor expected Emilio to take a guilty plea, as most people did. But if they went to trial, the good news was that the standard of proof in criminal cases was "beyond a reasonable doubt." Only then could the jury pass a guilty verdict. In this case, it was Evelyn's word against Emilio's.

Kyle sounded confident when he said, "I want the jury to pass a not guilty verdict in Snohomish County Superior Court."

Blanca smiled for the first time, and Kyle leaned back in his chair, as if ceding the stage to Laura.

"After we clear Emilio's record," Laura said, "we have to prepare for his individual hearing in immigration court. We need to pay for an expert witness. It's called a Country Conditions Expert for Central America, which covers Guatemala, El Salvador, and Honduras. For a thousand dollars, we get a form letter from this expert, explaining how bed—I mean bad—things are there. If we want the expert to testify at the hearing, it costs extra."

"I can get a thousand dollars," Blanca said, biting her lip. "I can sell more things from our house. I can do another tamales sale at our church."

Laura hated to go on. "Then we need to pay a psychologist to evaluate your children."

"What is wrong with my children?"

"You told me Jacob has been struggling in school since his father's arrest. An expert would recognize that Jacob doesn't know how to express his anger and pain."

Blanca nodded. "He was suspended from school because he had a fight with another boy. When I tried to talk to him, he locked the door to his room. He is not doing his homework. Not answering when his teachers talk to him. Not going to his boxing training after school. He had problems before, but he always got better. I pray to God for him to get better soon."

"We need the expert to tell the judge how hard it's been for your children," Laura said.

"I'm so sorry." Blanca teared up. "Emilio and I…we should not have kids because we have no papers. We were so selfish to make David and Jacob…"

Laura thought of Alice. "Don't say that, Blanca," she whispered.

Kyle shook his head. "Yeah, don't do that to yourself. David and Jacob are lucky to have you and Emilio as their parents."

Blanca wiped her eyes. "How much? This expert."

"Two thousand dollars for each evaluation." Laura decided to shorten this painful conversation, so she went on. "Kyle's fee is twenty-five thousand. And if you want Emilio out on bail, you need another hundred thousand, more or less. Bail bond agencies don't work with undocumented immigrants because of the flight risk. Which means we can't secure his bond with just a ten percent down payment. But you'll get the bond money back when it's all over."

Blanca hid her face in her hands, like Emilio that day in court.

"You own your house free and clear, right?" Laura said. "Can you get an equity loan?"

"I tried. The bank doesn't want to work with me."

Laura had half-expected that. If Emilio was deported and stopped paying the equity loan, the bank could just seize his house—but even banks were now afraid to work with certified undocumented immigrants.

"Okay," Laura said, trying in vain to come up with a different plan. "Okay…"

Blanca turned to Kyle. "Promise to clear Emilio's criminal record?"

"I promise I'll do my best," Kyle said. Ethics 101: you can't promise success in a trial.

Blanca pressed her lips together and nodded. "I will have the money."

×

David worked in his bedroom all afternoon, using a scanner on the little bits of paper recovered from Waltman's shredded compost. In between rounds of scanning, he practiced the chords of Leonard Cohen's "Hallelujah" on his guitar for next time he saw Alice.

He had just launched another scan when he heard a car pull into the driveway. Probably Jacob's ride, bringing him and his friends back from a basketball game. David glanced out the window and saw Evelyn Brunelle and a tall man with a briefcase getting out of her Mercedes SUV.

David was at the front door before the bell rang.

Evelyn smiled and said, "Hi, David," with the tone of an adult talking to a child. "Your mom's waiting for me."

David stepped aside, a bit confused. "Your shoes."

She peeled off her black pumps, as if grateful for the chance to rest her feet on the hardwood floors. The man took his shoes off and stashed them under the bench in the mudroom.

David's mom came downstairs, rubbing her hands and smelling of lotion.

"I brought my boyfriend with me," Evelyn said. "Todd, say hi to Mrs. Morales and David. And check out this awesome house."

Todd nodded. He unbuttoned his winter jacket and passed the briefcase to David, who took it to the dining room and opened it on the table. It was filled with money: twenties tied with rubber bands and hundreds secured with bank-issued bill straps.

"All there, two hundred thousand," Evelyn said, "but only if you agree to vacate the house by Thursday night. I'd like to start updating the appliances this weekend."

David couldn't believe it. "You're selling the house?" he asked his mom in Spanish.

She didn't answer. She picked up a bundle of cash marked $5000 and started counting. It took a long time, during which David felt about five thousand emotions rush through him.

Selling the house was a betrayal of his dad, who'd built it. Why was Mom doing this? It was their family's only home. Hadn't David and Fernando and Father Nicolas come up with enough money for the bond? They could raise more, even if it took a while. David could take a job at Grocery Outlet. Where would they move if Mom sold the house? A motel? He wouldn't have his own room anymore. Would they live in the pickup truck? What would they do with all their stuff?

"Looks like is all here," his mom said in English. She'd stacked the money on the table in piles.

"Awesome." Evelyn took a blue folder from her purse. "Now the papers."

David felt a jolt of anger. "Our house is worth more than a million," he told Evelyn. "You can't have it for—"

"Ugh," Evelyn said, hand slicing the air. "Obviously, this isn't all of it. This is the non-refundable deposit your mom and I have agreed on."

"A deposit?" David said.

Todd shrugged, as if he didn't understand either.

"Listen, son," Evelyn said, "I'm doing you all a favor. If your mom sells the house the normal way, she only gets five percent, max, in earnest money when she accepts a buyer's offer. That money goes into an escrow account, and she doesn't see a penny until closing. But I'm giving her a non-refundable deposit, so she can have the money she needs for your dad's lawyers and bond and whatever else she wants—right now."

David turned to his mom. "You're letting her steal the house from Dad."

His mom pinned him with such a pained look that he took a step back. "I'm doing this for him," she whispered in Spanish. "His criminal case will cost us more than a hundred thousand."

"But, Mom…" David understood they needed the money—in two short weeks, their family had lost both incomes and their health insurance—but he still couldn't accept it. He turned to Evelyn. "Just withdraw your false statement about my dad!"

"That cat's out of the bag, I'm afraid," she said with an infuriating shrug. "And you need money now."

"Mom, you can't sell. Think of Jacob. He needs this house. His home." Jacob's needs always came before David's, but this time he was okay with it, as long as it changed his mom's mind. He held his breath, waiting.

"As I explained before," Evelyn said, "you're transferring your property to me by signing this deed. This here is the description of your property. Read it and sign there that it's accurate." She held out a pen.

"Please, Mom, please!" David said. "This can't possibly be legal." His lower lip trembled.

"I assure you, Mrs. Morales," Evelyn said, "this contract is well within legal bounds. And I know an escrow officer who can handle the rest for us, no questions asked."

David wanted to grab the pen from Evelyn's hand, as if that was the critical weapon whose capture could win him the battle.

"Oh," Evelyn said, "and I need to make a copy of your power of attorney."

David's mom opened a drawer and took out a few pages held together with a paperclip.

Evelyn leafed through them. "Specific power of attorney… Description of property…Good." She passed the pages to Todd, who pulled out his phone to take pictures.

David grabbed Evelyn's pen, but his mom found another and wrote her name or initials where Evelyn had marked the documents with yellow sticky-arrows. There were a lot of places for her to sign. David kept hoping she'd stop before it was too late.

He leaned over the table, trying to see what she was agreeing to. "Evelyn Brunelle and/or assigns…" he read off a page. "Come on, Mom, do you even know what that means?"

"David, enough." She kept signing, then put the pen down. "When do we get the rest of the money?" she said in an exhausted voice.

"Thirty days, normal closing period." Evelyn smiled like a good salesperson. "But you don't pay any real estate commissions in a direct transaction, so I'm saving you a ton of money."

David's mom looked pale, as if developing another migraine. But this time he didn't care about her suffering and wouldn't help her up the stairs. She deserved her pain.

He heard the front door close. Evelyn and Todd had left, taking their empty briefcase with them.

"Don't tell your dad," his mom said in Spanish from the stairs. "Not yet."

David stood in the middle of a house that wasn't his anymore.

"And, David? No school until we finish packing. I'll send an email to your admin."

"No need," he said, spitting out the words. "It's mid-winter break."

"Oh, yeah, I forgot."

David walked around in a daze. He looked up at the air vent on the living room's far wall, where his security camera was. He hadn't told his mom about it because that would lead to questions. Maybe he could use today's recording to invalidate the house sale, somehow. He'd have to ask Ms. Holban.

21

LAURA ARRIVED IN Tacoma just before the Monday afternoon rush hour and prepared for the ambush. She parked her Prius in the NWDC's wire-fenced lot, beside a mound of plowed snow. There was another half-hour left on the day shift. With any luck, she'd be back in Seattle before the evening road-freeze. Now she just had to keep warm and wait.

For days, she'd been sending emails to and leaving voice messages for Emilio's deportation officer, Ken Masters. Since he never replied, she'd decided to talk to him face-to-face. She learned all she could about him from Emilio. Masters was at least six feet tall, White, with a goatee and a shaved head. And he worked the day shift.

Laura had to talk to him today. Because Emilio was being prosecuted in Snohomish County, he had to appear in front of a judge there but couldn't do that while detained at NWDC. Since ICE and the county prosecutor both represented the interests of the government—one federal, one state—they should be able to make arrangements for Emilio to appear in court. But only if the right documents were filed—and Laura didn't know which documents those were, because ICE changed its requirements on a weekly basis. Not even the county prosecutor knew which forms Laura was supposed to file. But if Ken Masters knew, she had to convince him to tell her.

Laura waited and watched as the day shift ended and officers and other personnel left the building, but she didn't see Masters. At half past five, she started the car to get the heating going and called Alice to ask her to take the chicken breasts out of the freezer so they could thaw.

"Anything else you want me to do?" Alice asked, sounding snarky.

It had been a long day for Laura, and she was anxious about meeting Masters. Soon she'd have to drive home on icy roads and then make dinner. She was cold, her stomach was tied up in knots—and she just snapped.

She switched to Romanian. "Because I'm asking so much of you, aren't I? You know what? Just order a goddamn pizza."

"Sure," Alice said in English. "I don't like your crappy food anyway."

Laura lost it. "You've had a bad day, I get it, but listen to me, Alice. Your problems are nothing compared to what I'm dealing with here. Remember David Ramirez? His father's locked in solitary. Not living the good life in Romania with a new wife and a baby on the way!"

She realized what she'd said, but it was too late.

"What?" Alice whispered. "Daddy's having a baby?"

Laura groaned. Lashing out had felt good, but the damage was now real. It had taken her mere seconds to create an awful moment for Alice to relive again and again—alone, with friends, and a therapist too. She should have known better.

She bit on her thumb to keep herself from screaming. Through the windshield, she spotted a man who looked like Masters, walking toward a Nissan.

"We'll talk when I get home," she told Alice.

"Whatever."

Laura turned off the engine and got out of her car. She dashed after that officer, slipping on ice here and there.

"Officer Masters?" she called from a few feet away.

He turned, and his face told Laura that he knew who she was. But how?

"I'm not supposed to talk to you," he said and continued toward the Nissan.

Laura followed him. "My client must appear for his arraignment in Snohomish County Superior Court. But to take him there, I need your approval as his deportation officer. What documents do you need from me to make that happen? Please."

He stopped. "Like I said, I'm not supposed to talk to you."

"Officer Masters, my client is innocent of the crime he's being accused of. To clear his name, he must show up in court. Please, he has a family here. Two American boys."

Masters looked around. "You picked the wrong spot to ask me for favors, Ms. Holban. There are cameras looking at us right now."

"Microphones too?"

"No."

Laura thought fast. "Then look angry. Get in your car. I'll follow you to a place where we can talk."

He smiled at her nerve. In the next breath, he put his hands on his hips, and his face became an angry mask. Years of being in the deportation business had trained him to become frightening in an instant.

"Get the hell out of my face, lady!" he yelled, pointing at the exit.

Laura wasn't sure it was an act, and she felt like she'd been punched in the gut nonetheless.

"McKinley Park, main entrance," Masters whispered, then walked away.

After the spat with Alice and being yelled at, Laura just couldn't hold back the tears even though she felt hopeful for the chance to help Emilio.

✕

It was dark when Laura arrived at McKinley Park. Masters pulled up a few minutes later and rolled down his window. He dictated a list of necessary documents while Laura took notes on her phone. The moment he was done, he rolled up his window and drove off.

On her way back to Seattle, Laura called Kyle. "I have the list. If we get an order signed by a judge, NWDC must approve the transfer based on legal sufficiency. Can you get an order?"

"Sure," Kyle said. "When the prosecutor submits a motion to the judge for the criminal case, I won't object, so they'll skip the hearing, and a commissioner judge can sign the order in their chambers. Then the sheriff will pick up Emilio and hold him in county jail until the arraignment."

Emilio wanted to be deported, not locked up in county jail. He'd hate Laura for this maneuver, but she wouldn't let him make the same mistake as Gabriela. Clearing his criminal record was critical if he was to have a future in America.

"Can Emilio get bail after the arraignment?" she said. NWDC would specify no bail on the transfer papers.

"That'd be up to the judge alone."

If Emilio could go free, even for a while, he might not hate Laura that much.

"I'm going to grab dinner," Kyle said. "Care to join me?"

Laura was supposed to go home to Alice for a tearful evening of recriminations. She drummed her fingers on the steering wheel.

"Sure." What the hell. She'd text Alice she'd be late, work stuff. Maybe Alice would be asleep when Laura arrived home. Then they could fight in the morning.

She suggested a restaurant on Broadway, nothing too fancy. Kyle had been there before and liked their Indian-inspired small-plates menu.

Laura stepped on the gas and took I-5 North. She recognized the tune on the radio and turned up the volume. Bonnie Tyler's "Holding Out for a Hero" had been a popular song in Bucharest almost thirty years ago, when Laura was a teenager. Her best rendition had always been "I need a hero, la, la, la, la, la, la," because she couldn't pick up the rest of the lyrics. But now, as Laura nodded her head in rhythm with the music, Bonnie's words were clear as day.

For that teenage Laura listening to American music in the '90s, song lyrics had always been opaque if not unintelligible. Back then, it had been all about the melody. She wondered what it would have been like to grow up with songs that spoke to her teenage angst. Songs that didn't make her long for the magic, faraway country they came from. Good thing Alice didn't have to wonder about that.

✕

In the restaurant, Laura and Kyle sat by a window speckled with snowflakes. Laura browsed the menu and spotted an eggplant spread similar to something her father used to prepare. Tasting that would surely sink her spirits. Instead, she ordered grilled trout with fennel salad and salsa.

"How long until the trial?" she said.

"Still talking work?" Kyle's smile put a dimple in his cheek. "Okay, then. I'll need six months to prepare, so I'll ask for a continuance if they set the date any sooner."

Laura didn't skip a beat. "If Emilio gets bail, he could have six months of freedom. In theory anyway. I wonder what Mason Waltman would say then."

Kyle made like his head was exploding.

Laura laughed. "You know he threatened to revoke my citizenship if I kept representing Emilio?"

Kyle's eyes widened. "He can't do that, can he?"

Laura waved her hand. "Empty threats." She sounded confident but wasn't so sure.

The waiter brought their drinks: a glass of zinfandel for Laura and a Sapphire martini with a twist for Kyle. Laura took a sip. She needed it to calm the nerves in her stomach. Sitting across the table from Kyle made her feel guilty but in a pleasant way. Why guilty, she didn't know.

"We can't let Waltman throw you out of the country," he said.

We again. Laura felt herself blushing. "My daughter, she's not my biggest fan—teenagers—but she'd hate to see me thrown out." Why she'd brought up Alice, she had no idea. Some kind of self-defense mechanism: I can't possibly be desirable; I have a kid at home.

Kyle didn't flinch. "High schooler?"

Laura nodded. Now how was she supposed to continue the conversation? Asking about Kyle's family wouldn't help if she wanted to keep their relationship professional. "You had a successful career in New York," she said, sipping her wine. "Why did you move to Seattle?"

"There was a case," he said, gazing out the window for a second. "It brought me here, a bunch of trips, back and forth. Then I met someone here and decided to take a chance. It didn't work out." He shrugged.

Laura didn't want to dive into the personal. "What kind of case?"

"It involved PSB, if you can imagine. As do a lot of my cases, still. Many of my clients have no choice but to live and work on their turf."

Laura took it to mean that he sometimes represented PSB members in court, and because of that he was off-limits for the gang. Still, he probably put his safety at risk sometimes. She leaned over, wanting to ask him if he was ever scared.

"Tell me," Kyle said, saving her from making that mistake, "why did you become an immigration lawyer?"

Should she bring up her ex-husband's job at Microsoft? She could tell Kyle of those long, dark years when she hadn't been allowed to work, but he'd probably say she had it easy, with an immigration lawyer supplied by a huge corporation. She decided not to go there. And she definitely wouldn't tell him that she felt some kind of need to prove to her mother that she had a right to stay in America because her work here was important. All that baggage would stay packed tonight.

"When I finished law school at U-Dub," she said, "I thought I could do corporate law, but I missed working with people. And immigrants need more help than most clients. Here, the government tries to keep people out. When I was growing up in Romania, the government tried to keep us in." She felt incoherent, floating on wine fumes. "Besides, what else was I supposed to do with my life? Like they say in Romania, I didn't want to cast my shadow on the ground in vain."

Kyle inched closer. "I have a confession to make, Laura." Hearing her name on his lips made her stomach flutter. "I've seen plenty of lawyers who act like the great White savior to their clients. Before we met, I thought you might be one of them."

"That's me all right." She laughed, but his words hurt.

"But seeing your work for Emilio and Blanca…" His voice was deep and enveloping. "Just wanted to say I was wrong and glad for that."

Laura felt her body warming up in a way she'd almost forgotten. She felt emboldened. "You know," she said, "I can almost pass for one of them."

"One of whom?"

"White people born in the US." She drank more wine for courage. "I'm pasty-white, though my ancestors have more to do with the Ottoman Empire than the Victorian one. So, White people are usually friendly to me. That is, until I open my mouth."

Kyle lowered his eyebrows and puckered his lips, as if not buying it.

"No, it's true." She felt flustered. "I read in some history book that, back when neighbors all looked the same—um, I mean, alike—the only way to spot a stranger was by speech patterns. We're hardwired to listen for that slight accent or unfamiliar turn of phrase belonging to someone who might look like us but lives across the river or beyond the hill. Someone outside our tribe, someone not safe, who brings in dangerous germs. Or ideas."

"You mean like the story of the Shibboleth in the Book of Judges?"

Laura was out of her depth when it came to the Old Testament, but she nodded and went on. "Discriminating against accents kept our ancestors alive, long before they started traveling far from home, where people looked and dressed differently, so you could spot a stranger from a distance."

"Now you're calling me a stranger?" Kyle looked amused, but Laura felt her heart sink.

"No, no, of course not." She waved the subject away. "I should get a lawyer before I say anything else."

"I'm right here." He leaned back in his seat. "So, which tribe are you?"

Laura shrugged. "I have a few Romanian friends on the Eastside but don't see them often."

"The immigrant tribe then?"

"Ha! Immigrants are not all one people." She brought the wine glass to her lips. "Maybe I belong to a tribe of one." Alice would definitely agree with that.

"Nonsense," Kyle said, "you're an American."

"With a foreign accent."

"All right, let's lay down the facts," Kyle said, and Laura agreed with a flick of her wrist. "You're never going to sound like a native. Your vowels will still come out just a bit off. And I'm never going to be White." He put his arms out as if showcasing himself. "I say, own it."

"It's not just my vowels. I make mistakes when I'm tired or angry or anxious."

Kyle scoffed. "I still have to stop and decide between collusion and collision. Crossed wires my brain can't sort out. But I don't care. Everyone makes mistakes in their native tongue. You worry too much about sounding perfect."

"I can't not care, now can I?" Laura said with a grin.

"When you hear other immigrants making mistakes, do you have a hard time understanding them?"

"No, of course not."

"Because our brains don't need to parse every word to get the meaning. But you listen to yourself with fierce attention, don't you? Always hunting for that tiny, little imperfection." He waited for Laura to nod once. "You don't do that in Romanian, right? Native speakers don't do that in English either."

"Easy for you to say. When a native speaker makes a mistake, it's because they're tired or distracted. When an immigrant makes the same mistake, it's because they're dumb."

Kyle conceded the point, sighing. "When a brother says 'ain't'..." He pronounced "brother" like "brutha," which reminded Laura of her own accent. She'd already overshared, and the alcohol was going to her head. She hoped the food would arrive soon.

Kyle touched her hand over the table. "Laura Holban, I think you're a good person. You should take a beat and relax a little."

He held her hand for a moment. His touch made her skin tingle. But how would she explain a new boyfriend to Alice? Especially after delivering Adrian's baby news?

She pulled her hand back. "I'm not looking for a relationship right now..."

He winked, all carefree as before. "You change your mind, let me know. Now," he said, sitting up straight, like a lawyer at a conference table, "please explain to me the difference between an expat and an immigrant."

22

EMILIO COUNTED EIGHT push-ups, then stopped. He used to do them by the dozens when he was younger. Now he was tired, even though he did nothing all day. And it was only Tuesday. He forced another rep. He had to get stronger in case Janaab was coming. A few times over the years, Fernando and the guys at work had taken him to a shooting range. Mastering the nail gun was just not good enough, they'd said. Emilio tried to remember how to handle a weapon, in case he needed to protect his family that way. He'd never had a chance to use Lucio's pistol before the pollero confiscated it.

He heard the guard's key in the lock and got off the floor, wiping his hands.

"Pack up your stuff, Ramirez," Officer Perkins ordered.

Emilio had been expecting his lunch tray. "Where am I going?"

"Don't know."

"Then I'm not going." This could be an ambush ordered by Janaab.

"Take it up with your lawyer, who's doing this. My job is to get you out of here."

Emilio picked up his toothbrush, toothpaste, and deodorant and dropped them all in a plastic bag the guard gave him. They marched along bright corridors and through secure double doors to a place where someone told him to take off his uniform and put on the clothes he'd worn when he was arrested.

The sight of his faded, paint-stained jeans brought a knot to his throat. He put on his old clothes, cinched up his belt, and grabbed his jean jacket. He'd lost weight on the NWDC diet, but with his clothes back on, he felt like a person again, not just an Alien Number.

"Ramirez," a man called.

Emilio turned to find Officer Masters scowling at him, thumbs stuck in his belt.

"Where am I going?" Emilio said.

"First, sign here," Officer Masters said.

Emilio wanted to say no, that he needed to read the document first, but Officer Masters pushed a pen in his hand. Emilio stole a glance out the window at the parking lot, where a van marked SNOHOMISH COUNTY CORRECTIONS BUREAU waited.

"Am I going there?" he asked Officer Masters.

"Talk to your lawyer. Now sign if you want out."

Emilio took the pen. He trusted Laura. And it was worth signing those papers just to see the gates of the Northwest Detention Center open before him.

×

Laura hoped Emilio's transfer was going well. She'd receive word later that afternoon. For now, she had a few hours to herself until Alice came home from school and the fight they'd avoided this morning caught up with them. Enough time for a run, then for processing a set of birth and marriage certificates for a Czech American family who wanted to relocate their parents to Seattle with green cards.

Laura had tried to convince them not to make that mistake, but the wife was pregnant and wanted her mother to help with the baby. In Laura's experience with green cards, she'd seen only one case where a parent thrived after becoming an "expat," as Kyle would say. Most retired transplants had no pleasant way of spending their days, especially if they were busy with grandkids. They did chores while pining for their hometowns, relatives, and friends. They fell ill with back pains and stomach problems, not to mention all those American germs they hadn't encountered while living in a different microbial environment. The only exception was a vibrant and chatty Romanian mother of a

Nintendo employee. In one year, Mama Sanda's restaurant in Bellevue had become a hub for Eastern Europeans in the Seattle area. Soon she was making more money and even feeling happier than her son.

Laura put her earbuds in. One day, when Romanian food didn't taste like regret, she might go sit at Mama Sanda's table and have cabbage-leaf dolmas with sour cream and polenta. She opened the front door and—

Two men in ski masks shoved her back, forced their way in, and shut the door.

"Excuse me?" Laura said, realizing how silly she sounded.

Her heart pounded in her throat. Were they there to rob her, to rape her, to kill her? They wore blue surgical gloves, so they wouldn't leave fingerprints. She couldn't tell whether they had guns. Whatever they wanted, the thick walls and insulated windows would block any screams or cries for help. And the windows were hidden by trees and rows of bamboo.

She stumbled back into the living room, grabbed the lamp off the side table, and threw it at the intruders, who had no problem dodging it. Her chest hurt from forgetting to breathe. She tipped the piano bench their way and dashed to the stairs. But they were faster.

They grabbed her and twisted her arm behind her back. A sharp pain in her shoulder took her breath away.

She felt like throwing up. "Did Mason Waltman send you?" That was her first thought, that he'd sent them to punish her for moving Emilio out of NWDC.

"Who the fuck is Mason?" one of them said. He sounded American.

He held her in his armlock while the other guy slapped her. Her cheek throbbed and burned, but she forced herself to memorize as many details about her assailants as possible. She'd never be able to identify them from police mugshots, and she'd never heard that voice before. The man who'd hit her was about five ten, with a square jaw, and brown eyes. He had a wide nose and a chipped front tooth. The other one was about Adrian's height, six two. Their clothes were common: jeans, black boots, and gray hoodies. They were going to ruin her floors with their boots.

Laura realized what a bizarre thought that was at a moment like this. Many of her clients recalled not thinking straight at the time of their first arrest. That kind of warped thinking was their—and now her—brains' way of trying to make sense of the danger staring them in the face. Her hands turned cold and started shaking. She took a deep breath but felt no relief.

"What do you want?" she said, trying to sound calm.

Chip-Tooth leaned close. "For you to back off," he said. He sounded American too.

So, they weren't there to kill her. "Back off what?"

"Drop. The. Ramirez. Case." He raised a handgun and pressed it against Laura's cheek. It felt cold and surreal.

"That's what this is about?" she said. "But if Waltman didn't send you—"

"She talks too much and doesn't listen," Chip-Tooth said and hit her with the gun.

It hurt—a lot. She heard a loud ringing in her left ear. Chip-Tooth was right-handed. Not a terribly useful detail. She couldn't taste or feel any blood. They weren't there to kill her, just to scare her. They needed her alive to drop the case. A dead lawyer would bring too much attention.

Chip-Tooth grabbed Alice's school portrait from the mantelpiece. Laura wailed as though he'd laid hands on the real Alice. She wanted to bite his head off, but the other one tightened his grip on her neck. It was hard to breathe now.

"Think what we can do to her," Chip-Tooth said, and the two men laughed. "You feel me?"

Blood pounded in Laura's ears, pain pulsing with her heartbeat. She strained to free her arm, but her captor's grip was too strong.

Chip-Tooth grabbed Laura by the throat. "I didn't hear a yes." The gun came back up, against her cheek.

Laura heard herself whisper. "Who are you?"

"Trust me, you'll thank us later. Do as we say and our boss will leave you alone. Don't, and he'll go after your whole family, you hear me?"

"No," she cried with whatever breath she had left. "Not Alice."

"I need a yes." He looked away, then hit her again.

Laura felt an explosion of pain inside her head. She tried to hang on to the world around her—

✕

She woke up on the floor. The front door was closed. How long had she been out? There was blood on her hands and a sticky puddle on the floor, where her mouth had been a moment ago. She tasted blood. A broken lip. A bitten tongue.

She sat up. There was a muffled rumble in her left ear, but her right picked up the ticking clock on the mantelpiece. What time was it?

Oh no, Alice would be home any moment now. She couldn't see this.

Laura stood up. Her head felt heavy. Her jaw, ear, and throat hurt. She leaned against a wall until the dizziness passed, then found her way to the kitchen. She grabbed the cleaning spray bottle and a roll of paper towels and went back to the living room to scrub the floor. The smell of the cleaner made her dizzy again, so she held her breath while wiping up the blood, taking small breaks to sit up and inhale. When she was done, she tied up the garbage bag and took it outside to the bin. She locked the front door before heading upstairs to take a shower.

In the bathroom, she checked her face in the mirror. The purple bruise on her jaw hurt to look at. Her lower lip was split. Was there anything else wrong? Her body didn't feel like her own. What would her mother say? *You moved all the way to America to be attacked in your own house?*

Laura stepped into the shower and let the hot water run down her body, her head—

She dropped to her knees, screaming. The pain in her left ear was like a hot needle piercing through her brain. The water burned like acid. She shook her head, but the earache was still there, drilling into her skull.

She finished her shower as fast as she could, got dressed, and took some ibuprofen. Then she sat on her bed with her laptop and checked the weather in Tacoma. No snow until midnight. No snow in Amsterdam either and some snow but stable conditions in Bucharest. She bought a one-way ticket to Bucharest via Amsterdam, leaving tonight, and added the unaccompanied minor service. Airline personnel would make sure Alice got from one flight to the next. When Laura was done, she emailed Adrian and asked him to pick up his daughter at Otopeni Airport the next day.

23

DAVID WAS TIRED after half a day spent packing the house with Jacob, while their mom browsed the internet looking for an apartment. He was sick of taping boxes and filling them with stuff. He needed some big moves that taxed his muscles and stretched his back in a healthy way.

Jacob's eyes were puffy from stealth-crying, and he needed a break too.

"Don't be late," their mom told them as David grabbed the truck keys.

He and Jacob drove to their neighborhood boxing gym through light rain flecked with snow. Cruz was happy to see them after so many days. A few people were here and there on the machines, plus a couple wrapping things up in the boxing ring.

David hung his jacket by the water fountain. The spot of honor on the wall belonged to one of his photos, taken after a youth boxing competition. Sweaty torso, one victorious fist high in the air, Coach smiling in the background.

"If you train all the time, you're prepared at any time," Coach always said. "If you learn your routines, you don't have to think when you're under attack. You just fight, instead of freezing in shock."

The theory hadn't worked out so well that time with Waltman. "Let's practice our routines," David told his brother.

Jacob picked up a jump rope, while David climbed on a treadmill and set the speed at seven miles per hour. After a few minutes, he was sweating.

"Yo, David," Cruz called out from the water fountain. "Your phone's beeping inside your jacket."

David kept going. His mom wouldn't text if she needed anything important; she'd call. So would his dad from NWDC. Anybody else could wait while he finished his fifteen minutes on the treadmill. He glanced at Jacob, who had his gloves on and was going through their boxing warm-up routine, punching the stationary dummy's body, head, then body again. Three-two-three, Coach called it.

When he finished his run, David strapped on a pair of gloves. "Let's see you hit the bag," he told Jacob.

Jacob took an upright stance and started jabbing and cross punching the bag. He had good legwork—after years of Coach calling him out for lazy feet—but David could see the apathy in his moves.

"Try some hooks," he called out.

Jacob obeyed, but his rear fist didn't hit the bag as hard as it should. David took his annoyance with his brother to the speed bag, fist over fist, again and again until his arms felt heavy. If only he could obliterate the last couple of weeks that way. If only he could bring his dad home and get the house back from Evelyn Brunelle.

He glanced at Jacob, who was still just going through the motions with the punching bag.

"What are you doing, man?" David said. "You're not committing to the punch." His shoulders burned as he shook his arms. "Come here." He marched into the boxing ring, motioning at his brother to follow.

Jacob shuffled over and climbed into the ring.

It was time for an intervention. Time to shake Jacob out of his stupor. "We're sparring now," David said.

"Dude, phone's beeping like crazy," Cruz called again.

But David had already started chasing after Jacob, who dodged and ducked and danced around the ring. When David threw a hook, Jacob blocked it with his elbow but didn't go on the offensive. Instead he sidestepped and dropped back into guard stance.

"Just throw a punch, man," David said, and snapped his fist forward. The sound of his glove landing in Jacob's gut felt liberating.

Jacob stumbled back, groaning.

"I just want you to fight me," David said, dropping into a semi-crouch.

"Fighting got me suspended," Jacob said, panting. "And it won't bring Dad home."

"Crying all day long won't bring him home either."

David went after Jacob, who bobbed and weaved but left his torso open. David landed an uppercut. When Jacob's arms dropped after the impact, David nailed his shoulder. Then his chin. He could beat Jacob senseless—because Jacob wanted his ass kicked—but that wouldn't do any good. It would just give him reasons to sink even deeper, so David stopped.

"I need a drink." He stepped from the ring, ran to the water fountain, and started gulping. The truth was, Jacob's silences and angry outbursts were scary. As if having their dad in lockup wasn't enough shit for David to deal with.

His phone beeped again. He stripped off the gloves and unlocked it. He had eleven unread texts, all from Alice.

My mom is sending me to Romania! Tonight!!!

She was flying KLM through Amsterdam. She was going to live with her father in Bucharest for a while. She didn't know how long.

David's clammy hands shook while texting her back.

Coming to the airport!

He looked at his brother. "Sorry, Jacob, I've got to go."

Jacob perked up. "I'm coming with."

This could be the last time David saw Alice. Like, ever. Jacob could wait a day. "Nah. I'll drop you off on the way to—"

"I'll just walk home," Jacob said, looking crushed.

"It's raining, yo."

Jacob shrugged. "So?"

David had no time to explain. Alice could be on her way to the airport already. And Everett was twice as far from Sea-Tac as Seattle.

×

Laura, head hurting and feeling nauseous, pushed Alice along the check-in line for KLM. Alice had cried in the car, all the way to Sea-Tac. Now she just sniffled and wiped her eyes under her glasses. Laura couldn't tell her daughter she'd been attacked. Better to have Alice angry with her than terrified for their lives. She'd used a lot of foundation on her face. She also invented a work emergency that forced her to retrieve a detained client's children from Tijuana, Mexico and get them settled in Seattle. She told Alice she'd have to spend time in California and Mexico, sorting out paperwork for those visas.

"What about me?" Alice had said. "Why are your clients more important?"

"It's only for a few weeks," Laura kept saying. One day, when Emilio's case was behind her, she'd tell Alice that she'd only wanted to keep her safe. But for now, a lie was better. And for Claudia too. If she learned about this, she'd fake a heart attack to force Laura back to Bucharest.

"Listen to your dad," Laura said, "and be nice to your stepmom."

"I'll call her Mama," Alice said.

Laura felt like throwing up.

"Daddy and I," Alice said, "and Mama, we'll go skiing in the Carpathians, like, all the time."

Laura held her tongue. They checked a large suitcase—two pounds over the weight limit because of all the textbooks Alice took with her so she wouldn't fall behind in school—and paid the extra fee. Laura picked up Alice's boarding pass and her own escort pass, which allowed her to accompany her child through security and then to the gate.

They entered a snaking line marked by retractable belts between movable posts, and inched their way forward in silence.

"Ms. Holban! Alice!"

What was David doing here?

He skidded to a halt on the other side of the barrier. "Please wait." He panted and doubled over for a moment to catch his breath.

Seeing him made Alice cry again. "I don't want to go." At least that was what Laura thought Alice had said. She couldn't quite hear with her left ear.

Some of the people around them seemed excited to watch the drama. Laura nudged Alice along. David asked something, and Laura struggled to read the question on his lips.

Alice answered before Laura could figure out what David was saying. "She's going away for work. But that doesn't make sense." She said something else Laura didn't catch. "—that I could go with her. I could do my homework there, but she won't take me. She doesn't want me with her." Her last few words were loud enough for everyone around to hear.

"You're dropping my dad's case?" David said.

More faces turned their way.

Laura wanted to scream. "He's in good hands for now," she said. "Just go, David. We'll talk later."

"How long will Alice be gone?" he said.

"Just for a few weeks."

"A few weeks? That's such a long time." David said something else about his dad, but Laura missed most of it when she turned to glare at the woman in front of them, who was dragging her carry-on at a snail's pace.

"I'll have my phone with me," Alice told him through whimpers. "I'll write."

"Me too," David said. "I promise."

"What's going on with you two?" Laura said.

"Nothing," Alice said with a hard stare. "We're just friends."

Their line turned to where David couldn't follow. He remained standing by the far wall, waving at Alice, who waved back until she and Laura passed through the metal detectors and the screening machines. Then they cut through the shopping area on their way to the gate. Outside the plate glass windows, night had fallen, pierced by airport signs and runway lights.

They walked to the gate in silence. Laura found the customer service agent, informed him that Alice was an unaccompanied minor, and gave him the filled-in paperwork.

Alice slung her backpack over her shoulder and got in line to board the plane.

"It won't be for long," Laura managed to say.

Alice shrugged and took another step.

"Come, give me a hug," Laura said in Romanian, holding back tears.

Alice groaned. "Why would I give a hug to my worst enemy?" she said in English.

Laura tried to smile through a growing headache. "I'm not your worst enemy, silly. The flu virus is! Make sure you always wash your hands. They have different germs in Romania, remember?"

"Whatever."

Laura pulled her daughter into a hug Alice didn't return. "I love you."

Alice let go and walked away. Laura didn't leave until they closed the boarding gate. Her head throbbed, and the nausea was getting worse. She sat on a bench and pulled out her wallet. She hadn't expected to ever call Waltman, but she did have his card. She tapped in his number and held the phone to her good ear.

He answered after a few rings. "Who's this?"

"Laura Holban." Raw emotions chased away her words. "Are you happy with yourself?"

"I will be if you tell me you dropped that case."

"So you did send those people to my house. They hurt me, all right, but they won't stop me."

"What people? What's this about?"

"And they won't get their hands on my daughter, you son of a bitch, because I sent her away."

"I'm not following—"

"Your people threatened my daughter! You're a father, aren't you? Shame on you!"

"What does this have to do with my kids?"

"Very convincing," Laura said and hung up.

×

Mason stood in the middle of the gym's locker room, speechless. He put his phone in the side pocket of his workout bag, still trying to understand what Laura Holban had just told him. Someone had attacked her in her house. There was only one possibility.

She'd sent her daughter away to safety. Away where? Romania? And she was more determined than ever to fight for Ramirez. How did things get so out of hand? Threatening her citizenship should have convinced her Ramirez wasn't worth the trouble. A smooth maneuver. But sending thugs to intimidate her was heavy-handed. Now there might be a police investigation. Why was Saravia so rash now, when all this time he'd been cool and deliberate? He was expecting

Ramirez at Nuevo Laredo next week—something Mason knew would never happen. And what would Saravia do when he didn't get what he wanted? Would he send his thugs to Mason's house to teach him a lesson too?

Saravia was out of control, and control had been Mason's top priority since the days of Pa Kirk in Yakima. He zipped up his gym bag, even though he'd just arrived. He had to talk to Saravia, and—as Saravia had predicted—it wouldn't be a polite conversation this time.

He hurried back to his Audi and connected his burner to the car's speakers, then sped out of the parking garage. Once on the street, he made the call. Saravia took his time answering.

"Did you send your thugs to intimidate the lawyer?" Mason said.

"What if yes?"

"This is America, not Mexico. That shit doesn't work here."

"Why you not deliver?" Saravia said. For the first time, he sounded like he was losing his temper.

"You don't understand. The American government has him, and they're not letting go of him yet, no matter how much you lose your shit."

"You not understand. I wait a long time to look that cabrón Villeda in the eye again. No one can take that from me."

"Villeda?" Mason said. So Saravia wanted Ramirez for himself? That changed things.

Saravia paused, as if he'd caught himself in a mistake. Then he let out a bitter cackle. "You not know? Ramirez is a name false, of course."

"Do tell. Our arrangement says you supply that kind of information."

Saravia cursed in Spanish, a first during their conversations. "No. I come up there and deal with him myself." The man thought he could extract Ramirez—or Villeda—from NWDC.

Mason had to stop him from trying. "You can't come here, sir." His voice betrayed panic, and he struggled to control it. "The police will look into the lawyer's assault."

"They find nothing."

Mason was scrambling now. "NWDC is operating under heightened security protocols. There was a detainee suicide, and the media's watching. The warden put Ramirez in protective custody because he was attacked by PSB gang members. Everything you do is making things worse. You can't get to him, so why endanger our valuable arrangement for a few more months of waiting? He's not going anywhere."

"I. Not. Like. To. Wait."

He sounded like Mason's kids at the end of a long day. But now that Saravia had revealed that there was no outside force pressuring him, Mason felt he had some breathing room.

"Let me tell you something," Saravia said with a loud sigh. "In America, you have TV shows and books and blogs about how to embrace your mortality, yes? Use it as reason to do the things you mean to do in life, right now. They say, you work too much, and you let the things good in life go away, until it is too late. Right? So you spend money on T-shirts and coffee cups that tell you to find joy in life. Love yourself. Stop neglect your heart."

Mason didn't follow this turn in their conversation.

"But where I live," Saravia said, "we know life is short and hard. We take every joy we find every day. We know we die one day. Probably soon. No need for guru wisdom. We walk out of the house, and we see the world like it is. Kill or be killed."

Mason couldn't stand being lectured by this Mexican thug. "Sir—"

"But when you live like every day is your last day, the worst thing that happen to you—other than die—is when fools waste your time. So, if you live in America, go ahead and talk about accept your mortality and about fulfill your potential. But in my world? ¡Deja de hacerte pendejo y no estés perdiendo mi pinche tiempo!"

Mason didn't know much Spanish, but he understood what Saravia had just barked at him: Stop wasting my fucking time! But Mason was also angry. "That's too bad," he said, "because now we have to take it even slower. The lawyer's digging in."

The moment he said that, he realized he'd painted a target on her back.

"She is weak," Saravia said. "She has a child."

"She sent her daughter away."

"Where away?"

"I don't know." Bastards like Saravia liked to make grandiose statements: You can't escape our wrath, even if you hide at the end of the world.

Saravia scoffed. "Then what you know?"

"Sir, just let me do my job. Just give me Ramirez's real name and let me take care of this once and for all."

A long pause. "Miguel Ernesto Villeda Lujan," Saravia said.

Mason committed the name to memory and pocketed the burner. His other phone rang now. He snapped it up.

"What do you want, Sheldon?"

"Sorry to bother you, sir, but I thought you should know that Laura Holban somehow transferred Emilio Ramirez to the Snohomish County Jail today."

"And you're only telling me now?"

"I called you as soon as Ken Masters called me, sir."

Mason hung up. "Motherfucker."

24

THE LIGHTS ON the highway hurt Laura's eyes and made her want to throw up, so instead of heading home, she took the exit for Swedish Medical Center. She called 911 on the way and told the dispatcher she'd been attacked in her home in Capitol Hill. The dispatcher said a police officer would meet her at the hospital.

Laura left her car at the emergency room door and the keys in an attendant's hand. He gave her a ticket and told her to text the printed number when she was done. Parking was free for patients.

The doctor confirmed a ruptured eardrum and a concussion, but found no sign of intracranial hemorrhage. "Still, you shouldn't be driving," she said. She prescribed anti-inflammatory and pain meds and recommended a CT scan in the event of vomiting, confusion, or blackout. The eardrum would heal in a few weeks. A nurse brought Laura's first dose of painkillers and discharged her.

Seattle PD Detective Brent Crowley met Laura in the triage area, after she filled her prescription at the pharmacy. He was tall, and looking up at him made Laura nauseous, so they sat down in the waiting room. The bright lights bothered her, and she wished she were home in bed, but she focused on Crowley's questions and told him as much as she could remember about her attackers, especially the one who'd hit her.

"You'll have to come down and look at pictures of guys with broken teeth," Crowley said, scribbling in a small spiral notebook.

Laura told him she'd cleaned the crime scene before her daughter came home, and she'd showered, so there wasn't much hope of finding evidence, except maybe on her jogging clothes. "They wore blue surgical gloves. They were careful not to leave traces."

"You're not giving me much to work with."

"I know. I'm sorry." Laura rubbed her forehead, but the pain was still there.

"By the way, where're you from? Your English is very good. I work with a lot of immigrants, and I can tell."

On a different day, Laura would have remarked on being singled out as the articulate immigrant, but she had no energy for that now.

"Romania," she said.

"Never been," Crowley said. "Do you suspect anyone in particular of doing this? Romanians maybe?"

Laura was about to tell him about Emilio's house being ransacked, but then realized she'd draw attention to Blanca and her undocumented status.

"No." She shook her head, and that hurt too.

Crowley made a note. "What do you do for a living?"

"I'm an immigration lawyer."

He didn't say anything, but his mouth puckered for a moment, and he looked away, clearing his throat. Immigration lawyers didn't have many fans in police departments. No surprise there. Laura thought of mentioning Waltman's threats, but after their phone conversation, she wasn't sure he was involved. And bringing up her threatened citizenship status would make her even less likable among the police.

"I'll take you home now," Crowley said. "You can return for your car tomorrow."

Laura got up too fast and felt dizzy.

Crowley took her arm. "Easy now."

She winced—a bruise was there somewhere.

They drove up Broadway in silence and into the heart of Capitol Hill. Red and yellow lights swirled around Laura, and she rested her head against the cold window and closed her eyes for a while, until she felt the car turning left onto her street.

It'd started snowing again. If it kept falling all night, she wouldn't be able to pick up her car tomorrow. Then again, she had no scheduled court appearances.

A police van was waiting outside the house. Two forensics analysts—Laura didn't catch their names—were there to look for fingerprints and other evidence. Laura stretched out on her sofa while the analysts walked around her living room wearing rubber gloves and shoe covers, looking at things and taking notes. They asked questions: Did the broken piano bench hit the attackers? Did they handle the child's photo on the mantelpiece? And so on. There were fingerprints everywhere, but they wouldn't belong to the bad guys. The analysts picked up some hairs—long ones, most likely Alice's. They treated the floor with luminol and saw where Laura's blood had been. But none of that was useful.

They bagged Laura's jogging clothes for the lab.

"You should stay somewhere else for a few days," Crowley said.

"They're not running me out of my house."

"Your choice." He had her sign a statement. "Come lock the door."

She turned off the lights and armed the alarm but felt too weak to go upstairs. She returned to the sofa, thinking Alice would need dinner soon, then remembered that her daughter was on a plane to Amsterdam.

Her phone rang. It was past nine but she saw Kyle's name on the screen, so she answered.

"We're lucky Emilio's case is in Snohomish County," he said. "A friend of mine is a prosecutor there. When our case comes up, he's willing to litigate in court instead of fighting us for a plea deal."

Laura's head was swimming. "Can we talk tomorrow?"

"Um, sure. You're right. It's late. I wanted…Sorry. Good night."

"I'm sorry…" Laura couldn't speak because of her tears.

"What's going on, Laura?" His voice was so soothing, and that tiny sign of compassion broke her resolve to keep quiet.

"I was attacked." She sounded hysterical, even to herself. "In my own house. The police just left."

"What?" There was a long pause. "I'm coming over."

"No need. I went to the ER. I'm going to bed."

"Listen, you can't spend the night there. I'll come pick you up. Where do you live?"

"I have a monitored security system, with police response. I'll be fine." She sniffled and cleared her throat. "Sorry to bother you. We'll talk tomorrow."

Her moment of weakness had passed. Kyle was a nice guy, but she couldn't muddle things now. She needed to focus on getting better and helping Emilio—and then bringing Alice home.

✕

Mason finished reading the twins their bedtime story, a chapter from a book about time-traveling kids messing with history. Orsetto sighed at the foot of the bunk bed and settled his head on his paws. The medicine was working, and he was looking better.

"Are you okay, buddy?" Mason asked him.

"He can sleep with us tonight," Oliver said.

"We'll take good care of him," Chloe added.

Mason turned on the turtle lamp and flicked off the light. Constellations and a crescent moon appeared on the ceiling. He tucked the kids in, Oliver in the upper bunk, Chloe in the lower, and gave each a kiss on the forehead.

"Daddy, can you check the room for monsters?" Chloe said with a yawn.

Mason took out his cell phone and opened his Pokémon GO app. "There's a Vulpix in the closet," he said, happy with his discovery.

The kids jumped from their beds, rooting for Mason to capture the little fox-monster into a Poké Ball, and cheering when he did. Orsetto joined in with a loud bark.

"What's going on up there?" Helen called from downstairs.

"Nothing!" Mason ushered the kids to bed, laughing together. After another round of tucking and kissing, Mason said goodnight.

"Good catch, Daddy," Oliver said. "Um, is that what you do at work all day? Catch people who want to come into our country?"

"Why do they want to come here, Daddy?" Chloe said.

"Because…" Mason had never explained his work to his kids before. "Their countries are all messed up, but instead of fixing them, they'd rather take advantage of America's good heart."

"So their countries are bad?" Oliver said.

"Well, yeah," Mason said. "But they should fix them, not flee them."

"Like really, really bad?" Oliver said.

Chloe sat up on her pillow. "Do kids there even have Pokémon?"

"I don't know," Mason said, annoyed with their questions.

"But why not let them in?" Chloe said. "Each Pokémon is good at something. You can't have just Squirtle and Bulbasaur."

"Yeah, Daddy," Oliver said, "you need Pikachu and Glaceon. Gotta catch 'em all."

"And what if," Chloe said, "people in other countries have special powers? That'd be good for us, right?"

"Let's talk about this when you're a bit older, okay?" Mason said.

The kids settled back in their beds. Mason closed the bedroom door behind him and stood there, thinking of how to handle that conversation when it was no longer avoidable. He'd have to do a better job than he had with his sister Margot. But how to explain a wicked world to his innocent kids?

Just that morning, an ICE special agent in the Seattle office and one of Mason's trial attorneys had filed a joint criminal complaint against a Kosovo national who was planning acts of terrorism in the city. The police had confiscated false passports, explosives, and contraband weapons from the man's apartment. Lives had been saved today. Meanwhile, Mason was coordinating an investigation into a gang that smuggled children over the Canadian border. Little boys brought to the US to be slaves in illegal sweatshops. Little girls used as prostitutes and child porn fodder.

No, Mason had no idea how to explain that wretchedness to his kids. Though, if he did, he was sure they'd understand that their father's work was important—and just.

×

Laura woke up to the doorbell's ring. The red-LED clock on the bookshelf read 9:53 p.m. Somehow, after everything she'd been through, she'd fallen asleep. She got up, her head hurting less—the painkillers must have kicked in—and found her way to the door in the dark. It had to be that detective again.

"Laura, it's me."

Kyle? How did he get here?

"Please open up."

Her hand hesitated over the alarm control panel on the wall. She was safe now, though she didn't feel that way. Opening the door would mean explaining things—in English—when all she wanted was to be left alone with her thoughts—in Romanian.

"Not leaving you here alone tonight," Kyle said.

She killed the alarm and opened the door. Kyle bumped into her in the dark, door closing behind him. Laura found the light switch and turned the dimmer down, then rearmed the alarm.

"I'm fine." She stepped away from him. No hugs or other things, especially now.

"Not with that bruise on your face, you're not. Listen to me. We're going to go upstairs and pick up a change of clothes for you. And your medicine—you got some, right?"

Laura nodded.

"Then we'll get in my car, and I'll take you to my house in Fremont."

"But—"

"We'll argue tomorrow. Tonight, you rest, and I'll take care of you."

Laura had been in charge of everything for so long. Alone. Having someone else take that burden from her, even for a night, left her disconcerted. Like she'd lost gravity and was floating. It was a weird feeling.

Kyle took her hand. She didn't fight him.

"Let's go pack your stuff," he said.

Her lower lip quivered. "Okay."

25

MASON WAS THE first to arrive at work on Wednesday morning. He checked the digital portal for new arrests and deportation decisions. There was Gloria Carrasco, a Mexican woman who'd overstayed her visa. She'd been arrested while working for a residential cleaning company, now under investigation for using undocumented labor. Her biometrics had not yet been uploaded to IDENT. Then there was Ansel Lumaban, a Filipino man who'd been in the States for fourteen years after crossing from Canada. He'd been denied asylum and would be flown to Manila next week. Later tonight, Mason would upload their details to Saravia's secure site.

For now, he focused on urgent matters. He logged into the Interpol database and searched for Miguel Villeda—and any other Guatemalan Villeda he could find. He looked at crime reports, from drug dealing to kidnapping, money laundering to murder, including the Drug Enforcement Agency's records and intel gathered from other countries. It was late morning when he found something on a man who might have been Ramirez's father: a Guatemalan police officer on the border with Mexico. The pictures in his file had been uploaded years before—taken in Bethel, El Petén in August 1997.

The dead man was in his late forties, tortured and murdered, his heart removed through a cut in his abdomen, through his diaphragm. His wife and younger son had been shot dead and burned in their home the same day—and his only surviving family was Miguel Ernesto Villeda Lujan. The same name Saravia had given Mason for Emilio Ramirez. The timing worked too: Ramirez had crossed the US-Mexico border in January 1998. With such a gruesome personal story, he could have applied for asylum during his first year in the US. Instead, he'd chosen a life of crime.

One of the photos showed a message in Spanish on a bloodstained paper. There was an English translation in the file: Tell the reporter to bring his camera to Frontera (Corozal, Chiapas).

Mason sat back in his swivel chair, content with what he'd found. A camera meant pictures. Ramirez had been too young to be the reporter with the camera, but maybe he knew the reporter's identity. That might be what Saravia had been after all along: investigative findings of some sort. Pictures—but of what? Probably some crime that would still ruin him now. But wait, Ramirez must have the actual photos or else what were Saravia's thugs looking for inside the Everett house?

If Mason could make a deal with Ramirez—legal US residency in exchange for those pictures—he'd have leverage on Saravia. And how lucky that Ramirez was now locked up where Saravia couldn't reach him. Not the most convenient location—his fanatic lawyer had managed to transfer him to county jail—but at least he was safe from Saravia's allies, the PSB gang.

All Mason had to do now was convince Ramirez to give up the photos.

✕

When Laura woke up, she didn't know where she was. She wore her blue T-shirt and her pajama bottoms, but she wasn't home. Then she remembered. She'd taken refuge with Kyle Jamison in Fremont, which in the light of day seemed like a complication she couldn't deal with right now. She sat up. Her ear, head, and jaw were all tender. She needed painkillers.

She looked around the bedroom. A Lego airplane caught her eye. It sat atop a walnut dresser. The plane was a colorful, complicated structure. It must have brought a lot of joy to whoever put it together. She wondered if it had anything to do with that relationship Kyle had mentioned at dinner the other night, the one that hadn't worked out. Was there a child in his life?

No, she didn't want to know. She'd learned enough about his professional life, and his personal life was none of her business. She changed from pajamas to jeans and a sweater, one gentle move at the time. Other parts of her body hurt too. Her neck, where she'd been choked. Her shoulder, where she'd landed when she fell. Her knees.

She found Kyle in the kitchen, wearing cargo shorts and a printed T-shirt with an octopus hugging a nuclear warhead. He was humming and mixing something in a pot on the stove. The place smelled of vanilla pudding. Laura's purse was on the counter. The scene looked so domestic, it spooked her.

"Thank you, Kyle, for everything, but I have to go home now."

"Have you heard of my world-famous cornmeal porridge?"

She could see he was trying to cheer her up, and she didn't want to hurt his feelings. She sat on a barstool and waited for him to put a steaming bowl in front of her. It smelled of nutmeg and vanilla and had blueberries on top. She sank her spoon into the milky porridge and for a moment she felt good.

"Tastes a bit like polenta," she said and saw him raising an eyebrow. "A Romanian kind of cornmeal I grew up with."

But she swallowed with a sore jaw and was soon reaching for the painkillers. Kyle handed her a glass of bubbly water that tasted like peaches.

"Thank you," she said after taking the pill.

Kyle brought his bowl and sat next to her. "I thought you'd like it. Soft food."

Being there, with Kyle, it all seemed so normal. So safe. "How can you always look so carefree?" she heard herself asking.

"Carefree? Me?" Kyle blew over his spoon before his lips touched it. "You should see me out on the street. Everywhere I go, I know exactly who's behind me, ahead of me, across the street. I've this extra sense, and the memory to go with it. I keep track of everyone out there, and I remember them an hour later. Which makes every stroll in the park as intense as studying the textbooks in the first year of law school."

Laura's strolls to the food truck were her time to get lost in thoughts, not catalogue everyone on the street for fear of getting in trouble with the next casual racist. But she didn't know what to say to Kyle that might not sound privileged in some way. Definitely not "I understand," because she didn't.

"Where did you learn to make this?" she said.

"My nana. She learned it from her people, who arrived in the States on the *Mayflower*." He chuckled.

Time slowed down for Laura. If she joined in his laughter, she'd be saying, yes, what a funny concept, a Black person arriving on the *Mayflower*. But Kyle had made that odd joke, so not laughing with him would seem rude.

"I'm just messing with you," Kyle said.

The sense of safety was now gone. Laura didn't feel she could navigate Kyle's cultural markers. There'd be more *Mayflower* moments waiting in ambush, like that time when she was "cutting the cheese" while everyone laughed at her.

She'd been with men from other cultures over the years, and she'd learned her lesson. After her fling with Tadelesh, and a catastrophic dinner with his Indian parents, she'd resolved to only date men whose traditions were easy for her to follow. There was no point in a relationship that wouldn't survive a visit with Kyle's nana.

"I have to go," she said, pushing up from the stool. Her body protested the sudden move.

"I was just going to tell you about my plan for Emilio's trial."

She wanted to hear it but not now. She'd call about it later. She needed to pull off a clean exit.

"Thank you for everything, but I have to go home and finish some work." She remembered her car was in the ER parking lot.

"I'll drive you…"

She put a hand on Kyle's shoulder. "You've done so much already. I'll call a cab."

"Who calls a cab anymore?" he said with a forced smile. "Uber, Lyft…"

Another joke Laura took as a reminder of how different they were. She knew she was cutting Kyle off because he belonged to an outside group. Discriminating against him, doing to him what she accused the world of doing to her. But she was overwhelmed this morning, heartbroken over Alice, and in physical pain. Going back to known territory would make her feel safe again and allow her to regroup.

26

EMILIO DRUMMED HIS cuffed hands on the metal table in the attorney's room. He was back in Everett, this time the county jail. He was less than five miles from home but knew in his heart he'd never go there again.

After all sorts of contradictory emotions during his first day here, he'd settled on anger. He was angry with Laura for going behind his back and moving him to the Snohomish County Corrections Bureau. Though in truth he couldn't complain about the place. No one had treated him badly. In fact, they'd become downright friendly after his new defense lawyer, Mr. Kyle Jamison, visited.

Emilio expected Laura or Mr. Jamison to enter the attorney's room. Instead, a stranger walked in. He wore an expensive suit and had a scar on his left cheek.

"Hello, Emilio," he said, sitting across the table. "Or is it Miguel?"

A cold hook cut through Emilio. It had been more than twenty years since anyone called him that. "Miguel" had been his mother's last word, just before her face was blown off.

Emilio had no idea whether this visitor was a friend or an enemy. He looked Latino but had no accent and behaved like he was in total control. The best thing Emilio could do was keep quiet.

"My name is Mason Waltman. I'm Noah Sheldon's boss."

Now Emilio could place him. ICE meant enemy.

"You have something I want," Waltman said. "I have something you want. If we make a deal, Sheldon won't argue against your asylum application in court. He might even tell the immigration judge you deserve to stay. You and your wife."

For a moment, Emilio dared to imagine this as a real possibility. Then the white walls around him, the harsh light in the ceiling, and the chill of the room reminded him what his heart had been telling him for some time now: he'd never go home, no matter what Waltman said.

He settled in his chair, waiting for the visit to end.

"Miguel—"

"Don't call me that," Emilio said, his throat parched.

"You talk." Waltman laughed. "You had me worried there for a moment. Now that I know you can understand me, I need to talk to you about Javier Saravia. You know him, don't you?"

Emilio shook his head.

Waltman put a photo on the table. It looked like two men at a party. One of them was Waltman and the other was…Janaab? He had less hair than Emilio remembered and puffy bags under his eyes, but it was him. A sickening feeling came with that revelation.

"I can tell you know him quite well." Waltman took the picture back.

Emilio's worst fears had come true. After all these years, Janaab had found him. And he wanted the photos. That was why he hadn't set Emilio's house on fire, as was his way. He couldn't risk the pictures surviving in a fireproof box and being found by firefighters or the police.

Why Janaab still wanted them, Emilio didn't understand. They couldn't prove he'd killed Papá. And even if Emilio testified to that, who would believe him? Janaab wasn't going to be tried for murder just because of those few pictures.

"We can both agree that Saravia is a bastard," Waltman said. "He sent those thugs to ransack your home. He was looking for something. What was he looking for? Maybe some photos?"

"I need my lawyer." If anyone could protect him now, it was Laura. And Mr. Jamison.

"Not for this, you don't. This is just between you and me. Your immigration lawyer can't do anything to protect your family from Saravia. But I can. Saravia already knows your address, but he also knows not to step on my turf. And if I look the other way…We both know that when Saravia goes after someone, he goes after their entire family."

Emilio knew that all too well.

"Give me what Saravia's after," Waltman said, "and I'll do my part."

"Was it you?" Emilio said. "Did you tell him where to find me?"

Waltman didn't bother to say no. If he and Saravia worked together, then Emilio's arrest photo was enough to identify him. At NWDC he even wore his mugshot on his wristband.

Laura and Mr. Jamison would know what to do next, but Emilio didn't. He'd call them the moment Waltman left. Phone rights were more relaxed in county jail.

"You're a hard nut to crack, aren't you?" Waltman said. "I'll be back tomorrow. Remember, I'm the only one who can protect you from Saravia. And not a word to your lawyer if you know what's good for you and your family."

Was Waltman threatening Emilio's family now?

"My arraignment is tomorrow," Emilio said, his voice hoarse. "I'm in court all day."

"Two days, then. The warden will let a visitor bring you the photos."

Emilio nodded, and Waltman left.

Emilio looked down at his cuffed fists. A sound escaped him, unbidden—a wounded man's wail. He had to talk to Blanca, had to tell her to take the boys and hide. He hoped to God she'd stay strong for the family.

✕

David and Jacob finished loading boxes into the pickup. David checked his phone again to see if Alice had texted or emailed. Nothing. Maybe she was still on the plane, or maybe her phone didn't work in Romania, and she needed to get to a computer.

He put the phone away and helped his brother secure the load. Jacob seemed resigned to the house move. David had been afraid they'd wind up in a motel, but their mom had rented a one-bedroom condo in Lynnwood, fourteen miles south of Everett. Someone from her old cleaning job had told her about a couple of young doctors moving to Brazil for a year. The residential complex in Lynnwood looked nice—it even had a small swimming pool in the interior garden. The condo was on the second floor of a three-story yellow building.

The doctors' furniture was still there, so David would put most of his family's stuff into storage.

He hadn't had a chance to talk to Ms. Holban about Evelyn Brunelle, and now that his mom had dipped into the agent's money to rent the condo, the house sale could no longer be cancelled.

His phone rang, and he picked up. "This call is from an inmate at Snohomish County Corrections Bureau. This call is subject to recording. If you accept, press one."

David pressed one.

"With the money I have in my account," his dad said in Spanish, "I can only talk for a couple of minutes, so listen to me, son. You have to convince your mom to take you and Jacob and go into hiding."

Hiding? What now? "Oh, because of the break-in? Don't worry about it—" But he realized his dad didn't know about the house sale and the move to Lynnwood. His mom had told them to keep quiet for now.

"Yes, the break-in," his dad said. "I worry about other people getting the same idea. Please, just for a while. And don't call here to leave the address. Just keep it secret for now."

"Okay."

"And David, remember your tenth birthday?"

David had to think hard.

"I need you to dig two feet out toward the water. Bring it here tomorrow afternoon."

David's tenth birthday must have been when they planted the Guatemalan fir tree in the orchard.

"Don't show them to your mom or your brother. They—"

The call disconnected. The account balance must have hit zero. How much did these people charge for a phone call?

A secret mission sounded cool. David cut through the house to the backyard.

"Where're you going?" his mom called in Spanish from an upstairs window.

"I'll be back in a minute."

"Don't take too long. And leave your house key on the counter."

David wasn't going to leave Evelyn his key. He needed access to the house so he could remove his security camera from the living room air vent, but only after it spied on Evelyn for a while. If he filmed anything illegal, he might convince her to give back the house.

He sprinted through the orchard with its leafless fruit trees, then the sun garden with its raised beds where tomatoes grew in the summer. At the shed, he stopped to grab a shovel, then climbed down toward the water and found the tree.

"This fir tree is called a pinabete," his dad had told David on his tenth birthday. "In Guate, people cut them down for Christmas, so they're dying back there. We're planting one here. I hope it won't freeze this winter."

The pinabete didn't freeze that winter. Instead, it had grown taller and stronger with each passing year. Now, almost seven years later, little shoots poked through the dirt around it.

David pressed his back against the tree and walked two feet toward the foggy waters of Possession Sound. Then he thrust his shovel into the frozen ground. It barely made a dent. He kept at it until he reached softer layers.

He dug for a while, glancing up the hill now and then to make sure his mom wasn't coming, because he didn't know how to explain this to her. He wondered what his dad buried there. He thought of his own treasure hunt through Waltman's trash. He'd finished scanning all the tiny paper bits late last night. Once he had the digital images, running them through a reassembly program had been pretty straightforward. Most of the recovered documents were bills and receipts, but when David reconstructed a page with his father's name and picture on it, he knew Mason Waltman was up to no good. As soon as he was done digging up treasures and hauling boxes to storage, he had to talk to Ms. Holban.

He felt the shovel hit something. He scraped around and there it was: a rusted metal box. He picked it up and opened it to find a stack of color photos and a few pieces of folded paper, all tucked inside a plastic bag to keep them dry. He stashed the bag inside his windbreaker and covered up the hole as fast as he could, then ran uphill to the shed. He wished he could look at those pictures, but his mom was outside the kitchen door, waving at him to hurry.

"Jacob's all done," she said. "Let's go."

David went through the house again, not giving a damn that his sneakers left mud smudges on the hardwood floor. Jacob was already in the truck's passenger seat, earbuds in place.

David's phone vibrated with a text from Alice.

Just landed in Bucharest and I miss home already

She'd only been gone a day. It didn't feel like she was far, but she was half a planet away. He thought about what to text back.

"Can we go now?" Jacob said.

David typed, *When you come back, do you want to join my band?* and hit send.

27

LAURA'S HOUSE WAS cold without Alice, as if the colors had drained from it. Even though her daughter was on a plane, Laura wasn't feeling her usual anxiety about flying, not as strong anyway. It must be the painkillers. And then Adrian called to tell her that he'd picked up Alice at Otopeni and to complain, again, that he'd been given no choice in the matter.

"It's only for a few weeks," Laura repeated for the hundredth time.

"I have my own life, you know," Adrian said.

"Your daughter is part of your life. And it's only for a few weeks."

He went on and on. And on. She set the phone down to dull his whining. She hoped their daughter wasn't overhearing this. Alice was probably thrilled to be with her beloved father, who right now saw her only as a burden.

When the call was over, Laura powered up her laptop and opened Emilio's prehearing statement. She wrote an entire section describing the hardship David and Jacob had gone through and another section about Emilio's great contribution to his community in Everett.

The doorbell startled her. It was dark outside.

"Who is it?" she asked through the door. She imagined the two men in ski masks waiting outside, and her hands turned cold.

"David."

Her hearing was better than yesterday.

"Wait a minute." She rummaged through her purse, looking for her small jar of foundation, and smeared some over her bruises in the powder room by the door.

When she was ready, she turned off the alarm long enough to let David in. He looked upset as he started taking his sneakers off.

"Don't bother," Laura said. The house had been trampled by her assailants and the police, and she hadn't had the time or energy to clean it.

"My dad wants me to bring him this." David took a plastic bag from his jacket. "Pictures. And a letter."

In her medicated state, Laura found it hard to muster curiosity, but she took the bag from David and waved him to the dining room table.

They sat, and she took out the first photo and set it down, careful not to leave fingerprints. There was a yellow timestamp in the lower right corner: August 1997. The picture showed a group of people posing in front of rows of excavated stone steps. It looked like a work group photo taken somewhere in the Maya Biosphere Reserve. Based on Emilio's bio, she assumed it was the Mirador Basin, with its ruins of pyramids and cities. The people in the picture looked like archeologists and volunteers.

"I think this one is my dad," David said, pointing.

Laura squinted at the face under the blue cap and had to agree that the young, skinny man had to be Emilio. He was just a kid, maybe eighteen or nineteen.

"Is this what the burglars were after?" she said. "Where did you find them?"

"In our garden. My dad told me where to dig."

Emilio had told Laura he'd brought nothing from Guatemala. She took another photo from the stack. David pointed to Emilio in a group of young men and women under a big tree, all holding beer bottles.

Laura smiled. "Look at their clothes and hair." Emilio's hair was short, but the others reminded her of styles popular when she was in high school: bangs and frosted tips. It was the same with the clothes: baggy jeans and colorful shirts. Another photo was of a beautiful middle-aged woman in a kitchen, working on a pot of tamales.

"That's my grandma, I think," David said. "There's another picture with my dad and maybe his brother—a selfie."

The next photo was of a man driving with a rifle on his knees.

"That must be my grandpa. He looks a lot like my dad."

The images seemed ordinary. Why would anyone ransack Emilio's house for them?

David turned his eyes away from the remaining pictures.

There was a close-up of a jade mask with freaky-looking eyes and an open mouth.

"A Mayan death mask," Laura said. "I watched a documentary about them once. They were meant for royalty."

David shrugged as if he didn't care.

Two men in handcuffs, one with a beard and another with long hair and a mustache. And a man with slicked-back hair in a tense exchange with Emilio's father.

"This is definitely important," Laura said.

"Janaab," David said, pointing to the folded pages that came with the photos. "My dad wrote in his letter that the guy's name was Janaab."

In another image, Janaab poked Emilio's father in the chest, ignoring the rifle between them. Then there was the selfie David mentioned: Emilio, his brother, and their mother.

The last picture made her gasp. It was a dead body on a cement floor, covered in a stained sheet. The face was bruised but it was clearly Emilio's father.

Laura arranged the photos by date and time. Whatever had happened between the argument and the dead body was the real story, and it wasn't there. Even so, someone wanted those pictures, badly, so they must tell more than Laura was seeing. She reached for the letter. There were four pages, all numbered, all in Spanish. The first sentence read, "My name is Miguel Ernesto Villeda Lujan."

"My dad wrote it while running north," David said. "He thought that if he died trying to get to America, it'd help the authorities identify his body. And tell them what happened to his family."

Laura went to the kitchen to get a glass of water. On any other day, she would have felt annoyed with Emilio for lying to her. But the medication had numbed her emotions. She hated feeling so disconnected. When it was time for the next dose of painkillers, she'd switch to good old ibuprofen.

In any case, she wasn't surprised. In her experience, many refugees ditched their former identities while trying to escape horrendous pasts. She'd suspected that about Emilio from the start. The revelation shouldn't hurt his immigration case though. While his name was fake, it only served to demonstrate how terrified he'd been of the people who'd murdered his family. And keeping that secret for decades showed that he was worried they might find him here. Which, apparently, they had. All of it could work in their favor in immigration court—if the judge believed Emilio.

Laura stopped in front of the fridge water dispenser. If Waltman had nothing to do with the attack on her, could it be this Janaab? Emilio was Laura's third client whose past had caught up with him soon after being arrested by ICE. Waltman wanted Laura to back off so Emilio could be deported. He'd been living under a false identity for more than twenty years—but his photo and other personal information had been collected by ICE. If so, the timing couldn't be a coincidence. There had to be some connection, but how would someone like Janaab get access to ICE records?

She felt exhausted—damn pills. She drank a glass of water and went back to the dining room.

"It's late, David, you should go home. I'll read the letter and scan the pictures."

"My dad wants them tomorrow."

"Which can only mean one thing: Janaab or his friends got to your dad. They want the photos. But he shouldn't play their game. I'll talk to him after his court arraignment."

"Then you take these," David said. "I've made copies." He took out his phone. "There's something else." He showed Laura the image of a shredded document that had been reassembled.

She took the phone from his hand and zoomed in. It was the first page of Emilio's IDENT report: his biometrics, his height and weight, eye and hair color, date of birth, and birthmarks. The full report would contain his fingerprints too.

"Where did you get this?" she said.

"Mason Waltman's house."

Laura was alert now. "What were you doing at Waltman's house?" She knew she should feel more annoyed but admired David for working hard to help his dad. "Were you going through his garbage?"

"Technically, it was his compost."

"Don't get technical with me, David. Was his compost bin placed at the curb?"

David shook his head.

"You went inside his yard? That's illegal."

David shrugged. "Is it legal for him to have this page about my dad at his home?"

"I don't think so."

"And there're two more like my dad's."

He showed Laura a couple of reassembled pages on his phone. She didn't recognize the names, but the arrest dates were both within the last month. Those immigrants should still be in the US, either at NWDC or out on bond. In any case, this kind of sensitive information was not supposed to leave the ICE building, let alone be at Waltman's house.

"These pages were shredded," Laura said, "which means Waltman didn't want to go through the trouble of taking them back to work. It must be hard enough to bring them home. So why do that?"

If Waltman had extracted immigrants' personal information, it could only be for illegal reasons. Like using it to open credit cards or bank accounts in the names of unsuspecting immigrants, which ICE personnel had done before. But that didn't explain how Janaab had found Emilio.

Unless the information on the shredded page had been sent to Janaab by Waltman himself. Was that even possible? It seemed too bizarre. Why would he do that, and how would he even know someone like Janaab? Still, that could be the missing connection.

"Listen, David, I want you to promise you'll never go to Waltman's house again. This stuff is dangerous."

"I promise," he said. But Laura had been around kids long enough to smell a lie.

"I mean it, David."

"I promise. But Ms. Holban? I can use aging software on these pictures to figure out what Janaab looks like now."

Laura raised an eyebrow. "Is that a thing?"

"Not the most reliable, but it'll give us an idea."

Laura rubbed her face. "Janaab might be connected to the people who—" She stopped herself before saying the people who'd attacked her. If she told David, and David told Alice…In the morning, Laura would ask Kyle and his private investigator to fill in some of the missing pieces.

"Connected to the people who ransacked our house?" David said.

"Could be worse than that," Laura said.

"That's why my dad told us to go into hiding…"

"He did what? When?"

"When he called about the pictures, he told us to go somewhere safe and secret. We're moving to Lynnwood anyway, so…"

"Right." They were moving to Lynnwood.

David nodded and started toward the door.

"Alice thinks I'm in California," Laura said. "Please don't tell her I'm in Seattle." She saw his frown and hurried to say, "Don't ask."

"Okay," he said. "So…when's Alice coming home?"

Laura cleared her throat so she wouldn't tear up. "In a few weeks."

28

DAVID'S FIRST NIGHT in the Lynnwood condo was tough. He wasn't used to sharing a bed with Jacob and discovered that his brother whimpered and ground his teeth in his sleep. David lay awake, thinking of what it meant that Ramirez wasn't his father's real name. He turned Villeda around in his head, and it sounded all wrong. The name was the least of what he'd read in his dad's letter, but everything else in there was just too terrible to think about, so he focused on the name. Jacob had once complained about things not being real or true in their lives. It was so strange that he'd been able to see the truth when David couldn't.

Close to morning, David managed to drift off with his pillow over his head to dull the sound of Jacob's teeth grinding. At first light, he was up again. He went to the only bathroom in the condo to get ready. Winter break was over, but their dad wanted them to stay in hiding, while their mom expected them to go to school. David needed to be in class or he'd fall behind in trigonometry, and Jacob needed to keep busy or he'd just get more depressed. If they skipped school today, maybe Cruz could bring their classroom notes and homework assignments. They could meet after school at the gym. Janaab's heavies wouldn't know to look for them there.

David brushed his teeth while texting Cruz. Then he checked his email. A new message from Alice!

Hi David,

Romania kinda sucks. Bucharest is all dusty and smoky. Only been here a couple of days and everyone points out my accent. Apparently I don't speak Romanian like a native even though I've been speaking it my whole entire life.

My dad's new wife hates me. She got angry because I didn't say thank you nicely for the godawful food she gave me so she threw a tantrum and made my dad send me to my grandma's. That's another story.

Turns out my grandma never noticed my purple streaks during our video chats, mostly cause I only say hi and bye and don't really waste time on her. She was all like, what kind of mother lets her child dye her hair so young? No wonder she can't discipline you. That sorta stuff. I don't wanna sound dramatic but I'm starting to get why my mom isn't a big fan of her mom.

When she's not annoying me she tries to be friendly, which makes her even more obnoxious. To hear her say it, she built all of Bucharest singlehandedly back in the day when she was an architect. Oh, and she wants to take me to her friend's house, a retired music teacher with a grand piano. I guess she still feels guilty for not giving my mom lessons when she was a kid. Though I don't mind practicing while I'm here. Then maybe we can talk about that band when I get back.

David hadn't thought about music in a while. Yes, wouldn't it be nice if they could all go back to that?

How are things in Everett and Seattle? How's your dad's case going? I know my mom had to go to California

David didn't like having to lie to Alice on behalf of her mother, especially since he didn't even know why.

but I hope she's still doing a good job for your dad (now I sound like her mom).

Maybe chat later? Bucharest is 10 hours ahead so anytime in the morning for you works for me too.

David closed his eyes. His life might be a mess but so was hers. He couldn't wait to video chat and tell her she should definitely hit that grand piano.

✕

Laura felt better after sleeping. Her ear didn't hurt if she didn't touch it, and the bruise on her jaw had lost its painful edge. She took some ibuprofen to keep the pain dull and her head clear. Now that the stronger painkiller's effects were gone, she could contemplate what she'd seen and read the night before. Emilio's—or Miguel's—entire family had been killed in August of 1997. She couldn't imagine the trauma, the heartbreak, the scars.

The thought of Alice so far away made her want to hear her precious voice. She dialed Alice's number—she'd told her to enable roaming—and waited as it rang. No answer. She got out of bed and went in search of her laptop. She needed to see her daughter, now.

When she went downstairs, the motion sensor blinked red, and the alarm started beeping. Laura found the control panel by the door and punched in the code to disarm the system, then she rearmed it without the motion detectors, just windows and doors.

Her laptop was on the dining room table, where she'd left it the night before. It was just after six in the morning, so four in the afternoon in Bucharest. The video chat jingle went through its cycles before ending with a disappointing *boing*. "The person you're trying to reach is not available at the moment. Please try again later." She called Adrian next. Same thing. Maybe he was still at work. Claudia was marked active though, so Laura tried her.

The face that popped up on the screen wasn't Claudia's though. "Alice?" Laura's joy was instant. "What are you doing there?"

Alice didn't smile. "My dad's crappy wife kicked me out. I'm staying with Bunica now." She'd called Claudia by the Romanian word for grandma, which was a good sign.

Anger flooded through Laura, bitter anger at Adrian and his wife. "What happened?"

"When do I come home?"

"Soon, my love." Laura's voice caught in her throat. "I just need to wrap up this case."

"You're obviously not in California."

"I'm traveling a lot."

"Why don't you just tell me you don't want me there?" Alice shook her head. "I've got the worst parents in the world."

"Sweetie…"

"It stinks here." Alice crinkled her nose. "Literally. Bunica's house smells of cigarette smoke. And it's not just her. Everywhere I go, people smoke in my face. My clothes stink." She coughed to make her point. "All the nonsmoker places are downwind from the smoker ones. I'm sure they do that on purpose. Mom, I want to come home!"

Laura had to change the subject. "You look a bit pale, my love. You might need iron supplements, like before."

Alice rolled her eyes. "I told you it's pronounced i-urn, not i-ron."

"I-urn, yes." Laura knew that, but she was still waking up and rattled, so of course she'd messed up.

Claudia appeared in the frame. "Alice, move aside," she said in Romanian.

"Good morning—um, afternoon," Laura said. "What happened with Adrian?"

"Can't blame him." Claudia scoffed. "Your daughter has such a bad attitude."

"Oh, come on," Alice said in English, storming out.

"See what I'm talking about?" Claudia raised an eyebrow. "She did that a couple of times with Vera, and Adrian sent her packing. Don't worry, I'll talk some sense into her head. And speaking of her head, why did you let her dye her hair at such a young age?"

"It's not a big deal here, Mama. Many kids in her class do it. I don't want Alice to be the one who—"

"Laura, I'm your mother, and I raised a child too. This is not the way to take care of your daughter. You let her run wild. You abandon her."

Laura wouldn't need coffee that morning. Her heart was racing on its own. "I didn't abandon her. I have important work—"

"More important than your own daughter? The one time it was really important for you to separate from Alice, when your father was dying, you didn't do it. But you abandon your daughter now, for work?"

Laura forced herself to breathe. "You always complain you don't get to spend enough time with your granddaughter." She waved her hands. "Now you have time. Maybe Alice can help you go to a furniture shop and buy a new swivel chair."

"You think this is a joke?"

"No, Mama, it isn't. It's a mistake. I'll send airplane tickets as soon as possible."

Claudia frowned. "Now you think it's a good idea to put that poor child on a plane. So soon after she's crossed half a planet? She's still recovering from jetlag, you know. Maybe that's why she's so cranky."

Laura couldn't believe the change in tone. "Then maybe you can make her a cup of chamomile tea? She likes that."

"I suppose. I'm trying to make her feel welcome here. I even stopped smoking in the house since she arrived."

"That's wonderful." Though it'd be better if she stopped smoking altogether. "And do you still have the vinyl records from when I was little? The fairy tales and the theater plays?"

"They're in a box in the closet."

"The turntable too?"

"The needle might be a bit blunt."

"Then give it a try, Mama. Just give it a try…"

✕

Everyone was home at the Waltman house Thursday morning because it was still mid-winter break at the kids' school.

"Good morning, sunshine," Mason told Chloe, who emerged from her bedroom fussing with her ponytail. "Good morning, champ," he greeted Oliver, who sat on the floor, fighting with a stubborn sock.

Orsetto barked once to welcome Mason in the kitchen, but he sounded weak.

"What's wrong with him?" Mason asked Helen, who was making breakfast. "He was fine after seeing the vet." He was about to land a kiss on her neck when the burner in his pocket rang. She'd already tilted her head so he could truly nuzzle her and seemed confused when he pulled away. "Just a moment, love."

He hurried to his office down the hall. Saravia was the one person Mason didn't want to hear from right now. He let it go to voicemail. He expected the phone to ring again, and it did. He almost let it go to voicemail again, to punish Saravia in that small way, but he knew it would just keep ringing until he answered. Saravia never left voicemails.

"Where is Villeda?" The voice was seething.

"I'm taking care of it as we speak," Mason said.

"In your place, I finish this business long ago."

"It'll be done tomorrow." If Mason got his hands on those damn photos, this could all be over. And not the way Saravia wanted.

"It not matter now," Saravia said. "I come get Villeda myself."

"What? No! You won't be able to get him out of county jail. You can't come here, sir."

Saravia laughed. "I go where I want."

"Please don't do anything today. I'll call you tomorrow."

He hung up before Saravia could say anything else. He was shaking. His other phone rang.

It was Sheldon. "Sorry to disturb you, sir, but I wanted to ask your opinion—"

"Just do your fucking job, Sheldon," Mason said and ended the call.

That bastard Ramirez had better have something big on Saravia.

✕

Laura was ten minutes late for Emilio's arraignment and bail hearing because a light snow had bogged down traffic on the highway to Everett. She entered the Snohomish County Courthouse, which had such an easy, welcoming process compared to the one at NWDC. Even the security check felt casual. She took a seat in the back row of the gallery.

Emilio now wore a striped shirt and black pants and had belly chains, handcuffs, and leg restraints. He and Kyle stood before a judge Laura didn't recognize, but whose voice was raised as she questioned the district attorney—probably the friend Kyle had mentioned.

"Are you telling me, sir, that ICE forbids me to approve a bond? In my own courtroom?"

"That was the condition on which ICE agreed to transfer the defendant to county jail," the DA said. "He's to stand trial here and be returned to NWDC once a not guilty verdict is reached or a sentence is served. But he cannot go free."

The judge smirked. "Constitutionally, it's invalid to ask ICE's opinion about bond. We're looking at an assault case in which the defendant is pleading not guilty."

Kyle made to speak, but the judge held up a hand. "Bond is set at a hundred thousand dollars. Counsel, what were you going to say?"

Kyle had an endearing smile. "Nothing, Your Honor."

"You'll get your trial date. Next."

Laura couldn't believe Kyle had pulled it off. Then the armed marshals came for Emilio, and she reminded herself that victory for her clients was always relative.

She intercepted Kyle at the back doors, and they sat on a bench outside the courtroom. He didn't seem to hold a grudge for the other day.

"Your bruise looks better today." With the tone he used, it sounded like a compliment.

"I can't believe the judge just ignored ICE's directive," Laura said. "Can Emilio really get out on bond?"

Kyle looked pleased with himself. "The judge probably thought Emilio wouldn't have a hundred grand. She thought she could give ICE the finger and still keep our client in jail. I could accuse her of bias and discrimination, except it's all good for us."

"So, what now?"

"If Emilio's found not guilty, he'll be returned to ICE with no criminal record. Until then, he'd better stay out of ICE's reach—if he has a hundred grand to spare. His wife said she'd have the money."

"She sold the house. To Evelyn Brunelle."

Kyle's smile vanished. "That vulture."

Laura nodded. "ICE could place a detainer on Emilio." She meant a request that the jail hold him for up to forty-eight hours after he posted bond so that ICE had time to take him into custody based on his outstanding immigration issue. "But I didn't see Sheldon in court.

Maybe because of the snow? If we're lucky, he won't have time to file a detainer today. I need to talk to Emilio."

"They're not going to let you see him until all the arraignments are done. If things run long, you might not see him at all today. You want to grab lunch while you wait?"

"A little bit early for lunch," she said.

"Coffee then?"

Laura could use a coffee break. Still, she shouldn't send mixed signals. "I have to go to NWDC to see another client."

Kyle got up to leave, and Laura felt sad he wasn't trying harder.

She reached into her tote and took out the bag with Emilio's letter and photos. "I think this was what the burglars were after. And we have a name to work with: Janaab. I'll also text you three documents David recovered from Waltman's house. One of them concerns Emilio. Looks like Waltman is tipping someone off about upcoming deportations."

Kyle took the bag. "Do you have copies?"

"Yes. Can you read Spanish though?"

"My trustworthy PI does. Don't worry, I got this. See you soon, partner."

Laura watched him saunter from the courthouse and was sorry to see him go.

29

DAVID AND JACOB spent the school day hanging out at Alderwood Mall. They watched a couple of movies, got something to eat, and browsed the shops. They also worked on Janaab's photo with the age progression app. David didn't give Jacob the details, just said that Ms. Holban needed his help. Janaab was supposed to be in his fifties, so the app rendered him with thinning gray hair and small, puffy eyes. The old Janaab had slicked-back hair like the young one, but his eyebrows were lower and shot with gray. The app kept a small mole under his right eye. The aged photo looked a bit like a video game avatar, and David wasn't sure he'd recognize the man in that rendering if he saw him on the street.

After the mall, they went to the gym. Cruz brought a bunch of math printouts and a couple of library books he said they needed to read, pronto. On their way to Lynnwood after the gym, they drove to Our Redeemer's Church to pick up their mom. She was visiting with Father Nicolas to return the money they had borrowed from his congregation, using another chunk of Evelyn Brunelle's cash. She'd called David to say her car wouldn't start because of the cold weather. A friend had given her a ride.

So this was it. David had to come clean about the damage to the pickup. "I'll tell Mom someone rammed our truck in the parking lot at Grocery Outlet. Okay? Back me up on this one?"

"Yeah, dude, whatever," Jacob said.

Driving to church on familiar streets made David sad. He forgot to check the rearview mirror, but when he did, he noticed a gray SUV some distance behind. He tried not to panic. Ever since his dad's arrest, he saw danger everywhere. Just like his mom.

The SUV turned away, and David exhaled. He tried to keep his eyes on the sedan ahead while also paying attention to the mirror. There was a silver Volkswagen a hundred feet back. Behind it, a black Suburban that could be ICE. What would they want with him and Jacob? He realized he was speeding and took his foot off the gas. The Volkswagen passed him first, then the SUV.

A moment later, another black SUV came in right behind him. David turned left on Mukilteo Boulevard. The SUV followed. David's heartrate went up. He took the first right he could find. The SUV drove on.

David took a series of lefts to get back to the boulevard. One time he cut too close, and the back tire grazed the curb. Jacob tossed him an annoyed glance as they turned onto Olympic Boulevard, then into the church parking lot, which was quite full at that hour.

Jacob unbuckled his seat belt. "Dude, my life's in danger every time I get in this truck with you." He slammed the door and took off across the lot to the church.

David locked the truck and followed, still shaken. Their mom was waiting on a bench outside the tall wooden doors with Father Nicolas beside her.

"Ah, David, Jacob," Father Nicolas said in Spanish, rising when he saw them. "So good to see you both." He smiled but his eyes focused on something behind them.

David turned and saw a black Suburban pulling into an empty spot close to his pickup. He didn't stare because he didn't want to worry his mom. Maybe it had nothing to do with them.

His mom got up. "Thank you, Father Nicolas. You're always there for us."

"I'll try to visit Emilio again this weekend," he said and headed back into the church.

"Let's go, boys," she said.

They cut across the parking lot, making for their pickup. Explaining the truck damage to his mom had been David's biggest fear for days. Not anymore. He couldn't tell if she noticed the Suburban among the parked vehicles, and he didn't know if he should bring it up.

"Everything all right?" she asked David. "You look worried." Just like her to spot every muscle twitching in his jaw.

The SUV just sat there, dark and quiet. David unlocked the pickup's doors with the remote. Jacob opened the back door while their mom rounded the front of the truck to get to the passenger side.

David heard Jacob cry out—a shapeless sound. When he turned, two men wearing sunglasses and body armor labeled "POLICE ICE" were grabbing his mother.

"Blanca Morales?" one of them said.

A world of guilt crashed down on David. He'd brought them to his mom. He should have stayed hidden, like his dad had told him. His dad had been worried about ICE, not Janaab. How could David make such a terrible mistake?

"What's going on here?" Father Nicolas said, coming their way.

"We're arresting this illegal alien, Father," one of the officers said.

"I need to stay with my children," David's mom cried.

"You're on church property," Father Nicolas said. "And churches are on the list of sensitive locations. You have no right to arrest her here."

"This is a parking lot belonging to the city of Everett," the officer said.

"You're desecrating this place," Father Nicolas shouted.

"We were ordered to bring her to NWDC, Father, but she's changed her address recently."

"Please don't take me from my children," she said, tears on her cheek.

"You followed us here," David said with what little strength he could muster. "You followed us."

"And a ton of goddamn work too," the officer said. "Sorry, Father. These two skipped school today." He turned to look at David. "But you showed up at the gym."

"I'm an American citizen," David cried. "You followed me when you had no right to."

"Whatever," the other officer said, dragging David's mom and shoving her into the Suburban.

Jacob stood still the whole time, barely blinking. The SUV pulled away. Father Nicolas ran after it, shaking his fist. David called Ms. Holban, but she didn't pick up, and he left her the shortest voicemail, saying only, "They've got my mom."

Everything was falling apart around him—everything. He and Jacob were on their own now. Neither of them spoke on the way back to Lynnwood. Father Nicolas hadn't wanted to let them go at first, but David convinced him they'd be fine and promised to call if they needed anything.

He took a few wrong turns, heading for the old home out of habit, but in the end, they wound up in Lynnwood and parked in their assigned spot. Inside the condo, Jacob dropped his things by the door and went to the living room. He sat on the cushioned window seat, pulled his knees to his chest, and stared out at the gardens.

David knew he had to hold it together for both of them. "You hungry?" he said, looking through the fridge and trying not to think of anything else but their food.

They still had a few tostadas from yesterday and a leftover bowl of shredded cabbage mixed with seasoned chopped onions, green chilis, and carrots. He found a jar of tomato sauce in the cupboard. He set his ingredients on the counter with an opened can of refried beans to spread over the crunchy tortillas his mom had deep-fried. In the summer, she'd pick the cucumbers, tomatoes, and radishes right from her garden, but David managed to find some store-bought veggies in the deep drawer of the fridge. He now had everything except for the boiled eggs to prepare his mom's Salvadorian enchiladas, which his dad always criticized as not being the real deal, like the Guatemalan enchiladas. Which were nothing like the Mexican ones served in school cafeterias.

Jacob hadn't answered the question though. David closed the fridge and glanced at his brother. Jacob's face was turned to the window, his cheeks wet with tears. He didn't have a private place to sulk anymore.

"Why is this happening to us?" Jacob whispered.

"I don't know. But we'll sort it out. Somehow."

"What if we can't?"

"Come on, Jacob. Pull yourself together. Ms. Holban will get Mom out, for sure. We'll take care of each other for a few days, but I need you to—"

Jacob shot up from his seat and headed for the bedroom. The door slammed shut a moment later.

David clenched his fists. Everyone he cared about had been taken away, and he was still supposed to hold it together. He let out a low growl, which made him want to do it louder. It felt good to growl. He looked around for something to smash. The first thing he saw was the new lamp he'd bought after the break-in. He grabbed it, snatched its power cord from the socket, and threw the lamp against the wall. The explosion of shards felt so good, he screamed with relief.

He looked around for something else to obliterate. A glass by the kitchen sink. He threw it at the fridge and watched it shatter. Jacob could use some of that too. Cleaning up broken glass was easy, though the dent in the wall from the smashed lamp would need to be patched and painted over. Fernando would know how to do that.

David stomped to the bedroom, breathing like he'd just run a mile in six minutes. "Yo, you can break shit up too!" The door was locked. "Jacob?" No answer. "Fine, whatever."

He went back to the kitchen to look for another glass to break when a sudden dread choked him. What if Jacob was cutting himself again? He ran back and put his ear to the bedroom door but heard nothing. His hands went cold, and his stomach balled up. Without another thought, he hurled himself at the door. Once, twice. It didn't budge. He stood back and gave it a kick. The door cracked open, but something was blocking it on the other side.

"Jacob!" He pushed against the door until it opened enough for him to squeeze through.

Jacob was on the floor, his belt tied around his neck and the door-knob. The color on his face was a sickening bluish-red, and his tongue was halfway out.

"Shit, shit!" David dropped to his knees and scrambled to release and undo the belt, but he couldn't find the buckle at first, his fingers missing everything they could miss. He cursed. Tears kept him from seeing clearly.

With every second he fumbled, his brother drew closer to death, if he wasn't already dead. David screamed in terror and rage, pulling on the belt with all his strength. Somehow it came off, and he grabbed Jacob and lifted him up.

"Breathe, Jacob, breathe!"

He shook him hard until Jacob gasped and coughed and opened his bloodshot eyes.

David hugged him, whimpering. "Why, Jacob, why? What were you thinking?"

Jacob didn't pull back. He let himself be hugged for once.

David held his brother tight with one arm, while he pawed through his pockets until he found his phone. He dialed 911 but didn't hit call. The doctors would just put Jacob in a nuthouse. Then ICE could argue that Blanca was a bad mother and deport her.

Ms. Holban—she might know what to do.

×

Laura slid into her car outside NWDC, coming back from a client meeting. She answered her ringing cell. It was David, crying like a child. "I want my mom…I want my mom…" he kept saying, and Laura didn't know how to calm him down. Eventually, he told her about Blanca's arrest and about Jacob, who was alert but could barely talk.

"You have to call 911, David," she said. "Take Jacob to a doctor."

"Would they use Jacob to deport my mom?"

"It won't help her case, no."

"Jacob is fine for now, and I'll keep him safe. Go get my mom, please, hurry."

Laura made him promise to keep vigil at his brother's bedside until she got there, then she ran back to the building.

"You don't have another appointment," said the security guard with the German mother. Officer Madeleine Riker was her name. They'd chatted earlier, and Laura thought she could reason with her.

"I don't know my new client's Alien Number," Laura said, out of breath. "But her child is really sick, and I need to get her out on bond. Tonight."

"But all the judges have already gone home," Officer Riker said, sounding sympathetic.

"Then first thing in the morning?" Laura said.

Officer Riker pursed her lips, as if thinking hard, then let Laura through security. "Go check with the clerk."

Laura ran to the court clerk's window, where Chris Mair was getting ready to go home. He'd been with NWDC for a few years, and Laura knew him well. He was a stickler and a family man. That last part could help. She explained to him that she needed a bond hearing for Blanca Morales first thing in the morning.

"If every lawyer could get a hearing whenever they pleased…" Chris said.

"Come on, Chris," Officer Riker said, joining Laura at the clerk's window. "Her client's kid is really sick."

"Please, Chris," Laura said, hands clasped together. "I wouldn't ask if it wasn't a matter of life and death."

Chris typed at his computer. "Doesn't this kid have a father or some other family?"

"His father's in jail. His sixteen-year-old brother is looking after him now, but his brother's just a kid too."

Chris sighed. "I can squeeze you in before the first hearing tomorrow. Judge Derek Brown Gibson."

"Thank you so much," Laura said, though Judge Gibson was the one who'd rejected Gabriela's application.

Before driving to Lynnwood, she called Jennifer and told her to expect Blanca's bond hearing documents in her inbox early in the morning. Jennifer had to review them, print them, and bring them to NWDC.

When Laura arrived at the Ramirez condo, David looked pale and in shock. Jacob was in the bedroom, and he could barely talk because his throat was swollen, but he seemed out of danger. Because he couldn't see a doctor, Laura did the next best thing. She'd been a nurse to Alice many times over the years, so she checked him for symptoms of intracranial hemorrhage from blunt trauma. She tested his cognitive skills and made sure his pulse was healthy. She made him mashed potatoes, gave him a dose of ibuprofen, and watched him and David go to sleep. Then she sat in a chair by the bed with her laptop and worked on the documents needed for Blanca's bond hearing the next morning.

David moaned a lot and once jolted up to check on Jacob.

"He's safe, you're safe," Laura told him. "Go back to sleep." She watched him settle next to his brother—two children missing their parents. Laura couldn't be a substitute, but she could work hard to reunite this family, starting with Blanca's hearing statement.

After a few hours of work, she caught herself nodding off, but losing a night's rest was no longer the debilitating event it'd been when Alice was little and Laura was chronically sleep-deprived.

30

LAURA WOKE DAVID early on Friday morning and told him to ask Fernando or his wife to come over to help him watch Jacob. Because she always kept an extra set of court clothes in her car, she left directly from the condo for Blanca's bond hearing.

Her phone rang on the way. She pressed the button on her steering wheel and talked to Brent Crowley, the Seattle PD detective who'd seen her after the attack. There were no leads in her case and no incriminating evidence, as—Crowley stressed—Laura had cleaned the crime scene before calling the police. She thanked him and hung up. Her own case was the last thing she cared about right now.

Father Nicolas and a few dozen people from Our Redeemer's Church stood outside the detention center, protesting ICE and demanding justice for Blanca's family. Someone held up a sign that mentioned the Russian man who'd killed himself. The protesters were sure to make the local papers. While she was glad to see their support, Laura didn't have time to stop and chat.

Once she was past the security checkpoint, Officer Riker stamped the back of her hand with invisible ink and gave her a temporary pass to get through the three doors to the courtroom. Instead of waiting to be called and explaining herself to the guards, Laura showed them the pass, and they called for the doors to be unlocked for her.

She was one of the first people in Judge Gibson's courtroom, but the place soon filled with applicants, lawyers, and guards. Blanca was brought forward, dressed in a low-security yellow uniform. Laura passed her bond submission to the judge. Josh Peterson stepped forward as the government's trial attorney.

"What happened to your face, Ms. Holban?" the judge said.

"Nothing," Laura said, wasting no time. She asked for bond approval but didn't bring up the DUI, focusing instead on the support Father Nicolas's church was showing for her client outside the courtroom that morning. Then she moved on to showing that Blanca wasn't a flight risk, hoping she could present her arguments without hurting her case. "Her younger son, Jacob Ramirez, tried to kill himself after her arrest. He's only fourteen, Judge. He needs his mother. She wants to go to him."

Laura saw the shock on Blanca's face and motioned to her to stay calm. Blanca gave her the smallest nod back, though her eyes were wide with fear.

"For the sake of mother and child," Laura said, voice quivering a little, "please release Ms. Morales on bond today so she can go be with her son. That's the humanitarian—I mean, humane thing to do."

"If his life's in danger," Peterson said, "he should be in a hospital."

"His whole life is in danger," Laura said. "The trauma—"

Judge Gibson lowered his bushy eyebrows. "You tried that argument with Judge Felsen once, but it won't work with me."

"Judge," Laura said, "we all know that as soon as the press gets wind of this poor boy's misfortune, we'll make no more progress in this case. The department will resist Ms. Morales's release, and I'll threaten to sue. Months will go by. But that boy needs his mother. Today. Now."

Laura didn't clarify that she intended to keep news of Jacob's suicide attempt quiet, and she hoped Judge Gibson would be worried enough about getting caught in another scandal. There had already been a damaging article in Crosscut about the unnamed Russian detainee, and Gibson's name had been mentioned as the judge who'd rejected his relief from deportation. He now seemed to be pondering his options. The news of a fourteen-year-old trying to kill himself would be compelling, and more people would get involved and voice their opinions.

"ICE first arrested Jacob and David Ramirez's father," Laura said. "Then their mother. These two boys are American citizens."

Still, the judge was thinking. Peterson was thankfully quiet, as he probably hadn't had time to prepare for Blanca's rushed hearing.

"Jacob tried to hang himself with a belt," Laura said. She didn't have any graphic pictures, but words would do. "His brother David saved his life. David is in shock too, and he's only sixteen. Both boys need help right now. Please, Judge, approve Ms. Morales's release on bond."

Judge Gibson's jaw twitched. "His brother found him and saved him?"

"Yes." Laura wondered if David's situation reminded him of something in his own past.

"That boy," the judge said, "the older brother—"

"David Ramirez."

"David. He'll be scarred for life." He uttered those words as though announcing a decision.

"Will you help him then?" Laura said. "He's an American citizen."

"Even if he wasn't. Does your client have twenty thousand?"

"I believe she does, as she was recently forced to sell her house after her husband's arrest. That house was the only home David and Jacob had ever known."

"You have your bond," Judge Gibson said and waved her away.

Laura was glad to see that Peterson was preparing another file, which meant he'd be in court for a while, unable to report back to Mason Waltman.

×

Outside at last, Emilio could breathe again. He stood in the snow-lined parking lot of the jailhouse, hugging David and Fernando. He was surprised ICE hadn't arrested him on his way out, but maybe they didn't expect his family to afford such a large bond.

Jacob was at the hiding place in Lynnwood, with Fernando's wife babysitting. Blanca had just been released on bond and was on her way there. Emilio wished they could all go home, but ICE would probably arrest him there. Maybe Janaab was waiting there too.

Seeing his pickup truck parked in the lot brought tears to Emilio's eyes. It was the silliest thing to shed tears over, and he took a deep breath to stifle it.

"Thanks for everything, Fernando," he said in Spanish.

"You're welcome, my friend."

On the way to the truck, Emilio could tell something was wrong with David. He put a hand on his son's shoulder. "You saved your brother's life, and I can't thank you enough."

David stared at his feet.

"From now on," Emilio said, laughing, "you can do no wrong with me."

David looked up. "You sure about that?"

"Yes, I'm sure." He wiped his eyes and laughed. It felt good to laugh.

But David took off. When he reached the pickup, he pointed to a big scratch along the side.

Emilio couldn't care less. "It happens, son."

"I told you you'd be fine," Fernando said.

"But this dent, here—"

"Doesn't matter." Emilio watched David's face relax. "Now, do you have the pictures?"

"I gave them to Ms. Holban."

Emilio didn't know how to feel about that. "I'll talk to her. But right now, I just want to drive."

They all got in and buckled up, David in the back seat. Before putting the key in the ignition, Emilio had to ask Fernando. "The bond money. One hundred thousand—all from Father Nicolas?"

"Not Father Nicolas." Fernando took his time before he continued, "Blanca, she couldn't get a mortgage with you in jail and her out of a job."

"Then how?"

Fernando narrowed his eyes and bit his lip.

Dread gripped Emilio. "No," he whispered. "No, no, no!" It couldn't be. Not his house. His home!

"You built that house, Emilio," Fernando said. "You'll build another. What matters is that you still have your family and your friends."

"I'll help you build the new house, Dad," David said.

Emilio's home was gone. He wanted to scream. His house, his only home…

"Evelyn Brunelle?" he said.

×

In his office, Mason checked his morning email while sipping hot coffee. The last twenty-four hours had been bad for him. Ramirez had pleaded not guilty in Superior Court, and the judge had allowed his bond, spitting in ICE's face. That shithead Sheldon had taken the initiative and ordered the arrest of Blanca Morales. And if that wasn't enough, Saravia might already be in Seattle. Mason's consolation was that Saravia wanted to look Ramirez in the eye one more time, which limited that bastard's options and allowed Mason a little room to maneuver.

Sheldon appeared in the doorway, looking quite satisfied with himself. "Having the wife in jail should help Ramirez choose voluntary deportation."

"She'll be out in no time," Mason said. "Holban will use the kids to bail her out. You've wasted everybody's time and money arresting her."

Sheldon looked crestfallen. "But, sir, I thought you wanted me to. You told me on the phone to do my job."

Mason jumped ahead. "Did you place a detainer on Ramirez?"

Sheldon looked even more distraught. "He doesn't have money for bond, does he?"

"What the hell, Sheldon! You know what? I'll deal with it myself."

Sheldon scurried away without another word. Mason picked up his desk phone and called the Snohomish County Corrections Bureau. He identified himself and asked to place a forty-eight-hour hold on Emilio Ramirez after he paid his bond.

"Too late," the warden said. "He's already out."

Mason clenched the handset. "Who got him out?"

"Umm...His employer and his son."

Could Saravia have arranged that? Mason hung up before he started cursing. His first impulse was to report this and have ICE send a team to arrest Ramirez, but if Saravia had him, that could mean open war on the streets of Everett. And if it wasn't Saravia, then who had the money to free Ramirez?

Mason found Ramirez's home address in his A-File, the document ICE kept on each alien. He grabbed his car keys and ran out the door. Two minutes later, he started up his Audi and sped out of the garage. Soon he was on I-5 North headed to Everett. He called Saravia's number, but it went straight to voicemail, which could mean a lot of fucking things.

Time to improvise. First, he'd try to find Ramirez and convince him to hand over the photos. Maybe he could use the jailed wife as a bargaining chip before Ramirez figured out how weak that hand was.

Mason didn't have much trouble finding the house, but the sight baffled him. A moving van was parked at the curb, and two men carried a red couch into the house. Why was Ramirez's family having furniture delivered? It all became clear when he stepped inside and found Evelyn Brunelle in the middle of an almost empty house, talking to an electrician on a stepladder.

"You got the house," Mason said, not really surprised.

Evelyn turned. "As you can see. More prep work than I expected but yes. We're staging it for an open house. And have you seen the orchard going down to the beach? I'm subdividing the property and selling it to developers." She smiled, smug as hell. "A pretty awesome deal."

Mason swallowed his disgust. "Do you happen to know where the family moved to?"

"Ask at the church, they might know."

As if they'd tell a stranger walking in. "In that case," Mason said, "congratulations are in order. You're making a lot of money. You've achieved your goal after all. And you might be the only one still winning when this is over."

Back in his car, Mason weighed his next step. If Ramirez was out there, where would he go? His wife had just been arrested. Which meant her new address must be in her A-file. Mason would drive back to work and find out where the family had moved. Then he'd tell his secretary he had to leave for the day for some kind of family emergency.

31

EMILIO'S FIRST IMPRESSION of the Lynnwood condo was that it was tiny compared to the home they'd lost but bigger than a jail cell. He hurried to check on Jacob, who was asleep in the only bedroom, his back to the open door. For a moment, Emilio couldn't tell if his son was breathing or not. Pure dread wrung his gut, but just as he lunged to shake Jacob, the boy turned on his back, sighing.

Emilio wiped away a tear, the thought of almost having lost his son as painful as the memory of his dead family in Guatemala. He joined Blanca in the small kitchen—a narrow walkway between two walls with shelves and appliances. After her arrest, and what had happened to Jacob, Emilio had expected her to be stuck in bed, but she was on her feet, preparing food. Sometimes a migraine would drain her nervous system to where the next one couldn't develop right away. Blanca had already suffered her share since this whole thing had started, so Emilio hoped she'd have a few days before another episode.

"Listen," he told her in Spanish, "we can't stay here for long."

"We can manage here." She started chopping peppers on a cutting board.

"That's not it." He couldn't tell her about Janaab, but if that murderer was coming, he had to get his family out of here—and fast. "The ICE prosecutor in charge of my case, he's a corrupt man."

"But what about Ms. Holban? She'll be arguing our cases. I think she could win."

"This is beyond her reach, love. I don't think she can do any more for us than she's already done."

Blanca put the knife down. "You're serious?"

Emilio nodded and pulled her closer. He kissed her forehead and whispered, "I'm thinking California."

"But leave everything behind? Fernando and Father Nicolas?"

"We've already lost our house. But we still have some money for the road. We can't say goodbye to anyone though."

"We'll lose the bond money," Blanca said.

"I know. But we're hard workers."

"The kids…"

"This change will do them good. We'll be with Jacob day and night. And David, he needs us after all he's been through."

Blanca bit her lip, but in the end she nodded. "We'll use different names?"

If he told her about Villeda now, she'd feel betrayed when he needed her trust the most. Jacob wouldn't handle it well, either. No, it should stay between him and David for now. Emilio used to think David was strong, but the haunted look in his son's eye worried him.

"Yes, different names," he said. "Different phones, different cars."

Blanca started breaking eggs in a bowl, one crack after another.

"We'll sell your car east on I-90 for cash," Emilio said, "then take the pickup down I-5 South and sell it there."

Blanca nodded. She took a wooden spatula from a drawer and began beating the eggs.

Emilio squeezed her shoulder. "We'll all be together."

He left her to her omelet and went to the living room to talk to David, who was on the couch, typing on his phone. He told him they'd leave the next day.

"We're running away from Janaab?" David whispered.

"His real name is Javier Saravia." Real names again.

"How do you think he found you after all these years?"

"Mason Waltman."

"Makes sense, yes." David got up. "And your Guatemala pictures? I can go get them from Ms. Holban. I also have copies on my phone."

Emilio thought for a moment. "Tell her to keep them safe, for now."

"I should go to the store. We'll need a few things for the road. Like burner phones."

"Don't be long. And be careful out there, son. They don't know we're in Lynnwood, but we won't be safe here for long."

×

Laura pretended not to notice Kyle's warm smile when he walked into her office. "Come in," she said, offering the chair in front of her desk.

After Blanca's hearing that morning, Laura had gone home to take a nap, knowing that Jacob was safe. She had woken up to the sound of hail on her windowsill and went in to work wearing jeans and flat shoes. Now she was glad she'd gone casual, so Kyle wouldn't think she'd dressed to impress.

Kyle took off his winter coat and dropped it on another chair, then returned the bag with Emilio's photos to Laura.

"I've an idea what our friend Mason Waltman has been up to." He sat down and unbuttoned his suit jacket. "His home address puts him in the high-end property bracket. He wouldn't have that kind of money just from his government salary. His wife takes care of the kids full-time, so no income there—unless a fat inheritance dropped in their laps. But with a little bit of help from a good accountant, the IRS wouldn't suspect anything amiss there."

"So where does the money come from?"

"Waltman has unlimited access to A-Files, and it looks like he's selling the aliens' personal information. He's in charge of overseeing that data, so who's going to stop him?"

Laura wasn't surprised by Waltman anymore. "Who's buying though?"

"That'll take some time to figure out. But I'd venture to say that whoever wants Emilio deported knows he's on the market because Waltman told them so. Right there we have a lead: this Janaab fella."

"Waltman told Janaab, but how did Waltman find him? And not just Janaab? How did Waltman find the local people who wanted Felix dead? Or Gabriela's old sex trafficking ring?" She cleared her throat. "Whatever we do, we can't let them take Emilio. Janaab will kill him in Guatemala."

"Don't doubt that."

"Can we go to the police with what we already have?"

"Not the local authorities," Kyle said. "Waltman might have friends around here."

"The FBI then?"

"Only if we're sure the feds aren't working with him." Kyle scratched his ear. "Honduras, Mexico, and now Guatemala. Waltman wouldn't have the means or the time to put together something on that kind of scale. Not alone, anyway. He's probably working with one person who's already connected to all these other criminal groups. But we don't know if that person is FBI or someone local, like PSB."

"In any case," Laura said, "Waltman is sending information to this point man, or whatever you call it."

Kyle nodded, leaning back in his chair.

Playing detective intrigued Laura. "Waltman sends the pictures of these immigrants, not just their personal data. That's how Janaab recognized Emilio, even though he changed his name. So Waltman prints the first page of an immigrant's IDENT report and brings it home, where he must scan it and—"

"Upload it to a secure site somewhere," Kyle said. "If he's fancy, he uses a VPN—a virtual private network—and tunneling protocols to conceal his IP address."

"No idea what you just said, but I understand that once he's done uploading the biometrics report, he shreds the page and puts it in his compost."

"Like a true Seattleite."

Laura let out a long breath. "So how do we proceed?"

"The best course of action is to use electronic surveillance at Waltman's house. Tip of the hat to David, but we need to up our game here. My PI can intercept Wi-Fi and cell transmissions. They'll be encoded, though burner encryption is not super sophisticated. Still, it'll take time to crack."

"We don't have a lot of time though. The men who attacked me wanted Emilio's case dropped. You don't have months to go to trial in Snohomish County."

"Already working on plan B. Do you have a browser open?"

He came around her desk and stood at her side while typing an address, username, and password. Laura could smell his laundry detergent and feel the warmth of his body, but she didn't pull away. A webpage appeared on the screen, with Emilio's scanned pictures. His old letter had been translated into English.

"Here's all the stuff we already have," Kyle said. "The website is on a dead-man's switch, meaning it'll auto-send to the police and the media, unless I tell it not to, once every twenty-four hours." He closed the browser.

Laura was relieved that they had some kind of safety net. "Oh, David sent me an aged picture of Janaab, something he created with an app." She found it on her phone and showed it to Kyle. "Janaab might lead us to Waltman's point man."

"Do me a solid and text that to me, will you?" Kyle put his coat back on. "You want to grab lunch? Not too early, is it?"

Laura wanted to. "Another time," she said. "I have a green card application to finish and a citizenship one after that." She smiled and explained, "Things that keep the lights on and pay the mortgage." Then she'd need a good night's sleep.

32

MASON UNLOCKED THE front door, expecting Orsetto to bark and leap at him, but the hallway was quiet. Then he remembered: Helen had taken the dog to the vet clinic that morning because he seemed lethargic, and the vet had decided to keep him overnight for observation. It could be a reaction to the anti-inflammatory medication Orsetto was taking.

"I'm ho-ome." Mason hung his coat in the closet. He was bummed that the address listed in Blanca Morales's A-File was the old one. Once again, he had no lead on Ramirez. "Honey, I'm—" He smelled cigarette smoke, which was odd. And the Pokémon encyclopedia lay on the floor.

Mason darted to the living room.

Saravia sat on the couch, smoking. He was flanked by three guards with weapons. His eyes were narrow and frightening. "I like your lake view," he said. "My money buy this, yes?"

Something moved in the corner of the room, beyond the side table. Mason's knees went weak. Helen and the kids were on the floor, duct tape over their mouths. They were shaking and whimpering. Tears on Helen's face. Chloe and Oliver looked terrified. Mason rushed to them, but one of the guards grabbed him and pushed him back.

"I tell you I come," Saravia said. "And surprise, the Jade Jaguar just receive a shipment of Mayan artifacts. They fish it out of Lago Petén Itzá, not long ago. Too bad they are only for sacrifices of animals." He shook his head. "And too bad your dog is at the doctor." He took a long drag from his cigarette. "I want to try my toys on your dog."

Mason's head throbbed with intense panic. The man was out of control. But Mason needed to stay calm. He raised his hands and took another step in. "There's no need for this."

The guard came up to Mason, forced his hands down, and bound his wrists with a cold zip tie.

"You like to make me wait." Saravia put his cigarette out on the tabletop, then said something in Spanish to one of his men, who went to the kitchen.

"I have the situation under control," Mason said, his voice trembling.

His interlocked fingers turned cold and sweaty. His kids were on the floor, scared, and he didn't know what Saravia would do next, and he had nothing to barter with. He didn't have Ramirez's photos yet.

Saravia's man brought a glass of whiskey on the rocks and handed it to his boss.

"So, you have Villeda, yes?" Saravia said.

"Not exactly. But soon. He's out on bond. I'll send ICE to arrest him again."

"We are here." Saravia glanced at his men, who nodded. "We take care of things now."

Mason was about to say that Ramirez had moved. But he didn't know where, which made him useless and disposable. On the other hand, if he claimed he knew where to find Ramirez, Saravia would do whatever necessary to get the address from Mason. He'd threaten or hurt the kids. Mason would give him an address, and at that moment he'd again become useless and disposable. He had to think this through, but the whimpers coming from the corner made it hard to think about anything but Helen and the kids.

"You still need my reports," he said at last.

"I find another Mr. Waltman soon enough, one who not make me wait. That lawyer who work for you, Noah Sheldon? He can become the new ICE chief—"

"But why start all over again?"

"I start all over again all the time, Mr. Waltman. You think you are the only American who work for me?"

Mason raised his chin. "I work with you, not for you, Señor Saravia."

"Not anymore." Saravia finished his drink. "Take us to your office, Mr. Waltman."

Saravia's prints were on that glass. Why wouldn't he care about leaving prints behind?

"Please, let them go," Mason said, his voice cracking with panic.

The man who guarded Helen and the kids let out a chuckle that made Mason want to throw up.

"They're not the right kind of twins," Saravia said with obvious displeasure.

"What do you mean?" Mason said. He should have studied more on those damn Mayans all these years, ever since that party at the Jade Jaguar. Maybe he would have known how to sway Saravia now.

The other two guards pushed him down the hallway, with Saravia following. In the home office, one of them forced Mason to sit at his desk.

"Take his computer," Saravia told one of his men, who kneeled under the desk to unplug the cables. "Where is your safe box?" he asked Mason.

Mason nodded toward a corner and gave them the combination: his and Helen's wedding date. Saravia's other man began turning the dial, first fast, then slowing down, until he pressed the handle and opened the thick metal door. He stuffed the contents into a duffel bag: the family's passports, house deed, birth certificates. None of that was of any use to Saravia—and a man like him didn't need the kind of cash Mason kept in there. Unless he was trying to make this look like a robbery.

Mason had to stall. "Just give me one more day. Waiting today might save you precious time tomorrow." He realized it was the wrong argument with Saravia.

Saravia turned to one of his men. "Take care of them."

"Them who?" Mason said.

Saravia's man left the room, one hand reaching for his holstered gun.

"No, no, no, wait!" Mason jolted up from his chair, but the other henchman forced his face against the desk.

Mason took quick, shallow breaths. "Ramirez!" he cried. "He's not at his place. I know how to find him." He clenched and unclenched his fists. "Wait!" They wouldn't hurt Oliver and Chloe. That'd be absurd, unreal. He felt so sick, like fainting. He had to keep it together. Distract them. Help Helen and the—

Three shots, one after the other.

"No, wait! Wait. No. No. You didn't—"

"I give them a favor," Saravia said. "Not burn alive with the house."

"Wait," Mason said, laughing. "You're just trying to scare me, right?" His lips trembled, and his words came out slurred. "They're just fine…Just fine…" Now he understood why Saravia didn't care about leaving prints all over the house. Still, he couldn't believe it. "They're fine, of course. And you need me."

"No."

Saravia's guard forced Mason to stand up. The other gunman returned with Helen's guard and a duffel bag, and they started taking out and unwrapping what looked like Mayan artifacts. Saravia set them on Mason's desk, one after the other, with reverence. Ceramic bowls, obsidian blades, and then the jade mask with horrible eyes.

And then Mason understood. "No, no! You can't do this." He shook his head over and over. He threw up in his mouth and swallowed back, his throat burning.

"Quiet!" Saravia said. "We begin."

He nodded again, and all three of his men grabbed Mason. They pinned him to the floor by the legs and forced his arms over his head. He felt so weak he couldn't kick. They fastened a neck restraint to keep him from moving. It hurt his burning throat. The jade mask dropped over his face, and Mason's world went dark. He could still breathe through the mask's open mouth. The sawing sound in his ears was his harried breath inside the mask.

"This is not happening," he whispered, his jaw clenched.

He felt something warm down the inside of his leg. He'd peed his pants, like a kid. In all his awful years with Pa Kirk, that had never happened to him. His heart was beating so fast it ached. He was covered in sweat. His mother's face appeared before his eyes, smiling at him.

"Orsetto, my little bear," she said and vanished, leaving him to face another nightmare alone.

"Mama?" he whimpered. "Mama!" He fought to get up, but strong arms kept him down.

He gasped as a cold blade ripped through his belly, sucking the air out of his lungs. He screamed, but the mask muzzled his cry. Pain all around, naked pain, burning like no other pain before. He gulped a mouthful of air and felt the pain anew, solid like a wall crushing him.

He shrieked and struggled against the choking neck bind, against the iron claws that nailed him down.

Something made of fire was working its way through his insides, under his ribcage. It hurt like hell.

They were digging for his heart. For his own warm, beating heart.

"Nooo!" The air rushed out of his lungs and never returned. His lungs were gone, and he was suffocating inside the pain, in the dark.

Then the pain grew distant, replaced with a sense of illness, as if the world had just vanished and the earth had swallowed him.

He tried to scream, but he had no breath.

A final rip, deep inside. A sound like water and something heavy sloshing inside a bowl. He thought of Oliver and Chloe, and—

33

WITH ALICE AWAY, Laura was in no hurry to get home Friday evening. Her office windows were dark, and she was tired but had work to finish: plowing ahead on a citizenship application. She heard the office suite's outer door bang open, too loud to be Jennifer. She got up from her seat to go check, when a young man barged in with a gun in his hand.

A sickening jolt went through Laura's stomach. She grabbed her phone. Her thumbprint wouldn't unlock it. She began typing her security code when another man grabbed the phone from her hand. A third, older man, yanked her desk phone from its socket and threw it on the floor.

Laura glanced out the window, seeking help. She saw nothing but the brick wall through her reflection and the alley under the streetlight. She stood behind her desk, shaking. How could this happen again?

"They are mine," the older man said with a Spanish accent, grabbing the bag with Emilio's photos from her desk.

Laura realized she was looking at an older Janaab, like the one David had generated with his age-progression app. In an instant the world shrunk, and in its center stood a murderer who was now coming for her. She clutched her arms to her chest and stumbled back against the window. Her mouth turned dry.

A gun appeared in her face, and she squeezed her eyes shut. All she could think of was Alice.

"What do we do with her, boss?" one of the younger men said.

Laura would know that voice anywhere. It was Chip-Tooth, one of the goons who'd attacked her in her own home. She opened her eyes and there he was, but this time he wasn't wearing a mask. That was bad.

"Patience, Utah," Janaab said. "We need her. She break Villeda."

The words took a moment to sink in. Through her terror, Laura felt a slight sense of relief. Janaab needed her alive for now. That was good.

Utah grabbed her arm, twisted it painfully behind her back, and marched her to the elevator.

"Help!" she cried, though she knew the building was empty after business hours.

"Shut the fuck up," Utah said, tapping the elevator's call button, "or I'll give you another bruise to go with the one from Tuesday."

He pushed her through the opening doors. Janaab and the other man took the stairs. The doors closed, and Utah pressed the button for the first floor. Before the elevator started its slow descent, Laura already felt the small space crushing her, so she focused all her attention on Utah, who grimaced back. Small eyes, face scars, dirty blond hair. But he couldn't kill her now, on his boss's orders, so she threw herself at him with all her might.

The elevator was small, and Utah's head hit the wall. His teeth chattered, but he grabbed her by the throat, strong-armed her to turn around, and pushed her into a corner. He pressed her bruised face against the cold wall and forced her wrists into a zip tie.

She panted, in pain, on the verge of tears. Trapped again in a tight space. Her life in danger. Again. She kicked her leg back and hit Utah.

"Fuck," he yelled and slapped Laura over the head, over her healing eardrum.

She lost her breath from the shock.

The elevator doors opened on the main floor, and both of them stumbled out. At least Laura was free from that metal box, even if her hands were tied and her head was hurting from the blow. Utah pushed her through a doorway into the back alley, where a car idled in the cold. Someone was in the driver's seat.

"Where're you taking me?" Laura cried.

Utah grabbed her by the elbow and made her turn so he could slap a piece of duct tape over her mouth. The car's trunk popped open like a hungry maw, ready to swallow her. She didn't need to be told she was going in, but she had to tell him she couldn't possibly be locked in that extra tight space. No, no, no, she'd lose her mind in there.

She tried to back away, but Utah lifted her off the ground and dumped her into the trunk. With her hands tied, she landed on her side, saving herself from another blow to the head at the last moment. She flopped on her back and kicked at the trunk lid to keep it from closing.

Utah pulled out a handgun and pointed it at her. "You're getting on my nerves, bitch." He looked livid. Would he remember his boss's order to keep Laura alive?

She wasn't so sure, so she folded her legs and let the trunk lid slam closed. It was dark inside, and it smelled of wet dog, pee, and cigarette smoke. Even with her eyes wide open, Laura could see nothing. The car trembled with new people climbing in, and its doors closed with consecutive slams.

Laura screamed but the duct tape over her mouth and the rumble of the engine drowned it out. She tensed her body and kicked at the trunk lid. Her flat shoes slammed against a metal plate; the trunk was reinforced on the inside, perfect for kidnapping people. She tried to scream again, terrified to the bone. And then panic took away her breath. Her skin crawled with a cold shiver like electricity.

Her left shoulder she was lying on almost pulled out of its socket when she tensed and released again to kick the trunk lid above her.

The car turned and sped up. They were on the highway now. But were they heading south, toward Tacoma, or north, toward Everett? Laura's muscles tensed with a fresh bout of panic that seemed to last forever. She focused on her breathing. She hated feeling helpless. She hated being afraid. She kicked at the trunk lid again. The car braked, jolting her, then accelerated again: the driver's warning to quiet down back there.

Laura tried to calm herself, if only to be able to think. Her last therapist had taught her how to take deep belly breaths during panic attacks. Inhale for four seconds, hold for four, exhale another four. But the idea behind that method was to remind the body that there was no real danger. How could it work now, when Laura was in mortal danger?

She tried it anyway. Her breaths came tight and fast. It felt like her skin was burning. One, two, three, four. Breathe. It didn't work. She was in danger, and she couldn't fool herself otherwise.

Her hands were cold, her chest muscles tight, her heartbeat relentless. Were they taking her somewhere to torture and kill her, the way they'd tortured and killed Emilio's father? Utah hadn't hidden his face this time. Janaab either. That could only mean one thing: she'd die tonight. Alice would learn about it tomorrow or the next day—after Laura's disfigured body was found in a dump somewhere, half-eaten by rats and crows—and she'd live the rest of her life knowing her mother was murdered.

Deep breaths. Still not working. Electricity still shooting through her skull and skin.

Alice's last memory of her mother would be of their fight at the airport and the hug she didn't return. Once she learned what had really happened, she'd beat herself up for rejecting a mother who'd only been trying to protect her. She'd never forgive herself for those wasted last moments together. And Laura wouldn't be there to help her. Alice would have nothing but Claudia's harshness and Adrian's indifference.

Laura's eyes hurt with the first burst of tears. She doubled over in the dark, knees drawn up to her chest, stomach squeezed. She didn't usually cry in moments of shock or pain. The tears always came later. After her father died, she didn't cry for months. But now, the thought of Alice alone in the world was the greatest shock and pain of all, and the tears came like a breath of scalding air.

Laura stopped struggling and let herself slide into that place she'd resisted all her life: a place of sorrow and no hope. Tears pooled inside her damaged ear, causing more pain. Crying made her choke, but the duct tape kept her from sobbing. She remembered how proud Alice had been when Laura agreed to help David's dad. That was how Laura wanted Alice to remember her, not as Janaab's helpless victim. In life, she'd failed her father and her mother, but in death, she'd try to make her daughter proud.

First though, she'd have to admit the truth to herself: she was indeed a coward. Adrian had been right about that much. The year her father died, no airplane had fallen from the sky because of a snowstorm. Alice would have never been in real danger had they boarded that plane to Bucharest. Laura hadn't had to choose between her father and her daughter. She'd used the excuse of a snowstorm to avoid going to see her father because she was too scared to watch him die.

She'd spent years obfuscating this simple truth and blaming Adrian and the whole world for her own cowardice. Had she been in Bucharest when her father had first fallen ill, she would have stayed with him until the end. Holding his hand while doctors ran their tests, bringing him homemade food, telling him stories about Alice. It would have been a natural progression. Father and daughter together. But because she chose to live on the other side of the planet, and because he'd never told her he was ill, she could only drop in as he lay dying.

And here was another truth: she was glad she hadn't watched him die. Glad she'd never seen his body on a morgue table, then locked in a coffin, and buried underground. No regrets about that. Somehow, she knew he'd understand.

She wished Claudia could hear this mental confession spurting between muted sobs, but Laura was alone. Locked in her small, metal box. Listening to her own whimpers and struggling to breathe. Was that what it had been like for her father in his last moments? Alone, yes, but the man who'd once tried to swim across the Danube at night in search of freedom, the man who'd survived beatings and hard labor, that man wouldn't have been paralyzed with fear in his last moments. If only she could be like him. Not a coward.

Those thoughts came to her in a jumble of Romanian and English, words that sounded broken in both languages, and Laura saw herself at last as a pathetic human being struggling to reach for wisdom and depth, but in her darkest, most crucial moments sounding incoherent. A cackle broke through the duct tape. Laura was going to die, and no amount of blubbering nonsense in Romanian or English was going to stop it. And how much time had she wasted in her life worrying about speaking properly and sounding smart? Now she wished she had that time back so she could spend it all with Alice.

A sudden quiet fell over her. Her breath, she'd forgotten to count it, but it knew again how to go on, all on its own. The panic had somehow vanished. Instead there was only wordless anger at those assholes who would take Laura away from her baby.

She didn't know how long she'd been locked in the dark, but when the car stopped and turned right, she knew they'd left the highway and were close to their destination. Her mind returned to the present moment, and she felt nothing. She was as empty as her house after Alice left. She stared into the dark in front of her, waiting.

When the trunk lid popped open, the low brightness of the streetlights hurt Laura's eyes for a moment. The air was cold on her hot, wet face. She looked out and saw Janaab throwing away a cigarette stub.

"Come out of your underground chamber, Princess," he said. "You see any of your gods in there?"

A Mayan reference, no doubt, but Laura didn't care. Utah grabbed her by the elbow and pulled her out, all in one jagged motion that hurt her body in so many ways. She was now back on her feet, staring at her captors. Her hands were tied, but she was ready to fight those fuckers with everything she had.

34

DAVID WAS BACK home in Everett, but it felt strange to fit his key in the lock when Evelyn's key box was hanging from the doorknob. He'd come to retrieve his security camera from the living room air vent. With any luck, he'd find something he could use against Evelyn.

Inside, the house was dark except for a new floor lamp in the empty mudroom. David flicked the lights on. Everything looked so different. The kitchen was decorated with a porcelain coffee set, but the shelves were empty. A vase had been placed on a new dining room table. In the living room, a big red couch sat on a Persian rug, facing the bay windows. The couch was flanked by black recliners. There was a can of air freshener on one of the corner tables. Everything looked awful. And the air freshener smelled gross, like Evelyn.

David's old room had pink curtains, a white wooden bed, and a bookshelf with dolls and girly books. There was a rainbow comforter on the bed but no sheets underneath. David thought of the damage he could do here. First, he opened the windows. Maybe raccoons would sneak into the house tonight. He smiled at the thought of Evelyn arriving in the morning to find a freezing house infested by raccoons.

David's new burner phone had a cheap camera but also internet access, so he snapped a picture of his ridiculous room to send to Cruz. He opened the browser and logged into his email account to find that Alice had written to him again. No matter how pressed for time he was, he had to read her message.

Mind-blowing conversation with my grandma today. She was in the kitchen reading a tabloid and she told me, look at this, scientists discovered that fathers of daughters live longer than fathers of sons. And I told her, are you saying I'm somehow responsible for my dad's longevity? And she said, no, of course not, this stuff is nonsense. My Tudor had a daughter and he died so young, only 58. True, his daughter wasn't here to take care of him. And I said, that's because my mom had to take care of me in Seattle. David, you shoulda seen her face. So yeah, just wanted to tell you I can't wait to come home. Chat tomorrow?

David typed a hasty *You got it!!!* and hit send, though he was supposed to be on the road tomorrow. He put the phone away and went back to making Evelyn's life miserable. He turned off the thermostat. Maybe the house would freeze and a pipe would crack. He left the front door open while he went out to get the stepladder from the garage, if it was still there.

He set the ladder under the air vent in the living room and climbed up, a screwdriver in his back pocket. He was unscrewing the vent plate when he heard a car pull up outside. Someone was coming. Could only be Evelyn.

He slipped the screwdriver in the breast pocket of his windbreaker and climbed down. He pushed the ladder away from the vent and crossed the dining room to skid into the sunroom. He found a wooden screen in the dark and hid behind it. He unlocked the side door to the backyard—a quick way out if he needed it. But he still wanted his security camera, so he'd wait until Evelyn left.

Car doors slammed outside. David realized he'd left the front door unlocked and the living room lights on.

Soon there were men's voices in the dining room, speaking Spanish. Someone cursed in English. Didn't sound like Evelyn.

"No one lives here," a man with a smoker's voice said in Spanish. He switched to English. "Where is he?"

A woman's whimper followed the sound of something ripping.

"I don't know." What was Ms. Holban doing there? "He sold the house and moved." Her voice was low, her tone calm.

David's impulse was to go to her, but her whimper from earlier gave him pause.

"Go look around," the smoker told someone in Spanish.

A moment later, the lights came on in the sunroom. David stood still behind the screen, a cheap Japanese imitation with painted wooden panels that hid David well. Two men came in—David could tell by their footsteps. Two here, the smoker guy, and Ms. Holban in the other room—that made four. And there might be more.

"We shouldn't have killed Waltman," a man whispered in Spanish, sounding bitter.

Mason Waltman was dead? That was impossible. Then these people were his murderers, and they could kill David too. He felt nauseous. Sudden yellow spots danced against the wooden screen in front of him. He had to calm down. Everything was going to be okay. He should call 911.

"Keep your mouth shut, Nacho," the other man said, sounding closer.

David held his breath. The men passed by the screen and moved to check the laundry room and the guest bathroom. The laundry room led back to the kitchen, so David hoped the two men wouldn't return to the sunroom.

"Go check upstairs, Utah," the smoker said. "You know your way around here."

"Sure, boss," said a fifth man. He spoke English with no accent. A moment later, the floorboards creaked upstairs.

David listened with dread to the voices coming from the dining room.

"Call him," the smoker said.

"I don't have his number," Ms. Holban said. "I met him when he was already in jail. He didn't have a cell phone in there."

"Unlock it with her thumb," the smoker ordered in Spanish. Nacho and the other guy must have finished checking the laundry room and were now back with their boss. It sounded like Ms. Holban struggled for a moment. Then silence. Whoever had Ms. Holban's phone was probably going through her contacts.

"Found a David Ramirez here," the smoker said. "Flaco, untie her hands so she can type."

"You should type," Ms. Holban said.

"No," the smoker said. "It must sound like you. But no funny business. Tell him to bring his family here."

But the number would be David's old phone, which was now in Lynnwood, its battery removed. He pushed the side door open and slipped into the freezing backyard. He dialed 911 on the burner, but his thumb trembled over the call button— just as it had yesterday with Jacob. If the police found him here, they'd take him in for questioning. Then ICE would interrogate him and force him to give up his dad—

Something heavy fell on his shoulders, and he hit the frozen ground hard, cell phone flying from his hand. A man grabbed his arm and pulled him to his feet.

"Who do we have here?" he said in perfect English. Utah, then.

David turned to fight but found a gun pointed at him. His knees went weak. His phone glowed on the ground. Utah saw it too and picked it up.

"Inside." He pushed David toward the house.

David expected to go in through the sunroom door, but Utah took him around the front. In the dining room, David saw the smoker's face. He looked like the age-progressed Janaab, aka Javier Saravia, the man who'd murdered David's grandfather. Sheer terror gripped him. The muscles in his legs tightened, and he was ready to bolt. His breath came in fast as he looked around for something to grab and throw. Nothing.

Ms. Holban stood by the new table, guarded by a guy with an AR-15-style rifle on his shoulder. Judging by his skinny frame, he was the one called Flaco.

David had never been so scared in his life, but Ms. Holban seemed calm, and that helped a little.

"Check out his phone, boss," Utah said. "Only three contacts: Mom, Dad, and Jacob."

"You are David then," Janaab said in English, lighting a cigarette. "Good job, Utah." He picked up the phone. "Calling Dad," he said, winking at David. He took a drag from his cigarette, blew out the smoke, and pressed the call button.

David heard ringing, then his dad's voice—the sound of safety just twenty minutes away.

"Long time, Villeda," Janaab said in Spanish, heading to the sunroom.

Utah pushed David into the living room. Ms. Holban and Flaco followed, but Nacho stayed behind with Janaab.

"Hands," Utah said, and David understood he was to put his trembling hands behind his back. Something thin and cold tightened around his wrists, then a gun pressed against the nape of his neck.

"…if you want to see your son alive again," Janaab said in Spanish, coming back with Nacho in tow. "And if we see or hear the police, the boy dies." He hung up. "Now we wait," he said in English. "What we do in this country." He sat on the red couch and stretched his arms on the backrest. "In the day, this is another great view, yes? Expensive view."

"Do we still need the lawyer, boss?" Utah said, standing behind David.

Janaab laughed. "You want her?"

"Wouldn't say no."

"Patience, Utah, patience."

Ms. Holban didn't seem to care about that gross exchange. She sat on the floor, her hands behind her back, and Flaco's rifle pointing at her. Her calm gave David strength not to start crying like a baby.

With Utah's gun pressing on his neck, he moved to the back of the room, his weak legs bumping into things. Utah pushed him down to the floor, against the wall. David resisted the temptation to look up at the vent, where his hidden camera was still recording. One day, someone would find it, and David's death would go viral. But he didn't want to die to nail Janaab and his crew. He wanted to live and tell the story.

Now his dad was coming to the slaughter, and it was all David's fault. He glanced at Ms. Holban, who was right beside him. She had a steely face, as if she was in control of the situation—even though she was sitting on the floor with her hands tied behind her back, just like him.

No, wait. Her hands were behind her back, but they weren't tied. Flaco had forgotten to retie them after she texted on her phone. David's capture had interrupted things, and now Ms. Holban was doing her best to make Flaco think she posed no danger.

If David could tease the screwdriver out of his breast pocket and drop it on the floor between them, maybe she could pick it up. And do what with it? He couldn't imagine Ms. Holban attacking someone with a screwdriver.

Still, he slumped his shoulders and felt the tool move a little against his chest.

35

EMILIO GRIPPED THE steering wheel of Blanca's Camry. He drove into the night as fast as the speed limit allowed but no faster. He had to get to his son, not be pulled over by the police and handed back to ICE. He'd told Blanca and Jacob to hide, not tell him where, and take the batteries out of their new phones. He hadn't told them where he was going, but he assured them that David was safe.

He parked down the street from his old house and took the crowbar from the trunk before starting up the path, light steps on icy ground. He'd thought he'd never return, yet here he was. It didn't feel like home though. More like a trap.

All the downstairs lights were on, but the upstairs was dark. Emilio avoided the streetlamps, keeping to the shadows as he slipped through the hedges and circled around to the backyard. He peered into the living room windows, but the blinds were closed. Shadows moved inside. The sunroom door was open just a crack. He pushed it wider and slipped inside.

He could hear voices through the open door to the dining room, far enough to come from the living room. He recognized Janaab's husky tone from their earlier phone call. He and his men were probably armed. Emilio's crowbar wouldn't stop a bullet, but he might take some of the men down and give David a chance to escape.

He listened to make sure everyone was in the living room, then crossed the sunroom, making for the laundry room, where the lights were on. The floor creaked beneath him, and he froze. After holding his breath for a moment, he crept into the laundry room, gripping the crowbar.

A thin man stood by the open bathroom door, his back to the sunroom. Emilio saw Laura inside the bathroom, by the sink. What was she doing here?

The man glanced over his shoulder toward the kitchen door, as if to make sure no one was coming, then squared his shoulders, and took a step toward the bathroom. Emilio recognized the gait of a man ready to attack an easy prey and have his way with her. "Prestigio, dinero, armas y mujeres" was many gangs' motto. Status, money, and guns, yes. But women, always.

Emilio raised his crowbar.

The man pounced at Laura, who locked eyes with Emilio for an instant—long enough for her guard to notice. He turned just as Emilio swung the crowbar and hit him on the side of the head with the sickening sound of a watermelon cracking. He collapsed to the floor and lay still.

Emilio waited to see if anybody in the living room had heard anything through the laundry room, the kitchen, and the dining room. Chatter still rang in the distance.

"Where's David?" Emilio whispered.

"They have him in the living room, hands tied." She had a screwdriver in one hand. "He gave me this. I was going to stab this asshole when he got close enough to me."

Emilio grabbed the man and turned him on his back. He was alive but out cold. There was a handgun in his waistband. It looked like a 10mm semiautomatic pistol with integrated trigger safety. Just point and squeeze, as Fernando had once taught him. He took it and held it down by his knee.

"Does he have a phone?" Laura said.

Emilio knew that gang members didn't use passcodes on their phones, for speed of action and easy internal review by their bosses. And no print readers either, for fear of getting their thumbs chopped off in a pinch.

He checked the man's pockets. "There's no one else outside?"

"Not that I know of. We all came in the same car. Janaab, Utah, Nacho, and…Flaco here."

"Found it," Emilio said, holding up a phone. But the screen was shattered, and the phone was dead. Flaco must have fallen on it.

"Fuck!" Laura whispered. "You don't have a phone?"

"I didn't want to be tracked after Janaab called."

Emilio told her about the unlocked sunroom door, and she took off quietly to get help, screwdriver in hand. She'd have a few minutes head start at best. He gripped the pistol in both hands and inched out of the laundry room into the kitchen, where he hid behind the counter. He tried to remember what he'd learned about aiming at the shooting range years ago.

He took a deep breath and stood up to face a different-looking main floor. The people in the living room would spot him any moment now over the length of the dining room.

Even after all these years, Emilio recognized Janaab, sitting on a red couch like an aging king on his throne. His mean face looked just like it had when he'd argued with Papá by the river. Seeing Janaab in the flesh turned Emilio's stomach into a hard ball of anger. That was the man who'd murdered Papá and was now threatening David's life. But where was David?

Janaab looked unarmed, same as last time, but that didn't mean he'd grown less deadly. Another man stood by the window with his hand on an AR-15. Emilio trained his pistol on that one, then switched to another man in the far corner, whose rifle was aimed at someone sitting on the floor. David!

Fury exploded inside Emilio. Still, he had to be careful because David's guard could shoot if startled. Emilio aimed at Janaab instead and squeezed the trigger.

"Watch out, boss!" someone shouted in English.

The gun bucked in Emilio's hands, its blast deafening. People scrambled through the living room. A bullet flew past Emilio and shattered a cabinet window behind him. More shouting and cursing. Bullets flying. Something hit Emilio's right shoulder.

Then silence. No one moved. Both rifles were now pointed at Emilio.

"Don't kill him," Janaab ordered in Spanish. He pulled himself up from the floor, where he'd dropped when his man warned him, a split second before Emilio fired his gun.

"Dad!" David cried.

"I'm here, son," Emilio said. He came from behind the kitchen counter, but when he tried to lift his gun, his shoulder wouldn't engage. He glanced at it and saw a dark stain on his jean jacket. He'd been shot, but it didn't hurt yet.

He switched the gun to his left hand, pointed it at Janaab, and crossed the dining room. The guard in the far corner aimed his rifle at David's head while the other kept his gun on Emilio.

"I remember your father, Villeda," Janaab said in Spanish. "Burning his warm heart brought great pleasure to King Pakal and his gods."

Emilio took another step onto a thick Persian rug. His right shoulder was waking to the pain. "Let my son go," he said in Spanish. Blood trickled down his arm.

Janaab grinned. "I must confess though, it also brought great pleasure to me."

His man pressed the muzzle down on David, who closed his eyes, whimpering.

"My father...protected me with his life," Emilio said, trying not to wince from the pain taking hold in his shoulder.

Janaab nodded at his man, who hit David over the head with the butt of his rifle. David screamed in pain, but Emilio kept his aim. Tears came into his eyes, and he blinked them away.

Janaab craned his neck. "You killed my man Flaco back there? And where's the lawyer?"

"You can have me if you let my son go," Emilio said.

"You're in no position to bargain, Villeda. But let me tell you why I'm here. First, for my photos, which I took from your lawyer. Second, to kill you and your family and to set your house on fire."

"Your photos," David said in Spanish, shifting in his place on the floor, "are already on the internet."

Emilio hoped that was true.

Janaab sighed with impatience. "Then I'll cut off your balls, and you'll take the photos down while bleeding like a tapir."

"Except," David said, "the abort script can only be run from the IP address of the Everett Public Library."

Emilio felt certain that wasn't true but hoped David's lies would at least slow Janaab down, buying enough time for Laura to bring help.

Janaab shrugged. "Then we'll go to the library tomorrow morning, shoot the place up, and take down what's mine." He laughed. "You people here—unbelievable! At least in Mexico, people know when there's no hope and stop struggling. They just accept death. But here in America, you imagine you stand a chance, don't you? Then let me teach you a bit of Mexican wisdom, boy."

He moved closer to Emilio. "Put the gun down or Nacho will blow your son's leg to pieces."

Nacho moved the rifle from David's head to his thigh. The other man still had Emilio in his crosshairs.

"Don't keep me waiting," Janaab said in a sing-song voice. "Don't fucking keep me waiting, not another second."

Emilio had no doubt they'd shoot David's leg off. They'd keep him alive until they knew there was no website to worry about, but they'd make him suffer like hell until then.

Emilio lowered his gun, and Janaab took it from his hand.

"Flaco's gun?" he said and pressed it to Emilio's forehead. He turned to the guard by the window. "Utah, go find the lawyer," he told him in English, then switched back to Spanish. "I have you now, Villeda."

"Why do I matter to you?" Emilio clutched the wound on his shoulder. Shards of white pulsed before his eyes, but as long as he kept Janaab talking, Laura might still arrive with help.

"At your family's funeral," Janaab said, pressing the gun harder between Emilio's eyebrows, "I learned of another son. You. And then you were nowhere to be found." His breath stank of cigarettes. "I made my name by wiping out entire families. But because I let you slip away, someone called me a fraud. Me!" He laughed. "Oh, he's not alive anymore. But people, they started whispering that I might be weak, you see. And so, I had to kill twice as many people—because of you. Not that I didn't enjoy killing them, but once in a while, I would've liked to just take it easy, you know? But you—you didn't let me. Now those who ever doubted me—and are still alive—will know that I. Always. Keep. My. Word."

"They already know that," David cried. "You don't have to hurt my dad."

"Even if I didn't have to," Janaab said, "do you know how many times I dreamed of killing him? And now, I almost don't want it to be over."

"Then stop!" David yelled, before Nacho hit him over the head and sent him shrinking in his corner.

"Leave him alone," Emilio groaned, feeling the blow himself.

For a moment, Janaab seemed to consider the request, then he winked at Emilio. "You know that's not how things go, Villeda. Your whole family must die, and your house must burn. End of story. So, where are your wife and son?"

David sobbed. "Why does he keep calling you Villeda, Dad?" He knew why but was trying to buy time.

"You didn't tell him?" Janaab said, thick eyebrows raised in amusement.

Emilio shook his head, Janaab's gun pressing against his face.

"Ah, such a good—no, great—story," Janaab said. "And he doesn't know it?"

"Why don't you tell it?" Emilio felt so tired.

Janaab shrugged. "I don't have time. You're already bleeding."

Emilio realized that Janaab wouldn't shoot him in the head. He needed him whole for that sick and twisted ritual Lucio had tried to make sense of on the day Papá was killed. Emilio had run away from Janaab once. Not anymore. He'd die fighting for David.

He slammed Janaab's arm aside with his right fist—a cry of pain as he engaged his injured shoulder—and punched him in the gut with his left.

"Utah, no," Janaab cried, just as Emilio heard the shot and felt a bullet shatter his chest.

He crumpled to the floor, unable to breathe.

"Dad, no! Dad!" David cried.

"What did you do?" Janaab yelled at Utah, who now stood over Emilio with his rifle. "You shot him through the heart, you moron."

"He tried to kill you, boss…" Utah answered in English.

Emilio struggled to take a breath, but no air came in, as if his lungs were full of water.

"Find the lawyer," Janaab growled at Utah.

Emilio turned his head to take one last look at David.

36

LAURA RAN FROM the house and made her way to the street. The neighborhood looked deserted. She could stop a car and ask the driver to call 911, but she saw no cars anywhere. She could run to a neighbor's house and ring the doorbell. The closest house was…She looked around. Emilio's place stood alone in the middle of a large, dark lot that spilled down the hill to the beach, the reason Evelyn wanted it so badly.

She spotted another house in the night. It wasn't close, but it was all she had. She took off, running on the sidewalk, David's screwdriver still in her hand. She skipped over frozen puddles to keep from slipping. She breathed in the rhythm of her feet hitting the pavement, and she warmed up in a few minutes.

High beams whipped around a curve. Laura stepped into the street and waved her arms, but the pickup truck blasted its horn and sped past. Asshole.

She ran along the street until she reached the house. Up the front stairs, under the porch lights, she rang the doorbell. Her breaths came fast and hot. She pressed the button again and waited, but the place was quiet. After another minute, she walked around the house. There was a light on in a sitting room, but no sign of life. Friday night. The family was probably out.

Could she pry the front door open with the screwdriver? There could be a phone inside. But if she tripped an alarm, the police might come with sirens. Sirens would get David killed. She turned around— and bumped into a tall man who smelled of cigarettes.

"Thought you could get away?" Utah said. In the dim light, he looked like a crazed wolf ready to sink his teeth into Laura's flesh.

She shrieked, and her hand stabbed on its own. The screwdriver must have hit a rib because it turned sideways and slipped from Laura's sweaty hand. Utah stumbled back, cursing. It couldn't have been a deep wound, but it bought a few seconds for Laura to dash past him into the dark gardens behind the house. She couldn't go back to the street. It would be too easy for Utah to catch her there.

She ran, her heart in her throat. The thought of Utah's claws grabbing her from behind kept her going. She pushed through brambles and found herself running past trees, downhill. Branches whipped her face. Frozen, uneven ground threw her off-balance. She slipped and slammed her shoulder into a tree trunk but kept going.

At the bottom of the slope, she looked around, trying to figure out where she was. A lighthouse beam sliced the night. Possession Sound. Which made this place the bottom of Emilio's orchard, by the beach. Crap. She'd run all the way back, in a big circle in the dark. Now she was far away from the street. And there were no lovers taking selfies on the beach, not on a freezing February night.

Only one way to go. She aimed for higher ground and started again. Her muscles burned as she climbed uphill on slippery, lumpy ground. Her hands were cold and numb. She pushed ahead until she saw the lights of Emilio's house, then stopped to catch her breath.

A branch snapped somewhere behind her, downslope, so she sprinted to the backyard. Utah would be here any moment now. She had to find her way back to the street, but just as she rounded the house, she saw someone coming up the driveway with a duffel bag. Nacho. She slipped between the side wall and some bushes and noticed a row of windows to an unlit room. She remembered two closed doors off the living room. If she could find a way to force the window open, she could hide inside for a moment. But when she reached out a hand, there was no glass pane. Someone had left it all the way open. On a night like this?

She pulled herself over the sill and into a small bedroom. She moved to the door, cracked it open, and listened to the voices coming from the living room.

"The blade, Nacho," Janaab said in Spanish.

"What are you doing to him?" David sounded scared out of his mind. Laura listened for Emilio but didn't hear his voice.

"Here you go, boss," Nacho said.

"This, my boy," Janaab said, "is what King Pakal did to his prisoners." He grunted. "He...tore their heart out." He groaned in frustration. "That motherfucker Utah's going to pay for this—oh, he will. Because the heart was supposed to be whole."

"No, don't!" David cried. "Don't touch him."

Laura's stomach lurched, and she felt lightheaded. By the sound of it, Emilio was dead. Janaab had his prize and was now enjoying it—in front of David. She had to stop him. She looked around the staged bedroom. She grabbed a chair by the heart-shaped hole in its backrest, then opened the door and peered out while staying hidden in the dark.

The scene in the living room made her press a fist to her mouth to keep from screaming. Janaab was on his knees on the floor, mumbling something and cutting up Emilio's shirt with a knife. The jade mask from the old photos lay on the floor beside them. David shrieked from the corner, while Nacho craned his neck to watch what his boss was doing.

No one was looking toward Laura as she raised the chair and threw it with all her strength. It hit Janaab in the face, then crashed on the floor, shattering the jade mask.

Nacho swung his rifle at Laura, but David kicked him in the knee, and Nacho fell sideways. Janaab stood, blood running from his nose. He stared at the shattered mask and bellowed with rage.

Laura bolted from the bedroom door and knelt next to David. She found a shard of jade on the floor and cut the zip tie from his wrists. David sprang to his feet, but so did Nacho. David charged him before he could bring the rifle up, fists pounding into the man's ribs.

Janaab rushed at Laura in a fury. She swept a can of air freshener off a table and sprayed him in the eyes. He halted, his scream hurting Laura's tender eardrum. She stepped aside and shoved him into the wall.

David kept pummeling Nacho, who went down with his finger on the rifle's trigger. The room exploded with sound—bullets tearing into walls and ceiling. Laura's injured ear felt like it was being stabbed with a needle. She threw herself down. Chips of drywall leapt through the air. Windows shattered.

A moment later the room fell quiet. The air smelled of gun smoke, winter frost, and air freshener.

Nacho lay still on the floor, blood on his shirt. A ricochet bullet must have hit him. Laura couldn't tell where it came from. The walls around them were pierced and the windows broken. Maybe that fiberglass ladder had sent it back. She checked herself for blood but found no wounds.

Janaab reached for a gun in a holster at his back and turned to David, who leapt at him and slammed a fist into his side. Janaab lost his footing, and Laura grabbed his gun.

She held it out in front of her, the way people did in movies. The smooth grip was slippery in her hands. But could she squeeze the trigger—and kill another human being?

David yanked the rifle from Nacho's hands and turned it on Janaab. It was probably out of bullets by now, but if it wasn't, Laura couldn't let David kill someone. She knew what it meant to live with the burden of another's death, in whatever form.

"David, don't shoot! We don't need to kill him." Which was the last thing Janaab needed to hear. "We just need to take him."

"You're not a murderer, son," Janaab said in Spanish, snorting the blood in his nose.

David seemed torn for a moment, then put the rifle down.

Janaab looked ready to bolt.

"I'm not your fucking son," David said. "And you're not going anywhere."

He dropped into a boxer's stance and charged. Janaab parried the first punch, but another came fast, landing in his round gut. The old man was out of shape, not used to fighting his own fights anymore. He dropped to the ground by Emilio's body but hooked David's legs as he fell. David crashed to the floor, and they scuffled there for a moment, then both got up, fighting close-in. Even if she wanted to shoot now, Laura couldn't risk hitting David. She picked up the rifle to keep it away from Janaab and slung it over her shoulder, then dashed to the dining room to look for her phone.

The fight went on behind her. The smash of a punch. A curse in Spanish. The thwack of a fist against flesh. David's grunt and moan. Janaab's jeering.

Laura found her cell on the table and dialed 911.

"Please state your emergency," said a woman's voice.

"They killed Emilio," Laura said, panting.

"Where are you, ma'am?"

Laura recited the address, committed to her memory after all those immigration filings, and kept track of the fight in the living room. David punched Janaab hard in the stomach. The old man, his face bleeding more than before, stumbled back into the stepladder against the wall. But he used it to steady himself and stomped down on David's foot. David cried and jumped back, then came in again and grabbed Janaab by the neck. He forced him face down on the floor.

"I need to tie him up," he yelled at Laura. He looked around. "My dad's belt."

"Please, hurry," Laura told the dispatcher and ran to get Emilio's belt.

There was blood on the rug around Emilio's body. As a child, Laura had seen plenty of dead people in open-casket funeral processions through the streets of Bucharest. But they'd always looked asleep, if unnaturally gray. Emilio looked almost alive. His face was serene, but there was a bloody hole in his chest.

"My dad's belt," David cried. "Give it to me!" He was still on the floor, pinning Janaab down, who was thrashing his arms.

"Oh, look at you," Utah's voice came from behind Laura. "Rifle and gun? You're quite the badass now, aren't you?"

Laura turned to face Utah and his rifle. He swung it back and forth, pointing it in turn at her and David. She had to give David a chance to take cover. She was not losing him too.

She raised her gun, but an explosion sounded before she could pull the trigger. She felt a blow to her stomach and stumbled back. It felt like she'd been punched, but the hand she touched to her belly was now covered in blood. Her knees buckled, and she fell beside Emilio, green jade shards all around them.

There was a sound in the distance. Sirens? If she could hold on for another few minutes...

At least Alice was safe and far away. In a few years, she'd be old enough to return to Seattle as an adult. After her time in Romania, she would have made friends, she'd know the culture, maybe even learn to like the food...

David saw Ms. Holban fall. Just like his dad. They'd both been too good for this world. With a scream of pain and anger, he dragged Janaab up and put him in a chokehold.

"Let him go," Utah said.

Janaab gurgled and panted in David's hard grip.

Utah aimed his rifle at David's head. "Let. Him. Go."

David tensed his arm around Janaab's neck.

"Let him—"

A gunshot sounded. Then two more. Utah fell to his knees, then tumbled onto his side.

A policewoman appeared behind him. "Son," she told David. "Let go of that man. You're choking him to death."

David pushed Janaab away and fell on his knees, covering his face. He hadn't tried to kill that bastard, just hold him down until someone took him off his hands. He wasn't like Janaab. He hoped to hear his dad's voice telling him he'd done good. He waited, wishing it with every fiber of his being.

"Hijo de puta," he heard Janaab mutter before breaking into a throaty cough.

Laura heard a man's voice calling, "Ma'am? Can you hear me, ma'am?"

The lights were too bright, and she closed her eyes. She felt hands lifting her up and a mask covering her mouth and nose. She was rolled along on a gurney. Dull pain radiated from the center of her belly. She turned her head to the side, trying to take in the scene.

David was standing by the wall, crying. He looked unharmed. Janaab was on his knees in handcuffs, and a medic was wiping the blood off his face. A police officer took Emilio's pulse and shook her head.

Laura felt the gurney quiver a little as it was carried out the front door. Her stomach felt a jolt of hurt. She moaned.

Snow fell from a black sky, cold and white. It fell on her cheeks, on her forehead. If not for the oxygen mask, she could have tasted it.

Smelled it. The image of snow from before all this, when her father was healthy and she was little, came to her through muted pain. She remembered one afternoon, with a bit of sun peeking through the clouds, when the powder was fresh and soft. She and her father built a snowman together, with real coal chips for the eyes and buttons. The black and the white swirled together, turning into a black hat in a photo on a white marble cross. She wondered if that was where her grave would be, with her father, and if Alice would come to visit.

...*the graves of your loved ones...mormintele celor dragi...*

Snow fell from a black sky, pushing her down, deep into darkness.

When Alice came home, they should go skiing together at Snoqualmie Pass.

Alice loved snow.

37

LAURA'S RECOVERY took five long months. After a couple of weeks in the hospital and a few more at home with a nurse, she was able to walk around the house without help. At first, she could only have liquid food. People took turns bringing her chicken soup and smoothies. Jennifer, Blanca, Fernando, Father Nicolas, and a couple of Romanian friends—all came to check on her and keep her company.

Claudia offered to come to Seattle to help, but Laura asked her to stay in Bucharest and take care of Alice. For the first time in Laura's memory, Claudia didn't argue. Alice spent her time in Romania learning to appreciate eggplant salad, stuffed peppers, and cabbage rolls with sour cream. She started asking her grandmother for a sprinkle of lovage in soups. Claudia baked pastries for her every weekend: salty breadsticks, baklavas, and on special occasions, panettones. She found the old turntable, and they listened together to the stories Laura had grown up with. Once a week, Claudia took Alice to see a friend who had a grand piano and plenty of time to give Alice lessons. Laura was grateful for her mother's help.

Sometimes David visited with Orsetto, the dog he'd rescued from the Seattle Animal Shelter after the Waltmans were killed. At first, Blanca had been against adopting the golden retriever. A dog was expensive and distracting, but David promised he'd take good care of Orsetto, who wasn't responsible for Waltman's sins and needed a home. Just like Emilio had when he first arrived in the US. In the end, Blanca relented.

Kyle had come to the hospital once, but Laura couldn't let him see her lying bloated and bruised in bed, so she'd sent him away with the message that she was resting and had everything she needed. He'd sent flowers and offered to help at the beginning of her recovery, but she wouldn't let him see her limping through the house, holding her belly. Then he gave up on her.

In the silence that followed, she had plenty of time to think of him. Their work on a case he called "ours." Kyle holding her hand once, at a restaurant. Showing up in the middle of the night to rescue her. Making her cornmeal porridge and trying to cheer her up with a clumsy joke after the other attack. She couldn't even remember what she'd been afraid of when she'd pushed him away. Something about cultural differences. Goodness, how ridiculous that sounded now, after all that had happened. But the more days that went by, the more she accepted that Kyle had moved on. Sometimes she thought about texting him, but no, it wasn't fair to bother him now, after months of no communication.

When Alice returned to Seattle, she brought with her a newfound passion for all things Romanian. She sat down at her piano and played a piece by George Enescu, the great Romanian composer. She accompanied Laura to Pike Place Market, where they bought a fresh jar of lovage, though they kept the expired one in the cupboard. And they started cooking together.

One evening, while preparing a potato salad with olives, pickles, and dill weed, Laura said, "The last time I had this, my dad made it for me. Before you were born."

"It sucks that we sometimes don't appreciate what our parents do for us," Alice said.

It was the closest she'd come to acknowledging that her mother had sent her away to protect her, but Laura didn't press the matter. There was plenty of time to talk about that later. Right now, she was grateful for every day together.

✕

David was quiet on the drive to the Seattle Immigration Court that July morning. His mom didn't try to make conversation either, and Jacob kept his earbuds on. They took the elevator to the twenty-fifth floor of a downtown building, went through security, then sat next to Ms. Holban and Alice in the windowless waiting area outside three courtrooms.

While his mom and Ms. Holban whispered something about the individual hearing that was soon to begin, David leaned out of his seat and waved at Alice.

"Welcome back," he mouthed the words, and she smiled, nodding.

He wished they could talk, but this was not the place. Besides, she felt distant, like she belonged to another universe, whereas he had lost so much since they'd last seen each other.

As soon as his mom and Ms. Holban went into the courtroom, Alice scooted over.

"I'm Alice," she told Jacob in a low voice, extending her hand over David's lap.

Jacob nodded and shook back.

"It's so good to see you, David," Alice said. "Your suits look great."

David cringed. Both he and Jacob wore the black suits bought for their dad's funeral. This was the second time David had worn his, and the symbolism wasn't lost on him.

"Did you feel the earthquake last night?" Alice said.

"What earthquake?" David hadn't slept much, but somehow his anxious brain hadn't registered their new apartment shaking.

"I did," Jacob said, and David felt annoyed that he was the last one to find out.

"So," Alice said, "about that band? Who's in? I'm at the keyboard, you're the lead guitar. You said your friend Cruz is your bassist? A girl in my class plays violin. Jacob, do you play an instrument?"

Jacob shook his head, then pointed at his earbuds. "I'll be your number one fan though."

David couldn't think about that right now. "I don't want to talk about it here. It seems wrong. Besides, if my mom—you know." He didn't want to say the word "deported." "Then we'll leave. To El Salvador."

"That won't happen. My mom's going to help her stay, you'll see."

"Now you're really jinxing it," David said, and his hushed, angry tone made her pull back in her seat and cross her arms.

"I'm so stupid," she whispered.

"No, you're not," David said, staring ahead. "You've got every right to dream about the future."

"Well, so do you. And Jacob."

"For us, it's up to the judge behind that door."

×

After a five-month absence, Laura was back in the Seattle Immigration Court for Blanca's individual hearing. To protect the applicant's privacy, the courtroom was empty except for Blanca, the attorneys, Judge Felsen, and her clerks. Everyone present was on edge because of the 4.6-magnitude earthquake that had woken up the greater Seattle area at two in the morning. All, except for Laura, who'd slept undisturbed in her sturdy little house in Capitol Hill.

In her opening statement, Laura explained that Blanca would have to stay in the US as long as the investigation into Mason Waltman's crimes was active. She'd also have to be here during Javier Saravia's trial, where David would be a witness for the prosecution. Blanca was already on ICE's non-detained docket, with an employment authorization card that allowed her to live and work in the US. She hoped to attain permanent resident status—a green card—through an approved asylum application or a cancellation of removal.

The criminal conspiracy between Waltman and Saravia, to which a few thousand immigrants had fallen victim over the years, had been all over the news. Footage from David's hidden camera had gone viral across the globe, including in Romania. The investigators had also linked Saravia to a PSB-affiliate organization dealing in stolen Mayan artifacts through the Jade Jaguar Gallery in downtown Seattle and to the recent murders of foreign archeologists in Guatemala. The investigation was ongoing, though with Utah dead and his identity still unknown—save for the state he might have been from—there was still no lead on his American accomplice who'd helped assault Laura in her home.

"We're all terribly sorry for what happened to you, Counsel," Judge Felsen said.

"Thank you, Judge."

Emilio's assault charges had been withdrawn after Evelyn Brunelle admitted to being intimidated into false testimony by the now-deceased ICE chief Mason Waltman. She kept Emilio's house because the real estate contract was unassailable and the rest of the money had been transferred between the parties, but she was yet unable to make the sale she'd wanted so badly. Not many buyers for an infamous house, and Evelyn was so far unwilling to drop the price. But she probably had the resources to weather this rough patch and close on that "awesome deal" sooner or later.

"Our office is working hard to erase the stain left by Mr. Waltman," Josh Peterson told the judge, looking sad and smug at the same time.

"Then start with affirming my client's right to live in the US," Laura said. Her "live" came out sounding like "leave," but she didn't care about her accent anymore. They all knew what she meant.

"Mr. Waltman's methods might have been flawed," Peterson said, "but he was right to pursue extreme vetting of illegals by connecting ICE with foreign intelligence providers. The government should do that all the time."

Laura explained that Blanca and her children had already gone through hell. Though Nacho and Utah were dead, and Flaco and Saravia were awaiting trial in federal court, Blanca and her sons had received threatening letters from Americans who hated undocumented immigrants. They had to move several times.

"They deserve a break," Laura said in closing and asked Blanca to the stand.

Blanca told her story in a soft voice, tearing up when she spoke Emilio's name. Judge Felsen's brow furrowed with annoyance every time Peterson interrupted.

After Blanca, Laura brought David in and asked him about his father's arrest, his younger brother's suicide attempt, and his father's murder. He still had that haunted look on his face, and Judge Felsen seemed burdened by his testimony, especially when he mentioned Cruz and Clara Dominguez's father, who'd also fallen victim to Waltman and Saravia's conspiracy. Laura argued that sending Blanca away would cause David and Jacob irreparable damage. They needed their mother, and they needed professional help to deal with their trauma.

The judge dismissed Peterson's irrelevant questions and let David go with a warm, "Take care, son!"

Next, Laura had Father Nicolas vow to Blanca's good moral character and her standing in the community. When the time came for Kyle Jamison to explain the criminal conspiracy against Blanca's family, Laura asked her questions while searching for a sign from him that he still cared about her. There wasn't one, no smile, no glimmer in his eye, just professional answers to professional questions.

Laura thanked him for his testimony, and he left. She forced herself to refocus her mind on her case. Things were going well with the hearing, but there was still Blanca's eighteen-year-old DUI. With no statute of limitations under US immigration law, even long-term residents could be deported for minor convictions they'd received decades ago. Laura was sure Peterson would bring up the DUI, so she'd pleaded for leniency in her prehearing statement.

After Laura's last witness, Fernando Harris, left the courtroom, Peterson argued that a DUI implied a lack of good moral character.

Laura was ready with her rebuttal. "Not only did Ms. Morales pay for her mistake, but she also learned from it. And she taught her sons to respect the law and take responsibility for their actions."

"That's a weak argument," Peterson said. "David Ramirez can walk out of here today and run a red light—"

"And there wouldn't be a thing you could do about it," Judge Felsen said. "He's an American citizen, over whom you have no authority whatsoever. Making your statement irrelevant."

"But—"

"I think I've heard enough." Judge Felsen squeezed the bridge of her nose. "This is how I see it. Asylum is a prospective form of relief. While I'm moved by Ms. Morales's recent predicament, I believe she's now out of danger. Both here and in El Salvador. Asylum application denied."

Blanca covered her mouth, fingers shaking.

"That still leaves cancellation of removal," Laura said, fast with her next line of defense. "The law states that a person who has been here at least ten years and is of good moral character—and whose US citizen children would suffer 'exceptional and extremely unusual hardship' if the parent were deported—can stay."

"The good-moral-character argument is nonsense," Peterson said from his table. "Judge, please deny this petition as a matter of discretion based on the DUI."

If Blanca's cancellation of removal were denied in the way Peterson requested, Laura would be unable to appeal the case to the Ninth Circuit Court. There would be only the Board of Immigration Appeals, which would review Blanca's file and—most likely—reaffirm the Seattle Immigration Court's decision. Laura had to win the fight today.

"This case," Judge Felsen said, "has attracted national attention. The president himself has tweeted that people like Mr. Ramirez and Ms. Morales bring trouble to our country."

"Thank you, Judge," Peterson said with an exaggerated nod.

"But Judge," Laura said, "Ms. Morales—"

"Please approach the bench, Ms. Holban," Judge Felsen said.

That was unusual. Laura frowned, as did Peterson, but she did as instructed.

Judge Felsen pushed her microphone away and covered it with her hand. "Here's the thing, Ms. Holban," she whispered. "Some time ago, you made me feel responsible for the death of your client, Mr. Felix Dominguez. I never held that against you, just so you know, but I've thought a lot about your point since then. A lot. And you know what? I'm just a cog in the system. If I refuse to fulfill my quota, or if I quit, someone else will take my place."

"Yes, but you might inspire other judges to do the same."

Judge Felsen scoffed. "Like that would ever happen!"

"Judge, Ms. Morales's family has already been hurt. Please give them a chance to fight another day. Lots of people are rooting for them out there. The world is watching."

"Are you suggesting that if I deny, Seattle activists will be protesting at my house?"

"You'll be a target for protesters no matter what. If you allow my client to stay, you might have to put up with angry letters coming from all over the country. But you should do what's right by Ms. Morales and her children."

"Commendable words, Counsel, but if I take up this fight at my age, I'll find myself unemployed."

"With all due respect, Judge, there's a great need for experts in our field. You could join any immigration law firm in the city, and you'd be welcomed with open arms." Laura couldn't believe she was poaching an immigration judge.

Neither could Judge Felsen, whose pale cheeks turned red. "Go back to your table, Counsel."

Laura returned to her place. What the judge did next was out of Laura's hands, but she knew she'd done all she could to make her case. Sweet-talking the judge wouldn't have cut it, not when all the incentives went toward rejection. In any case, the fight wasn't over, and Blanca was prepared, for the sake of her children, to put up with a lengthy appeal and also to litigate the matter in the court of public opinion.

Silence fell over the courtroom. Laura gave Blanca's hand a soft squeeze. Judge Felsen looked at the ceiling for a long moment, as if weighing her next words. Peterson fidgeted, unable to contain his glee.

The judge brought the microphone back to her mouth. "Ms. Morales's application checks all the requirements under the law. Cancellation of removal is approved on the merit."

Laura was surprised and relieved.

Peterson shot up from his chair. "What about the DUI?"

"As you said, Mr. Peterson, it's a matter of discretion. My discretion. You can appeal if you like." Judge Felsen got up to leave.

"You bet I will," Peterson called after her.

"What happens now?" Blanca asked Laura when they were out of the courtroom.

"Now you go home and try to build a life."

Alice, David, and Jacob were in the waiting area. Alice had asked to accompany Laura today to show her support for David and his family. The kids saw the smile on Blanca's face and jumped around with silent cries of joy. Alice threw Laura a thumbs-up. That was something Laura could get used to.

She also spotted Kyle reading his phone in a seat by the door. It wouldn't be too much to stop by and thank him for his testimony today, would it?

"Mom," Alice said, heading her way. "We're going out to celebrate. Want to come?"

"I still have work today. Where're you going?"

"I think I'll ask them to go up the Space Needle with me."

Laura's smile vanished. "That sounds great, except we've just had an earthquake and might get aftershocks. Save the Space Needle for another day. Please?"

"Oh, right," Alice said. "I forgot about the aftershocks."

"But you can still go to the Seattle Center. There's plenty to do there. Maybe go watch the dancing fountain and eat at the Armory?"

Alice nodded, then joined David, Jacob, and Blanca. Laura waved to them as they headed for the exit, then she turned to Kyle.

He got up when he saw Laura approaching and glanced around as if he had somewhere else to be.

"Blanca's getting a green card," Laura said. "Might take a couple of years because of the annual caps, but in the meantime she's safe. We couldn't have done it without you."

"She really deserves it," Kyle said. Then his face changed. "Did you feel the earthquake last night?"

And there, in his show of casual concern, Laura saw hope. "No need to worry," she said. "Our house is supposed to be the last one standing when the Big One comes."

Kyle nodded, hands in his pockets, waiting, the warmth gone from his eye.

"Your house okay?" Laura said.

"Just a crack in the wall, nothing major." He turned to leave.

Laura mustered up her courage. "Say, you want to grab an early lunch?"

He narrowed his eyes as if trying to determine whether she was joking, then his old smile reappeared. "What would you like? Italian? Mexican? Thai? French?"

"Actually, there's this restaurant in Bellevue, Mama Sanda's. The chef's a former client. Romanian. I've never been, but I'd like to try it. That is, I mean, if you want to."

"Sounds great, Laura. Never had Romanian food before."

Laura couldn't help a silly smile. She probably looked like a teenager in those South Korean high school dramas her mother loved so much. But she didn't care. She was thrilled to finally get to know Kyle—and she owned it.

38

LAURA CHOSE LAKE Washington Boulevard for her first run since the shooting. Sunglasses on to keep the late-afternoon August sun from hurting her eyes, she walked where the pavement sloped, and only ran on level ground to go easy on muscles she hadn't trained for half a year. Her shadow blurred and sharpened on the sidewalk as the sun drifted in and out of the clouds. After half an hour, the sidewalk changed to a dusty bicycle rut by the curb. After another hundred feet, Laura took the wooden steps down to the lakeshore.

The gravel path reminded her of the Danube shore on a hot summer day. Reeds swaying in the light breeze, drawing circles on the water. Trees wrapped in ivy. White and pink bean flowers. Dandelions and wheatgrass. Just like Romania, all of it. Even that same smell of fish and seaweed in the air.

Laura sat on the grass off the path, a few feet above the water's edge. It was a warm day, and there were boats everywhere. Across the shimmering lake, downtown Bellevue and the snowy Cascade Mountains looked like a picture from a glossy album.

Laura's phone beeped with a text from Jennifer. *Did you hear? NWDC is rebranding. Now they're calling it the Northwest ICE Processing Center (NWIPC).*

That will do wonders for their public image, Laura texted back with an eye-rolling emoji.

She heard an airplane descending into Sea-Tac Airport, no doubt bringing a few more immigrants like her to Seattle. She took a deep breath and felt the now-familiar tender spot in her belly as she exhaled.

She was exhausted but in a good way. She'd finally understood she could have only one home on Earth. Seattle, not Bucharest. No human being could straddle the planet and be in two places at once. Simple physics that had taken her years to accept.

The Skype jingle rang in her hand: Claudia Florea calling for a video chat. Laura pressed the green button.

"Where are you?" Claudia looked good, though still in poor resolution.

"My first run," Laura said but stopped before saying "since the shooting." "It's going well." She moved the phone around to show her mother the lake, then Mount Rainer covered in snow to the south.

"Is that the volcano?" Claudia said. "Are you sure it won't go off?"

Laura thought better than to answer. "So, what's going on?"

"Listen," Claudia said, "I've been thinking. Since Alice left. The house is quiet again, and I've had time to think."

That sounded ominous. "Whatever it is, we can figure it out together—"

"Everything's fine, just fine. But I need you to listen to me for a minute."

"I'm listening."

"You see, all these years I wanted to spend time with my granddaughter, just the two of us, to get to know her. And it'd never happened, and it broke my heart and made me angry with you. But now it happened, and we're building something together." She paused, as if choosing her words carefully. "And now I understand her more. Yes, she has Romanian-born parents, but she's as American as she can be. She belongs with her people, and you belong with her."

Laura wasn't sure she'd heard her mother right but didn't dare interrupt.

"And I belong here," Claudia said, "with my people, in my city. On every street, it seems there's a building whose blueprint I once drew. You've lived most of your adult life there. Alice speaks Romanian with an accent. Kids here ask her where she's from. She looks Romanian by features, but even the way she carries herself is foreign. Without a parent with her to bridge the gap between here and there, she couldn't belong. Though she did like my panettones."

Laura laughed. "Those with Turkish delight are the best."

Claudia sighed, as if relieved to get the hard part over with. "By the way, she did make me go to the furniture store for a new swivel chair. But she wasn't much help there because she didn't know the Romanian word for adjustable screw. In the end, I worked it out with the salesclerk by myself."

Laura kept quiet now. Whatever was happening with her mother, she didn't want to say the wrong thing and break the spell. She just nodded, glad she had her sunglasses on.

"Here's the truth, Laura," Claudia said. "After your father died, I didn't want to take care of the things he used to do because that meant replacing him. I'm not helpless, you know, though after Tudor died, I felt that way for a very long time."

Laura cleared her throat so she wouldn't start crying. "You know I'll get on a plane and come see you, Mama." It felt like a lie because she'd said the same thing to her father once. "It's just that I won't be there when you need me the most. It'll take me a couple of days to reach you, so for that first night in the hospital, when things are the scariest, I won't be there for you."

Claudia nodded. "Come visit when you can. Until then, I'll keep company with other parents whose children live in London or Cyprus or Australia. It's our generation's curse, I guess, and no number of tantrums will stop a changing world."

Laura slipped a finger under her sunglasses and wiped away a tear. Had she once known what she knew now about being an immigrant in America, would she still have come—and stayed? She wanted to tell her mother what she'd realized in the dark trunk of Saravia's car, to confess how sorry she'd felt for letting them down, but this wasn't the time to talk about herself. She let Claudia have her moment.

"And," her mother said, "try not to be alone if you can."

Laura thought to mention Kyle but again decided this should be Claudia's moment and kept quiet.

"One more thing," Claudia said. "Alice is a wonderful piano player. She should continue practicing with a teacher."

"Sure, but she should decide that for herself."

They said goodbye, and Laura put the phone back in her pocket. She stood up from the grass and took one last look at the lake and the blue sky streaked with white contrails, then she started back to the gravel path. Somewhere up the hill stood Mason Waltman's burned house. Those poor kids…

A man in his sixties strolled her way, all smiles. "Hi there. I couldn't help but overhear your conversation on the phone. Where're you from?"

Some battles would never be won. "Romania," Laura said.

"Romania? I would've thought Brazil."

"That's because Romanian and Portuguese are both Romance languages." She smiled. "Enjoy this beautiful day!"

"You speak English so well," the man said. "How long have you lived here?"

Laura thought for a moment. "Half a lifetime."

She waved at him and started running. She was going home.

ACKNOWLEDGEMENTS

I am an immigrant. I arrived in the US from Romania in 2001 with a job in software development and found a welcoming country where I began to slowly build a life and a home. Then during the 2016 presidential campaign, "immigrant" became a scary word for many American voters. And one day, I heard the new president compare immigrants to snakes, which tender-hearted people might take in and warm up at their breast, when they should instead throw them down and crush them. So much of what was being said wasn't based on the realities of immigration. Soon after, I started working on *Extreme Vetting*.

Unlike other thrillers that are more evergreen, this is a time capsule of February 2019, since the regulatory framework changes not just between administrations but sometimes from week to week. It wasn't an easy story to write because being an immigrant is never easy, no matter the reasons for moving away. It's also hard for the families left behind. My mother Angelica Aramă, my late father Georgel Aramă, and their entire generation saw many of their children leave Romania, my brother and I among them. That must have been heartbreaking.

Writing *Extreme Vetting* wasn't a solitary effort though. Many wonderful people helped me bring this book to life—and I'm here to thank them. I hope they know their gift means the world to me.

Half a planet away, my family in Galați, Romania encouraged and comforted me as I wrote about displacement, resilience, and searching for a new home. My best friend Cristina Doroftei, herself an immigrant, offered me perspective when I struggled, lifting me up and cheering me on. Ioana Miron, my friend and role model, who's also an immigration lawyer, graciously sat through hours and hours of interviews, then answered dozens (hundreds?) of more questions about legal intricacies.

James Crossley at Madison Books in Seattle recommended thrillers for me to read while I wrote my own. My neighbor Shawna Ader explained the finer points of the Seattle real estate market. John Robert Marlow at The Editorial Department helped sharpen the story and make it a thriller. My friends Milagros and Philip Welt read an early draft and provided insightful feedback, plus useful links and book recommendations.

The teams at Salt & Sage Books and Tessera Editorial guided me as I polished successive manuscript drafts. The editors at the *Write Launch* published an early excerpt in their literary magazine. Thriller author Karen Hugg pointed the path to publication when I was completely lost, then the team at Ooligan Press chose to work on this novel and turn it into a book.

My children Smaranda and Zamfira were patient and understanding when I needed another hour to work, then another. They also showed me how to write parents and children in my fiction. Before they were born, I'd only been my parents' child, with just one side of the story to tell—then they taught me how to also be my children's parent. Of course, my writing wouldn't have been possible, let alone become a book, without my husband Tracy Sharpe, who gave me the idea for *Extreme Vetting* and supported me throughout, at every turn and in every way. He and my children are where my home is.

ABOUT THE AUTHOR

Roxana Arama is a Romanian American author with a master of fine arts in creative writing from Goddard College. She studied computer science in Bucharest, Romania, and moved to the United States to work in software development. Her short stories and essays have been published in several literary magazines. *Extreme Vetting* is her first novel. She lives in Seattle, Washington, with her family. More at https://roxanaarama.com/.

OOLIGAN PRESS

Ooligan Press is a student-run publishing house rooted in the rich literary culture of the Pacific Northwest. Founded in 2001 as part of the Portland State University's Department of English, Ooligan is dedicated to the art and craft of publishing. Students pursuing master's degrees in book publishing staff the press in an apprenticeship program under the guidance of a core faculty of publishing professionals.

PROJECT MANAGERS
Ashley Lockard
Devyn Yan Radke

EDITORIAL
Sienna Berlinger
Rachel Howe
Rachel Lantz
Kelly Morrison

DIGITAL
Amanda Hines
Anna
  Wehmeier Giol

ACQUISITIONS
Amanda Fink
Kelly Zatlin

PUBLICITY
Tara McCarron
Emma St. John

MARKETING
Sarah Bradley
Sarah Moffatt

AUDIO
Paige Zimmerman

DESIGN
Katherine Flitsch
Elaine Schumacher

SOCIAL MEDIA
Riley Robert
Nell Stamper

BOOK PRODUCTION
Rachel Adams
Jenna Amundson
Elliot Bailey
Alex Burns
Francisco
  Cabre Vásquez
Hannah
  Crabtree-Eads
Rachel Done
Ivory Fields
Frances K.
  Fragela Rivera
Alexander Halbrook
John Huston

Jackie Krantz
Ashley Lockard
Savannah Lyda
Agi Mottern
Luis Ramos
Rachael Renz
Alexa Schmidt
Phoebe Whittington
Em Villaverde

A NOTE ON THE TYPE

This book was set in Arno Pro, Rift, and Courier. Styled to mimic the classic typefaces of 15th and 16th century, Arno is an elegant serif font created by Robert Slimbach for Adobe. Rift, the tall font used to style chapter headings, was created by Mattox Shuler and was inspired by fonts used in sci-fi. Designed to be used in typewriters, Courier created by Howard Kettler is a serif font that has become a classic that is easily recognizable. Finally, Webdings is used as section breaks to match the geometric styling of the chapter headers.